Time
for
Once

Time
for
Once

WELLIUM
publishing

Published 2023
Printed in the United States of America
Print ISBN: 979-8-9863946-6-4
E-ISBN: 979-8-9863946-2-6

www.jessmyth.com

Cover Design by Kari Brownlie

Wellium Publishing, LLC

To those rare moments in life when the clouds of time part and
the rays of someone familiar shine brighter than the sun

Prologue

She pressed against the trunk of an old oak tree and hoped the wild beating of her heart would slow down. He was supposed to be in the lecture hall preparing his dissertation. Yet, there he stood next to the bike rack. His tall frame was bent over as his long arms maneuvered a chain around the thick metal bar.

His nerves were clear even from this far away—though it could be a projection of herself in his shoes. Her trepidation grew tenfold as she watched him move across the street. The twinkling morning dew on the grass below chilled her bare toes.

He approached the base of the steps at a speed too fast, but he was running late and time was never on his side when that happened. He halted as he began his ascent into the lecture hall, and looked around. Had he mistaken the time of his thesis presentation? No one was around. The sidewalks were empty of their regular, manic footsteps.

Across the narrow road, the park stood still, suspended in a mist of fog, looking more like a moment caught in a dream. It was then he noticed the woman standing underneath an oak tree, shifting ever so slightly. Her long skirt gave the illusion of weightlessness. He was about to run up the steps when his name echoed off the brick walls.

She prepared to approach, gathering the hem of her sundress. He raised his hand to shield his eyes, as if sunlight blocked his view, even though the sun was behind him and not her. She couldn't be certain why, but she didn't advance. His voice shot across like an arrow to its target, pinning it in place.

"I'm late."

He watched her drop the hem of her dress at the sound of his voice. The movement disappointed and intrigued him all at once. The nakedness of her slender ankles had evoked a sense of unexpected familiarity, like the sight of a beloved runaway cat dashing across the road. He lowered his hand from his eyes.
If only he could make out her face, he thought as her voice spiraled back across like a loosened coil.

"I'll wait."

He raced up the steps at a speed too fast, but he was late and time was never on his side when that happened.

She pressed her body against the trunk of the tree again, hoping she would see him before too long. It had been years since the last time.

One

December 2004

Waiting was the worst. Jolie had always thought so. Until she found herself sitting in the lobby outside her Thursday morning lecture, her head snapping to attention each time the door swung open. Jolie knew what she had to do once he walked out those doors, and wished she could skip to the part where she had already done it. Instead, time crawled forward, suspending her in endless anticipation. Waiting wasn't the worst—no. Time was.

It was only later that she would look back and marvel at how true this thought would be for her and Jace.

Jolie rubbed her eyes from behind her glasses, then focused on the ticking clock on the wall ahead. Sunlight streamed through the east-facing window and glared off the marble floors. Why were the earliest mornings in her school week the most eye-burning? Jolie loathed classes before nine o'clock and, up until the start of this semester, had skipped them often. Then a perfectly good reason to never miss a class showed up and early Thursday mornings became a fail-safe how-to on perfect attendance.

Her friend Alix emerged from the lecture hall and slumped down on the bench next to Jolie.

"That sucked." A resounding statement and one of defeat—typical of Alix post-examination.

"I'm sure you did fine. We studied enough."

Jolie's canned response echoed off the tiles of the empty

lobby.

Alix stood up and jammed her arms into her oversized jacket. Thick brown bangs covered Alix's eyes while Jolie watched her struggle with the zipper. "Does staring at words count as studying? How quickly did you finish? I looked up once and you were already gone." Alix sat down again and jiggled her legs.

Jolie poked at the bench's faded black vinyl. "The first one to finish. I think. It's adrenaline." She eyed Alix's round face as a wordless conversation passed between them. The plan for Jolie to approach Jace, which she hashed out with Alix the night prior, would go into effect as soon as he walked out those double doors. "So, let's just...sit for a while."

Alix hesitated before leaning against the wall. "Sure, we can sit for a sec. I don't think I slept last night. You probably slept less, huh?"

Jolie nodded and closed her eyes. An image of a broad smile and wavy hair flashed behind her eyelids. Her stomach jumped. Her eyes popped open. This was the same pattern as last night. "The tossing and turning were cardio-worthy."

Alix patted Jolie's hand. "Well, at least you like to exercise."

"I like to sleep more." And she would have slept more throughout the entire semester, had she said something to him when they made eye contact during their first class together. Instead, Jolie had flinched and looked away, her mind racing. She spent the rest of the class trying to process how someone she didn't know—at all—could make her feel like he'd just re-turned from a long absence. The urge to ask him where he'd been all this time had overwhelmed Jolie, making it impossible to introduce herself. Jolie was well aware she was shy, but her reaction to seeing his face was next-level. And that ended today.

"He's taking his time, huh?" Alix cut through Jolie's rumina-tion over the same unanswered question.

Why him?

Jolie squinted at the clock again. Ten minutes remained until class was officially over. Time was *not* the worst. The worst was going after the unknown once her time ran out.

"It's possible he went out the front exit," Alix added.

Jolie let out a long breath. She hadn't considered that option, but it was possible. Today could be the day he broke his semester-long pattern of exiting the door she had planted herself in front of. Her heart plummeted at the thought but her mind caught it before it broke for no reason. "No, I don't think so. It wouldn't make sense."

"How about we give him two more minutes?" Alix said. "If he's not out by then, we can assume he left through the front and you won't—" Alix stopped talking as the lecture door swung open.

Jolie's back straightened. He was done. And walking. Right past the bench. His messenger bag was slung over one shoulder, and his stride purposeful—like he couldn't wait to get out of the building.

Jolie stood up, trance-like. Her heart beating a sprinter's pace. *Go catch up*, it would say if hearts had mouths. But her feet had turned to puddles, followed by her calves and then her knees. All she could do was stand still as her body dripped into a puddle across the tile.

Alix glanced at her. "Jolie, what are you doing?"

"I... I can't." Jolie's voice shook.

Alix remained quiet. The significance of what Jolie had set out to do, and that she couldn't see it through, didn't need highlighting. "You never know," Alix whispered while Jolie's eyes tracked his legs moving him further away. "He might come through the Union again and I can give him your number or something."

"That happened once. In three months. Those odds are not favorable." Jolie watched him stop in front of the exit. Inevitably, he would walk out those doors and the "Where's Waldo?" of her college years would continue. It seemed where she was frequent on this campus, he was elusive. Not a single random, or even not-so-random, run-in outside of class. Yet, there he stood, mere steps away. The end of the beginning was within her grasp. All she had to do was go up to him and say what she'd lost so much sleep rehearsing.

Hello.

Time was running out.

"You've put way too much pressure on yourself, and on this person you don't even know. And—Why is he just standing there?" Alix's voice sounded far away.

The loud, rhythmic ticking from the lobby clock directly over his head had replaced the sound of his retreating footsteps now that he'd come to a stop.

Tick.

Jace was staring out the window. She noticed his headphones were pulled down around his neck.

Tick.

Jolie was standing only a few paces away from him.

Tick.

She could do this. She had to do this.

Go catch up.

Jolie clutched onto Alix's arm. Her expression, she imagined, was wild. Her face was an oven.

Alix rolled her eyes. "I'm going to use the bathroom," she said and mouthed, *Go.*

Reason took over emotion and Jolie launched herself forward.

She was out of breath when she reached him. His back was to her. She felt dizzy and slow like she was underwater, and reasoned the sunlight was playing ethereal tricks on her mind; Jace appeared to be glowing. Her hand trembled as she tapped his shoulder, the black leather from his jacket soft and cool on her index finger.

Don't pass out.

Jace turned and stared at her.

His expression was startled. His forehead was creased, and his eyes—not brown, like she'd thought originally, but more of a sage color in this light—grew wide. Probably because she was in full-on gawk mode.

"Hi." Her voice shook. She hoped he didn't notice.

"Hi..." He continued to stare.

"You don't know me—" She paused and released her clenched jaw.

Just breathe.

"We were in the same lecture all semester, and since this is our last class, and I never run into you around campus, trust me I've looked—" A strangled giggle released from her chest. Why had she said that? "I was wondering if you'd maybe like to hang out sometime?"

Those were the most words she had ever said to someone she'd never spoken to before—and it all came out in one breath. Jolie wondered, in the silence between her voice and his response, who had just occupied her body—and if they were to become good friends.

His gaze raked over her face. The corners of his mouth had curved slightly. There was no way of knowing what this expression revealed, other than how it made her feel. His face right now was like waking up from a really good night's sleep.

"Uh, yeah sure, yeah. That's cool," he said.

"Great!" Her voice cracked a full octave above her normal range. "I'll just give you my phone number." Jolie shoved the ripped piece of notebook paper with her number on it into his hand. She'd written it down ahead of time since her hands always revealed her nerves. Adrenaline was a funny thing.

He seemed startled by her speed. "What's your name?"

Right, he didn't know hers. "Sorry." She shook her head. As far as first impressions went, hers was a mess. "I'm Jolie."

She already knew his name. Jace.

But hearing him say it, and the tentative smile he offered afterward, was a memory cemented in a heart still under construction.

She pushed the bridge of her glasses up her nose as he ran a hand through his hair.

"You headed out?" he said, searching her face with a pair of eyes she couldn't believe were staring back at her.

"Yeah, I am." She pulled on her gloves and noticed Jace watch her put on her hat with the oversized maroon puffed topper.

His mouth twitched as if he was sharing an inside joke with himself. "I like your hat."

"I like you." Jolie's stomach dropped to the floor. *Why!* Why had *those* words come out of her mouth? She twisted her hands and attempted to unscramble her mind. "I mean, I like your jacket. It looks very leathery."

Jace's smile grew while he readjusted his messenger bag. "You're different. Aren't you?"

"You could say that." The heat radiating from her face was becoming unbearable. This was not going as planned. But, who was she kidding? Her only plan was "hello". Everything else was an awkward bonus.

Jace continued to smile. "All right. So, you want to go?"

"Yeah. Great!" Jolie glanced over her shoulder. The lobby was empty. Alix was still in the bathroom. She should tell Jace that Alix was waiting. But, *but...* Jolie worked her bottom lip between her teeth while she followed Jace to the lobby doors. Alix would understand why she left without warning, right? How long could the walk with Jace last? Once he went off in the opposite direction, she would rush back to Alix. *Problem solved.*

Jolie blinked at the glaring sun while her breathing adjusted to the frigid temperature. The sharp air choked her lungs, but walking next to Jace was more shocking than the cold.

"I don't know about you, but I'm glad that class is over," Jace said.

"Those early mornings weren't my favorite." Jolie bit her tongue to keep from saying more—seeing Jace had been her favorite.

"Tell me about it. I have to take a bunch of required courses in order to advance in my statistics program. This was one of them. And don't get me wrong, the different facets of psychological research were interesting enough. But I'm ready for the next step. I'm aiming for magna cum laude by graduation, which is crazy to say out loud." Jolie felt her eyes open wide. He was smart—*numbers smart.* She still counted with her fingers.

They weaved around a couple holding hands, then Jace continued, "Higher education isn't a big thing in small-town Iowa. I'm the first in my family to go to college, so I'm trying to do it right."

They stopped at a crosswalk. The roads were as white as the exhale of his breath. Yet, Jace seemed unaware of the cold. Beside her, his jacket remained open. "I don't know why I just told you all of that." He laughed. "And proceed to tell you exactly what I continue to think. Your turn."

The light changed. Jolie drew in a breath. "Let's see. I'm not from Iowa but from the second most popular state to attend this great university." Jolie felt Jace touch the small of her back and maneuver her to the inside of the crosswalk. Her body buzzed as loudly as her mind. She would *not* blurt out how insane this all was. Instead, she tried to focus. "I'm a psychology major, which took me two semesters to figure out, so I've been in a constant state of catch-up—and no, I cannot read your mind, but yes I may be a little nuts."

Jace barked a laugh. "Noted."

"I'm kidding. I swear I don't know what came over me earlier, giving you my number. I'm not what anyone would consider the 'outgoing' type." Jolie forced her mouth shut.

The pressure on her back disappeared once they reached the other side of the road.

She wondered if he'd enjoyed their fifteen seconds of closeness as much as she had.

"Can I be honest with you, Jolie?"

"Yeah. What's the point otherwise, right?" She attempted to laugh away her defensive tone. Her trust had been broken too many times to react any other way. And she hated that fact. She hated that someone's willingness to be honest felt like a commodity she had to earn.

"You're very easy to talk to, which isn't normal for me," he said. "It's like I've known you for longer than"—Jace squinted his eyes in the direction of a large digital clock hanging off the side of a brick building—"twenty minutes. I wish you would've approached me sooner in the semester."

Jolie's stomach jumped straight into her throat while the snow on the ground turned into pure glitter. She glanced in his direction and watched his wavy hair dance in the cold wind. How this wasn't a dream was beyond her.

"Me too."

They stopped at another intersection. Her apartment was a block ahead. Their time was almost up. "Which way for you?" Jace asked.

It took Jolie a moment to turn her attention away from Jace and look ahead. "My apartment is over there to the left." The crosswalk light changed and they moved into the road. Jace's hand returned to the small of her back and guided her in front of him as they approached a mound of frozen snow. Jolie's feet slipped over the pile. Jace caught her by the elbow. He lingered by her side while his scent, something musky like sandalwood or amber, drifted around her.

"My place is just past yours to the right," Jace said, pointing to the five-story apartment building Jolie saw looming in the distance daily.

"You mean the blue one with the red roof?"

Jolie stared at where he'd been hidden away only steps from her apartment. How had she not run into him? Remarkable really, and infuriating. He wasn't elusive. He'd been right under her nose this entire time!

He nodded and fiddled with his jacket zipper, the shadow of a grin plastered on his lips. Did Jace realize too how serendipitous their meeting had become? Or was she overthinking the little things again?

They came to a halt in front of her building.

"Wow. I am just now realizing how cold it is," Jace said. The tips of his uncovered ears were red and poked out from underneath his wavy hair. "So, Jolie…"

Her mouth went dry as the sound of her name rolled off his tongue. "So, Jace."

He blinked and cleared his throat. "I have, like, three finals next week, and a paper, and live with a bunch of dudes who never study and are loud and—not your problem." He cleared his throat again. "I was planning to use the weekend to catch up and study, is what I'm trying to say. But maybe I could call you on Sunday if I can break free."

Today was Thursday. Aside from the written take-home final she had to turn in next Wednesday, she was done for the semester. She and Alix had plans to celebrate tonight. Damn, she wanted to invite him along, but not with a weekend of studying ahead. And double damn at having to live in the memory of this moment for three days while she waited for him to call. Or not call. "Okay, yeah. Whenever is totally fine."

"Great. Well, until next time then. I look forward to it." He dipped his head and began to walk on but didn't go far before he stopped in his tracks, looked over his shoulder, and delivered a wide, devastating smile. A shiver coursed through her as the same sensation she felt at the beginning of the semester dangled on the edge of her own awareness. There was a uniqueness to his presence, felt not just once, but twice now—as if she'd been reunited with a stranger.

She shivered again in the frigid weather and continued to stare like a complete fool well after he disappeared into his building.

Don't freak out.

Just move.

Jolie rotated on her heel and took off in a run. *Alix.* Jolie had left without saying goodbye. She was pretty sure Alix wasn't still in the bathroom at the lecture hall, and more than sure she was pissed. Halfway between the lecture hall and their apartment, she saw Alix's petite frame hunched against the biting wind.

Her arms were crossed over her oversized red jacket. Her pace was set to "visibly annoyed" as she approached. As if the length of her tiny stride ought to be wider than what her legs could actually accomplish. Jolie sped up to close the gap.

"Alix! I am so sorry." The apology was sincere, but she couldn't hide the joy in her voice.

Alix's frown evaporated as she shouted in the icy mist.

"Tell me!"

"I gave him my number," Jolie said as Alix clapped her hands. "Wait! Oh my god. Oh crap." Jolie slapped her hand against her forehead. The sensitive skin was frozen; unlike her sinking dread. "I didn't get his. How did I not get his? What if he doesn't call?"

"So you did it!" Alix dodged the loaded, mostly rhetorical, question like a pro. Three years of friendship would do that, Jolie figured—form a callous against the constant second-guessing.

"I did. But it gets even crazier. We started walking, and talking, and asking questions, and before we both knew it, he's standing in front of our apartment, pointing to his a block away. Alix. He lives *a block away*! How is that even possible?"

Alix shook her head, wide-eyed. "All this time."

Jolie nodded and walked ahead in a daze. All this time. And in a week she would pack up to go home for a month for winter break. In a different state.

"He'll call," Alix said so convincingly it stunted Jolie's growing concern. "Why wouldn't he?"

They entered the front door of the apartment building and each let out a sigh. Time to thaw.

"Even though I look like this?" Jolie pulled off her hat to the sound of static electricity. She imagined her hair was similar to Einstein's in the dry air.

Eight a.m. lectures meant most students rolled out of bed and stumbled in smelling like the night before. Jolie had taken some effort this morning. She'd brushed the tangles from her boring, brown hair, dabbed some concealer under her unavoid-able-during-exam-time bloodshot eyes, and glossed her lips. Still, her black sweatpants and fluffy winter jacket had to be the opposite of a thrilling first impression.

"Stop it, Jolie. You're being ridiculous." Alix pushed open their front door and tugged off her stocking cap. Alix had brown hair like Jolie, but stood five inches shorter. Add in her tiny nose, and Alix's sweet and mousey appearance stood in stark contrast to her loud voice and mother-hen tendencies.

"Never mind, I'm just kind of..." She didn't want to say it out loud *—freaking out.* "I'm riled up, is all."

"How couldn't you be?" Alix gave her a look of, well, Jolie wasn't quite sure what that look was, possibly pride mixed with concern.

"What's with your face?" Jolie asked, circling her finger at Alix. "Why are your eyebrows going all over the place? It doesn't match your smile."

Alix's face dropped. "Fine. I'm going to say this, but please don't take it the wrong way."

Jolie stopped herself from opening the closet door and leaned against it instead. "Go on." She waited while Alix snapped and unsnapped the buttons on her jacket, her eyebrows pinched together.

"Just...tread lightly," she finally got out.

Jolie eyed her friend, knowing there was more. Alix was never short for words, but now she held back for some reason. Maybe Alix realized it would be wasted breath. The timing of Jolie's introduction to Jace had left her little choice but to dive in. Jace was a magical, pristine pool she thought could only exist in her dreams. She had no intention of treading lightly at all.

Jolie would have to race against the clock to make up for all the time already not spent in the warm waters of his presence.

Two

December 2004

J ace flipped his phone closed and tossed it onto the crumpled blankets on his futon. So much for taking the afternoon to study.

He walked past a stack of notes he needed to review before tomorrow and stared out the window of his tiny bedroom. The sky was ominous. It would be another day in a series of too many with no sunlight.

Chewing on the skin around his thumb, Jace mulled over what had just happened. Jolie's voice echoed in his head.

"I had to call. I had to ask."

He'd almost responded, *"I'll be right there."* Instead, he acted as dense as the thick, low-hanging clouds and declined her casual suggestion to meet for coffee. In response, she wished him luck but kept the door slightly ajar for him, *"If you feel the need for caffeine, I'll be here with a friend."*

He felt a need all right—to not fail the one exam that would determine his placement for the statistics honor's seminar. But the desire to know more about Jolie was unexpected and far too enticing. He couldn't get her off his mind. So, instead of waiting until Sunday to call, as he had promised, he dialed her number last night. He had to call, if only to make sure she was, in fact, real. She was.

He felt himself smile. It had been the quickest two-hour conversation *of his life.*

But why now!

Why hadn't they met at the start of the semester, when his time had been free of worries and exams? Leave it to fate—a concept he hated in the first place—to have him meet the biggest distraction of his semester during winter finals. Talk about bad timing. The lump of disappointment, which had grown heavier since turning down Jolie's coffee offer, settled into the pit of his stomach.

He turned away from the window and looked at his desk. There was no way he could focus on all those notes, his curiosity was too strong now. Jolie was under the assumption he wasn't going to show because he had to study. If he changed his mind and surprised her, would that make the pressure of showing up feel less intimidating?

He placed a vinyl record on his turntable, cranked the volume up on "Drive" by Incubus, and wondered how many layers of clothing would be necessary for his short walk to the coffee shop. By the looks of it, the sky could dump snow any minute.

"Hey man!" one of his roommates shouted from the kitchen. "Where you at?" Jace pulled on his wool socks and walked out to see Dru shoving a six-pack of beer into the fridge. A head of dirty-blond hair, born and raised in the Lone Star state, popped up over the open fridge door. "Want one?"

"It's three o'clock on a Friday. I'll pass." Jace sat at the chipped wood table and watched Dru twist the cap off his beer. "What are you up to?"

"Tryin' to find Bridgit." Dru pushed aside a piece of hair from his eyes. For a clean-cut guy, he seemed to hate close haircuts. "She's somewhere near Java House, but I had to make a quick pit stop first. What're you doin'? Oh wait, let me guess, studying."

Jace ignored Dru's jab. Jolie was at Java House. "I was thinking of getting some coffee. There's a girl from one of my classes that wants to meet up. Actually, that's kind of a crazy story." Jace stopped, unsure if he wanted to share more or if Dru would even listen. They rarely hung out solo. Dru was either with a group of guys from his fraternity or out with his on-again-off-again girlfriend.

Jace couldn't afford Greek life—he had enough friends without a bill attached—and hadn't taken the time to date much. Relationships and college were like oil and water, and he had zero interest in mixing the two. Until maybe now.

Dru drained the last of his beer, straightened the sleeves of his flannel, and stood up. "Let's go then."

Jace knew Dru wouldn't put up with the second-guessing Jace's brain wanted to entertain, so he went to search for his jacket.

Once outside and hunched against the stinging wind, Jace decided, *the hell with it*, and started talking. "So, this girl I mentioned earlier, I just met her, like yesterday. She's with a friend I've never met, and she probably thinks I'm not showing up." He fisted his gloved hands. The insides were damp against his skin.

"Didn't you say she's in a class with you or something?" Dru looked confused.

"That's true, and she was. Our last class was yesterday. I don't really know her." They were almost there. The dark, wooden door of Java House was just a few paces ahead. "She went up to me after class and asked if we could hang out now that the semester's over."

Dru's eyebrows shot up. "No shit."

Jace shoved his hands into his jacket pockets. "I did nothing. She had all the nerve."

"Well, you being so stubborn earlier, not leaving the house to study and all that, yet here you are." Dru clicked his tongue. "It always takes two." And with that sage advice, Dru pulled on the large, iron handle and ushered Jace inside.

It took a moment for Jace's eyes to adjust to the dim lighting. It was one of the few trademarks of Java House. Along with wickedly strong coffee and a few too many broken light bulbs.

Jace scanned the narrow space. An array of couches, over-stuffed chairs, and small, round tables were jammed in the back.

The faces of the occupants were shadowed. The walls, colored in crimson paint, were just as cluttered with local artwork of all genres. Jace enjoyed the gritty atmosphere of Java House as much as the actual java. Perhaps Jolie did too. Or maybe not. Girls were about as predictable as the wind with their likes and dislikes—or so his past experiences suggested.

"Why is this place like walking into someone's basement? Can't see anyone back there," Dru said. "Wait. Come to think of it, Bridgit hates it here. Too dark and dirty. Maybe she meant Cafe Java instead. You know what? I bet she did. Could've sworn she said House though." Dru paused with a blank look on his face.

It wasn't uncommon for Dru to think out loud. The first time it happened, Jace wasn't sure if Dru was having a conversation with him or someone else Jace couldn't see. Until it happened again and again and Jace soon realized Dru was having a conversation with someone: himself. "Oh well. Do you see her yet?"

"Not yet." Jace ordered a large coffee and kept his eyes straight ahead toward the counter. Maybe she would see him, on the off chance she was looking for someone who wasn't showing up. *Not likely.*

With his coffee in hand, Jace walked into the back area and scanned the rest of the room. He could recall in detail what it had felt like to be around Jolie yesterday morning—a restless comfortability—but her actual face was a complete blur. She could be the owner of an unrecognizable face, he thought as he gulped down a rising sense of panic. If she happened to be sitting on a couch or chair, he would have to walk past each one to find out for sure.

The sound of laughter from the back corner caught his attention. There, on a tired-looking couch, sat two girls. The one with brown hair leaned forward and picked at an oversized muffin on the coffee table. She seemed familiar. But the only physical feature he could confidently recall was covered by a curtain of hair. The other girl he could tell, even while sitting, was far too short to be Jolie.

He shifted on his feet and stalled. How could he go up to someone who looked like...that? And then her face turned toward his and her eyes, strikingly green even from this distance, landed on him while her lips, so red he felt himself heat from the inside, formed an *o*. His stomach did a weird bungee-like spring-back. Whoa. Jolie two-point-oh-wow.

She waved. Her cheeks matched the hue of her sweater. Jolie's friend turned in his direction and narrowed her eyes. She radiated protectiveness.

"That's her. The one in the red sweater," Jace said. Dru did a double-take. Jace felt himself tense. He hadn't anticipated her to hold that type of power over the opposite sex, and over a self-proclaimed "picky ladies' man" to boot.

Good to know, Jace thought.

"Well, lookee there. Nice job, man." Dru patted Jace's shoulder and shoved him forward at the same time. Right, he had to talk to this dazzling girl who, for whatever reason, liked what she saw enough to approach him. After an entire semester. No pressure or anything. Jace had to move, so he did, knowing if he stayed rooted in place, Dru would no doubt swoop in and lay down his charm. He felt her eyes on him as he approached and focused on not tripping over his feet.

"Hi! Did you change your mind? I mean, of course, *obviously*, you're here!" Jolie smiled up at him, her cheeks now a cute pinkish hue. She slid further toward the side of the couch and patted the cushion next to her. Jace shrugged out of his leather jacket and watched her out of the corner of his eye. She was clearly nervous but carried it well, like a rehabbed weakness, while she introduced her friend Alix. Jace said hello and sat down at the same time Alix stood up.

"Don't mind me." Alix walked to a chair opposite the couch and sat down. "I know couches are meant for more than two people, but no one enjoys being the third." Her hand shuffled the line of bangs on her forehead before Jace's gaze was returned.

"We've met before. I mean, kind of. I have a part-time job at the student union. You bought a Red Bull like, a week ago, maybe? I rang you up."

Jace smiled at Alix's full—and now that she was closer, not-so-threatening—face. He had no idea who she was though. "That's a daily habit I need to break." His nerves laughed for him. "I'm going broke because of it. But it's nice to meet you, officially."

"Thank you, Jace." A smile crinkled the corners of Alix's eyes, which flicked to Jolie before returning to him. "It's about time."

Dru, who had sat down in a chair next to Alix mid-conversation, looked at her like she had a second head. "Weird thing to say. Don't you think?"

Jace thought it was sweet if said sincerely, but never mind what he thought, Dru rarely did.

Alix focused on Dru, the look in her eyes turning into daggers. Jace cut in before Dru caused further reproach. "This is my roommate and friend, Dru."

"Dru, with a '*u*', y'all. 'Cause that's how my mama named me." Dru knocked his knuckles on the wood coffee table, twice, and picked off the muffin placed in front of Jolie. Jace cringed. So, this was the Dru he had brought—the obnoxious frat boy.

Jolie shifted next to him. "You can have the rest of that muffin if you want, Dru."

Dru licked his fingers then held up his hand.

"I can do you one better, Jolie. A round of muffins for the table instead! Alix, was it? You mind helpin' me?"

Jace sat up straighter. Dru was giving him alone time with Jolie. Whether purposeful or not, he no longer regretted bringing Dru along.

"That exit was a bit obvious," Jolie said. She shook her head as a piece of hair, the color of caramel, released from behind her ear. If he was a bolder man, he would have tucked it back behind her ear.

"I'm not complaining," Jace said, turning toward her as much as he could. It had been a long time since he'd sat on a couch with a girl this close. He wiped his palms down his thighs. "Can I be honest?"

"Always." Jolie smiled, her eyes dancing.

"I didn't recognize you at first." He paused to gauge her reaction. She nodded and bit her lip but didn't interrupt. "You look different without your glasses."

She patted her leg. "No sweatpants either. I thought maybe you'd change your mind— I don't know. I woke up feeling good. Sometimes the wardrobe follows suit."

Jace rubbed his bottom lip and watched as her gaze locked onto his mouth. "I liked the low-key look. This right here is deceiving," he said. The smile on her face dropped. "No, like, in a really good way."

Jolie's gaze darted to her hands and back to his mouth before returning to his eyes. "Can I be weirdly honest with you?"

"I'm all ears for weird honesty. Go for it."

"Okay. Well, it's more of a question." A look passed over her that brightened her face, like a light had just flicked on somewhere. "Do you ever wonder if a chameleon feels comfortable in a skin that's always changing?"

He stared at her with what was sure to be a ridiculous smile. He had never been caught off guard so many times by the same person. Jolie seemed to have the element of surprise in spades and a hand she didn't hesitate to play, either.

"I've never considered what it would feel like to be a chameleon. Do you change based on your surroundings?"

"Maybe," she said, reaching for her mug on the table and holding it in the palm of her hands. "Or maybe it's an adaptation to what's going on inside of me, so I can better handle what's happening outside of me." She took a tiny sip from her mug. "Clearly, I've been deep in the psychoanalysis textbooks." Her eyes looked up toward the ceiling as she shrugged. How quickly she'd humbled herself in the face of what he thought was a profoundly self-aware thing to say. "And another question hanging over my head these days: What happens after all this learning? Don't get me wrong, psychology is interesting stuff, I love studying it, but what the heck do you do with a degree in it, you know? I'd hate to go back after graduation to the same house I grew up in."

He nodded and sat back. "The doing is what you're doing, you don't have to decide the rest of your life anytime soon." Jace cracked a knuckle and glanced at her sipping her coffee. "So, what's your chameleon status right now?"

"Super nervous," she let out with a strangled laugh, "and red-sweater confident." The side of her leg pressed against his as she looked off ahead. "Maybe it's the constant change that's the comfort in the first place."

His tongue had grown heavier by her closeness and was now officially tied. She was striking, there was no doubt there, other than maybe in her own head. But the openness she willingly offered him was the most disarming. An intimate exchange he had only experienced in well-worn relationships. Of which he'd had one. In high school. Did that even count? Granted, her awareness of him far exceeded his awareness of her, by roughly ninety days, give or take, but why him?

"I'm sorry," she puffed out, "that was totally random. It's just, you're sitting here and we're talking, and I'm..." She shook her head. "I don't want to scare you off."

"You're not." He wanted to touch her by pure instinct. She beat him to it. Her slender fingers grazed the inside of his wrist. Her smell, lavender laced with coffee, circled around him. His stomach knotted. It had been far too long since someone of the opposite sex had touched him, and it felt far too good. Her voice came back into focus.

"I'm glad you decided to come feed the need." It took him a moment to realize she was talking about caffeine and not herself. His arm tingled as her hand left his skin. His eyes rested on her mouth while an internal curiosity begged him to find out: Did she taste as good as she smelled?

"But I think we may need to separate those two," she said. Jace followed Jolie's gaze to Alix and Dru.

They walked up with hands full of warmed muffins and mouths full of heated words, about the state Dru was from, which Alix took offense to apparently. The words "cowboy," "conceal," and "carry" drifted from their mouths.

Jace leaned forward to grab the muffins from Dru and Alix and looked back at Jolie. Her eyebrows were drawn together as she glanced between the two. He set the plates onto the coffee table and picked up a muffin. "I'll fix this," he whispered to Jolie, as she bit her bottom lip. *Dammit. This girl.*

He raised an eyebrow at Jolie, broke off a piece of muffin, and lobbed it at Dru. Dru flinched as it bounced off the center of his forehead, and Jace watched in horror as the same piece of muffin shot backwards onto Alix's nose. A sound much like a squeaking mouse came from Alix as the muffin exploded into a crumb-like confetti. Jace froze. Alix and Dru, who had broken free from their stare-off, turned to stare at Jace, mouths open in shock. Jolie made a noise. Was she laughing?

"I am so sorry, Alix. That was intended for my friend over there, the one who doesn't know when to shut up." Jace glared at Dru, who shrugged and mouthed, *"She started it."*

Alix skirted around Dru from behind and wrapped herself into a jacket far too big for her stature. "Here," she said as she shoved Dru's jacket into his stomach.

"Take it easy, lady," Dru muttered.

Jolie sighed and reached for a black wool coat. "Time to go, I guess."

Jace rose from the couch in slow, deliberate movements, feeling very much like a sullen child being forced to do something, and put his jacket on. Jolie stirred a curiosity in him he didn't realize existed, and he wanted more. But did she feel it too? Or did her mind change as easily as her clothes?

He reached down to help her up. "Your hands are freezing."

"I'm afraid that's always the case unless I'm stealing someone else's warmth." She laced her fingers with his. He looked down and back up, stunned by the ease of her affection, and stranded in the paradox of this stranger. To him she was unknown. And yet, there she stood, defying logic, with a pair of lips he knew, once kissed, would send reason straight into outer space. An anti-gravity for a new reality.

A punch fell onto Jace's arm and tore his focus away from Jolie's mouth.

"I'm ready when you are, man," Dru said. Jace felt Jolie's hand pull out of his grasp. Clueless Dru. Always trying to amplify the moment with his presence.

"We're all headed in the same direction, right?" Jolie asked as they walked to the front of Java House. Jace held the door open for Jolie. She looked up at him and said, "Thanks."

Dru looked confused as he shoved a stocking cap on his head and followed Jolie outside. Jace nodded. "Homeward bound."

"You guys live a block from us, apparently," Alix said, who was the last to exit. She spat out her words like they were rotten, while she pulled on a pair of thick gloves.

"Well, shit. Now that's bum luck. Ain't it?" Dru capped his response with a sardonic laugh. Jace looked back and forth between Dru and Alix, both standing with crossed arms. Those two had certainly struck a chemistry of volcanic proportions in a short amount of time.

"No, Dru. In fact, it's downright serendipitous. For Jolie. Not for me." Alix stormed off ahead with Dru in close pursuit, their backs blurred by the clumps of snow tumbling from the sky.

Jace captured Jolie's hand. "I'm glad I fed the need too," Jace mumbled close to her hat-covered ear. He hadn't thought about all the work still yet to be done this weekend since laying eyes on her again. In fact, he felt oddly confident that he was going to crush the exam come Monday.

She exhaled a plume of white. "Me too. So much."

"Would it be okay if I call you tomorrow?"

"As long as you mean it," she said, her smile tight. "I've been on the receiving end of a silent line one too many times."

"I mean it." Jace squeezed her hand. He had experienced hurt from others' carelessness too and hoped she believed him. Dru and Alix reappeared and walked silently to the corner separating their apartments. The four of them stopped as a car crawled through the intersection, and sooner than Jace wanted, they were all saying goodbye, again. As he and Dru walked the last block to his own apartment, Jace laughed to himself at how fated it all seemed now.

Was it the novelty of how she fell into his life? Her striking green eyes? Or his curiosity for the few inside layers she had already revealed? Whatever the reason, the certainty of her significance in his life did not alarm him. When, in retrospect, it probably should have.

Three

April 2005

Jace flinched awake in the low-lit bedroom. A freight train on the tracks outside hummed and moaned. Specks of dust floated on the slices of light streaming through the window. The plastic blinds moved in rhythm with the wind, tickling his exposed arm—air too warm for April. The day, well underway, had seeped into the room he didn't want to leave. Not just yet. Not with Jolie lying next to him, with a face so calm, her breath so even, and her lips so swollen from their night together. She stirred as if his stare on her body alarmed her internal clock.

"Hi, you." Jolie's voice was gravel. Her arm flopped over his bare chest. He'd spent almost every night in her bed this week. And yet, her first words of the day, meant only for him, left him amazed. How did he get so lucky?

He flipped on his side, pulled her between his legs, and trailed his mouth against her neck. "Hi," he breathed out. Her flesh was bumpy under his lips.

"I have morning breath," Jolie said as she began to wiggle her butt under the covers. Her smile was growing.

His legs tightened around her attempted retreat. "So do I." He locked her into place as a squeal released from her perfect lips. The slam of a kitchen cabinet rang through the bedroom door.

Jolie went quiet and pushed onto her elbows.

The bedsheet pooled at her waist. "Darn it." Her tank top revealed her waking chill. "I can't make you pancakes if Alix is in the kitchen slamming things around."

"You can be my breakfast," he said. His stomach growled as the uncharacteristic words came out his mouth. Four months of Jolie and he was more himself than ever before and yet still a stranger in his own skin. She turned him inside out and outside in—it was an exhilarating confusion.

"I'm going to pop my head out and see what's up." Jolie pecked him on the lips and darted from the covers before his hands could stop her. He leaned back and watched her hurry into a pair of black leggings. Her legs, extraordinary in their length, seemed to run from ground to neck whenever she wore those leggings. She reached for his white t-shirt and pulled it over her head.

"I love it when you wear my clothes," Jace heard himself say, as if his mouth was possessed by the beauty in front of him. He would never tell her the number of times she brought him to his knees by simply being her. Jolie was midway to the door when she stopped, turned around, and walked back to the bed.

"Morning breath be damned," she whispered, and proceeded to straddle him. Her face was radiant as it lowered to his; the silky ends of her hair tickled his shoulders. He gripped her hips and dug his hands into her backside. The scent of lavender was everywhere.

Jace studied her lips for a moment. His mind was lost in the desire she so easily stirred. He craned his neck to close the gap between them. They kissed, tentative at first but then quicker, with hungry tongues and nibbling teeth, as if they were starved for each other's nutrients. *This* was what he couldn't get enough of, consuming a remarkable creature such as Jolie.

How many times in the last month had he fought the urge to tell her what he couldn't truly comprehend. After only four months. Those three words were pounding on the door he'd kept locked since his last relationship, where the very definition of love had been synonymous with toxicity. The urge was there, to tell Jolie he loved her, but those words, once ushered in, would reveal the weak spot in his armor. Which left him questioning whether it was time to let go of what protected him so well and risk the hurt.

Jolie pecked his lips with a finality he knew well by now and said, "I'll be back," before she untangled herself from his arms. He stared at the ceiling and tried to tamp the emotions bubbling from inside, waiting for her to come back.

When she returned moments later, a frown had replaced her dazzling smile.

"She's in a mood." Jolie shut the door behind her. "*He stayed over again*," she said, mimicking Alix's voice. "It's probably a good thing I have to work late tonight."

Jace sat up. His urge to protect Jolie from a temperamental roommate muted his lingering second-guessing about the L word. "She has a problem with me staying over?"

"A misdirected problem. I think she misses our single-girl hangs." Jolie sat on the edge of the bed and gazed at him for a moment. "Our time here is coming to a sharp point we'll have to touch eventually. Graduation is in a month."

She trailed off, but he knew the empty space she left asked, *Then what?*

During winter break, when two-hour phone calls had been the norm, they had shared their post-graduation plans with each other.

"I need to live near a big city, and away from a bunch of undergraduates who don't know their alcohol limit," Jolie had said. "What a tiring learning curve that has become." Jolie seemed more than eager to distance herself from the country fields he had known all his life. Her move away was imminent once her lease expired at the end of July; the low number in his bank account would keep him shackled to his part-time job until he found something else.

Jolie had also admitted she was bummed to be separated for the holidays and after only a week of knowing each other.

"I like you, Jolie. I'm not going anywhere. I can barely think about anything else right now," he assured her. His fall for her had only sped up during those long winter phone calls. Looking back, he wouldn't change a thing if given the option.

A long-distance relationship, if needed, seemed feasible while they both organized their post-graduate professions. Or at least, it was for him. He was too chicken shit to ask where she stood, too enticed by life in a cliché no longer beyond his reach. They were young and in love. Why ruin it with a reality still a month away?

"How about I make breakfast for you and Alix instead?" Jace suggested. He could help mend the bridge between Jolie and Alix. After all, his relationship with Jolie was the biggest strain on their friendship. Food was the least he could do.

She looked at the nightstand next to her bed. "I don't think you'll have enough time before you go to work."

The digital clock blazed four red numbers he wanted to ignore but couldn't. One day he would say no to filling in for someone else. And find a profession outside of retail and electronics. Her body pressed into his side.

"I'll call you when I'm done tonight," she said. "Maybe we can sleep at your place or something."

"Hey, not so fast. I have a few minutes." He wiggled his eyebrows.

She smiled, an unmistakable twinkle in her eye. "Come on then. We can brush our teeth together."

"That was not what I had in mind."

"Clean teeth first. What you had in mind second."

He sprang out of bed and pulled her up with him.

"I very much appreciate your quick commitment to the unknown." His hand snaked around her waist and squeezed the most impeccable ass he had ever touched.

Her breath caught. "I trust you, Jace."

He released his hold and motioned for her to move ahead of him. "Then, by all means, after you, Lady Lover."

She laughed. "We need to work on better nicknames."

"Kitten Lips," Jace offered in his best serious voice. He peered around the corner. Alix's bedroom door was shut tight. The thumping bass leaked into the main living area.

"That's a weird one. Even for you," Jolie said. She darted into the bathroom located opposite her bedroom—a convenience Jace had underappreciated until today—and flicked on the light.

Jolie grabbed her toothbrush and got to work. Jace found his—yes he had one here—and did the same.

"Babycakes," he said around a mouth full of toothpaste foam.

Jolie spat out toothpaste and swished some water before answering. "Absolutely not." She wiped her mouth on a hand towel and looked thoughtful for a moment while a pink hue saturated her face. "Shower with me?"

Jace rinsed then smiled. "Well, that's an unconventional nick-name, but I can get on board with it."

Jolie swatted at his arm. He took hold and pulled her to his chest. She smelled of mint, sleep, and day-old lavender. He pressed his hand into the small of her back to meld her hips to his. She shuddered against his growing desire as it nestled into the soft part of her upper thigh.

"I have a confession," she said. "I've never showered with anyone before."

Jolie bit her lip. He dipped his head and captured her mouth.

Every first she offered him made Jace fall for her even more. "I get to be your lucky first?"

Her forehead fell to his shoulder. He felt her head move up and down. "So, before I change my mind..." She stepped back and lifted the t-shirt above her head, tossing it to the ground.

Jace's eyes bounced down to her chest then back up to her face. "Right. No chameleons allowed. Got it. Let's do this." Jace began to remove his pants while Jolie removed hers. "But don't go thinking because you're semi-naked my quest for nicknames has fallen to the ground alongside your shirt and pants."

She bent over and turned on the water. Once she straight-ened, Jace watched her remove her underwear.

Jace's palms itched. "And those too. Yep. Who showers with underwear on anyway? Oh speaking of." He kicked off his boxers. "All right. So. What's next?"

Jolie pushed back the shower curtain and tugged him inside with her. Every weekend could start like this, for the rest of his life, as far as he was concerned.

"The prodigal fifth roommate has returned!" Travis proclaimed with lifted arms as Jace entered the kitchen. "Join us."

Jace hesitated. He had just clocked in a five-hour, almost enjoyable shift at work, and felt desperate to lie horizontal for a second before meeting back up with Jolie. He wasn't surprised, though, to find himself here at the end of a day gone too well, bombarded by all four of his drunk roommates.

Dru raised his beer from one of the many cluttered cans on the table in an exaggerated salute. "Welcome home, Romeo."

"I'm surprised you didn't go straight to the ole ball 'n' chain tonight."

This came from Chad, notorious for straight-up assholery and limited direct eye contact.

"She's working 'til ten tonight," Jace said, undoing the top buttons on his shirt. The weather was too nice for an April night. During his drive through town earlier, it had seemed everyone on campus was taking advantage of it. He felt a familiar itch to be out and about, more pronounced now with graduation right around the corner.

"Oh, so we're your default crew, huh?" Chad burped, shuffled a deck of cards, and continued to not look at Jace.

"Lay off dude. He just got in." Tony offered Jace a beer. The peacemaker. Jace nodded his thanks and took a swig. His friends weren't being total dicks; Jace hadn't been around since the start of the semester. Any leftover time he had after his classes, his honors seminar, and work, went to Jolie. He'd run himself into the ground in an attempt to be enough for her, to be enough for his studies, and to save whatever money he made so he could eventually move out of state. And he was failing on all three counts. It would be worth it in the end, but he was exhausted.

"Jace, buddy," Dru said to him directly. "This is a mandatory roommate bar-hopping extravaganza. And that beer is your second wind. We're leaving with you once it's gone."

What other choice did he have—he kind of owed it to his friends at this point—than to change, scarf down a slice of cold pizza, and join the fun?

Many libations later, Jace found himself seated in a loud, crowded beer garden just off the pedestrian mall, drunk off his ass from multiple shots of Jägermeister. This had not been the plan, at all.

What had been the plan? Something with Jolie.

He looked down, plucked his t-shirt away from his stomach, and snickered. His plans usually involved Jolie these days and he liked it that way. The ground moved when he brought his eyes back up. *Where was she anyway?* He wanted her next to him. So she could tell him he needed food to soak up all the alcohol sloshing around in his stomach. Time to hit up the gyro stand.

What time was it?

He stood up too fast and sat back down.

"You okay, Cowboy?" Dru chuckled, slapping Jace's knee.

"How much has he had?" a female voice asked, its tone as tight as a pinched nerve.

"I haven't a clue, Little Lady. I'm not his mama." Dru put his hands on his hips.

Jace focused on the vertically challenged girl next to Dru. "Alix! When did you get here?"

Alix squinted at him. "A little bit ago." She turned to Dru and asked, "Can I talk to you over there?"

Jace watched the two move into a corner near the open patio doors. Maybe he would try to work his legs to an upright position again. He braced his hands against the armrests of the wrought-iron chair and pushed up. Success. Now food.

"Hey-hey-hey." Travis bounded up and grabbed Jace's elbow. The ground evened out from its previous tilt. "Where you headed, man?"

Somehow Jace's hand had found a cup of water. "This is not a gyro," he grunted, but gulped down the clear liquid. Alix placed another plastic cup in front of him. More water. "Alix! Where did you come from?"

"We've been through this, Jace." Alix adjusted the sleeves of her tunic dress—what Jace wouldn't give to see Jolie in a dress right about now—and placed her hands on her hips. "Jolie is waiting for us, and *this*," she waved her hand up and down in front of him, "is going to freak her out."

He missed the last part of whatever Alix had said. Jolie was close and he needed to see her. Now. "She is waiting for me, isn't she? God, I love her." Jace smiled to no one in particular, although he noticed Alix's head cock to the side.

"Dru, let's get him some food."

"Gyro. It's not food. It's just *gyro*," Jace said. He felt Dru grab him by the shoulders while Travis supported him on the left.

Alix was ahead and cut a path to the exit, like a tiny, protective, fire-breathing dragon.

Alix spun around. "I'm going to see if I can spot her. You"—Alix eyed Dru—"deal with this."

Alix marched away as Jace said, "She's always in a mood, isn't she?" His words sounded slurred, even to his own ears. God, why did he do this to himself?

"Buddy, she's doing you a favor right now," Dru said. "But who knows with that one. Cold in a hot-ass body. She's a she-devil I'd visit hell for, ya know? Shit!"

Jace stumbled over something and felt his body pitch forward at an angle too severe to correct. The next thing he knew, his face and the brick sidewalk were making out. The taste of iron bloomed across his tongue. He pushed himself up, his palms stinging, and touched his lip. "Shit." His fingertips were red. He felt a rush of wind and someone's hand on his forehead.

"Jace, you're bleeding." Jolie's voice was in his ear. He tried to look up but her hand pressed him down. "Don't move."

There was a flurry of movement around him. Too many pairs

of shoes rushed back and forth in a nausea-inducing blur. A set of arms lifted him from underneath his armpits. Jolie's voice moved in and out of range.

"This cut looks deep. I think he might need stitches," Jolie said to the person who had lifted him up.

"Nah, his blood is thinned from all the alcohol. It looks like a lot, but it isn't," Dru said or wait— Chad, that was Chad's voice. Where had he come from?

"He's had that much to drink? But, how, why?" Jolie asked.

Jace saw Chad shake his head. "That's what we do, get drunk."

"Y'all, we need to get him outta here ASAP before the cops come," Dru said.

Jolie's voice, slightly more cracked than moments before, was back in his ear. "Crap. You're right."

"Can you walk?" Chad asked. Of course, the guy who had pissed all over his relationship with Jolie from the beginning, and who had fed him shot after shot tonight, would come through in a moment like this. Jace tried to nod, but couldn't. Jolie's hand was still on his forehead. Was that blood dripping down her wrist? "Hi, Jo-Jo."

Jolie's hand faltered. "Don't, Jace. Let's get moving so we can fix your face, okay?"

"Okay. Jo-Jo."

"Dammit." He heard her mumble under her breath. "I'm covered in your blood. Walk now. Nicknames later."

"You got it. Jo."

His feet somehow began to move in unison with Jolie's and Chad's. He heard Jolie say "something's not right," before everything went black.

A week had passed since Jace woke up in the emergency room. He couldn't recall much of the experience but knew what had been missing: Jolie's face. Jace called to apologize the next day but Jolie had cut the conversation short.

"I have to study."

It was an excuse she used to get off the phone for the rest of the week.

Jace touched the tender spot on his forehead where five stitches held together his wound. The dull headache had been around for as long as Jolie hadn't.

Jace surveyed the empty hallway then leaned against the cement wall. Any minute Jolie would walk through those doors, see him, and then what? Run in the other direction? His chest tightened. She had no idea he was here. But he had to apologize again, in person this time, and make it clear he did not want to lose her. He had to try.

The doors banged open. A flurry of bodies filed out in a crescendo of footsteps and chatter. Jace scanned the heads until he found hers. Jolie's eyes were cast down while she struggled with her bag, the sleeves of her sweatshirt pushed up her forearms. Her hair tumbled out of her ponytail and covered her face. Jace pushed off the wall and watched as two people weaved around Jolie, one bumping into her from behind. Her bag dropped to the floor. Loose papers and a flattened granola bar spilled out in front of her feet. She audibly sighed and looked up, catching his stare. Her eyes flashed a vibrant green as he walked over and bent to gather the scattered papers. Jace stood up and handed her the pile.

Jolie's fingers grazed his hand.

"Thanks," she said, shoving the papers into her bag.

Jace ran a hand through his hair. "I hope this is okay—me showing up unannounced."

She tossed the granola bar into a nearby trash can, then looked at him. Her expression gave away nothing. "I know why you're here. But can we go outside and talk? I need fresh air. I hate this basement lecture room."

Once outside in the warm sunlight, they sat down on a wooden bench near a tree in bloom. Jace reached for Jolie's hand. She offered it without hesitation. *This was a good sign.*

"I want to say how incredibly sorry I am for my behavior," he said. "There's no excuse. I acted like a complete jackass. And I'm so sorry you had to see me like that."

"I'm used to it," Jolie mumbled. She squeezed his hand before letting go. "The thing is, Jace, I've heard this apology before. So many times. Too many times." He noticed the bottom of her eyelids had grown damp. He reached for her hand again, but she pulled away.

A lump in his throat began to form. "Who would need to apologize to you for drinking too much?"

Jace watched a tear slide down her cheek.

"My mom." Jolie took in a shaky breath. "The reason I don't want to go back to that house after we graduate."

Jace stared at Jolie, unsure of what to say. "I had no idea."

Jolie rubbed her chin as the tear dropped off it. "The only two people who know are Alix and my childhood best friend, and even then it's surface. But my mom is my mom. I'm stuck with her. You, though—" Her gaze raised to his forehead. "I have a choice."

Jace suddenly felt nauseous. "A choice? What does that mean?"

She looked at him with even more sadness in her eyes. "I don't know." She stood up. His body had gone numb so he remained seated. "I'm late for my next class. But I'll call you later." She offered a small wave before walking away.

Four

July 2005

"So you're definitely going to the party," Jolie said. The tightness in her voice was evident.

Jace cradled the phone on his shoulder. The dark-blue concrete wall scratched at his arm as he leaned against it. "I just don't know when it'll ever happen again," he said.

He felt suffocated most days in this spot, having to navigate yet another argument with Jolie, bickering to avoid what neither of them wanted to talk about. Her leaving. Him staying. Jace wiped the sweat from his forehead. The summer humidity was only an insult to injury at this point.

"This is my last weekend in the same town as you," she said, sounding tired. After his drunken fall in April, they decided to stay together—well, a loose interpretation of the word 'together'. Which was all his fault. His nights out and weekends away were, in his mind, a "last hurrah" before real life began. His urge to run away from reality, while Jolie stayed back working, came all too often. He still wondered if him staying would have prevented her from randomly kissing that one guy back in June?

Jolie had confessed to her terrible mistake the moment he returned from his weekend away at a music festival. Her voice had been hoarse from crying and his ears hadn't stopped ringing since. He cracked a knuckle and then another.

He knew wishing a single moment differently wouldn't change the actual problem, one he wasn't ready to see yet.

Jace ignored the burn in his chest and adjusted the volume to *low* on Jolie's comment.

"You know most of my friends from back home are planning to move soon, too," he said. "This could be the last time I see any of them. Why don't you come with me?" He threw the idea out there even though he knew she had to work. Sweat trickled down his back while he watched two cars in the overcrowded parking lot almost back into each other. Why he continued to take his breaks outside and in the middle of this chaos was beyond him.

"Sure, okay." Her laugh that followed sounded like a warning. "I'll drive two hours to your hometown by myself, arrive well after everyone else has been partying all day, and then drive to Illinois the next day."

The less-than-fun Jolie had landed. Someone who appeared more often these days, in random spurts, and for reasons unknown to him.

Jace thought back to when he'd taken Jolie to his hometown for the first time last month. Back when he thought running away from their problems together was the answer. But he couldn't outrun the fact she had kissed someone else.

She'd been drawn to the river that broke his town in two—a replica of her own hometown—and declared later, over a second glass of wine, that they were fated for each other.

His mom was warm and welcoming; he never expected anything less. Jolie ate little of the home-cooked meal, admitting to a sour stomach that had been around for days. In response, his mom poured Jolie lemon-ginger tea. Jolie stared in silence as his mom placed the mug in front of her. A protectiveness washed over Jace and made him reach for Jolie's hand. He squeezed it.

Yes, people will care for you with no consequences, Jo, he wanted to whisper to her.

After a few rounds of Blackjack, they retreated to the basement of his tiny home. The mattress his mom had found, especially for Jolie's visit, was so old it folded like a taco when they climbed in. Jolie laughed uncontrollably as he pushed her butt out from the middle. He spread the comforter on the floor, and she straddled his lap, eager and frantic with need. She kept most of her clothes on while they made love.

Her bite mark on the side of his neck, a poor attempt to stop her moans, turned purple the next day. She apologized for the mark, more than was necessary. He forgave her. Like he had a few weeks ago. "Let's leave the past in the past."

And he continued to try. As best he could. Which made his unwillingness to sacrifice a drunken couple of nights with his friends on his last weekend with Jolie seem all the more justified. This truly was his last hurrah. And Jolie could easily join him in the fun.

"Just...think about it." He didn't know what else to say. "I have to go. But I'll call you later."

"Okay." She sighed and hung up. Jace leaned his head against the wall. There were four hours left in his shift and then he would be off doing exactly what he did so well when reality was too heavy to carry—leaving.

To his surprise, Jolie drove up to spend a few late-night hours with him. He watched her as she sat around the firepit outside his friend's newly-mortgaged house. She wasn't actively engaging in the party, but she was responsive when brought into a conversation.

"Jo-leeeeee."

Dave approached the fire and draped his arm around Jolie's shoulders. Dave was Jace's childhood friend and had always been a touchy type of guy. Jace could tell it made Jolie uncomfortable. "Why do you have to leave our boy Jace for Illinois? It's really not that different from Iowa."

Jolie kept pulling at her shirt as if she didn't want it touching her stomach. Her eyes were blank. Sad. Like she was present but not.

"It's time to move on, I guess," she said.

The pit in Jace's stomach grew wider. Dave removed his arm from Jolie, the relief in her posture evident. Dave eyed Jace and asked, "How do you feel about all this, J-man?"

Like crap. Jace stood up and offered his hand to Jolie. "Like it's time Jolie and I got some sleep. She has to be up early tomorrow."

Not long after, they lay in bed together in the guest bedroom of Dave's house.

"Thank you for coming," Jace whispered into Jolie's hair. Jolie rubbed her feet against his as she normally did and mumbled something while she drifted off to sleep. It was the first time Jace realized how much he would miss the little things that made Jolie everything.

Early the next morning, he stood next to her car. The inside was crammed with boxes, suitcases, and random plastic bags. No room for him. He cupped her face and kissed her tightened lips. She was close, yet miles away already.

Jace pulled away from her, his head throbbing. "Do you want to figure this out, Jo?"

She kept her eyes cast down. "What's 'this', Jace? You drinking with your buddies every night while I'm stuck at home with my mom, searching for a way out and trying not to eat"—she shook her head as if a fly had landed on top of it— "and trying to maintain a long-distance relationship?"

He stepped away from her spiteful tone. "That's a bit harsh, considering your actions last month. I'm willing to try. Or at the very least, I don't know, not lose you forever." He felt his chest tighten. Not this again. "But you know what? Maybe I'm the idiot. Maybe I should have ended things when it made more sense."

Jolie's eyes, red-rimmed and brimming, met his. "And maybe if you hadn't gone to the ER drunk off your ass I wouldn't have freaked out and kissed someone else in the first place!"

He didn't react. Having heard it all before, he was numb to her point.

"Wasn't it you who said the past is in the past?" she said.

Jace crossed his arms. "And don't you have it written down

somewhere that the future is yet to be determined?"

Jolie's mouth twitched. Sometimes they argued in clichéd quotes unintentionally.

"There needs to be a future to determine one," she said. "We can't control what we can't grasp."

He was lost. "I'm lost."

Jolie took a deep breath. "I think it's best if we officially... I don't want to say it." She rolled her shoulders back. "Okay. It's probably best if we break up until circumstances change. I mean, do you really want to do long-distance? I just... I don't want to fall into what is expected of us versus what is realistic. Right? I'm probably not making sense."

Jace looked down and pushed his shoe into the gravel driveway. She was making sense and he wanted to hate her for it. He licked his lips and braved looking at her face. Rosy cheeks. Forest-green eyes. The home of his heart. "Dammit, Jo. Fine. Distance can break us up. Not the stupid kiss last month. No. We're going to part ways because of distance. It's all poetically ironic, isn't it?"

Jolie stared at him for a moment then rushed into his arms and immediately wilted into his chest as if she could no longer keep fighting. "I'm sorry."

Jace breathed in her familiar scent and squeezed her around the waist but was startled by her sudden retreat. "No, you're not sorry," he said. "If you were, you'd keep trying."

She wrapped her arms around herself. "I am though. I'm sorry for the timing of it all."

His insides began to boil, the steam rising up into his lungs, something he hadn't felt since his last failed relationship. Hurt. "Stop. I don't want to hear it. Go off and have fun in Illinois. Forget about me. That's what you want, isn't it?"

"No, of course not, Jace."

Jace stared at Jolie, breathing as if he'd been running up and down a flight of stairs, repeatedly, since last month. "I get it. It's time. It's been nice knowing you."

Jolie hiccupped a sob and covered her mouth. Her eyes spilled tears freely.

He hadn't meant to say that last part out loud. "Can you just...calm down before you drive away?"

She nodded and wiped at her face. "I'll need you to go back inside. Okay?"

A number of minutes may have passed while Jace fought against instinct, reason, and reality. He nodded, his tongue stuck to the top of his mouth, then turned and removed Jolie from his view. Time to move on.

Five

August 2005

The overwhelming absence of noise bounced off the faded walls of Jolie's childhood home. A buzzing reminder of her current situation: no job to distract her, no income to save for her own apartment, and an abundance of loneliness to choke on. What she wouldn't give to hear the purr of her childhood cat, to feel the comfort of distraction. Instead, she had busied her hands, and her mouth, with an entire package of Oreos. She sat forward and twisted her back left and right. Each crack was a reminder of how long it had been since she last moved.

The phone rang, scattering her hazy thoughts right under the couch. Better off under there anyway.

"How's the day?" Carrie asked, the soft tap of computer keys sounding in the background.

Jolie stood up and cradled the blocky portable phone between her ear and shoulder. Carrie had decided to fill the role of mother lately while Jolie's actual mom was off doing...whatever. Jolie had avoided her mom after her first night home.

"I changed from my nighttime pajamas to my daytime pajamas." Jolie looked down and patted her bloated stomach. "Might go for a run soon."

"Okay, Lady-of-Leisure, you think you could swap the PJs for a bathing suit tomorrow?" Carrie had a full-time job and energy to burn on the weekends, and no doubt had something up her business-casual sleeve. Probably a party—as if booze and a bunch of people were the solutions to Jolie's problems.

A place to go during the day, and a steady income, would do the trick. Anything but another round of cringe-worthy socializing surrounded by a bunch of employed, post-grad professionals.

"I lost my bathing suit," Jolie told her friend. The truth was her bathing suit, which she'd worn only a few weeks ago, had become too snug.

Carrie took a breath. "You can borrow one of my bathing suits."

Jolie laughed despite Carrie's serious offer. "You do realize you're at least two cup sizes bigger than me."

"I don't think so, Lady. You've got a set on you. Have you looked in the mirror lately?" The sound of the keyboard stopped.

No, she avoided the mirror too.

Carrie lowered her voice, "I invited some people from my work. Palmer will be there with a few of his friends too. Mostly people we already hang out with. You can invite whomever you want as well."

"I have two friends and one of them is you. The other is in Iowa." Jolie picked at a loose thread on her shirt. She missed her *other* friend. Alix had offered Jolie her couch to crash on in July, but Jolie had declined. She was sticking to the promise she made to herself: a new life in a bigger city. The current roof over her head was just a teeny-tiny detour to bigger, better things. So, she hugged Alix farewell. And, with a fake brave face, which had quickly turned to tears and turmoil, Jolie had said goodbye to Jace and their relationship.

It would be easy to fall into the darkness of what had al-most-been with Jace and get swallowed by the endless what-ifs. What if their summer together had gone better? What if June hadn't happened at all? What if he already lived closer? What if she had a job?

What if I hadn't gotten so scared when he drank too much that one night?

But Carrie fought firmly against Jolie's wallowing and had

essentially reattached Jolie to her hip. Jolie admired Carrie's strength and tenacity—even if Jolie felt a bit suffocated by her best friend at the moment.

"It'll be a solid group of people, regardless." Carrie's voice brought Jolie out of her thoughts.

"Right. A group of mostly Palmer's friends." Jolie stared at the small hole from the pulled thread on her shirt.

"Well, I mean, it is his parents' property," Carrie said slowly, like Jolie had lost a brain cell or two since starting the conversation. Which was typical whenever it came to Carrie's cousin.

Palmer.

Boisterous in a jovial way, tall like a pro basketball player, and a rumored heartbreaker with his single-dimpled smile. Possibly two dimples, Jolie wasn't sure. He showed up at his parents' pool unannounced a few weeks ago—him in from work, her sitting anxiously in a pool towel—and said in his casual way, "How's it going girls?"

Jolie watched his long legs sprint up the deck steps of the two-story house. Even then, in a pair of faded jeans and scuffed black boots, it felt inappropriate to stare at something so wildly out of her league. Palmer was display-case worthy, as if he should be surrounded by multiple do-not-touch signs.

"As much as I love you," Carrie said gently, "I don't think I can spend another weekend alone with you."

Jolie rolled her eyes—a normal reaction to Carrie's unnecessary dramatics.

"Yeah, I know. I just hate huge groups of people," Jolie said, leaving out the real reason for her hesitation. It was one she had never voiced to Carrie before: extensive time with Palmer around.

Her heartbeat sped up at the thought. Which was ridiculous really. She'd spoken a total of ten words to Palmer in her entire life, give or take nine. The infrequency of their interactions had made it easier for Jolie to rationalize whatever looks they did exchange as nothing but polite curiosity. Even though, when she had spoken her one word to him, his brown eyes had sparkled like she'd just whispered a secret into his ear. But she wasn't anything special, nowhere near sparkling—certainly not in the eyes of her friend's older cousin—so she chalked it up to imagined nonsense. Palmer should mean nothing to her, even if it had felt like something. Because Jace was still more than nothing to her. Even now, in the empty space she put between them, Jace's absence loomed more present than ever.

"Come on, Jolie. Give that couch a break from your ass," Carrie insisted. "And hang out in the sun, in a wide-open space, and in the company of other humans."

An impressive indent in the ancient, brown corduroy couch stared back at her. It was a testament to her hours-long retreat into daytime television and cooking shows. The only way she could turn her fragmented brain into a mush-like quality at the end of the night. She couldn't last on baby-food thoughts forever though. "I am going a little nuts."

"Then it's decided. You're coming."

Jolie cleared her throat. "Yeah, okay. There's only so much Rachael Ray I can stand."

"That woman's voice is grating." Carrie sounded distracted. "Listen, I gotta go. But I'll call you later and we'll figure out the details for tomorrow." Carrie clicked off, leaving Jolie in the silence of her childhood home once again. She stared at nothing, a blankness in both sight and emotion, before looking at the empty Oreo package.

No fewer than ten packages lined the trash bin by now; with the huge life change, her quarter-life stress had turned itself into mindless eating. To the point of stuffed nausea and forehead pimples. A run would help.

She stretched her arms up to the ceiling in an attempt to release the overcrowded feeling in her stomach and padded down the carpeted hallway to her bedroom. Her undernourished reality was fed by the empty calories of others' expectations. For now, she would have to accept this. Once she found a bathing suit that fit, somewhere in the boxes filled with her old life. Another problem entirely. As was the state of her room, and her heart.

She would find her footing. On her own. And unpack her life. Eventually. But not today. Instead, she located her car keys—no problem there—, slipped on her flip-flops—easy enough—and got in her car to drive to Target, where the bathing suit section was impossible to miss.

The sun burned relentlessly the following day, as if it had concentrated its most brilliant beams onto the dried-up world below while the air swelled with moisture. A sheen of chlorine-scented sweat covered Jolie's body within minutes of leaving the pool. The atmosphere was stifling, and her only relief was to jump back into the pool.

A handful of people, most of whom she knew, floated on inner tubes or pool noodles, with drinks raised to avoid chlorine contamination from the splashing. As carefree as inebriation could be.

"Good news!" Carrie shouted over a squeal of someone getting unexpectedly dunked. She doggy-paddled over to a floating Jolie. A coworker of Carrie's reemerged from the water with the face of a raccoon— *Who wore mascara to a pool, anyway?*

"Mark is coming with Jay and they're bringing stuff to grill."

Carrie was notorious for rattling off names as if everyone—namely Jolie—knew who they belonged to. Jolie's blank stare must have tipped Carrie off to her cluelessness. "A couple of Palmer's friends. They're bringing food."

"*Food.* I need food like I need a good ole make-out sesh," Jolie said with a hiccup-like giggle. Yeah, she was tipsy and everything in her view had softened; like Carrie's cheekbones up close, or the wooden posts in the fence surrounding the pool's patio from far away. Maybe drinking on an empty stomach hadn't been the best decision. The only solid food she had laid eyes on since breakfast was the squeezed wedge of lime in her gin and tonic.

She felt okay in her bathing suit, however. Which was perhaps a result of not feeling much of anything at the moment. Either way. Food was required now.

Two guys approached the edge of the pool and startled Jolie out of her haze. They chugged their beers, as if it were a televised race, and shouted incoherently before jumping in. Right over Jolie's head.

Jolie attempted to grab the edge of the pool but missed. The back of her hair went underwater, but she somehow saved her face. Which was a relief. Water and contact lenses—a brand new pair she had worn more often than her glasses this summer—did not go hand in hand. Although she wondered if perhaps the prescription had changed somehow in the last hour. Or perhaps her vision was as overwhelmed as her hearing. It was so loud. And so...splashy.

Jolie took a gulp of her drink and focused her attention, as best she could, back on Carrie. "Have I met them before? Mark and...James?"

"Jay. And yeah, at that happy hour we went to when you first moved back. Remember?" Carrie reached for a passing pool noodle and straddled it, all while holding her beer can above water.

Jolie raised her eyebrows, impressed by Carrie's seamless maneuver. "Uh, you might need to remind me." It appeared she had entered the hazy-memory phase of summer drinking.

"Maybe O'Bryan's? Mark had his eye on you all night," Carrie said. "He's the one with the nose."

Jolie laughed before she could stop herself.

"That's not nice." She was able to place his face though. "Wait, didn't you and some guy kiss that night? Was that Jay?"

Carrie shushed her and paddled closer. "Yes, and Palmer would totally not approve."

Jolie glanced around and lowered her voice to ask, "Do you really need your cousin's dating approval?"

Carrie shook her head. "I just don't need to hear all the

reasons why it's a shitty idea."

A whooping noise from the deep end of the pool drew their attention away from what was sure to be a circular conversation anyway. Palmer stood tall—there was no other way for him to stand—and bounced on the edge of the diving board. Beer in one hand, pool noodle in the other. His gaze latched onto Jolie, and his face split into an ear-to-ear grin.

Two dimples.

"Look out!" Carrie cried moments before Palmer launched himself into the pool. Water heaved over everyone and sprayed onto the cement patio.

Jolie tipped precariously to one side, while Carrie mirrored the chaos. Both reached for the other in order to avoid a watery demise.

Palmer surfaced with a pool noodle between his legs, much like a knight riding a horse, his sword a can of beer, raised high in victory. Jolie sputtered from the overflow of water and absurdity.

"On a scale of one to forever annoying, you're off the frickin' charts, Palmer." Carrie swiped her wet hair from her eyes and moved to the pool steps. "I need a break from the water. Jolie, you coming?"

"Yeah. I'll dry off for a bit," Jolie said.

Palmer and his wet, glistening chest waded toward Jolie.

Jolie watched Carrie's eyes flick to Palmer. Carrie's eyebrows raised higher and her mouth tightened before she stepped out of the pool.

"I was aiming for Carrie, more so than you," Palmer said.

Jolie waved away his comment and the stare she caught herself in.

"No worries. If you're in a pool, you get wet."

Palmer nodded solemnly as he approached. Before she could register what was happening, he'd wrapped his long arms underneath her legs, lifted her up from the water like a long-lost treasure, and launched her, with impressive force, directly into the deep end.

She surfaced with a drenched mind, and a body just as wet but impossibly on fire. After a series of eye blinks—her contacts hadn't washed away, thank god—the face of her best friend's cousin came into focus. His irresistible, playful brown eyes, tinted with humor and challenge, tracked her every movement.

"Oh, Palm Tree, that was a bad idea," Carrie chirped from the lounge chair on the grass a good distance from the water. "Jolie is known for her ninja-like revenge."

Palmer smirked and raised an eyebrow at her. "Is that so?"

Sure, Jolie could strike in good-natured retaliation when least expected, but that side of her had quieted, along with her ability to flirt. "Guess you'll find out," she said, surprising herself.

Okay, that was kind of a flirt.

Palmer's other eyebrow jumped up to join the first. "I look forward to it."

Carrie sighed, loudly. Right, time to stop the tip-toe flirting with Palmer. Jolie was certain her capacity to handle any sort of male attention at the moment was null and void.

She swam to the ledge of the pool and tried not to stare as Palmer bounded up and out—*wet swim trunks, good lord*—and walked to greet his friends at the wooden gate.

Emotions, messy and clumsy ones, sloshed around inside Jolie like a stomach adjusting to a ship out at sea. A constant rocking between loneliness and curiosity. If she wasn't careful, she would wind up with seasickness, and she hated throwing up.

Jolie decided the best course of action was to find a water bottle, eat something soon, and leave the rest of her insides right where they belonged, hidden and out of sight.

Six

August 2005

J olie walked along a path behind the pool house, water in one hand, food in the other. She stopped at the wooden fence. The sun had begun to dip below the horizon; a blazing exit of deep oranges, saturated purples, and delicate pinks.

Her head and her heart were filled with a tumult of emotions. She felt a sense of relief in the spectacular view beyond the flat green field and comfort in the smell of freshly cut grass but she couldn't fight against the longing in her thoughts of Jace. He'd given her a framed photograph as a gift for their first Valentine's Day together: a brilliant setting sun behind wisps of moody clouds. It was a night he planned meticulously, ensuring all four roommates would be out of the apartment—no easy feat—so the two of them could have a candlelit dinner on the old kitchen table. After their meal, Jolie followed a trail of rose petals to his bedroom. The smell of bloomed flowers was so concentrated in his tiny room, she felt dizzy. The memory was so vivid she could almost feel the velvet petals on her fingertips now. It was their first time together, completely. She had never considered herself a romantic until Jace came along.

Sadness from all her replayed memories crawled to her ankles and twirled around them like roots, locking her into place.

"Have you tried my famous butter-grilled corn yet?" A voice from behind startled Jolie back into reality. Palmer stood next to her at the fence line. The bass from the large speakers by the pool thumped, muted and stale. The rhythm matched her beating heart.

"Oh hey. Wow. Hi. I didn't hear you walk up. Or see you. No, that's impossible, you're too tall." Jolie clamped her mouth shut and nodded. "I have tried the corn, yes. Consider me a transformed Midwesterner." Jolie pointed to a hollowed-out corn husk on the plate balanced precariously on the fence post. The combination of grilled, tender corn in melted butter, fresh basil, and a hint of paprika, had been unexpectedly mouth-watering.

Kind of like Palmer.

The unexpected part. Well, maybe the mouthwatering part too.

"Never underestimate the power of paprika," he said. His eyes landed on her. His signature smile was in place. "And the power of perfected grilling skills."

She wiggled her toes in the soft grass. The long blades were wet with evening dew. She focused on the slow-moving dairy cows grazing in the distance.

"The only thing I underestimate these days is myself." She rubbed her forehead as heat bloomed across her face—*Where had those words come from?*—and hitched a thumb over her shoulder. "I should probably get back."

Palmer's arm touched her shoulder. "Hold up. You okay?"

She froze against the sudden heat. There was no way she could possibly walk away. His skin against hers felt like silk had caught fire. "Yeah. Maybe. Actually, I'm pretty sure this is what a quarter-life crisis looks like."

He laughed and shook his head. "You're doing it entirely wrong then."

"Is that so?"

"More than so."

He grabbed her hand—another body part heated—and led her straight to the massive speakers set up under the open-air roof of the pool house.

"I know you're a music snob—"

"Hey now," she said. "I take offense."

"In a good way, Jolie."

He wasn't off his mark though; unknown bands were a passion of hers. One she had shared with Jace. But how Palmer knew this information was unclear.

Did it even matter? No. Maybe.

Because it meant he had paid attention at some point unknown to her. Which called into question the certainty of being off his radar.

She wrapped her arms around the sudden sparks in her stomach. "I'm not sure I believe you, but go on."

"If you can find it, I will play it."

Palmer pointed to the iPod set atop a vibrating speaker, then mimicked her crossed arms.

She fought against a smile. Was he flirting with her? "All right. Let me see what you have on the good ole iPod. But I'm not playing DJ for the night."

She reached for the iPod right as Palmer pulled her into his side. His heavy arm laid around her shoulders, and his bare chest was entirely too close.

"I'm afraid your obscure taste in music will not be appreciated here. This is your one and only chance. My gift to you. To kickstart a proper life crisis."

"Okay, yes, seems fair," she squeaked out, while her brain scurried to catch up. Palmer was totally flirting with her. He leaned forward as she scrolled and selected her current favorite summer jam. It was a song popular enough for the radio stations to play, with a beat that left no room for frowns or stillness.

Palmer leaned even closer and squeezed her when the song came on. "You are not at all what I expected."

She stilled as the smell of him—chlorine, sunscreen, and fresh pine—took hold.

"Jolie!" Carrie screeched from the pool. "Get your booty shaker over here!"

Palmer released her. "I would never get in the way of the beauty that is a good booty shake."

Her insides vibrated. "I'm gonna go"—she pointed to Carrie—"attend to that."

He rubbed his thumb against his bottom lip. "All right. Go have fun, but don't go too far. I plan to find you later."

She watched him take off for the diving board. No doubt in pursuit of yet another cannonball.

As signature as his smile, she mused.

She hoped he would find her later. Whether she was ready for it or not, she was definitely on the brink of a not-so-innocent interest in Palmer. An edge within reach, even if slightly shadowed by her heartache.

"Your song is on! Come over here!" Carrie moved in her direction to the beat Jolie had a hard time denying herself. If only she could feel as carefree as everyone wanted her to be.

Her friends, her mother, herself even, and her stubbornness not to compromise on what she wanted, all encouraged her to live life as best she could. There was no way Jace was sitting at home, night after night, mourning the reality of their situation. The thought of him at a bar with friends, talking to younger girls, enjoying himself, drinking way too much, and not acknowledging what they had abandoned—

Screw that.

She was done. So, fine. She would have fun—and would dance her ass off to prove it.

A cool breeze danced across her skin not long after dusk and beckoned her to visit the hot tub's promised heat.

The music had mellowed to easy guitar strums while the earlier sun-drenched commotion faded into the shadows. A decent fire had formed, perfect for s'mores-making and other guilty pleasures.

Jolie roamed in search of Carrie, unsure of the last time she had seen her. Her face was not among those lit by the fire or bobbing in the pool beyond. Jolie suspected Carrie was somewhere with Jay, not totally naked, hopefully, and making semi-respectable decisions. She should probably find her; that's what best friends did right? Checked in. But, for whatever reason, she couldn't muster up enough concern to continue making the effort. Oddly enough, she wasn't even concerned about where she would sleep tonight. She knew she would find a place somewhere by the pool, under the stars.

Young, and wild, and free—Right?

"Hey, there you are," said a voice the moment her toes skimmed the hot tub's surface. "I was hoping we'd have a chance to catch up. I haven't seen you all afternoon."

Jolie forced a smile in Mark's direction. His unmistakable nose was silhouetted by the house lights. She slipped into the bubbling water opposite him. "Hey, are you enjoying the night?" Jolie knew he was harmless, but Carrie was right, he was eager.

"Heck yeah, I am! It couldn't be more perfect for an impromptu pool party, you know? And you're here, so it was destined to be amazing." Mark beamed, the effort of his desperation like an emergency brake on any hopes of her feeling attracted to him. Not that he realized it.

"I wish all nights could be like this," Jolie said.

She sighed and closed her eyes. The water wavered and raised. Someone else had joined.

"Hey man."

Palmer.

She popped her eyes open and watched him hand Mark a plastic cup. He then offered one to her.

"I'm good, thanks," she managed to say as the spike in her heartbeat pulsed in her ears. She switched to water after the sun had set. It was a decision she was sure her less-hungover self would appreciate tomorrow.

Palmer settled next to Jolie, much to her surprise, and—

Was that his hand grazing her knee? Oh crap, it was.

Maybe it was an accidental brush. Jolie gulped—his hand remained—and she attempted to listen to Palmer talk about the high school kids who had crashed the party earlier in the evening.

With his closeness and the bubble of a pure summer night, she was newly intoxicated. Their eyes connected for a brief moment, and an unspoken acknowledgment passed. *Okay.*

His hand, still underwater and still on her knee, crept an inch higher. His touch was like oxygen to the embers inside her slowly heating abdomen.

On instinct, she squeezed her inner thighs together, an attempt to defuse the heat from spreading further.

"Hey, you two. Where have you been?" Mark chuckled.

Jolie forced herself to look up, so distracted by Palmer's hand on her she had barely noticed Carrie and Jay enter the hot tub. They appeared as one in the dim light with grins the size of proper crescent moons on both their faces.

Jolie felt Palmer's hand move away, much to her disappointment, as Carrie and Jay sank further into the bubbling water. But her letdown was short-lived. Palmer's breath caressed the exposed skin on her neck, his velvety timbre in her ear. "Come join me in the pool."

Sexy. The man was sexy.

"I want to make sure she isn't in over her head," she said, motioning in Carrie's direction.

Palmer nodded and rose to leave, with Mark close behind.

"Carrie," Jolie said over the bubbling water. "Come here a sec, would you?"

Carrie's delayed reflexes eventually kicked in, and she moved across the hot tub, landing next to Jolie with a splash. Spaghetti-like arms wrapped around Jolie's waist— Carrie was definitely in rare form.

Jolie asked, as delicately as possible to a person who had been drinking all day *and* all night, if everything was okay.

Carrie hiccupped. "I'm *fine*. Like, super freaking great, actually. Well, soon-to-be anyway. Once you get outta this hot tub like the other two." With a wicked gleam in her eyes and a kiss on Jolie's cheek, Carrie returned to Jay's lap.

Message received. Jolie hoped Carrie knew what she was doing; although if Jolie was being less pessimistic, it looked like Carrie was...having fun.

Jolie climbed out and made her way down to the pool, leaving a trail of wet, hasty footprints. Her heart raced along with her legs. Palmer was waiting. For her. To join him. A thought as staggering as his apparent interest in her.

All in the name of fun. She was having fun. Okay, at the very least, she was open to the invitation of having fun. Granted, she would never be able to let loose like Carrie, pulling men in for passionate, tongue-filled kisses, but—old news there.

Palmer bobbed in the water, a buoy she tried not to see as a warning: *No swimming past this point.* She stopped once the water hit her chest and looked up at the stars.

"I always thought you were the quiet one," Palmer said, flicking water in her direction. A few drops landed on her cheek, a watery pinch to what felt like a dream. "Yet here you are, proving me wrong with your awesomeness."

Jolie dipped her chin into the water. The instinct to swing her legs around his waist was strong. A reaction she should *want* to drown in the deep-end of denial. Yet the precarious tap-tap-tapping on the glass ceiling of her desires could no longer go unnoticed. So, she did it. A bit robotically, but she successfully crossed the imaginary line between them and wrapped her legs around his waist.

His eyes sparked. There was zero hesitation in his next move. She held on tight as he pushed into the deep end. The rise and fall of his breathing and the feel of silky water on her skin were all that mattered. The details of his face sharpened the more she stared.

Yet, she was too tired to read his warning label. If he had one in the first place. His arms tightened around her waist, his mouth so very near to hers.

Why not wade in the ease of Palmer? she found herself thinking, *Even if only for one night?*

"So, I was wondering…" Jolie gathered herself. "Would you be a willing participant in my quarter-life crisis?"

"Tell me where to sign."

Her gaze flicked to his mouth. The desire to act outside her normal boundaries grew rapidly. Palmer felt safe, like a flame surrounded by water— So why not?

"You can sign right here." She tapped her lips.

He inched closer, his breath mixing with hers. "You sure?"

"Yes—" She had barely voiced the words when their lips connected in a soft, tentative kiss. She released into it with a sigh and parted lips.

One of his hands held her face and guided her on the journey of kisses, while the other kept her lifted and floating. He was quick, then slow, with a few deep, toe-curling, mind-numbing, don't-ever-stop kisses, followed by a series of shy ones.

He gave it all to her— *Good lord, the man could kiss.*

She was fit to burst at the need to be touched. Everywhere. *I know this girl*, she thought, the one currently acting as her. Once upon a time, Jolie had thrived in life with her but had hurt others along the way. She had forgotten about her. Or ignored her. And was now reminded who required the warning label. Herself.

They floated together for a moment longer before she broke away. Her thoughts stumbled at the sight of Palmer's two dimples, more pronounced than ever before. She swam to the pool's edge, reaching for solid ground as the thought of Jace's absence flooded her mind. What was she supposed to do but endure the symptom of their reality? He lived in Iowa. She lived here. She could no longer deny the inevitable. She would have to find a way to let go.

"Why'd you swim away?" Palmer said from the middle of the pool.

Jolie inhaled, avoided his dark, distracting eyes, and exhaled. "You're Carrie's cousin."

He drifted closer. "So?"

"Palmer." His name felt like a speck of dark chocolate on her tongue, a taste of something she would need more of to feel completely satisfied. Maybe that need was reason enough to throw caution to the wind.

"Were you going to say something other than my name?" He laughed. "I mean, I loved hearing it, and I'm pretty sure that's the first time you've ever said my name out loud, come to think of it."

She would roll her eyes in good humor if she knew him better. The man was not only well versed in the art of flirting, but also skilled at voicing his observations of her, many of which she had assumed would remain unnoticed.

"I see what you're trying to do," he said, his body close enough to touch her again. "You're up there, in that beautiful head of yours, searching out all the reasons why this is a bad idea."

She blinked several times. "Aren't you?"

"Jolie," he said with a sigh, as if resigned to her emotional blindness. "Me being related to your best friend can't take away"—he tucked a damp strand of hair behind her ear. Flirtatious, intuitive, and romantic—"what could be a really great fucking use of our time."

Her face started to drop. *Oh.* Of course. He just wanted a snack, not a full meal. She had to fight to keep a smile plastered on, and nearly broke in two from both the relief and disappointment of it all. Of course he would suggest casual. She wasn't ready for whatever this was either. So that little letdown could just—*flick*—go away.

"Okay," she whispered.

"Okay?" He laughed again. "She says okay, like it's no big deal." A mumbled string of words followed, possibly not meant to be heard. The hour was late; who knew how coherent either of them would sound to an outsider anyway. He looked at her. His eyes were cautious yet clear. "So, you're okay to give me your phone number, and okay with me calling you, and okay if I ask you out for drinks—fully clothed unfortunately but appropriately—and you're okay if all of this happens, like, tomorrow?"

She nodded. "I'm okay. With all of that."

Palmer jumped out of the pool, presumably to find his cell phone, while water rushed up and down Jolie's body. *Ride the wave. Get wet.* She smiled despite herself—like full-on, not-forced-at-all, smiled, and thought that maybe she was going to be okay.

Seven

October 2005

Jolie wasn't okay. Not anymore. Her heartbeat quickened as her eyes, dry from the long drive, soaked up every familiar detail. The winding river cut the campus in half. The sidewalks were filled with bodies hunched over from backpacks. The row of bars she used to bounce in and out of lined the main street. All of it was still there, just as she'd left them.

Only a few months had passed. But what filled her eyes now had somehow changed; what had been before was there but faded. It looked the same. It felt different.

Jolie parked her old Chevy in a visitor spot and walked across the parking lot to Alix's apartment. She tried to focus on the potholes in the street. The cracked steps leading up to the four-story building. The chipped navy front door. Anything to distract her from the tightness in her chest. It didn't help. She could barely take a full breath. The air felt thin and burned her lungs. A symptom not of low oxygen levels, or too much caffeine, but of anticipation, of what she would have to face.

"You're here!" Alix squealed. Jolie had barely brushed her knuckle on the front door. "Dru, she's here!" Alix jostled Jolie into an uncharacteristic hug and pulled her through the door. How did Alix always manage to smell like freshly baked cookies?

"You look so different without your bangs!" Jolie said. She squeezed Alix back, careful not to mess up Alix's longer, curled hair, then readjusted her now lopsided glasses. If only her friend's energy could seep into her own tired bones. With the little sleep Jolie had gotten last night, and her subsequent work-day and four-hour drive today, she was standing at the edge of exhaustion, which only coffee—at seven in the evening (so college-esque)—could pull her back from.

Dru's blond head hovered in the background. "Hey, Dru. That's a pretty neat man-bun you got going on there." Jolie smiled through a full-on eye twitch. She wasn't sure how to treat her friend's live-in boyfriend, and her eye had picked up on the unverbalized stress.

Dru reached behind his head and patted his hair. "I'm guessing if you're anything like Alix, you don't much care for it. Which is why I'm keeping it for a while. Just to drive my baby crazy."

All Jolie could do was nod.

Alix and Dru. Dru and Alix. Two people who loathed each other for well over a year, certainly up until graduation, and then *boom*, sparks, and plans, and cozy, shared living quarters. A solid helping of enemies turned friends, turned lovers. Which only added to an already complicated weekend. But as the old saying goes, *nothing in life was free*...of emotional turmoil. Not even her sleeping arrangements for the next two nights.

Jolie followed Alix down the narrow hallway—it was time to enter this alternate reality. She walked past the tiny galley kitchen and into the airy living room.

Alix looped her arm around Dru's plaid-covered midsection. "Welcome to our apartment-in-progress," she said.

Jolie looked up at the cathedral ceiling with a single, wooden beam down the middle, and back down to the balcony doors. It was a definite upgrade from the apartment she had shared with Alix for two years.

"Is that Bob?" Jolie laughed when she spotted the overflowing spider plant in the corner.

Alix laughed in a pitch much higher than Jolie was used to. "Yup, he lives."

"I brought him back to life," Dru said.

Jolie opened her mouth to reply with something nice, or at

least an attempt at cordial, when a body appeared from the adjacent hallway and floated into the room. Like an unforgettable
ghost.

Jolie dropped her bag from her shoulder, the weight of it
suddenly too heavy to hold, and took him in.

Jace.

His hair was split like a curtain against his cheekbones. The
curled ends hovered just above his shoulders. The stubble on his
jawline suggested ease, but his collared blue-and-white striped
shirt, the same one they found together at a second-hand store
earlier in the year, implied thoughtfulness. He was just as lean,
just as tall, and just as familiar. Yet, seeing him again felt brand
new.

Holy crap, she had missed him.

"Hi!" Jolie's voice cracked; her neck heated. She placed a
hand over the soon-to-be relentless rash, one she knew he
would notice. His mouth twitched. He'd caught it.

"Hey yourself." He leaned forward and then back, his body
seemingly stuck between movement and stillness.

She opened and closed her mouth. Twice.

"Jace stopped by on his way to dinner," Alix cut in. "Totally
unexpected. We had no idea." Alix glanced at Dru, who nodded
once in confirmation. Jolie looked at the two headstrong indi-
viduals who clearly expected to navigate as copilots in her and
Jace's incoming storm.

"Relax, you two," Jace said. His smile looked tight as his eyes
locked on Jolie's. The air crackled in her ears. "I thought I'd
try my luck and see if you were here yet," he said, as casual
as the hand that slinked through his long curls. Casual and
cataclysmic.

Don't freak out.

Jolie caught Alix's expression: eyebrows raised so high they
appeared to touch her hairline.

Oh, right.

Last week's phone call from Jace, and the masquerade of

all their unsaid words, had not been shared with Alix. After however many days, however many sleepless nights, and way too many failed attempts at convincing herself that Jace was truly gone, he had called to ask if she would be entering his stratosphere.

She had stuttered in response, unsure if a visit for homecoming weekend made sense. How would she feel seeing him? She had barely been managing when he popped up in her thoughts. Jace had suggested she consider joining the fun, and hung up not long after his three-word poem.

Unable to remove herself from the state of mystified chaos he continued to keep her in, she buried herself in bowls and bowls of cereal instead. A mouth full kept a mind empty.

Jace's voice interrupted her thoughts. Right, he wasn't just running laps in her mind anymore, he was right here in front of her.

"I called to see if she had plans to herd with all the other sheep to our lovely university on the most sacred of alma mater holidays." He spoke directly to Alix, his tone playful. He must have picked up on the tension vibrating through the room.

"I thought for sure her bags would've been packed and ready—any excuse to visit you, Alix. And enjoy the greatness that is fall football season. The only reason to really show up, in my opinion. Sports and booze." Jace closed his mouth abruptly as if he just noticed the last word he had uttered.

Jolie felt her mouth purse. She hadn't missed boozy Jace, but she had definitely missed rambling Jace. Longing from deep inside her bones, for a moment free of complications, rushed through her bloodstream and left her lightheaded. She ached to feel his strong arms wrapped around her again. To lie in his bed, content in his embrace, while all the other memories, so resilient and strong in her head, drifted away. She shook her head to clear the fog.

"What did she say?" Alix looked directly at Jolie as she asked the question.

Jolie's eyes bounced from Jace, to Dru, and back to Alix. Was she supposed to answer?

"Jolie—" Jace cleared his throat as if her name got caught on its way out. The sound of his voice, saying those five letters, however, softened everything. "—hadn't confirmed she was coming until she texted me earlier today."

Alix hadn't taken her eyes off Jolie; her smile appeared forced now. With no acknowledgment that she had heard Jace's response, she asked instead, "Can we talk in the other room please?"

Before Jolie could answer, Alix grabbed her wrist and pulled her down the hallway and into the first opened door. Alix released her grip on Jolie to close the door.

Jolie rubbed at her skin and looked around. "Is this a tiny room or a closet?"

"It's supposed to be a second bedroom, but it's my closet now." Alix examined her fingernails. "Dru wanted an office, but his desk and chair wouldn't fit. And since I make more money at the moment, I won the argument."

"Badass," Jolie said.

She turned in awe of her friend's many articles of clothing. Alix was actually doing it—and doing it well, the whole adulting thing. Jolie pushed her glasses up her nose. "I still have clothes in boxes."

Alix put her hands on her hips. "Jolie, what the hell is going on?"

Jolie frowned. "I don't know what you mean."

"What happened with Palmer?" Alix said.

"I called you like two weeks ago. You were on your way out, headed to the city with him. You sounded excited."

Jolie toed the faded tan carpet. "He wanted more than I could give. I didn't want to lead him on if he was falling in love."

"He said he loved you!" Alix shouted. The volume of her voice was partially absorbed by the rows of hanging polyester and cotton. Still, Jolie's balance faltered in shock.

"His eyes did." Jolie crossed her arms over her chest. "We were on our way back from the city, his brother was with us on the train and said something about us getting serious. Palmer looked at me and then put his head on my shoulder. The weight of it. Literally. I don't know." She shrugged her arms free. "I wanted to run."

Alix paced. Two steps one way. Two steps the other. The room was very small.

"But I thought you liked him."

"I did. I guess I probably still do." She sighed. "His pace was impossible to catch, and I couldn't convince my heart to speed up."

The room folded into silence.

"We should probably get back—"

"I knew about your text to Jace today," Alix spoke up. "Jace called Dru the moment he got your message, and according to Dru, he hadn't heard Jace that happy in months."

A spark flickered in her stomach. "Okay." She watched Alix tilt her head to one side. "He lives here. I don't. End of relationship." It was a truth so saturated it snuffed out all the sparks.

"He could move. Pretty sure he wants to."

"Stop." Jolie swatted her hand at the buzzing emotions. "Or I'll bury myself in the hole I just climbed out of and end up renaming it false hope."

And continue to eat mindlessly.

Alix captured Jolie's waving hand and squeezed before releasing it.

"He has been an ass to you. A drunk ass."

A lump formed in Jolie's throat. "Not entirely undeserved," she said.

"Are you talking about June and that random tequila kiss with what's-his-name? Jolie, he forgave you. It's been four months."

"With only one month of damage control. Then I ended our relationship and left the state. Maybe I forced him out by sabotaging everything. Maybe I left him with no other choice.

It's the only thing that makes sense. Jace's words rarely match his emotions." Jolie shut her mouth. She had never admitted this out loud until now.

"Jolie, listen to me." Alix moved in close and lowered her voice. "You are not responsible for how Jace manages himself, emotionally or otherwise."

"I know," Jolie murmured.

Alix's eyebrows drew together. "And don't you dare feel guilty over something he's already forgiven."

Jolie felt her eyes sting, realizing how small her guilt had made her.

Don't cry. Don't cry.

"Okay."

A knock sounded on the door. "You two about done? I'm starving," said Dru's muffled voice.

"Almost." Alix rolled her eyes. "He's always hungry. Here." She handed Jolie a red V-neck sweater. The material was soft, reminding Jolie of rabbit's fur. "These too." Alix pointed to a pair of black pants and heeled boots.

Jolie picked at the sweater—the smell of vanilla profuse—and wondered if she was still a size six in pants like Alix. "Thanks. I won't be long."

After a quick face wash, some reapplication of makeup, and an even quicker wardrobe change—Alix's pants untouched so as to avoid the mental warfare—Jolie reemerged feeling less like herself and more like someone she hadn't met. A girl who could handle the look Jace gave her when he saw her enter the room. A girl who wouldn't fidget with her glasses—she'd swapped them for contacts anyway—and could smile back at him without feeling like it gave too much away. A girl who could pretend she was someone else and see past those broad shoulders that felt like home, as she followed Jace out the door and into the night.

Eight

October 2005

Two shared bottles of wine and a full meal later, and the itch to be near Jolie only grew stronger. Jace had ordered a second bottle of Malbec for the table—an epic failure to dull his thirst for her—and had sat on his hands after his knuckles refused to crack anymore. Jolie was a force in red; her eyes glowed sea green because of it, and all he wanted to do was touch her. The moment he knew she was en route, that was it. He was done for. To have her this close, this magnified; his underprepared senses were drowning in the depth of emotion her presence ushered in.

Jace needed, more than he realized, the short walk to the bar they moved to after dinner. The smell of stale beer was as prominent as the number of bodies. People were everywhere, shouting, drinking, and spilling. Hopefully, his head had cleared enough to handle the rest of the night.

Jolie nudged his elbow and pointed to an empty spot at the standing counter underneath the front windows.

Once they claimed their sticky-floor real estate, Alix clapped her hands together once. "Dru, honey, you know what to do. Drinks please!"

A queen's summons, Jace mused.

"But of course, Sugar." Dru motioned for Jace to join him. Man, his friend was whipped, but at least he was agreeing to reasonable demands.

Jace felt a pull on his sleeve as he turned to follow Dru. Jolie offered a small smile. "Can you get some water too?"

He nodded. "Good call. I'll probably do the same."

Jace followed Dru to the back. A massive mahogany bar, lit up like Christmas with neon beer lights, spanned the length of the room. The place was a throwback to drinking in the '70s. Everything was shaggy and a bit sticky.

"Gotta say, man, and no offense, but I was half expecting a huge emotional reaction the moment Jolie saw you. Considering how off-the-rails things ended with you two all while the train was still going." Dru let out a low whistle as they waited in line. "Seems to be going okay, though."

"Why wouldn't it be going okay? Jolie's just visiting for the weekend. End of story."

It wasn't that simple, but he needed to pretend it could be. Last he heard, Jolie had dated someone after her exit and smack in the middle of his own denial of their situation. He hadn't pried. But Dru, and his tendency to overshare, had dumped the information unprompted before Jolie arrived. Jace had wanted to punch Dru in the face, which wasn't a normal reaction, so he asked Dru to mind his own business instead. Jolie could still be dating this person, but Jace would rather remain ignorant of Jolie's other life.

Dru's voice sounded over the thumping bass. "Not trying to stir up feelings and what not, relax. Just calling out Mopey-Jace's absence. Glad he's not here. 'Cause that dude is a major drag."

Jace grunted. "I don't fucking mope."

Dru looked at him like he had just announced he was giving up red meat to go vegan. Sacrilegious to a Texan like Dru.

"I'm just not as excitable...lately," Jace said. It was an excuse. He knew he'd been a shell of himself. Grumpy too. But what creature was meant to live in a shell? Jace smirked at what he imagined Jolie would say to his dramatics: *a hermit crab.*

"Sure seem to be excited tonight. Glad to have ya back." Dru slapped him on his upper back and moved forward to order drinks.

Jace walked back with his hands full and nudged Jolie with his elbow. A sheet of hair moved over her right shoulder as she turned. Her smile was wide. Her eyes were bright. A look so unfiltered and so uniquely her—and one he'd seen many times before. He gripped tighter onto the glass he transferred into her hand. Dru was right, as much as it bugged the shit out of Jace to admit it. Having Jolie back in the fold, even if only for the weekend, balanced him.

"You look happy," Jace said, leaning against the counter. He watched her gulp down the cup of water before switching to the wine he'd also brought over.

Her body pressed into his then moved away. He knew it was the natural ebb and flow in the limited space but he wasn't complaining. No fucking way. Still, he resisted the urge to kiss the top of her hair, to inhale her calming scent, and to find out if she still used the same shampoo.

Jolie bobbed her head to the music and sipped from the glass. "Oh god, I probably look like a zombie. I am having fun though." She looked down and appeared to be lost in thought, until she snapped her head upright.

"Also!" she said, revealing a faded copper penny in the middle of her palm. "I found this."

He exaggerated a grimace. "Did you extract a penny from the glue down there"—he pointed a finger down—"also known as the floor? Not possible."

Jolie laughed, her tone high and free. Would there ever be anything better than knowing that beautiful sound was his doing?

"I guess I did. In fact, it released itself willingly." She gazed up at him. "Although, I should probably wash my hands."

"Jolie!" Alix pushed her way through the crowd and grabbed Jolie from his side. Jace stopped himself from pulling her back, and instead watched her go. She glanced over her shoulder. Her lips pulled into a playful smile as she mouthed, *save me*.

Damn, he'd been an idiot. A fool. A willing participant in the hurt he'd turned into anger then fear. A fear reinforced by the pile of job rejection letters on his bedroom floor. All from jobs in her state. The downpour of rejection had drowned his hope and left him sopping wet. He pretended, however unconvincingly, and with way too many bottles of alcohol, that life without her could still carry on. And it could, it had, it did. There was an application for a master's program sitting on the top of his desk right now. Proof he was trying to move on.

Jolie returned with a slim camera in her hand and pointed at his mouth, which he realized had descended downward.

"Don't worry," she said. "It's for a new photo project titled *Alix and Dru: The Early Years.*" Her sarcasm danced with laughter. "She wants a few photos of them together."

After a series of snaps, most of which Alix seemed to be curating for an art studio, Alix snatched the camera from Jolie and announced, "You two now!"

Jace's instinct to step away almost took hold, but Jolie wrapped an arm around his waist, with the other rested on his chest and that damn penny pinched between her thumb and forefinger. She moved her hair to the side—yeah, same lavender and vanilla shampoo—and he draped his arm around her shoulders, like a seatbelt clicking into place.

Click.

Alix nodded her approval and handed the camera back to Jolie. "At least you two are picture perfect."

Jace held Jolie tighter and released. She lingered by his side, while Alix and Dru cuddled and kissed until it was necessary to look away. Jolie shifted her body into his.

"That's going to take some getting used to," she muttered from behind her glass.

"It's an odd match. I won't argue with you there." Tonight was the first time Jace had hung out with Alix and Dru since that one awful night a month ago, when Alix and Dru hosted. The pet names, and velveteen eye sex, and whispers between them had made Jace more nauseous than from a normal night of drinking, and left him feeling decidedly more alone.

"I really don't want to play photographer all night, either," Jolie said. She tucked the camera into her black sequined bag. Her gaze landed on his as she continued to button and unbutton her corduroy jacket. He'd forgotten how much he loved Jolie's understated uniqueness, like how she paired random sparkling accessories with otherwise utilitarian clothing.

She had turned heads back then, with an infuriatingly humble ignorance, and even more so now. He had counted at least five lingering stares in her direction since arriving at the bar. Not that he blamed those wandering eyes. Jolie was radiant. He couldn't control how far her light would reach, and he wouldn't dare try. He only wondered how long her flames would stay contained. His burns may have healed, but the scars remained.

"You're staying with them this weekend, right?" He faked a cringe and smiled at her. She shuddered and nodded.

"And you know how paper-thin those walls are," he added.

She lightly slapped his arm. "Not helping!" Her eyes, forest-green now, darted to his, while a delicate pink hue took over her cream-colored pallor.

He would bet all his money, which wasn't much at all, that she wasn't thinking about her two friends going at it right now.

"Remember that one day right before graduation?" he asked, hoping his instinct was right.

Her cheeks flamed red, and his heart swelled. There was no other face like hers. No other flame he would willingly step into.

"God, you're going there, all right. Of course, I remember. Alix wouldn't look at me for a full week," she said.

He fought against the need to readjust himself as she pulled her bottom lip between her teeth. Was she aware of the effect she was having on him?

"I enjoyed that particular vocal concert," he said. His voice sounded deeper, even to his own ears.

Her gaze fixated on his mouth while her fingers worked around those coat buttons again.

"Which is why I brought earplugs." She looked up. "Saving grace."

He poked her arm. "You wear earplugs now, huh? This is breaking news, coming from the world's second most finicky sleeper."

"That's a little harsh coming from the world's *first* most finicky sleeper." She held him in a weighted stare. "You're right, though. The feel of them is awful. But I do have this." She raised her glass to her lips, those he so desperately wanted to feel on his own, and took a tiny sip.

"That's not tequila, right?" he joked, knowing he had ordered the drink for her.

She grimaced. "Oh gosh, no. I can't even look at a bottle."

He was aware. She'd apologized for her mistake in June and promised to never drink tequila again. If only those words could heal his cut rather than slap a Band-Aid over the wound.

Between hiccupping sobs, Jolie acknowledged her slip-up had reopened the scars from his previous relationship. And she tearfully admitted he deserved better than what her mistake had proved—Jolie was just like *her*.

His ego had begged him to walk away. His heart, however, urged him to forgive, as she had done for his drunken fall months before. So he licked his wounds with his late nights out, hoping his forgiveness would see him through the hurt. It almost worked too, until she left for a new life away from him.

But she came back, didn't she? Jace cracked the knuckles on his left hand before picking up his water and chugging it.

"Let's do tequila shots, guys!" Dru shouted. An eruption of cheers broke out from total strangers who, in free-drink haste, swarmed Dru. Jace felt Jolie tense up next to him. Dru was a good friend—despite his tendency to throw around money while drunk. A good friend who would understand why Jace needed to go, and why Jolie was coming with him.

He took Jolie by the hand and walked out of the bar into the chilly autumn night. They walked across the street and into the section of campus lined with academic buildings—no chance of drunken crowds over here.

"This seems purposeful," she said once he slowed down.

Without much thought, he rushed to say, "Stay at my place tonight, Jo." A brisk wind cut straight through his shirt, but it wasn't the reason for his sudden shiver.

She halted. Right in front of the building where they had first met after class. Whether she realized it or not was unclear. She seemed to be in a silent fight with herself.

"Is that really a good idea?"

No. He was at serious risk of falling for her all over again, harder than before. Which meant heartbreak all over again. Hell, she could be with someone else or not love him anymore. Which meant time was moving at a burnout speed.

"I just said hello to you," he said. "I'm not ready to say goodbye again." His shoulders tensed as he squinted. Her exquisite light had searched out the cracks in the wall he'd hid behind since her absence. He felt disoriented and blinded by his need to keep her light near him.

She watched him with a wavering stance. "No funny business?"

Jace laughed before sobering. "I mean, if that's what you want, sure. No funny business."

She looked around, and he watched as realization dawned in her eyes. "There's no other way than overwhelmed with you, Jace," she whispered, her gaze trained on the building. "Or maybe it's you and me together that creates the overwhelm. And maybe sleep is the cure."

The only overwhelm he felt was how quickly their time together was ending. "Is that a yes? You'll stay with me tonight?"

She sighed, kind of smiled—closed-mouth smiles confused him—and nodded. "It's an...okay."

Nine

October 2005

The drive through downtown the following afternoon was Jace's first mistake. Not taking into account the football team's afternoon win and homecoming weekend was his second. But his third and most constant mistake was undoubtedly his crappy retail job. Forty torturous hours a week dedicated to sucking away any sense of meaning to life. But money was money. And he needed it to pursue a higher degree in place of his failing job hunt. In the amount of time he had spent drafting cover letters and submitting resumes, he could have easily produced his first midterm paper in a master's program by now.

At least that's what he kept telling himself while he sat in his rusty relic of a car. It sputtered and moaned in the long line of traffic that was moving at a corpse's pace. He was late, nowhere near his apartment, and wanted—no—needed to remove his work clothes. To then somehow, *somehow*, find Jolie in the masses.

Jace rolled down his window so he could breathe in fresh air. *Jolie.* It felt like home in his mind, to have his thoughts occupied by her all day again. He breathed in the late-afternoon air—a hint of crispness, a touch of grilled food—and took in the color-drenched trees. Near perfect. Once he found Jolie.

His cell phone rang. "What's up?"

"Back in town yet?" Dru's voice fought against the noise of whatever restaurant he was calling from.

"Kind of." Jace stared at the hunks of metal in front of him. At this rate, it would be well past dark by the time he got out of the bumper-to-bumper traffic.

"Is Jolie with you?" a woman's voice shouted in the background. Alix.

Jace rubbed a finger above his eyebrow. "No. I just got off work. I'm still in my car."

Dru repeated everything to Alix in a booming slur. Jace felt certain a full-fledged headache was on the way if he didn't get off the phone soon.

"When did you see her last?" Jace asked. It wasn't unheard of, Jolie turning skittish, especially when spaces became too claustrophobic for her.

"Here at the restaurant." Dru stopped as the sound muffled. "Christ. Sorry man. Alix is fit to be tied. I guess Jolie left to make a call. Now she's nowhere to be seen." Another muffled pause. Jace moved a car's length before stopping again. Dru came back on the line, the background noise muted. "Here's the deal. Alix is trying to cover for Jolie. I saw her go outside with some guy. You should know."

Jace's stomach dropped. "I thought you said she went out to make a phone call."

"Alix did. Hell if I know. She might've had her phone with her. I'm certain there was a guy close behind and he seemed to know her well enough." Dru's words were a billboard Jace refused to look at. But the message was clear enough: *Claim your property!*

"So she recognized someone she knew," Jace said. His gut kicked him from side to side, urging him to find a remedy for the nausea. If only he could convince his emotions to respond as nonchalantly as his tongue had. It was so easy to manipulate a muscle with zero intelligence, he thought, unlike his brain. Or his guts.

He tapped his fingers on the steering wheel to an imaginary cadence.

Truth or lie. *Tap-tap-tap.* Truth or lie. *Tap-tap-tap.*

The past was in the past, he thought, as he bit around his thumbnail. He would swallow whatever he had to in order to settle his stomach. He looked down and stopped. The bed of his nail was near blood.

"That was an hour ago, man." Dru sounded defensive. Jace didn't blame him. Dru was holding true to an unspoken code when it came to women. Always have your buddy's back. Especially with one who was unpredictable.

"Well, shit. Hopefully she's okay," Jace said. He refused to believe Jolie would stab him in the back. Not this time. How could he even consider this possibility with the way she had looked at him last night?

They had stayed up talking until the birds announced the break of dawn. No funny business though, per her request. But that didn't stop him from cupping her face in the shadows of the disappearing night and asking for a kiss.

Her skin, as soft as he remembered, warmed against his palm when she nodded her head. His lips grazed hers, an aching touch so familiar and, as their kiss deepened, so needed. A lightning awareness of her presence struck him right in the spot he had tried to numb, quickening the relentless beating of what he'd hidden from her all along—his heart.

Did he believe she pranced off with some dude the day after all that? Ditched her friends and him, an hour before he was due to join the fun? No. Well, maybe. Was he a fool? Yeah. He would always be a fool when it came to her.

Jace got the name of the restaurant from Dru and hung up. His knuckles went white as he gripped the phone. He wanted to call her. A reasonable action would be to call her. The risk of her not picking up and further fueling all of his doubt stopped him.

He laid his forehead against the steering wheel. The knot in his stomach, thick and dense, weighed him down to the dirty floor of his car. *What am I even doing with my life?*

A determined tap on his window startled him out of his near

existential crisis.

Annoyed and prepared to fend off a drunken idiot, he turned in his seat. A pair of green eyes peered inside the car. Relief rushed down his spine. *There she is.* He leaned over to crank down the window. "Are you for real right now? How did you even find me in this mess?"

Jolie swung the passenger door open and jumped in.

"Easy! Thanks to this blue antique. You're still alive and kicking, aren't you old pal?" She patted the dashboard like it was a beloved tomcat returned home from a wild night out.

He resisted the urge to do the same and reply, *It's nice to have you back too, Jolie,* but he was too fearful she would spook and run away again.

"Besides, I was walking faster than you. It wasn't hard to catch up."

He peered out the windshield. "Where are you headed?"

Were you with anyone?

The smell of lavender and vanilla flooded the car.

"Somewhere. Anywhere. I guess." She scratched her sun-kissed nose, the spattering of freckles more pronounced than when he saw her last night.

"You were on the sunny side of the stadium today, I see." He wanted to tap her nose and be playful. He wanted to ignore the disappointment of missing the game because he had to cover someone's shift at work. He wanted to take her in with nothing but guileless adoration. None of that seemed unreasonable, which made it all the more unreachable.

"Yeah. Thanks for the sunglasses by the way." She dug into her purse and pulled out the pair he'd lent her. "You're coming back from work I see."

He nodded and reached for her hand across the gear shift. Their fingers automatically laced together. Her skin against his grounded him. It always did.

"I just got off the phone with Dru." He flexed his free hand on the steering wheel. He was going against the grain but owed it to himself to ask, to not ignore it. For once. "Alix was in the background. They were looking for you."

"Ugh. Right." Her knee started to bounce. "They were so busy making eyes at each other, I thought I could slip away to take a call."

He felt the weight of her stare on the side of his face but remained quiet in hopes she would keep talking. His eyes started to burn from staring ahead, unblinking, while he waited for her to continue.

"I wanted to tell you last night but..." She blew out a breath, and he knew, whatever was coming next, he wasn't going to like it. "I dated someone for a while and only recently ended it. For many reasons he seems unwilling to accept."

The traffic started to move, although pedestrians continued to weave in and out of the line of cars. It was a jaywalking nightmare. Jace focused on the road ahead rather than the ticking time bomb in his car. She was talking about her friend's cousin.

What was his name? The in-between guy. Christ. His own in-between relationship was aptly named hangover.

He felt dampness on his palms and wiped them on his khakis.

"Anyway, he was just checking up on me, said he was worried 'cause I've been quiet. And then everything got really loud, like a practical joke, or something. There was nowhere to go, the sidewalk was too crowded, you know how I get—and I just blurted out, *'I can't do this!'* like a jerk. He took the hint and we hung up."

"I see." He sat in the space of uncertainty for longer than necessary. "So, you didn't go off with another guy just now?" There was no way he could avoid sounding spiteful. As much as he wished he could avoid it. Even if he knew he had no place.

"What? No, of course not. Why—" She shook her head. "Dru, right?" Her eyes were on his face again, but Jace kept still. "There was this one dude tailing me like he stood a chance. Tried to get my number. I blew him off and ducked into Java House. I saw your car out the front window, and when I was sure that creeper was gone, I followed you on foot until I caught up. I swear."

He took in her slumped shoulders and pinched mouth. She had said those exact words to him during moments of, what was most likely, true honesty, so many times before, he'd lost count. *I swear.* She looked tired and was probably even more exhausted from having to say them once again. The urge to comfort her with his acceptance knocked him sideways.

"I believe you, Jolie," he brought her hand up to his lips. "I'm glad you're okay. Now I want to kick some college kid's ass."

"He might have been middle-aged actually."

"That's even worse." He kissed her hand again and placed it in his lap. "So, what's the plan? What do you want to do?"

She sighed. "Not go back tomorrow." She released her hand from his. "I know that's not what you meant."

The time apart from her only amplified the cryptic response. He glanced at her and said, "I'd rather talk about what's been going on with you. Up there in that head of yours."

"It's just...living at home stuff. My lack of independence and too much of the same. Nothing's really changed." She looked out the window. "I'm sure I'll move out soon enough." She reached for his hand again.

He took it in his and stroked her palm. He wanted more of her—touch, thoughts, dreams—but to push her against her will would remove the instinctual intimacy she rarely withheld from him. The tip of his tongue pushed against the back of his teeth. "Are you over it?" A question they used when a mental or physical escape was needed.

Jolie squeezed his hand. "Pretty much."

He knew exactly what to do. His car crept to an intersection. He turned left. The passenger window remained open, her hair tangled around her face, wild as they picked up speed, and got away from it all, and away from what it was all supposed to mean.

The hike was an uphill climb and steep enough to require a few switchbacks near the end. Dried leaves crunched beneath their feet as the crisp air became infused with the tangy scents of sun-bathed pine and dry dirt. The sky, blue and pale, blinked in and out of view from behind the canopy of peaking autumn trees. After forty-five minutes, they emerged onto a bluff surrounded by turquoise water. A former quarry now retired. Beautiful geological devastation. The perfect mirror to the memories they shared.

Jace fixed his gaze ahead as a cool breeze rose off the water. Jolie moved closer to him on the boulder they sat on, like so many times before. The heat from her thigh transferred to his.

"Promise me"—she stopped as if to mark the moment like one of the creased pages in the many books she owned—"no tipping the odds in our favor. I wouldn't know what to do with that sort of pressure."

Jace surveyed her profile, the view just as stunning as the duel of colors from the setting sun and reflecting lake.

"What do you mean?"

She tucked a loose strand of hair behind her ear and squinted. Her eyes were straight ahead. "Don't let location stop you from going after your dream job—or stop you from applying for a great master's program somewhere far away. You should pursue something you'd enjoy doing with your life. Here. There. Anywhere."

"You know that's statistical suicide." His jaw clenched. Why would she say that? Why not tip the odds in their favor? Hell, he could work and do classes online if it meant he got to sleep next to her every night. Anger simmered, but his confusion burned hotter.

A sadness moved across her face and washed away the happy glow she wore earlier. "If we're meant to do this part of our life together, then it'll happen."

His already split heart pulled even further apart. What else was there left to say? He didn't want to argue, and he knew kissing her worries away would only create another stiff problem for him, thus leaving two issues unresolved.

"Fine. I promise." He bit his tongue. Hard. She nuzzled closer as her slender fingers laced between his. This felt too natural to fight. Resigned, he was left with only one option: play the stoic card and act sincere in his reaction to Jolie's sentiment of fairness. His logic would just have to catch up to hers, so his anger could remain unseen, much like the bottom of the muddy lake below.

Ten

November 2005

An ear-piercing beep seared through Jolie's dream. Like a firefly, she was bright and satisfied, weightless in the pulse of her own internal glow. She jolted awake and blinked at the cracked white ceiling of her childhood bedroom. The furnace had been running more than normal with the colder November temperatures, leaving the air desert dry. Her tongue stuck to the top of her mouth as she tried to swallow. She needed water.

Rolling over, she hit the off button on her alarm clock and sighed. Yet another morning marked by her dusty past.

She was still here, living with her mother—barely—and going through the motions of imposter adulthood. Shower, coffee, forty minutes stuck in traffic—a ticker tape of unhappiness. She'd worked as a temporary employee at a title insurance company for two months now. Where pushing paper, quite literally, required none of her college-educated brain cells. In a soon-to-be automated world, she was an unnecessary human.

The numbers on the clock grew brighter as her eyes found focus. *That couldn't be the actual time.* She kicked off the covers.

It was the day before Thanksgiving and Jolie found herself in a rush.

"That's your breakfast?"

Jolie closed the refrigerator door—she forgot her mom had the day off—and turned around. Her mom gave her a look from behind her mug. The smell of instant coffee mixed with who knows what else made Jolie's stomach roll. She gripped her protein-shake. Jolie hadn't encountered her mom in the morning since starting her job. "It is. I needed something quick. I'm late already."

"You're not yourself," her mom droned. "You go to work, you come home to run, take a shower, and go to bed. When are you eating? *Are* you eating?"

"I think we eat at different times, Mom. We keep different schedules." Jolie averted her eyes and focused on the stairs near the front door. Her mom would undoubtedly recoil in disgust if she knew how often Jolie found escape in bags of potato chips and whole cartons of ice cream. Or at least, how often she used to. Leaving Jace last month after one too many kisses to make the goodbye feel final, and his continued absence in her daily life with no end in sight, had stifled her appetite.

"You're depressed because of him, aren't you?" This was so like her mom. She liked to cut deep when a scratch would have been just as effective.

Jolie shoved her foot into her boot, along with her emotions. "Does it matter?" she mumbled before closing the door behind her.

Forty minutes later, she rushed toward the building where her office prison awaited. The west wind cut through the layers of clothing she had put on for the day, prickling her skin. The air smelled of snow. Jolie loved the change of season, but the weight she'd lost had left little insulation.

The lenses on her glasses fogged up as she entered the front doors. The initial warmth had become a welcome, albeit false, sense of relief each morning for the last week. She rolled out the tension between her neck and shoulders, pushed her glasses down her nose—fuzzy vision was better than none at all—then slinked her way through the maze of cubicles.

"There you are." A sharp voice stopped her in her tracks.

Jolie stifled a groan. She'd hoped to go unnoticed for at least the first hour.

"Once you clock in, come see me," Tracey said.

Jolie's supervisor sat low and troll-like in her cubicle, surrounded by soft, insane-asylum walls. It seemed anyone who held a permanent position in the company—and not many did—was a supervisor to the many, *many* temporary workers.

Jolie pushed her glasses up and gave Tracey her standard response, "No problem."

Tracey swiveled to her computer screen. Her nest of blonde hair shifted to the side a half second later. Jolie's cue to keep moving.

Jolie walked deeper into the open-air office. The whole schematic of this place was draining—from the over-crowded cubicles, to the overinflated sense of superiority, to the revolving door of employees. She sighed as an acute need for caffeine hit hard. Right on schedule.

This was only a blip in her career, she reminded herself hourly. The money she made here and saved by living at home would eventually go toward her own apartment, with a new, tolerable, maybe even enjoyable, job. If only it were as simple for Jolie as it had been for Carrie. All Jolie could do was hope she wasn't completely jaded by the time she found *the* dream job amongst all the nightmares.

"Thanks for coming back so quickly," Tracey said the moment Jolie returned. Jolie felt her brows come together. Something wasn't right.

Oh.

Tracey was smiling. "As you may already know, EPOC has launched. Exciting times. Unfortunately, we're behind, way behind, and drowning in requisition forms on the new system."

Jolie's butt had barely touched the stiff chair—placed lower and opposite the massive desk of her boss—when Tracey delivered the news like winning numbers on a lottery ticket. One Jolie hadn't bought.

"We need all hands on deck," Tracey declared.

She went on to explain in her usual monotone how Jolie

would continue with her current duties, *swash-bucket wench*, in addition to the EPOC tasks, *more swash-buckets*, all while learning the new platform to perform said additional duties, *no mops but clean it anyway!*

And oh, since she was a temporary employee through an agency, there would be zero raise for the extra work. Or wait, how had Tracey put it?

"A great opportunity to put you in the running for a permanent position."

The very thought of permanency made Jolie's feet go numb, as if the boots she wore were too small. They weren't.

Tracey pointed to a towering stack of requisition forms, eyebrows raised. Jolie fought the urge to raise a middle finger in return.

"Okay," Jolie said and picked up the forms. Paper had never felt so heavy.

She weaved to the back of the cubicle maze and into her cell. The majority of 'tempers' were hungry for a permanent role. But that had never been Jolie's intent. This job was a pass-through. Although it had become more of a sewer tunnel than, say, a city skywalk, but nonetheless, not a stopping point. Her final destination was completely unknown, and the constant darkness prevented any enlightenment about what she was supposed to do with her life.

She didn't want to end up a sewer rat; she wanted to climb out. But how?

"You got EPOC'd I see." A deep voice chuckled from behind.

And the hits kept on coming.

Jolie turned to see Roy, one hand on his hip, the other holding a travel mug. A wannabe peacock in business-casual clothes. She hadn't been able to place his age when they had first met—his cologne suggested younger, while his hair, heavily gelled to disguise its thinning, hinted at older. One thing was for certain, he liked to hover.

"It appears so." She heaved a theatrical sigh, overcompensating for her discomfort.

"Well, if you're ever in the weeds with the new system…" He stopped to rub his chin, leaving his sentence incomplete. He did this all the time. And it bothered her to no end.

Finish your damn thought.

He let out a cough. "We could discuss everything over drinks after work tonight, if you're free."

She blinked rapidly. Roy finished his thought all right, it just happened to end in a pseudo date request. She wondered what number she was on his prey list. Roy walked around like his position, marked with a capital PERMANENT, was an aphrodisiac to the agency girls.

"You're at a full one-eighty, Jolie." Jace's voice rang in her ears, a quip he used when her mood was turning on her. Which happened more often than she liked to admit.

"Oh, well, I'm not free." Jolie shrugged, hoping the movement would release her souring disposition. It didn't help. Someone other than her usual, polite self took over.

Roy's pestering, Tracey's assumption of Jolie's goals, the emptiness Jolie couldn't fill… She was done being cornered into complacency.

"Oh sure. Tomorrow I have something but could rearrange my plans for you." Roy popped his hip out as if to punctuate another complete sentence.

She shook her head. "Let me be clear. I'm not free. Ever."

Roy's mouth twisted. "Are you quitting or something?"

Jolie stared at the white cinder block wall just over Roy's shoulder. How much was she willing to sacrifice in the name of a steady paycheck? The daily run-ins with a disrespectful coworker had become more than a tax on her fundamental need for employment. She would rather be broke than spend another day in this dead-end job. A warmth was building inside, one Jolie felt certain would soon morph into the same rush she had felt before. One of monumental change, like going up to Jace all those months ago.

"Actually, that's a great idea," she said, as a figure approached. Roy's boss, bald with broad shoulders, walked at a clip and called to Roy.

"Get out of the temp section, Roy, and back to work. Seriously!"

Roy's face turned tomato red. "Yes, sir."

He averted his eyes and backed away from the cubicle, leaving the exit unobstructed.

Jolie's knees bounced as she thought about what she wanted to do: get up right now, push past a stupefied Roy, and walk out the front door without a single goodbye. Instead, she watched Roy walk away then turned to her desk and stared unseeing at the stack of papers, aware it wouldn't be her problem tomorrow.

When the clock hit five, she put on her jacket as if everything was normal and calmly exited the building for the last time.

Wisps of relief floated up into the icy atmosphere as she walked to her car. The music blasted loud on her drive home, while she smiled with zero abandon. That night, while quiet snow blanketed the world outside, Jolie sat lit in the blue glow of her laptop, and applied to no less than ten jobs, all requiring a college education. Hope floated around her, a thousand specks of glistening light only she could see. And in that moment of impulsive clarity, Jolie deleted Jace's number from her phone.

Eleven

November 2005

We're pleased to inform you...

Jace leaned back in his tired leather chair, its signature squeak echoing under his weight. This was a job offer. Unceremoniously displayed in grainy digital letters on his computer monitor. The lowest rung on the corporate ladder: entry-level statistics analyst. But he didn't care. It was happening.

Finally.

"Jace, stop jacking off, and let's go, dude! We have a two-hour drive," his childhood friend said through the door. Dave had come down for a visit, and they were headed straight north to their hometown for Thanksgiving.

Jace would have been fine hanging solo for the holiday; rarely did he have a day off to himself. But his mom missed him, and being an only child—especially during the holidays—carried certain expectations. As did the day before Thanksgiving.

Dave had insisted that ditching *Blackout Wednesday*—a hometown holiday among their high school friend group, larger than Halloween, Thanksgiving, and Christmas combined—would have been next-level sacrilegious. Jace and his liver were less enthusiastic about the tradition.

"Hold on, just wrapping up," Jace shouted and scrolled down to double-check the location of the job offer. He had applied to so many, he'd lost track. A good number had been in Illinois, but following the events of last month, he'd turned reckless and applied all over. East Coast, West Coast, North, South, Canada.

Anywhere.

Like he'd agreed to do during their hike, having no say in the matter. Jolie had forced him into a corner. Which was why he'd kept a figurative distance as big as their literal one. Self-preservation was typically stronger in a controlled space—or so was his reasoning with each passing day.

He reread the email once more. "Well, shit," he muttered and raked a hand through his newly chopped hair. A single sentence. That's all it took. He was stunned speechless, yet the intense urge to fist pump the air took hold. So he did.

We'd love for you to join our team in our new sister office.

He cracked his knuckles and read it again. Then a third time. This was *the* winning hand in a high-stakes game he didn't qualify for, and all he wanted to do was show Jolie his cards before he laid them down.

"Dude!" Dave pounded on his door. Out of breath, Jace grabbed his duffle bag, swung his bedroom door open, and grinned at his annoyed friend.

"I knew you were watching porn."

Jace brushed past Dave and called over his shoulder. "I wasn't. Not even close. And I'm going to leave it at that."

Midnight. Call failed.

How many times could the line drop before it connected? He tapped his phone against his leg and leaned against the wall outside his hometown bar in middle-of-nowhere Iowa—where shit cell service was as standard as endless corn fields.

All he wanted, since reading the email hours earlier, was to hear Jolie's voice. To revel with her in what he had thought impossible to obtain under such unfavorable odds. A life together. One he felt certain was meant to be lived immediately and regardless of what he was leaving behind. Surely the unsent application for a master's program in statistics could find a new home in Illinois. Yet all he could do was check the time and wait.

The line trilled, finally.

"You're drunk." Her way of a warm greeting.

"It's only midnight." His denial. And truth.

"Fair."

It was quiet in the background.

"Are you out?" he said.

She took in a shuddering breath. A guarded *nope* was her response, followed up in record time with, "Why are you calling?"

He gathered what little courage he had, like a ball of energy in his hands.

Heads up Jolie.

"I got a job offer in Illinois."

The line went quiet. Except it wasn't silent. The faintest sound of a ticking clock piped through from her end. Then a heavy "*okay*" left her mouth.

Maybe it was her tone, or the weight of a single word, but he felt lucid and clear. He'd taken Jolie's love for granted—authentic even if complicated—for long enough. A realization that may have come too late.

Regret pressed down on him as if the night sky was caving in. A million glowing stars overwhelmed his view. Beautiful but already dead.

"We can do this." He could no longer hide the eagerness in his voice.

"Do what?" Her voice was quiet, cautious.

"Life."

A few of his buddies tumbled out of the bar, impeccable in their timing, and insisted, in loud shouts and hard body shoves, that he hang up his phone.

"Life." Her laugh sounded hollow. "It's just one big party for you. Isn't it, Jace?"

Not now.

He walked away from the noise. "Tonight doesn't count." A weak argument even in his head. "I've spent most of the night trying to find cell reception. To tell you we can be together again. That somehow it worked out."

"Right, of course." Jolie's tone arched high, like a cat's back, ready to pounce. He pinched the bridge of his nose and squeezed his eyes shut. Now was not the time to spar against the master of mood swings, but his insides burned. He'd worked his ass off with this job search and she seemed to not understand the time—the fearful hope—he'd put into it.

"Jo, you know this is temporary and not how I want to live the rest of my life. The going out and drinking and partying, all of that goes away once I move."

Another hollow laugh. "Excuse me for the cliché you're about to receive but, I'll believe it when I see it."

Click.

A sense of dread cascaded into the pit of his stomach so fast, hope gasped for air, while his ears rang in the silence.

Twelve

December 2005

"Where's the snow?" Carrie said. "Doesn't it usually snow by now? I don't want a brown, dead, depressing Christmas. I want a beautiful, musical-worthy, white Christmas. Oh!" She paused in the middle of her caffeine-induced rant and pointed. "Parking spot! Finally."

Jolie turned the steering wheel to squeeze her car between a minivan and a truck. Another dent in the car door was in her future, thanks to this micro–parking lot.

"Looks busy," Jolie said.

Just as Jolie's mom had stumbled in this morning from the night before, Carrie had pulled Jolie out of the house and into the throes of a holiday shopping in order to find a particular cheese. For a fondue party. Because this was Carrie after all, who thrived on food, friends, and Jay—well, men really, but Jay in particular for the last month. Maybe two months.

Jolie's rose-tinted glasses had turned gray, shading her view with ambivalence. Only packages of cookies and freshly popped avoidance caught her attention these days.

Carrie dug through her purse. "Of course it's busy. We're two weeks away from Christmas. This is a mission worthy of the greatness of melted cheese. Ah, there it is." Carrie whipped out a piece of notebook paper filled with large-looped handwriting.

"So, you plan to buy all the cheeses I see." Jolie locked her car and shoved her keys into her purse. The moment she zipped it shut, her phone buzzed.

"Is that you or me?" Carrie asked, patting her coat pocket.

"Me." *Buzz.* "You probably need a cart, right?" Jolie passed through the automatic doors and reached for the line of carts.

Buzz. Buzz.

Carrie flipped her hair over her shoulder and crossed her arms. "You're not going to check who it is?"

Jolie struggled to release the cart from the one in front of it. Dampness prickled at the top of her hairline. *Who jams carts to the point of near fusion like this?* She continued to tug on the cart.

Buzz. Buzz.

"Jeez," Jolie said. "That one is seriously stuck. You probably just need a basket anyway." She looked everywhere but at Carrie.

Buzzbuzzbuzzbuzz.

"That sounds like a phone call now. Who calls you other than me?"

Jolie found a basket. "Here." She was mid-handoff when Carrie dropped her arms and pointed a manicured finger at Jolie. She stomped her boot and proclaimed, "Jace."

The sliding doors opened and closed as more people walked through. A blast of frigid air blew through each time. Not unlike the state of her emotions. Rude and cold.

Jolie had no doubt it was Jace whose call was vibrating in the darkness of her purse. The number of times he had called in the last three weeks far exceeded that of the three months prior.

She'd answered once. In a moment of weakness. The details of his move had come tumbling out unprompted. A rush of assurances; his partying ways had finally come to an end; he would now pursue the image of a decent human being.

Whatever the heck that looked like in his brain, Jolie thought. She was unwilling to hear any of it and found herself recoiling at the earnest tone of his delivery.

"I'm doing this for you, for us."

Her anger, which she hadn't realized he had shaken, again and again, uncapped in a burst of wicked foam.

"Do it for you, Jace."

How unfair for him to place his life decisions on her, for him to hold zero responsibility when things go wrong. Or right. Her heart—no, her soul—could not be his saving grace. She was barely holding it together herself. There was no way she could carry the guilt of Jace uprooting his life to be with her, if, in the end, it didn't work out. She'd allowed his calls to go unanswered since. But she felt it, the stress on her endurance.

"Let's just go find your cheese," Jolie said. She backed into a person leaving the store and apologized, but it was too late. The squeeze in her chest, which radiated up her left shoulder, had taken over. She should have stayed home—where solitude and packages of Oreos were in abundance, instead of people and weighted stares from her best friend.

"You know, the invitation to join us tonight for the most amazing fondue ever still stands." Carrie took the basket from Jolie and moved in the direction of the massive cheese cooler. "And before you mention third-wheel status, Palmer will be there too."

"Which would make the night a pseudo double date. Not awkward at all." Jolie controlled her impulse to shudder. She hadn't laid eyes on real-life Palmer since October. He had, however, popped into her dreams at random times whenever her subconscious regret decided to seep through the cracks of her unconscious denial.

"He's bringing Mark, I think. Maybe a lady friend too."

Jolie's stomach clenched. There was not enough cheese in the world to convince her to spend time—of her own free will—with the aforementioned group of humans.

Nope.

"I have flowers to deliver tomorrow. For a funeral."

Carrie laughed and picked up a block of bright yellow cheese. "Wow, that's the best made-up excuse you've given me yet."

"It's not made-up. The flower company I've been temping for

couldn't find a driver, so I offered." Jolie sniffed a block of bleu cheese and placed the rectangle of mold back down. "Gross. Never understood that stuff."

"But you monitor their online orders, right? Have you ever actually been in the shop?" Carrie sniffed the same block of bleu cheese and placed it in the basket.

Jolie made a face. "Is bleu cheese meant to be in fondue?"

Carrie shrugged, not looking up from the cooler.

"Anyway, yeah," Jolie continued, "I went into the shop once, for uh, flowers," Jolie said, a half-truth. She had visited the shop last week, under the ruse of purchasing birthday flowers for her mom—whose birthday wasn't until June—but in reality, to ask for a permanent position. A romanced idea, she realized now, to work with flowers as a therapy of sorts. The owner had told her she was overqualified, while surrounded by the perfume of promised happiness.

"Does it matter? I can drive," Jolie said.

Carrie looked up from a triangle of brie. "You need to find an actual job."

Jolie drew in a deep breath. She'd been hopping from job to job for the last month, a life detail her own mother wasn't aware of. Carrie made up for this by being annoyingly present.

"I'm figuring it out. I promise." Jolie eyed a display of choco-late-covered pretzels. *Hello, Saturday night plans.* Who needed human contact when this perfectly sweet and salty treat could keep her company?

"And Jace? What's the update there? Other than the fact that you're not answering his calls." Carrie plopped in two more blocks of cheese. Her diamond stud earrings sparkled in the light from the display case as she moved toward the bakery section. She might as well be a floating cheese fairy.

"I don't want to talk about it." Jolie grabbed the pretzels in Carrie's wake.

"All the more reason. Otherwise, it festers. Right? And then you'll end up feeling like...how that block of bleu cheese looks."

Jolie eyed the cheese again. Leave it to Carrie to use profound food analogies, an extension of her expert skills in the kitchen. Yes, the Jace problem was in a closed room, aging and growing mold, and waiting to become something significantly less palatable by her own indecision. But she also didn't want to harbor disgust for Jace for the rest of her life—only for bleu cheese.

Carrie pressed her finger into a loaf of sourdough. "Can you find one that is a day past its sell-by date? I need it slightly stale."

In her search for labels with the current date minus one day, Jolie announced on impulse, "I'm going to answer my phone the next time he calls."

Carrie looked up from the bread display, her face stoic.

Jolie felt her shoulders rise as Carrie continued to stare at her.

"I know this has nothing to do with me," Carrie began, her eyes softening, "but I'm rooting for you two. I really am. I mean, Christ, he's moving here! Isn't that what you wanted all along? You need to talk to him, for a fresh start. Or closure. But you need this."

Jolie felt the back of her eyes prickle. The loaf of bread in front of her blurred. "Here. Day-old bread."

Carrie smiled. "Ah, perfectly imperfect bread. The true embodiment of life."

Jolie let out an obligatory laugh. "You're on fire today, oh wise one."

Carrie shrugged. "I read somewhere that the brain in love can increase blood flow, and I'm feeling the effects, girl."

"No, that can't be right. The brain in love mimics that of a drug addict." Jolie glanced at Carrie and took in her flushed cheeks.

Carrie fiddled with her earrings. "So, I guess my brain is witty on the love drug, then."

Jolie reached for Carrie's wrist. "Wait, *love*?!"

Another shrug, a *double* shrug. Oh no. Carrie was trying too hard to convince, not just Jolie, but probably herself too, that this wasn't a big deal.

"Maybe. Just don't tell Jay." Carrie winked and, in a breeze of sweet-smelling roses, sauntered past the flower section to the check-out lane.

Jolie followed her friend and wondered if countless amounts of cheese could replace the denial both she and Carrie seemed to have an appetite for.

Two weeks had come and gone before Jolie heard from Jace again. Following her cheese epiphany with Carrie, her thoughts of Jace were back in full rotation, and this time, he manifested in the form of a text message.

I'm safe and in your state.

And then silence again. She considered texting him back, something cute, and funny: *You're far from safe now that you're so close!* A low-hanging olive branch she could easily pluck and extend. But her hands had trembled. By the time she picked up her phone, she found those same hands were too busy shoving fistfuls of potato chips into her mouth.

Christmas came and went, snow had yet to descend, yet another kind of storm arrived at Jolie's front door. His hair was ruffled and his coat was unzipped despite the single-digit temperatures of a New Year's Eve night.

Jolie stared at Jace while a strange feeling came over her. She wanted to rush into his arms. *Badly*. Was this some hiccup in time? Why was he here?

"I know this is strange, me showing up unannounced," Jace said. Jolie grew stiff. Did he feel the time hiccup too? "My coworker Talon invited me to a party he's throwing at his house. I said no. I don't know him very well, so it was kind of unexpected. But then he mentioned the town he lives in, your town, and how it's right next to where the fireworks are happening, which is why he's throwing the party in the first place, and how it's going to be a wild time. And I thought if you don't already have plans, maybe you'd want to join me. "

Jolie was silent for a moment while her mind balanced the surreal with the real. Rambling Jace was in front of her, being brave, and asking her to...

"A party? I don't know. I mean, I'm shaking already with you in front of me, I can't imagine how I'd do in a house filled with strangers."

"Oh, not the party." He laughed and shook his head. "I guess I didn't get that part out. I meant just you and me, walking in the cold while we wait for the night sky to explode. And you don't need to shake. It's just me."

She wrapped herself in her cardigan as the cold crept into the fibers of the itchy wool. "I haven't showered in three days."

Jace looked at an imaginary watch. "I can wait. In my car. Or in your house. Or wherever. I'm here now. I'll wait for you, for as long as it takes. For...forever." He raked a hand through his short wavy hair, eyes drawn down to his black boots.

Jolie held Jace's gaze once it returned to her face. It was amazing how he could dry her tongue of speech yet drown her mind in unsaid words. All but one. "Okay."

Maybe it was time, she realized, to no longer try to let go of something that was always meant to be. Doors were meant to close *and* open, and she had kept her moldy avoidance sealed for long enough. Ready or not, she would turn the doorknob, release her fears, and watch them explode into the brisk night of a new year.

Thirteen

January 2006

He'd taken a chance and had shown up unannounced. A spur of the moment decision to end his time away from Jolie. The porch light had flicked on, illuminating the frozen night, and the door had opened to reveal two green eyes tucked into a face free of makeup and pretense. The sight of Jolie in faded black pajamas and a messy ponytail was the missing key to all the words he'd kept locked away, which he released in a plea. The tips of his toes hovered just above the stoop as he uttered the word *forever.* Or so it seemed. Regardless, whatever he said captured her enough to join him tonight. Sure, his mind wanted answers—was she lonely, bored, was this all just a whim? But he pushed them aside. The universe was paying it forward for as long as he waited it out.

He rounded the back end of his car as Jolie stepped out and pulled on a cream-colored stocking cap over her hair. It took everything in Jace to not openly stare. He hadn't laid eyes on Jolie since October. Although it seemed like much longer. Time made zero sense whenever Jolie wasn't in his life.

"I remember that hat," he said.

She patted the maroon fuzz ball on top. "This thing is hanging on by a thread."

Jace pulled his gloves on and zipped up his leather jacket. The air was face-stinging cold, but Jolie was next to him, so he wasn't about to complain about the weather.

They moved onto a paved path along the east bank of the

icy river. Parts of the unfrozen water blinked and danced in the streetlights' reflection, as if the exposed parts were overjoyed to still be in motion.

"Have you learned to sew yet?" Jace said.

"You remember that too, huh? No. But I probably will when it's absolutely necessary."

"Necessary. Like sewing a button on a teddy bear for one of your future kids or something?" He had no idea why that thought came out of his mouth. The mental image of Jolie as a mother was too square to fit her unique and ever-changing shape.

A squeal next to him startled Jace out of his thoughts. Jolie's body was veering dangerously close to the river bank, her feet sliding. He grabbed her forearm to stop her from falling into ice and wetness.

"Are you all right?"

"Oh my god, how embarrassing. Thanks. I must've hit a patch of black ice." She straightened her shoulders. "To answer your question. This pom-pom is absolutely necessary. So, I guess my New Year's resolution, aside from finding a job, is learning to sew." She looked at him. "How do you like your job? Would you consider it meaningful, or worthwhile, or whatever?"

Jace navigated around a pile of frozen goose droppings and considered her question. "I like my job, yeah. I haven't been at this new company long but already I feel lighter. Which seems impossible given the workload I'm expected to carry. But also like I was made to take it on regardless." Jace smiled as he spoke. He missed talking to her. It was always so effortless to open up and be himself when Jolie was around.

"Yes!" she said. "A career that you can be proud of, something that makes you feel accomplished, even on the worst of days. I envy that. The more data entry I do, in positions that only need me for one or two months, the more I question what happiness even feels like. I just can't figure it out. What to do with my life."

"You will, Jo. Just be patient."

Jace wondered if wrapping his arm around her shoulders

would be out of place, but before he could overthink it, his instincts had done it for him. He felt the weight of Jolie relax into him.

She exhaled and pulled away. "Wow, there are so many people out."

A large crowd milled about in a U-shaped park up ahead. In the middle stood three tall cement posts. To the left, a semicircular pavilion covered by a white trellis fence overlooked the river. On either side were two floodlights illuminating the park. Everything else was too cluttered to make out. It was odd to see all the bodies huddled against the cold at almost midnight.

"It's like a mob of cheerful zombies," he said, nearly reaching for Jolie's hand as their pace slowed near the pedestrian bridge.

A line of teenagers dressed in outfits more fit for spring crossed in front of them. Jolie bounced on the balls of her feet. The wind whipped around them, and Jace zipped his jacket higher. Loud shouts and fast-paced music echoed from across the river, where a two-story house stood tall and bright: the location of the noise.

"I think that's where the party's taking place, the one my coworker invited me to." Jace saw a rugged-looking man in the distance. "Actually that might be Talon on the front porch." Jace turned to Jolie, then looked past her. He wouldn't push going to the party. "Follow me."

"Where are you taking me?" Jolie looped her arm around his as he maneuvered around a group of people. He locked her arm against his chest while the urge to kiss the top of her ridiculous hat-covered head took hold.

Jace focused on putting one foot in front of the other and asked, "When was the last time you went to a playground on New Year's Eve and swung on a swing as snow began to fall?"

Jolie's laugh, light and sincere, changed the air around him.

As if the gravity holding him down had been reduced by the sound of her joy, he felt weightless.

"This will be the first," she said. "Except it's not snowing." The moment Jolie stopped talking, Jace saw a tiny speck of white, then another, and another, float down from the dark sky.

Smiling, Jace gazed at Jolie. Her eyelids fluttered against the descending snowflakes as she looked up. One landed on the tip of her eyelashes, a few stuck to the ends of her exposed hair. It didn't happen often to Jace, but it always took place around Jolie; when he knew without a doubt the present moment would turn into a cherished memory.

He wanted to pull her into his arms and breathe her in, to touch her as much as his mind had thought of her over the last few months.

They sat down on the curved blue seats of the swing set. Jace grabbed the rust-dotted chains, pushed his toes into the frozen mud, and launched backward. The joints overhead squeaked. A man and a woman from across the street turned to stare.

"Right. Maybe we just sit and chat while we wait for the fireworks." After a weighted silence, Jace spoke up. "Penny for your thoughts?"

"Who honestly carries change these days?" Jolie looked over at him, the corners of her mouth turned up slightly but in a sad way. "I'm feeling stuck, I guess. I'm still struggling to find *the* job, the one that is supposed to make sense, the one that will get me out of living with my mom, who is worse off than I want to admit, and it's just all...stuff I don't want to think about. But if you were wondering, the answer is definitely not at the bottom of an ice cream container." Her gaze moved back toward the river. Jace wanted to ask her more, uncover what she meant about her mom, help her dig up her buried dreams. But he let the silence take over. He didn't want to force himself into a space he wasn't invited to occupy.

"Honestly though, I can't believe you're here," she said, pushing off the seat in a crescendo of clinking chains and planting herself in front of him. He felt his throat go dry. "But you are. And I need warmth." She reached down and brought him to his feet. "Let's go to that party."

"Are you sure?" Jace was out of practice with Jolie's change-able side.

Out of practice and desperately starved.

"Jace, I can't feel my toes. Yeah, I'm sure." Jolie placed her hand in his.

Funny, he couldn't feel most of his body either, but in the best way possible. Jolie was walking with him hand in hand, through a land of frozen glitter, and into the promise of a new year ahead. One with her in it. If she chose him past the randomness of tonight.

They settled onto a loveseat not long after midnight's strike. With a firework backdrop, a chilly champagne toast, and Jolie glued to his side, Jace couldn't think of a better start to the new year. And it was still going. Jolie draped her arms across his chest, sitting more on him than on the couch at this point.

"Let's dance." Jolie's hand snaked down his stomach and squeezed his upper thigh.

He shifted to adjust himself. The finished basement of Talon's house had turned into a makeshift dance floor. Most of Jace's new coworkers had transitioned to the dance-with-zero-aban-don portion of the night. Talon himself was sandwiched be-tween two very animated blondes. The look of bewilderment on Talon's face was warranted, albeit comical. He was, after all, married and co-hosting with his wife. Wherever she was.

"Dancing is going to take a lot of convincing, Jo-Jo," Jace mumbled into the side of her head.

Just a few hours earlier, Jolie was shyly slipping on ice, grasp-ing for balance, but now she was this: a force who couldn't get enough of him. He was having a hard time keeping up. Strike that. He was keeping up. But he knew they should maybe also...take it slow.

Before he could decline Jolie's request to dance, he was pulled off the couch and guided by her determined stride toward a hallway leading to the bathroom.

She stopped and pressed him against the wall. His breath hitched up his throat. Wow, so this was Jolie tipsy on champagne. Her lips feathered along the base of his neck and up to his earlobe, her voice low and heated. "If not now, when?"

A fiery cold, like icy spikes on the tips of licking flames, coursed up and down his spine.

He cupped her from behind and squeezed. Her lips released a satisfied gasp. He was beyond tempted; the strain against his jeans made it all the more obvious. "Jo-Jo. I respect you too much to have sex with you in my coworker's basement bathroom."

She shook her head and dropped her hands to her sides. "No. You're right."

He swallowed down regret as Jolie moved away. What was he doing, turning her down? The gentleman he had fought with all night would just have to step aside and let bygones be hormones.

"My place has a bathroom though, and a kitchen, if you're hungry. An air mattress if you're tired." He was rambling, and Jolie looked confused. "I've only had one glass of champagne. The snow has let up. What do you say? I'll find our jackets and we can get out of here."

She took his hand and walked him to the stairwell like they were leaving, but was she agreeing? Jolie spun to face him. "You're getting your first 'okay' for the new year. Among many other things that I can't wait to remember. With you."

Leaving. She was definitely leaving. With him.

Later they laid together on the air mattress in front of the wood-burning fireplace in the main room, his limbs intertwined with Jolie's. When Jolie walked in earlier, she had joked a bearskin rug would have taken them to smutty-romance status. He'd done his best to prove her right.

Her bare backside pressed against his groin.

"I can feel that, you know," Jolie said with a giggle.

He leaned into her further, her softness the closest feeling to coming home he had experienced since…ever.

"How is this even possible right now?" he said.

She flipped so her legs locked around his waist. "Remediation."

"For what exactly?"

"The months and months of drought." She propped up on her elbow and traced his eyebrows with her finger, right then left. A mannerism he'd missed during her absence, just as much as her bare behind.

"You do need a proper mattress though." She unfolded her spider-like legs to stand and arched her back in an enticing stretch before slipping on his t-shirt. He watched her tie her hair into a knot, exposing the delicate skin of her neck. It was hard to resist the headiness of her. Their reconciliation felt like a rekindled honeymoon period, in an apartment with no roommates, and right on the heels of his move to her state.

Jolie had welcomed him back eagerly and hadn't spoken once of the journey it took for him to get here. She only said that she had missed him. An unprompted confession while tangled together, her words were as sweet and seductive as the pair of lips that had uttered them. He felt relaxed with her already.

Once the dust settled around them, he would ask Jolie to move in with him.

"We can shop for a mattress tomorrow." He rose up on both elbows, appreciating the view as she padded to the retro-yellow galley kitchen.

She turned as if she'd hit the wall with her elbow, mouth pinched, eyebrows raised.

"I, uh—" She patted her elbow. Maybe she had hit it after all. "That sounds mighty domestic."

"Isn't that what's happening here?" He rubbed a finger against his forefinger—the cuticle rough—and stopped himself from biting away the imperfection.

She folded her arms across her chest and pointed to her discarded pants across the room. "Can you hand me those?"

He stood up, butt-naked, and reached for her pants. The earlier calm had definitely rippled. "What's going on up there?"

She struggled to keep her balance as she pulled on the pants to cover her legs.

"I don't know."

Not good.

He knew what this was about. "Did I freak you out?"

"No. Maybe. It's just a bed." Her eyes darted around like she was caught in a pair of headlights not meant for her. And while he never understood what preceded her mood flips, he had enough practice to know how to juggle them. He found his pants on the floor and pulled them on. Her eyes landed on his face and he moved in closer.

"Is this all right?" he asked.

She nodded. He circled his arms around her and breathed. In four counts, out five. Over and over until her body softened. His scent mixed with hers quieted his mind into a calm state of reaffirmed certainty.

Her voice was muffled against his shoulder. "I've lived in the ambivalence of a future with you for so long, it's hard to let go of it."

His fingers moved up and down her back. "I want you here with me, Jolie. At some point. In a bed you like. That you can get a good night's sleep in. That isn't too soft. Or hard."

"I'm not the Goldilocks of mattresses, Jace."

She tipped her head back to look at him. "I just need time to adjust."

Jace swayed her from side to side in an effort to dislodge the force of her own overthinking while ignoring his own. "Adjust to what?"

"To not rejecting hope the moment it's linked to you." Her mouth moved to the side like she wanted to say more. Instead, she said, "I'm starving."

The whiplash subject change was a trademark of hers, as was the shooting pain in his head whenever he was witness to it. But he knew a hungry Jolie could easily take control of a sensible one, so he let it go.

"The usual then." He moved past her into the kitchen and opened the refrigerator. "Scrambled eggs or French toast?"

"Both." She wrapped her arms around him from behind, her fingers wandering around the exposed skin of his stomach.

He turned and kissed her. "I thought you were hungry."

Her arms circled around his neck. "I am. For you. And eggs."

She had listed him before eggs. He kissed her before his blooming grin turned ridiculous.

Scrambled cheesy eggs with French toast and maple syrup with a side of kitchen sex. Simple. Easy. A recipe he hoped to repeat in this new phase of their lives. Together.

Fourteen

January 2006

Jolie walked through the front door and pulled off her stocking cap. She hated feeling like a teenager out past her curfew. It was three o'clock on Sunday. But the car in the driveway meant her mom was home, and all Jolie wanted to do was sneak down into her bedroom. Over the last three weekends, Jolie had spent her time with Jace. His apartment was an escape from her life here, a distraction from a reality she would rather deny. There was a familiar comfort in sleeping next to Jace in his new bed and cooking side by side in his kitchen, but it would never fill what she knew was missing: a direction of her own.

"My only daughter has returned." Her mom's voice drifted down from the kitchen.

Jolie climbed the first few steps until her mother came into view. She sat in a razor-edge posture, a distinct slur in her voice.

"Hi Mom. How are you?" Jolie's autopilot response kicked in. Her mother habitually overcompensated when she was drunk: straight spine, excessive use of mouthwash. And the late-afternoon hour, on a weekend, was prime time for generous pours of vodka from various bottles hidden around the house.

Jolie hovered just outside the kitchen area, a subtle indication of her imminent exit. The house was split-level. A necessary separation.

"I see that...you and Jace are...playing house," her mom went on to say, or slur, rather.

Playing house.

Jolie swallowed back a less than constructive response, determined to ride the high of Jace right over the dark cloud named Mother. "It's nice having him close." She offered a tight smile. "I have a bunch of laundry to do, so—"

Her mom cut her off. "You should eat something, Jolie. You're so thin these days."

"Okay," she said and walked down the stairs.

Jolie closed the door to her bathroom and pressed her forehead against the faded wood. The material was cool against her skin. She breathed. Five minutes, that's all it took for her mom to get under her skin. Like a tiny splinter wedged underneath her broken-down trust.

She stared back at her reflection in the mirror and noticed the inward draw to her cheekbones. She had lost weight, but there was a glow there too, right? Her time with Jace had replaced her mindless solo eating. The urge to stuff her face with junk food was still there, but no longer constant. Except for right now.

Her phone vibrated on the edge of the bathroom sink and almost shimmied into the trash can below. She rushed to catch it from the ledge right as her thumb hit the answer button.

"Hey, you." A deep voice filled the tiny speaker.

Jolie's breath caught. There weren't many people who greeted her with such unmitigated familiarity. Palmer was one such person. After nearly two months of not speaking, she was unexpectedly pleased by his casual hello. Impressed actually, since their parting of ways had been less than amicable.

"To what do I owe the pleasure?" Her voice came out airy and flirtatious. She pinched the bridge of her nose and mentally slapped her wrist.

Don't do that!

"This call is a pleasure, huh? You're too easy, Jolie."

Palmer's tone swam in a pool of unreleased laughter. The image of his indented smile surfaced in her mind. However short-lived, her time with Palmer had been carefree. Uncomplicated. So unlike her history with Jace.

But she had never been *too* easy. They never slept together. Jolie reserved that type of intimacy for those she loved, could love. To seal the deal with Palmer would have been her non-verbal return of the sentiment he had already hinted at. One she couldn't return. Or at least that's what she'd assumed at the time.

If only logic could negate the curiosity of what might have been. Maybe great sex. Maybe not.

"I mean, yeah—after what I just walked into with my mom, yes. Anything would be a pleasure right now," she watched her reflection say with a now flushed face. "And lucky for you, the competition is unimpressive at the moment." She clamped her mouth shut. Where the hell had that come from? It was as if she'd forgotten her lines while standing center stage and improvised a completely different storyline. Jace was the competition, and he was far from unimpressive.

Palmer laughed for a few seconds longer than she felt necessary. "Which leaves you zero room to wiggle out of what I'm about to ask you."

Oh god, he had a question, and her stomach—the traitor—jolted in response. She heard him draw a quick breath, and then another. Was he nervous or speed-walking?

"I'm throwing a surprise birthday party for Carrie. Saturday night. Usual bar. She'd want you there."

Palmer's stilted delivery sounded more like an obligation than an invitation. Not that it mattered. She'd been so high up in her love nest with Jace she'd completely forgotten about Carrie's birthday. Come to think of it, she couldn't remember the last time she'd seen Carrie.

"Oh, sure. I'll be there," she said quickly. She would figure out the details later. Whether to bring Jace or not. This wasn't about debuting her once estranged boyfriend anyway. It was about Carrie. Her best friend. Whose face was fading into the shadow of Jolie's rekindled relationship with Jace. A balance had to exist, however temporary, until her two lives melded together.

"It's looking to be a big group so be there on time, all right?"

Palmer's voice cut in.

"Yes. Sure. Wait—sorry. Can you repeat that?" She missed most of what Palmer had just said. Other people's words were the first to get lost in her wandering mind.

The line went silent. She was about to ask if he was still there when he responded, "We're meeting at eight. Park your car behind the bar two doors down, on the street near...You know what? Why don't I just pick you up?"

"Oh, I—uh, maybe?" The thought of being alone with Palmer, dimple-smiled and seriously tall Palmer, in a seriously confined space, *seriously* did not help her balancing act.

Unaware of her internal struggle, Palmer asked, "It'll be just you, right? I'm thinking it's one less car to hide."

Jolie turned away from her reflection in the mirror as a niggle of discomfort settled at the base of her tailbone. Yes, just her, she decided...for the night. "I'm in the opposite direction of you, picking me up would add ten minutes."

"I'd say five minutes, max," Palmer said.

"No. That's not accurate," Jolie said, remembering how often Palmer corrected her. "From my house to the bar it's ten minutes. I've driven it more than once, you know."

"Ah that's the problem then. I'll be the one driving." His tone was light. Jolie squeezed her eyes shut. She could easily put this back-and-forth to an end. *Tell him you're bringing your boyfriend!* Or, worse, tell him he's wrong by five minutes.

"You can walk back to Carrie's place afterward. Not worry about your car being towed," he added, most likely sensing her hesitation. There was no reason to say no to Palmer's offer; it was logical and efficient. This was a problem of her own mind's making and the root of her freak-outs. Buried deep and spread wide in the rich dark soil of her own self-doubt.

"I don't want to inconvenience you," she said—a last-ditch effort to talk him out of it.

"Jolie," he said, followed by a huffing sound. "That will never be the case." Silence fell as his words painted a canvas with heartfelt sentiments, whether he knew he was an artist or not. "Just say yes."

Could she trust herself to appreciate the view from afar and leave it at that? Kind of like visiting a museum. She liked museums. Palmer was a museum. Look but don't touch.

So, she said, "Okay."

Jolie glanced out the front window. The night sky was painted an orange glow as the reflection of streetlights bounced off the falling ice crystals. It had snowed all day and showed no signs of letting up.

"You're going out?" Her mom's voice drifted down from upstairs. Jolie leaned against the door as she finished lacing her faux-fur-lined snow boots. A new retail-therapy purchase to navigate the snow.

"Yeah, for Carrie's birthday. I'll stay with her tonight." Jolie shrugged on her down jacket.

There had been a time when she wore nothing more than an off-the-shoulder sweater in the cold. Not anymore. Warm was the new sexy.

"Oh, okay, sweetheart." Her mom clutched the banister. A glass of vodka was absent in hand but present in her slur. "Tell Carrie hi. I'll see you tomorrow." Much to Jolie's surprise, her mom retreated down the hallway. Usually there were at least five follow-up questions prior to Jolie's departure.

Headlights flashed through the small glass squares on the front door, as if cued.

Mother is out of sight. Okay to proceed.

Jolie exhaled a breath she didn't realize she was holding in and slipped outside. No one—not Jace, or Carrie, or Alix—knew the struggle Jolie had lived with since high school. Only the fact that her mother drank. The emotional drain of her mom's problem, the vodka bottles hidden around the house, the number of failed confrontations, all of that Jolie kept to herself.

Jolie thought back to the last bottle she found over a year

ago. How she gripped the neck of it so tightly, her knuckles had turned white. She was desperate to strangle and kill the power it held over her mom. Jolie had walked straight to the back kitchen door and launched the bottle with such force, she'd shocked herself. The bottle shattered on the concrete patio below. Her mom shouted, red with rage, or embarrassment. Jolie didn't care. And even then, after all that, nothing changed.

Even then.

It was only during moments of deafening silence and ink-black darkness, when her defenses lowered, that Jolie could acknowledge the weight of unlived years passing through her. Her mom's addiction had required her to grow up. Had forced her to cope. Back then it was by way of McDonald's French fries and high school boyfriends. Totally unhealthy. Totally teenaged. Totally not how she planned to cope this time around. Jolie's permanent departure from the house of hidden bottles was so close. Another month and she would be out. She would be broke but free.

A blast of wind and fat snowflakes jolted her into the present.

Jolie shuffled down the icy driveway, the idling truck a blur through the snowfall, and hopefully from the house windows too.

Jolie pulled the door open and hopped up.

"Hi," she said, taking a deep breath. She stopped herself short.

The warmth of the car was a relief, but Palmer's musky pine scent was everywhere, and those damn dimples— Holy crap, he was sitting there being all...him, and she was nervous.

Staring straight ahead, she breathed through her mouth. It was a five-minute ride to the bar according to Palmer. Jolie had never wanted to be proven wrong so badly in her life.

"So, this is kind of weird," he said. Palmer put the truck in reverse and stretched his long arm behind the head of her seat. The air crackled in his nearness.

"You mean the snow in January? Not really." She bit down on her lip in an attempt to quell the wit that erupted in his presence.

"Fair enough," he laughed. "It's nice to see you again."

She felt his eyes on her but kept hers trained ahead. His truck inched along the unplowed roads. This was going to be the longest five—but more than likely ten—minutes of her twenty-three years.

"It's been a while, hasn't it?" she said.

"What have you been up to since, uh... October," he said.

"Well, let's see," she said, hoping her tone lightened the weight of his opener. "I was working that temporary job at the title insurance place. But quit before Thanksgiving. So, I've kind of been floating about trying to figure things out since. What have you been up to?"

"Good. You're so much more than that job," he said, dodging the returned question. She'd forgotten about this habit of his, the lack of reciprocation. It had bothered her then, but she'd ignored it. Now was no different.

"Well, my unemployed self appreciates the vote of confidence."

Palmer released an exasperated sigh. "You're applying for other jobs though?"

"Of course."

"Then it's just a matter of time."

She crossed her arms over her stomach. She wanted to shrug off his support, yet somehow, it was exactly what she needed.

"Tell that to my bank account."

Palmer tapped the steering wheel with his thumb and then cleared his throat.

The silence that passed between them felt purposeful.

"Listen," he said quickly. "My dad's furniture company is looking for front desk help. An in-between thing. If you need it."

"Does it come with housing?" She clamped her mouth shut, the words out before she could stop them. These random spurts of voiced frustration cropped up at the worst times.

He slowed to a stop at the red light as the intersecting traffic crawled through the slush. "It could."

She turned to look at him dead-on. "Seriously?"

His eyes met hers. "If it needed to, yes."

"But how?"

The traffic light changed, and he looked forward. "Well, other than you being more than qualified with that college degree of yours"—out came a dimple—"it's a permanent position, with health benefits, an hour lunch break, vacation time."

"And the housing you casually tacked on?"

He scratched his cheek, his eyes focused on the road. "It's nothing. I know an apartment that needs a tenant ASAP."

Jolie kept the skepticism out of her voice while she peppered him with additional questions. The unit belonged to Palmer's neighbor, two doors down, who had moved out after a failed marriage. His neighbor had also failed to keep his job and risked foreclosure if he didn't rent it out soon.

There was so much to consider, like how Jace would receive the news. She would be living in the same building as Palmer. But Jolie felt lighter, more hopeful. Jace would have to understand the separation from her mom trumped any possible discomfort he might harbor.

"Okay," she said.

Palmer maneuvered the massive black truck into a somewhat conspicuous parking spot and shifted into park. "I swear, Jolie. You're the only person I know who can break a single word into a million pieces just by saying it out loud."

She repositioned her gloves while a syrup-like warmth blanketed her heart. She loved the word *okay*. Because of its breakability. Palmer's comment shouldn't have taken her by surprise. He was the most intuitive person she knew. How effortless it had been for her to skate on his understanding back then, like ice covering a frozen lake. Until the ice started to crack, and then she got the hell off it. But she wondered, more than she liked to admit, if that thin ice had only needed more time to harden. Or if anyone would ever live up to the smoothness of Palmer's lake.

Regardless, the only thing that could shield her from over-thinking at this point was sarcastic deflection. "I've been known to break dishes, but not words. And I'm starving."

Food fixed anything, and it often took up space in a heart that desired more than was allowed.

Palmer laughed and shut off his car. "Remind me to hide the plates when you're around, okay?" He unbuckled his seatbelt and—

Did he just wink?

"Let's get you fed."

Fifteen

June 2006

Jolie tossed a third pair of pants onto her bed. The previous two lay strewn about like roadkill on a highway. Carrie was due to arrive at Jolie's apartment any minute and Jolie was running out of options. A long bohemian skirt would hide the weight she'd gained since January. If she could find one. Digging deep in the back of her tall dresser, she pulled out a wrinkled swath of fabric. She hadn't worn the floral patterned skirt since her puffy college days.

"So, we meet again." She snapped the fold open and sniffed. Musty but not terrible. And better than wearing jeans in June. A muffled knock at her front door left no room for further self-pity.

Jolie had ditched plans with Carrie one too many times over the last month. If she didn't put in some face-to-face time, she would lose her friend to old patterns. She sucked in a breath and pulled on her skirt.

Another knock, louder this time.

"Coming!" she shouted, readjusting the waistband en route to the door. The skirt fit, but the mental warfare raged inside of her.

"Sorry I was—" Jolie stopped and looked up. Way up.

"Not expecting me." Palmer's dimples flashed their high beams and blinded her for a moment.

Jolie's voice rose in pitch. "Hey, Palmer! Not Carrie. I mean, I was expecting your cousin." She sucked in a steadying breath of pine and musk and *Palmer*. Her nerves should not be like this around him. "Um...she'll be here any minute. You want to come in and wait, say hi?" Jolie opened the door wider.

Palmer kept on with the dimples. "Girls' night?"

Jolie's head nodded more times than the question warranted. Her glasses slipped down her nose. "It seems to be Carrie's go-to these days."

"That's why I'm here. To see Carrie," Palmer said, toeing the frame of her door with his work boot. "She's not answering my calls."

Jolie wrapped her arms around her waist. Her t-shirt suddenly felt too tight. "She told me about Jay and the engagement ring. For his, er, other girlfriend."

Upon discovering the ring, Carrie had called Jolie in a fit of rage and declared she was removing all men from her life, as well as five inches of hair from her now chin-length blonde bob. The let's-be-single-together flames licked upward, hungry for oxygen. But Jolie rained on Carrie's fire, a lot.

Jolie's weekday outings ceased to exist, due to a lack of energy and properly fitting pants, and most weekends Jolie spent on the road to see Jace. He rarely made the trip to her place; his job had become more demanding with all the overtime, or maybe it was because Palmer lived in the same building. Jace never brought it up with her.

Lately though, Jolie found herself spending more and more time alone by choice. Books and food had become her emotional support.

"Come on in." Jolie motioned for Palmer to follow her. She heard the door shut and turned to watch Palmer enter her living area. His large presence shrank the already small, one-bedroom apartment to LEGO size. He'd never been inside her place. But they saw each other every day at her job—maybe his reason, and excuse to stay away.

Palmer looked around. "I knew about Jay. Well, I knew what he chose to share with me. I could have sworn he told me they broke up, him and his girlfriend—sorry, fiancée—last August. But, yeah, she still showed up on the nights Carrie wasn't out with us. And Jay would disappear. I should have put two and two together. Now she thinks I was in on it." Palmer trailed off and scratched the stubble on his chin.

"Yeah. Carrie filled me in. I think we're all a bit shocked. Her rightfully so." Jolie pushed at a cookie crumb on the armrest of her microfiber loveseat.

The loveseat and her favorite reading chair filled the area. Tiny-living experts were not likely to applaud her usage of space, but it was only her. And she rarely had visitors.

"She'll forgive you, Palmer. She just needs a place to spread her pain."

Palmer slumped onto the reading chair. "I hope you're right this time." He raised an eyebrow at her. "I didn't pay much attention last summer, honestly. I was too distracted by this awesome girl I wish I'd taken the time to notice earlier."

The air around her thinned, as if his words had sucked up all the surrounding oxygen. He was always so capable in speech, like snapping two fingers together. *Poof.* Thoughts delivered.

Heat radiated up from her neck. "I, uh... Right."

At least he had the decency to look bashful for what he just said.

"Carrie is family," he said. "I should have said something, once I realized what was going on."

Her phone lit up on the table next to Palmer. "You think Carrie would have listened?" she asked.

Palmer picked up her phone and tossed it in her direction. "Doesn't matter. I'd rather have her not listen to me than not talk to me."

Jolie looked down at her phone then grimaced. "Do you want me to read this?"

"I think you're going to have to if it's from Carrie."

"I heard Palmer talking inside your apartment. Good luck with that." Jolie's eyes met Palmer's. "Oh boy."

"She's something else," he said and stood up. He opened the sliding glass doors and disappeared onto the balcony.

Jolie tapped out a short reply to Carrie.

He's here to talk to you.

Carrie seemed to be angrier with Palmer than with the one caught in the act. Which was frustrating to witness—someone placing blame on the wrong person, rather than facing the facts: Carrie had dated a shitty person.

"Is that her?" Palmer pointed to a car stopped at the corner waiting to turn. A large oak tree blocked the view of the parking lot below but didn't hide it entirely. "She's leaving?" He cupped his hands and shouted, "REALLY, CARRIE? REALLY!" The squeal of tires peeling out onto the main road echoed in response.

Whoa. Jolie had never heard Palmer raise his voice before or noticed the bulging vein on the side of his neck. A bubble of laughter escaped before Jolie could stop it. And then another.

Palmer turned, his eyes narrowed. "Is this...amusing to you?"

Jolie shook her head, but it was no use. Her inappropriate reaction only prolonged her laughing fit. Like that one time during a somber operatic performance in college, when a second-act spark of silent laughter had become nearly impossible to stop. Tears had streamed down her face while her stomach ached. A joyous misery she was reliving again, right now, in front of Palmer.

"No, no," Jolie said as a fresh round of laughter erupted. It felt great. Palmer crossed his arms, but the more Jolie struggled to stop, the more he seemed to soften.

"I've never seen you yell," she said after a few gulps of air, her voice strained. "You're usually the opposite of upset. But that was like watching the Stay Puft Marshmallow Man turn angry"—she exaggerated a frown, pulled her eyebrows together—"with his angry marshmallow face."

"I made you think of *Ghostbusters*." His tone was either one of disbelief or frustration. It was hard to tell.

A light wind moved across the balcony and danced with the hair she'd spent too much time curling earlier. Palmer stepped closer, his hand lightly touching the skin on her cheek.

Well, that was one way to stop her laughter. Her evening had taken an unexpected turn, and she was about to topple over.

"I...yeah, you do. Well...did...make me think of that movie. Yes." Her insides jumped while her mind tried to process the fingertip trail of fire against her skin. "Because you're sweet. Like melted sugar. Definitely not puffy though. I mean, you've been going to the gym, it seems." Her tongue had taken over, and full breaths felt laborious. Palmer was close, too close, even for the limited square feet of her balcony.

"Do you want to know what you make me think of?" The shimmer in his eyes transported her back to their first kiss, when they'd floated together in the cool, turquoise water of the pool.

If she was a pilot watching this storm in the once-empty sky, all of the warning signs would have been flashing, telling her to *abort.*

"You're making it impossible to say no." Her voice cracked.

He cocked his head. "Am I?"

"Palmer," she said, pointing at the little space he'd left between them. "Yes."

He nodded but didn't back away.

"You make me think of how boring and pointless and disappointing—"

"You're doing wonders to my self-esteem, Palmer."

"—and how disappointing all the girls I've gone out with have been. Since you."

"Oh. How many have there been?" The words were out, and on-trend with her absent filter this evening.

"Enough. Not enough. I don't know." He took another step. "They're not you."

By the look on his face, the refocusing of his eyes on her mouth, and the deepening of his voice, it was clear he wanted to kiss her. How was she supposed to resist him, with her back to the wall, and her knees weakened? She needed the support.

"But you're not an option. Are you?" Palmer continued.

She wasn't an option. Of course not. They had split up for reasons—many of which she couldn't pinpoint with him so close, but there had been reasons. The biggest one being Jace—who was sitting in his apartment an hour away having dinner alone because Carrie had begged Jolie for a girls' night out.

"We've done this already," she said.

Palmer offered a solemn nod. "You feel it though, don't you?" He reached for her hand and placed it against his chest. Heat shot down her arm and straight up her shoulder. She felt the aggressive beat of his heart like a prisoner pounding against steel bars. "This connection we have."

"Palmer," she said. "I'm with Jace, you know that." It was a truth as much as it was an excuse.

He dropped her hand and stepped back. "Jace." His sardonic laugh bounced off the aluminum siding. "The man that's never around. Maybe that was the problem with us. I was always there for you."

She hated that Palmer was tampering with her triggers. He *had* been there for her in a natural and effortless way. But there had been an absence too, one Jolie had thought was meant for Jace. Even now, with Jace close, she still couldn't find what was missing. The thought that Palmer could fill her void was too easy to get lost in, which made it all the more impossible to navigate. Jolie felt her hand grip the phone she'd forgotten was there. Why had Carrie sped off and left her alone with Palmer?

"I should probably call Carrie," Jolie said. "Figure out where she stormed off to."

"That was out of line, sorry. It just seems like you're settling."

Of course, he voiced what was in her head already. But whether to see her reflection in the mirror he held up was her choice, and at the moment, her eyes were cast down.

"You call it settling, I call it safety." She looked up and *holy cow* there he was again, surrounding her in his forest scent. The tips of his fingers grazed the insides of her wrists. His touch was soft and intentional. Her mind scrambled while her body urged her to wake up and live, to go off course, and *make a mistake*.

"Safety from what?" His chocolate eyes stared back at her.

Jolie felt reason slip down to the bottom of her feet. He was going to kiss her and she was going to let him.

"From you." Those two words ignited a fire built out of consuming desire. A beacon for her to wander to. He cupped her already raised face, and even Jolie couldn't be sure of the expression he saw in her eyes.

"I really *really* want to kiss you," he whispered.

"It would be impossible to say no."

He let out an audible sigh and claimed her mouth with his.

Sixteen

June 2006

Jace toed his shoes off and sat down on his bed. Closing his eyes, he inhaled the warm breeze coming through his window and rubbed his temple. "You have the tickets, right?" he said into the phone. "I'd hate for you to forget them."

Jolie's forced sigh distorted his phone's speaker. "Putting them in my purse now."

Jace nibbled on the skin of his index finger, broken and bloodied. The taste of muted iron was sour against the tip of his tongue. Jolie was in a mood, again. "So, I'll meet you at the train station tomorrow then. House of Blues isn't a far walk from the station once we get into the city."

"That's the plan."

If tones could kill, he would be a walking corpse. Instead, his cuticles bore the brunt of his stress. "Don't be crabby, please. Be excited." Such a pathetic request, even to his own ears. He was at a loss though. Ever since last weekend, Jolie had taken a turn. He couldn't remember the last time they'd laughed together.

Jolie released another sigh. "I'll try. I just wish the show wasn't on a Thursday. It's going to be a long day tomorrow at work, and Friday I'm on my own, which is always a shit show."

"So, no playing hooky with me I guess," he joked, testing the waters.

"I'm out of sick days," she mumbled.

"Really?" He was surprised. Jolie had taken a day here and there for minor health issues, a headache, cramps, whatever, but not enough to deplete her PTO bank. Although he knew very little about her job and benefits. They didn't really talk about what she did for forty hours a week. He would rather ignore the subject of *who* she worked with and how close that person was to *where* she lived.

He wasn't jealous. He trusted the rational Jolie. It was her impulsivity that made him wary. Especially when her tipping points were impossible to map.

"I'll take a page out of your book and just suck it up," she said.

Jace cringed. The best way to navigate Jolie at this point in the conversation was to exit. "It'll be worth it. And you can come over right after work on Friday. We'll sleep the night away to recover."

"Wine and quesadilla before?" Her voice turned quiet, tentative.

"Anything you want, Jolie."

"Okay." There was hesitation, as if she wanted to tack on a few more syllables to that favorite word of hers. "I just miss you, I guess. Living alone, it's...lonely, and only seeing you once a week, I'm struggling to..."

He knew the destination of her thought, having climbed aboard the same train months ago. "To keep going?"

"I want to do life with you, Jace. God, that sounds stupid."

Jace looked around. When he first moved here, he thought for sure Jolie would have been necessary to his daily life. But then work took over with long hours, and he began to savor the time alone. His apartment was clean. His record collection was alphabetized and in order, and the kitchen sink was clear of dirty dishes. He could breathe.

What he hadn't anticipated would fill the spaces of quiet was a buzzing question, like a fly coming in and out of view. Was living in the pause so bad for right now, when the end game was so obvious?

Where Jolie lacked patience, Jace needed time. They were walking on different pages in the same book, for now.

"You're it for me, Jolie." *You're the girl I want to marry. Someday.* "I'm sold. I just want to slow it down until I can hold you up."

"And if I'm a crumbled mess? How do you—" Her voice broke. Man, she was in a state tonight. He wished he could hug her.

"Jo, do you want me to come over?" The minutes on his clock had inched toward ten o'clock. His alarm was set for five. But he would do it. He would jump in his car and drive the hour to be with her.

"Okay," she whispered.

His back straightened. Here he thought she would say no, as was her pattern, to fight comfort with a shield of pain.

"On my way." He clicked off before she could talk him out of going.

Jolie's ashen face greeted him after a record-setting forty-five-minute drive. His stomach clenched at the sight of her. She didn't look like herself. Behind her round glasses, he could see her eyes were red-rimmed. She wore baggy sweatpants with an oversized, familiar-looking sweatshirt.

He followed her into the main room, the air stale. "Is that my sweatshirt?" He squeezed onto the couch next to her.

She looked down at the material, pulling it away from her stomach. A shadow of a grin passed her lips. "It *was* yours. A year and a half ago."

He circled his arm around her shoulders. "How are you?"

She shook her head and released her lavender scent. "I don't even know where to begin."

"If it's work stuff, we can talk about it."

She shifted and crossed her legs away from him. "Yeah, I guess it's related." Her ankle shook. She uncrossed her legs. Her toes tapped the floor. Then she was up on her feet and headed to the kitchen. "Tea?"

"Sure."

This wasn't good.

The formality of tea, or any beverage, was always a delay in delivering bad news.

"You need help?" Jace stood and walked toward the kitchen.

Jolie grabbed two mugs from the cabinet, turned to face him, and leaned against the counter. Sucking in a breath, she said, "Palmer kissed me."

"He—what?" Jace planted his hands on the counter, hoping he misheard. "How? I mean, when? Like, recently?" He watched her nod. The floor began to tilt. "Wow, yeah. Not at all what I was expecting you to say."

"I wasn't expecting it to happen," she muttered.

He rubbed his forehead as a dull pain bloomed. "Really? I would've expected you to slap him. But obviously you're doing what you want, I guess. So, all right. Why did you let him?"

A red hue flooded her cheeks. "I don't know. It just kind of happened. You know?"

"No, Jo. I don't know."

He pushed off the counter and searched for the nearest chair. Which wasn't far in this mouse-hole of an apartment.

"Are you mad?" she said, then shook her head. "That's a stupid question, sorry."

"Jo." He took a breath. "Some other dude kissed you and your face just answered a bunch of questions I didn't ask."

Her eyes darted to the whistling kettle. "Don't draw conclusions based on this catastrophe," she said, circling her face with a finger. He watched her pour hot water into a mug as her thumb held the tea string in place. She repeated the process before moving to the table he'd just sat down at. She lowered herself onto a seat across from him, her eyes trained on the mugs. She pushed one in his direction.

"Thanks," he said under his breath. Jolie's automatic movements were easier to focus on than his own emotions. He couldn't look at her, not yet, and found himself fixated on the swirls of steam inside his mug. A spider-like crawl of brown bloomed in the clear water. With a sinking feeling, his gaze reached Jolie's face. What he wouldn't give to take her by the hand and tuck her into bed. For her to dream away the conversation they were about to have. Instead, he asked, "When?"

"Oh." The chair creaked as she shifted her weight. "Last Friday."

Heat radiated down his back as if she had just dumped her mug of hot tea on him. "Last *Friday?* You didn't think to mention it all weekend?"

Jolie flinched. "I mean, yes. But I didn't want to ruin the day we had planned."

They had driven to an art museum in the city—a surprise she'd planned for weeks. He understood now why she'd been off, not as excited as expected. She checked her phone more than usual and had fallen asleep on his couch almost immediately later that night. He figured she was tired.

Tired.

He was so fucking gullible. It all made sense. In the worst possible way. An unwanted slab of dread situated itself directly across his chest.

"I'm waiting for you to say what I need to hear. But I don't think it's coming," he said.

"What do you mean?"

"Like," he leaned his elbows on the tabletop. "You're sorry this happened. Again."

"That was a year ago. Too much tequila. We talked about this. You *know* why that happened. How many times do I have to explain and apologize for the past, Jace?"

He shook his head. He wouldn't play dirty. It was unfair to bring up a past they had both worked so hard to lay to rest. "So, what's the reason now?"

She looked down and turned her mug by its handle. "There isn't one."

Turn, turn, turn.

He watched her mouth do a side-to-side tick.

"I don't want to lose you," she said. "But how can I keep you when I can't even find myself?"

"I don't get it, Jo." His legs tingled in their relentless bounce. "You said in January you wanted to be together, however imperfectly. You wanted this."

"I do want this, Jace. But we never see—"

"Does imperfection mean kissing other guys?"

The sides of her jaw flexed. "Maybe. I don't know. It should've never happened. But it did. And don't go on about how I should have slapped him across the cheek. This isn't a damn soap opera."

"Then why all the drama, Jo?" Jace shot up on his feet. "That's the problem. The lack of remorse for what you did. Like you're using it as an excuse, a justification, for what you're about to do."

A beam of light reflected off the tears now pooled at the bottom of her eyelids. "Oh, so you're a mind reader. Great. What is it I'm about to do?"

He strode for the door. "Leave me. Like I'm leaving right now."

"Jace!" She jumped up and grabbed his forearm. Her touch burned. He pulled away. After everything they had gone through to get to where they were, this slip-up proved what he had battled all along. How could he possibly dampen her impulses with patience?

The cold brass of the doorknob focused his rushing emotions. He loved her. Which was why he had to leave.

Jace turned to face Jolie. Her chin was raised, her eyes were round and wet. Jace slowly removed the glasses from her face and placed them on top of her head. He gazed into a void of green then arrested her lips with his. She sighed into his mouth and wrapped her arms around his neck. Whether Jolie realized it or not, each heated kiss was a letter in the spelling of his temporary farewell.

Jace muttered against her lips, "Maybe the pause isn't meant to be shared."

Her forehead pressed against his. "What are you talking

about?"

He steadied her shoulders with his hands then said, "Let's fuck up solo without fucking up each other."

Jolie brushed a thumb underneath her eye and destroyed the tear about to roll down her cheek. "Solo fucking is kind of an oxymoron."

Jace groan-laughed. He would always be hers, which was why he knew this time apart was vital.

"We can do this. Separately. For a little while."

"But we already have—"

"I'd rather we choose to take a break than choose to hurt each other."

"It hurts." Her voice cracked. This time he caught her rolling tear with his thumb.

Yeah. It hurt.

"Pause till further notice?"

"Okay. Okay."

The door he opened had never felt heavier. "Okay."

Seventeen

"You're canceling, aren't you?" Alix's voice came out flat. Jolie cradled the phone on her shoulder and pulled open the worn, brown curtains hanging over her bedroom window. She'd planned on replacing them when she moved in. *Ten months ago.* Now, she just lived with it. Like with so many other things in her life. The view out her frosted-glass window was a blanket of white. Jolie turned away from the window and braced herself for the inevitable.

"I heard someone at work today say we're supposed to get a foot of snow overnight," Jolie said.

That someone had been Palmer and he said it directly to her while she shrugged on her jacket. She offered a quick thank you in return then hurried out the door.

Palmer's unexpected concern for her well-being had seemed out of place, considering the polite yet sizable distance she'd placed between them. Perhaps it was his internal nice-guy script at play: *Inform all within reach of inclement weather.*

"So, I'm pretty sure Mother Nature is the one canceling," Jolie said, hoping Alix wouldn't argue with her about the uncontrollable scenario.

Alix's groan didn't last as long as Jolie had anticipated. "I bet if you leave now, you'll miss the worst of it. You don't want to be snowed in alone, do you?"

Yes! Jolie wanted to shout while stomping her fuzzy sock-covered feet.

No sane person chose to road-trip in a massive snowstorm.

Alix's weekly pleas to see Jolie's face had turned to demands, leaving Jolie no choice but to agree to a visit. But then the forecast had turned to snowmageddon and Jolie's shoulders had relaxed. All she wanted to do was stay in.

Jolie took a breath and managed a yawn so big it popped her ears.

"I barely made it home from work," she said. "My car was slipping all over the place. I don't even know how windy it's going to be and the blowing—" A loud boom from outside drowned out the rest of Jolie's excuse.

"That's a snowplow, isn't it? See! You're fine. They're out plowing and salting and it's not *that* bad out there. Hey, weren't you going to quit that job like, months ago?"

"Alix, you live four hours away. How would you know? And yeah, if I could find another job to take its place, you know 'cause I need the money, I'd quit." Jolie went to slide the curtains shut but a section got stuck. She moved the phone to her other shoulder and took a closer look. A single frayed loop had nestled into an indent on the curtain rod. She pulled again, harder this time. It wouldn't budge. The sudden need to jump out of her skin took hold.

"Well, if it makes you feel better," Alix said, "most jobs at this stage in life suck, and only an inch of snow fell here. I figure once you get out of your mess you'll be fine over here."

Right. If a drive through a snowstorm could remove Jolie from her mess, she would rush out the door without looking back. But running would never remove the immovable. Jace was physically gone, but occupied her waking mind as much as her dreaming one. Her mom was physically around, but not in a capacity Jolie was willing to subject herself to.

And of course, there was the ever-so-present Palmer. From the fateful kiss she relived almost daily, or whenever she saw him, which also happened to be daily, to the hovering desire deep within her soul, he was a forbidden answer to a question

Jolie hadn't figured out yet. Which was no surprise. She couldn't even figure out her own decorating style. Or whether she wanted to leave town for two days. Or what the heck she was doing with her life and—was it her or were the walls in her bedroom caving in all of a sudden?

She took a deep breath, put her phone on speaker, and tossed it on her bed. "My car probably isn't buried in snow...yet. So, that's something." She glanced around the ever-shrinking room. How quickly the blissful thought of being snowed in, by herself, had transformed into dread. "Maybe I can throw on my boots, see how the roads are, and let you know how it goes. I just have to do something first." Her eyes landed on the one thing that needed to go. Those curtains were too heavy, too ugly, and too damn suffocating. They were coming off. *Now.* Jolie reached up to lift the curtain rod away from the wall.

"Really?" Alix said, her voice muffled by the many blankets on Jolie's bed. "Did I convince you that quickly? Maybe I should go into lawyering."

Jolie tried to laugh as her arms strained. "I can't really see you as a lawyer. Especially since you just called it lawyering."

The curtain rod would not remove itself from the brackets. Jolie pulled again. Nothing. Clearly, a gentle coax was out of the question; this would require force. So she pulled harder. Again, and again, and— *Shit.* A sharp pop followed by a thunderous crack vibrated throughout the bedroom. Jolie shot backward—the six-foot curtain rod and drywall-encrusted brackets still clutched in her hands—and fell straight into her grandfather's dresser across the room. *Double shit.*

Her body ricocheted off the oak drawers and knocked her straight onto her ass. Sweaters and underwear and, of all things, Jace's old sweatshirt flew out like confetti as she gulped for air. Her favorite clay lamp teetered on the edge of the dresser—there was no stopping its fall in the chaos—and shattered with impressive force onto the floor. A sharp pain seared across Jolie's jaw.

"What just happened? Are you okay? Did your roof cave in?" Alix's voice sounded distant even though Jolie was close, albeit on the floor.

Jolie touched her jawbone. "Ouch." She pulled her hand away from the sting and peered down at red fingertips. "Uh, I need to call you back, Alix."

"Are you sure? Should I call someone to come over? That sounded really bad, Jolie."

"I don't know. I think it's okay. Can I call you back?" Jolie crawled onto her knees and reached in slow motion for her phone on the bed.

"I'm calling you in fifteen minutes if I don't hear from you. Got it?"

Jolie's temples throbbed. "Yes." She clicked off, her hands unsteady. A drop of blood landed on her comforter—thank god she had opted for a grayish hue over the more popular off-white—but...

Holy crap, how bad was the cut?

Once inside her tiny bathroom, Jolie peered at herself in the mirror.

"Really not good," her reflection said. She wadded up a clump of toilet paper and placed it over the cut. A wave of nausea passed through her as she bent down and opened the cabinet doors underneath the sink. If a box of bandages existed in her apartment, she would have stored them here. Which she hadn't. The sudden need for her mother overwhelmed her to the point of stillness, followed by a reality check; her mom was the last person to call on. Not far behind that unwanted feeling came a slightly more reasonable—and head-spinning—second thought. It made sense, more sense than any other option, which was none. So, she picked up her phone, texted a few choice words, found a washcloth to place over her face, and sat down.

Jolie's door opened after a swift knock, and like a modern-day knight in his black shirt and loose-fitting track pants, Palmer was there, filling her space—and her nerves—to capacity. Her jaw stung, while the hand holding the cloth over her cut faltered.

"Hi," she said, unfolding her legs to get up from the couch.

"No," Palmer said, setting a white plastic box on her end table. "Don't move. Please." He took two steps forward and kneeled in front of her. "Let me see."

Jolie secured the cloth to her face, shook her head, and held her breath. His pine scent was too close, his eyes were too concerned, and this instinctual craving she felt for him was too much.

"It's not bad," she said. "Just a scratch. I would've called someone else, like my mom, but she shouldn't be behind the wheel. Like, ever." Jolie felt her cheeks heat. Why had she said that? Palmer didn't know about her mom's drinking problem.

"No one should be behind the wheel right now," he said.

Jolie felt relief cool her face. *Of course, the snow.*

"Anyway. I'm pretty sure a bandage is all I need. So, if you want to leave one for me, or maybe a few. That'd be great. I'll run to the store first thing and pick up more. Tomorrow. When it stops snowing. Thank you, though. I don't want to keep you from your evening." Her ears rang in the quiet that followed her over-sharing voice.

Palmer scratched his chin while the corners of his mouth crept upward. "You know I don't have plans tonight. No one does. It's nasty out there. Lucky for you, though, you have someone down the hall to help." His eyes were bright. "Me. I'm that someone." She felt his hand circle around her wrist. "Jolie. Please. Show me." His skin against hers illuminated her insides and melted her false courage. He gently guided the cloth away from her face. "That's a good one you got there," he said.

"It's bad, isn't it?" She watched him reach for his box and open the latch.

"It's more than a scratch but it doesn't look deep."

He removed a packet of gauze, antibacterial ointment, and a large bandage.

His eyes, capable and reassuring, locked onto hers. Her face must have spoken her internal question. "You learn pretty quick how to assess and fix cuts when you grow up with two rough-and-tumble brothers. Building furniture has also kept my first-aid skills top-notch."

"I had no idea. I thought the pieces in your family's stores were from other vendors."

He tore open the gauze and steadied the left side of her face. His hand was rough. And touching her, *again*.

"Oh, right. Those aren't my designs. But I'd like to sell my own work one day. For now, it's a splinter-heavy hobby," he said, his gaze focused on her jaw. She inhaled his scent, no longer able to contain herself, and softened. He applied light pressure to her jaw, removed the slightly bloodied gauze, and squeezed a dab of ointment onto his finger.

"It looks like the bleeding has stopped, so I doubt stitches are needed." The ointment was smooth and cool when it touched her broken skin. The exact opposite of what her insides were signaling to her brain—pure fire. Palmer removed the bandage from its package and placed it carefully onto her jaw. He leaned back to assess his work. Serious and capable was the new sexy.

The wound was dressed, and by all accounts, Palmer's job was done. Yet, he remained close. "Although you may get an itty-bitty scar on that beautiful face of yours." The hand that had just fixed her face circled around her back and moved up and down her spine.

She wasn't sure if it was the rush of adrenaline from the injury or the unexpected closeness of Palmer, but she blurted out the only thing she could articulate at the moment.

"You think I'm beautiful?"

The corners of his eyes crinkled as a dimple flirted with his right cheek. "Uh, yeah, Jolie. You're, like, gut-punching gorgeous."

Her heart raced as she ran a hand over her tied-back hair. "I think maybe you need your eyesight checked," she said.

Palmer applied the same amount of pressure to her back as he had to her jaw.

"Nope," Palmer said. "Perfect twenty-twenty vision with corrective contact lenses, which are currently stuck to eyeballs that are loving the view. And even if I do need an eye exam, which again, I don't, what I see is just a bonus."

Everything in the room faded as his mouth came into focus. How long had it been since she felt lips on hers? *Six months.* Yes, she was tempted—Palmer excelled in that department—but he deserved more, didn't he? Like a woman who could return his affection equally, a woman who could love freely, a woman who wasn't her.

"It's here"—he tapped her temple and then moved his hand to the middle of her chest—"and here"—his hand moved in rhythm with her rapid breathing—"that continues to capture me."

Jolie dipped her chin down. *Well—shit.* Why did he continue to shower her with these words? And why couldn't she convince herself that she was worthy of him? He seemed to think she was. What would it take to convert her?

Memory loss.

"You're too good to me, Palmer. And I have no idea why." Jolie placed her hand over his. He lifted the bottom of her chin with a tender touch. His mouth opened as if to argue with her internal struggle—w*ould a kiss be so bad?* Instead, he removed the distance between them and placed his mouth on hers. It was soft. Tentative. And *so not* bad.

"Hold on," she said, her voice rough. Kissing Palmer wasn't supposed to happen right now, not when her head and heart were at odds with each other. He started to pull away as a wave of longing, impossible to ignore, coursed through her. "Wait," she said, pushing further into his chest. There was no stopping this. "Don't go."

"As you wish," he said and wrapped himself around her. His lips were on hers again, opening her mouth wide while their tongues pressed against each other. He tasted like cinnamon with a hint of excitement. Her hands moved up his arms and gripped his shoulders, deepening their kiss even more. Palmer's touch had always made her forget about everything, including herself.

A buzz from the side table seared through the room. She pushed away and bolted to her feet.

"Crap, that's probably Alix," Jolie said. "She probably thinks I'm stuck under something heavy. Injured and alone."

Palmer's hand—steady as ever—placed the phone into her palm.

"Thanks," she said, sounding winded.

Alix's voice rang out sharply. "That's how you greet me! After texting you repeatedly and then calling you like a stalker, you say, 'Thanks'? My god, Jolie. Where did you go? Dru was about ready to send Jace over there."

Jolie cringed and eyed Palmer, who pointed down the tiny hallway and disappeared into the dark.

Tea. She needed tea.

"Hi, sorry, yes. I'm okay. I broke stuff by accident—you know me—and got a cut, and was trying to find a bandage, so I didn't hear the phone." Jolie turned on the stove and watched the blue flame hit the bottom of her stainless-steel kettle. She lowered her voice and asked, "Did Dru call him?"

The pause in Alix's response was answer enough. "He did. But it went straight to voice mail. Jace doesn't really answer phone calls anymore."

Jolie felt a jolt in the pit of her stomach as if there was still the tiniest bit of electricity left in a dead wire. If only Alix would say what Jolie needed to hear: that Jace was busy but okay. If only Jolie had the right to ask.

"Seriously Jolie, you had me worried. Did you find a bandage?"

Jolie turned the stove off. She didn't need tea, she needed whiskey.

"Yeah. I found something to help." Her feet moved away from

the kitchen and walked her to the entrance of her bedroom. Palmer stood in the dimly lit room, his arms extended in front of him, his back muscles rippling through his t-shirt. He was repositioning the curtain rod back onto her wall, without the curtains.

Jolie leaned against the doorframe and stared, her thoughts picking up speed. *This is too much.* He must have sensed her presence and turned to face her.

"Hello, Jolie, did you hang up on me again? Where did you go?" Alix said.

A dozen wild horses on the brink of panic galloped inside Jolie's head, ready to be released. She held Palmer's gaze and cut Alix off. "I've hit a wall and I'm pretty sure sleep is in order. Can I call you tomorrow?"

Palmer nodded his understanding while Alix chirped her consent. The phone line went dead, and Palmer—with a swift kiss on her cheek—exited her apartment with the quietest of door clicks.

Jolie slumped onto her bed and gazed up at her window. What the heck just happened?

Eighteen

February 2007

The month of February was frigid. *Frigiduary.* Which made Jolie wonder in her teeth-chattering cold which sadist decided to put Valentine's Day, the dreaded day of expected romance, smack in the middle of it all?

Weeks ago Jolie had promised Carrie they would hole up in Carrie's apartment and binge-watch Johnny Depp movies like *A Nightmare on Elm Street* and *Edward Scissorhands*. All of Depp's less than swoon-worthy roles. Their version of an anti–Valentine's Day.

"We'll make stovetop popcorn with real, melted butter," Carrie had cheered over the phone as if Jolie was going to a coveted culinary experience. "And all the salt we want. Bloat away, baby!"

Jolie did her best to sound excited but her instinct to find an excuse not to go weighed her down. She would much rather mindlessly eat her way through the hours alone than acknowledge the last eight months during which she'd put her love on pause. Eating helped numb her growing heartache at the possibility of finding love again. With someone else. All bad habits and negative thoughts Jolie wanted to keep hidden from Carrie. She was fine. Everything was *fine*.

Jolie began the laborious process of removing ice and snow from her car while mentally throwing F-bombs at the weather. As she reached to scrape the windshield, her wool scarf suddenly tightened around her neck and pulled her back with such force her glasses flew off her face and landed…somewhere.

Seriously?!

"Hey, you."

Jolie squinted in the direction of the voice. Palmer came into view and loomed over her car. She released the end of her scarf from the door handle and attempted a casual smile.

"I swear I'm not a total klutz, you just have a knack for seeing me at my most clumsy." Jolie avoided his gaze and bent at her knees to root around for her glasses. Why was her body acting like she hadn't seen Palmer in ages? She saw him all the time now, and not just at work.

Ever since her December injury, Palmer had started dropping by to "check the bandage supply." The first time he actually went into her bathroom and called out, *"You're good!"* Then he stood by her front door and talked about the new sales position opening up at work. One he suggested she apply for. It was awkward in a comforting way. He returned the following week and did the exact same thing.

On the third Tuesday of his supply surveillance, Jolie made pancakes for dinner and invited him to stay and watch *Scrubs* on DVD. They sat separately but laughed together at all the funny parts. He balanced the plate on his lap and praised her perfectly round pancakes, suggesting he make waffles the next time she wanted breakfast for dinner. They were almost through the first season and smack in the middle of a never-ending frustration. Well, Jolie was. Palmer acted like a friend, a respectable and platonic one that Jolie shouldn't want to kiss every time he was around.

So going to Carrie's wasn't the worst idea. At the very least it meant Jolie would have distance from Palmer on the one day that begged the coming together of two lonely hearts.

"Here you go." Palmer handed Jolie her glasses, the lenses covered with fluffy snow.

"Thanks." She stood up and turned the temples around, frowning. The cloth to clean them was inconveniently located inside her apartment.

As if Palmer could hear her thoughts, he said, "You go inside and clean those off. I'll take care of your car here. You're headed to Carrie's, right?"

She nodded, trying to remember if she'd told him about her Valentine's Day plans last week. "Yeah. We're doing a movie marathon."

Palmer smiled. "I know."

Jolie pursed her lips. There wasn't much Palmer didn't know, it seemed. "You really don't have to clean my car. The movie can wait while I take care of this." Jolie held up her glasses as if he hadn't just witnessed the last five minutes of her life.

The way Palmer was looking at her put her on edge. Like the air around him was charged.

"It's no problem, Jolie. It just means you have to agree to me making waffles tomorrow for dinner."

Jolie hesitated while wisps of curiosity surrounded her. "I don't have a waffle maker."

"Well, it's a good thing that's not your problem." Palmer reached into the snow for her scraper. "Go. This won't take long at all."

Jolie stalled. Why was she having a hard time accepting Palmer's help? That's what friends did, right?

"I owe you one, Palmer. Thank you."

He pointed the scraper at her. "You owe me your willingness to eat my food."

Jolie laughed. "Okay. Deal."

One lingering hug and twenty minutes later, Jolie slowed her car near Carrie's apartment—a converted 1920s Craftsman house that had been split into two units. Carrie's place was a rare find with its private entrance and proximity to the nightlife of their hometown. The spot in front of the detached, shared garage, Jolie's designated visitor spot, was filled with cars, three by three in length and width. Carrie's downstairs neighbor, a Polish woman in her late thirties, fresh off a divorce, clearly needed additional support tonight. In the form of a huge party by the looks of it.

Carrie's head poked out her front door. "Change of plans!"

"Let me guess, we're invited to the raging party below," Jolie said as she stepped into the upper level of the house. A small hallway leading down to the front door separated the living and dining area. It was a replica of her dad's first house post-divorce, a slap in the face when she'd visited Carrie for the first time; warm oak flooring, glossy white door frames, and plaster walls heavy with loneliness. She spent more time at Carrie's than in the house her dad had since sold. He now lived with his new wife a few hours south.

She ignored the tightness in her stomach as she took off her jacket—and her perpetual daughterly guilt for not calling her dad—and laid it over the vibrant-red couch. Carrie lived in the big, the bold, and the messy. One of the many reasons they never discussed living together.

"You want to go?" Jolie asked out of obligation. The tone in Carrie's door-shouting excitement had seemed primed to argue with Jolie's indifference, like an old married couple.

"It might be a fun pre-salt-bloat adventure," Carrie said. "Helena's bar is always well stocked."

Jolie laughed. "Since when do you use phrases like 'well stocked'? You sound like someone twenty years older than us."

Carrie's eyes darted about like she was watching an intense match of tennis. "That's probably 'cause I'm seeing some-one...older."

"Older by twenty years?"

Apparently, Jolie wasn't the only one in their friendship withholding information. She had yet to tell Carrie about her weekly friend-dates with Palmer.

"Yeah, but he's not *old* old. Yeesh, since when did you become an ageist?" Carrie said, poking Jolie's arm. Okay, great. Jolie could roll with sarcastic humor. "But yeah, he's older, and he's married," Carrie added on. "Wait no. He's separated. Zero kids.

And even less sex with his wife."

Jolie could only imagine what her face had just expressed—based on Carrie's narrowed eyes, Jolie's face did not portray the neutrality she had intended. "No judgment, Carrie. I swear."

A single eyebrow in Carrie's porcelain-doll face twitched. "So quick to fold. Why is that?"

Jolie stared at the hardwood floor while a duo of thoughts fought. She could tell Carrie she deserved more than used goods covered in the scent of a sexless marriage, or she could come clean about Palmer. Jolie was certain Carrie would sniff around her *friendship* with Palmer like a bloodhound. She would have to avoid this entirely.

"As long as you're happy." Jolie faked a smile, every bit a fraud in the cop-out sentiment.

Carrie shrugged. "It's just for now, not forever."

"Honestly, I've always envied that about you." Jolie twisted her hands in her lap. "I seem to have a problem keeping the two separate."

Her friend laughed sharply. "Well, of course you do, Miss Relationship-Hopper. I'm surprised you've been single this long."

Jolie picked at a loose thread on the cuff of her sleeve.

Carrie's words had a bite to them. Enough to make Jolie want to run before blood was drawn.

Carrie continued to talk as she flipped the thick ends of her blonde hair. "Speaking of serial monogamists, you should have seen Palmer the other night, trying to pick up this Amazon of a girl. You'd think he would have more game, being randomly single like you for a while now, but it was *crash and burn, Baby,*" Carrie said, smashing her hand into her fist.

Jolie was glad to hear Carrie and Palmer were back to hanging out, but it was still hard to hear.

Friend. He was a friend.

"That must have been"—Jolie cleared the frog in her throat—"an entertaining spectacle."

"Oh, it was. All thanks to you, my dear."

Jolie tensed while Carrie pointed her finger at Jolie's forehead. "You're stuck in his head if I had to guess."

Palmer had been stuck all right, smack in the middle of last night's dream. A single candle had lit a make-believe bedroom, perfuming the fantasy as Palmer marked his place in her subconscious.

The turtleneck Jolie had chosen for warmth suddenly felt too hot.

"He might stop by tonight to grab it," Carrie said, cutting off Jolie's toe-curling memory.

"Sorry, who's stopping by where and grabbing what?" Jolie needed to sit, so she did, on the couch. Her ankle bounced in double time to the inaudible beat of dread, or possibly anticipation. It was hard to decipher between the two these days.

Carrie took her time enunciating each word. "Palmer, for my waffle maker. I literally just said this."

"Right. Duh." Jolie's chest tightened. She wasn't supposed to see Palmer so soon after that hug she still needed to pick apart, and *not* at Carrie's, of all places. Carrie sprang off the couch and trotted to the kitchen, out of sight. If only Jolie could verbalize her sudden angst to the one person who wouldn't judge her for being such a girl at the moment.

Cabinets and pans banged and echoed. "If I can find it, that is!"

Jolie took the opportunity to grab her phone and text Palmer.

She would offer to bring the waffle maker back and save him the trip. *A neighborly favor.* Except... The parking lot run-in— Had he been on his way to Carrie's? Maybe that's why he knew about her Valentine's Day plans. *Crap.* He could be here any minute.

Her phone vibrated and she thought maybe it was Palmer calling to let her know he was coming. Her mom's name flashed on the screen. *Double crap.* Her mom barely knew how to use her cell phone and never called past seven o'clock. Jolie felt her shoulders tense. Probably just a drunken butt-dial and nothing more.

"Hey, Mom, what's up?" Jolie walked to the front window of the main room and looked down at the snow-covered roads. No sign of Palmer yet.

"Jolie." A voice much too deep to be her mom's greeted her. "It's Bruce."

"Oh. Hi." Her tongue tripped over the second word. Jolie could count on her hand the number of times she'd spoken to the man her mom had started dating two months earlier—another in a long line.

"I'll get straight to the point," Bruce said. "Your mom hit her head and is in the hospital. She's fine. No concussion or anything. She slipped on the driveway, but her blood-alcohol level suggests a different story. You should probably get here as soon as you can."

Her vision tunneled while Bruce offered a few additional details before the doctor interrupted. Jolie heard herself declare she was on her way and hung up. What followed was pure motion.

Grab jacket. Find car keys. Slump on the floor. Cry.

Jolie felt Carrie's arm cradle her body like a security blanket. "Sweetie, what's going on?"

Jolie pressed her palms against her wet eyelids. "My mom. Again." She felt Carrie's arm tighten. Jolie's breathing regulated. She hated crying, especially with an audience. "Her boyfriend said she fell down and hit her head. Then a doctor came into the room, and he had to go." Jolie blinked and wiped her nose. The last time Jolie had entered an emergency room was in high school when her mom was admitted for 'dehydration'. That was the story anyway.

After a sleepless night, she returned home with her mom. The next day, Jolie had found a crumpled list of AA groups in the kitchen trash can along with a brochure for an outpatient program for addiction.

Tears welled at the thought of her mom tripping over herself on the shoveled and salted driveway. The hopelessness of the continued lies. "She's sedated now. I need to be there. I need to go."

"Let me take you," a voice echoed up from the front-door landing.

Jolie watched as a tall figure climbed the stairs to where she sat. How long had he been standing there? Why hadn't she heard the door creak, or felt the sudden grip of cold air? How much had he heard?

Carrie released her and took her cousin's hand to stand up. "Jolie, you're in no state to drive," she said. Carrie's concerned stare from above shrank Jolie further into the floorboards.

Jolie studied the hand Palmer held out for her to take. It was strange what her mind chose to focus on, what details she couldn't ignore. Like how smooth his fingers were close-up, not bitten down at the cuticles.

A chill coursed through her. Of course her dormant heart-break would decide to take advantage of her weakened state. She wanted the hand in front of her to be Jace's ruined one, didn't she? But he was busy living 'in the pause'. As if real life didn't happen all the time. And life was happening, right now, and in a very serious way. Instead, it was Palmer offering to live through this terrible moment with her. It was his hand that was here, his hand she would choose to take.

"Thanks," Jolie said, as he helped her up. The warmth was too comforting for the current moment. She released his hand quickly, exhausted from her varying concerns. "I don't know how long I'll be there. Besides, you probably have plans." Jolie looked at Carrie, her mouth pinched into a straight line.

"The roads aren't the best," Palmer said, looking from Jolie to Carrie's nodding head.

"I'll come with you, Lee," Carrie said gently. "In Palmer's very big capable-in-snow truck."

"Seriously, you guys. It's fine." Jolie repositioned the purse on her shoulder. Jolie's strength lived in her solitude. She would conquer this on her own again—just like last time. "I can drive my snow-worthy car across town to the hospital." The purse strap slipped off her shoulder. She pulled it up. "It just seems unnecessary to have Palmer drive." There went the strap again.

Pull. Slip. Pull. Slip.

"Oh, for *fuck's* sake!" She yanked the purse off her shoulder and hurled it down the stairs, where it bounced off the front door and exploded in personal effects.

Her breathing was labored as she stared at the strewn insides of her bag. Most of the 'Wine and be Fine' quote on the doormat was obstructed by her crap.

"I hate that doormat," she said.

It was pin-drop quiet.

"Babe." The word came from Palmer. Her eyes jumped in tandem with the jolt in her stomach. He had never used a term of endearment with her before. She hated that word, it sounded derogatory, objectifying. Except when Palmer said it just now.

The tension in her shoulders released as she took in the crease between his brows. She hated seeing him so worried. This part of her life was only meant to be shared in the many journals she'd kept over the years.

"I'm sorry. That came out of nowhere," Jolie said. She walked down to retrieve her bag. A sense of kinship to the exposed contents, spilled every which way, washed over her. After she shoved it all in, she stood and said, mostly to her feet, "I'm not used to having people around when shit hits the fan with my mom. But I do appreciate you both." She paused to look at Carrie and then Palmer. "So much."

Palmer held her gaze. His eyes were dark mahogany. "We've got you. Now let us be there for you."

"Be there for me. Right." Jolie spat out a half laugh, half sob. "What does that even look like? I see my dad from time to time, but not consistently. My mom, well, she's here but always in the company of friends." Jolie air-quoted the last word while her hand trembled. "And don't get me started on Jace." Her eyes jumped to Palmer's face. She should stop talking. This was all supposed to remain deep inside her until it turned into nothing but dark, corrosive mush. And yet... "So, thanks. I mean it. But I'd rather rely on myself like I always have. I'm the only person that can't leave me."

Palmer approached her. She couldn't look at his face.

"At the very least," he said as his hand moving to her shoulder, tentative, gentle, "we can make sure you don't jump out of your skin. We can keep you in you, if you is all you have."

Jolie swiped away a rogue tear. "That makes absolutely no sense."

"Sure it does. Now let's go, sweetie," Carrie said. She moved in and hugged Jolie before she could protest, and essentially dragged her out of the apartment door.

Jolie wanted to resist the nonsensical words that actually made a lot of sense, just as much as her mind wanted to treat the hug of a friend as a threat. But that's what she did best, reacted to help in the same way as to hurt.

Come tomorrow Jolie knew she would pull away from the forced support of both Palmer and Carrie. Because life wasn't fair, was it? Life was hard, which made living it all the more complicated. But the fact remained, Palmer and Carrie combined could never be what Jolie really needed at this moment—a healed mom.

Nineteen

December 2007

Jace leaned against the paint-chipped wall, took a gulp of stale keg beer, and tried to ignore the rising decibel level in his friend's apartment. The floor vibrated from the New Year's Eve party, which had his paranoia convinced the police would barge in any moment for a noise complaint.

Not likely to happen, Jace thought while shaking off the image of uniformed officers cutting through the cloud of weed smoke and arresting only him. This was why he did not smoke pot on a regular basis. Except for tonight, when he had—so far—given zero fucks about life decisions.

"There you are!" Esther materialized from the pulsing crowd. "I've been looking for you, for like, ever."

"Hey." Jace lifted the rim of his Solo cup to his lips and nodded. Him and Esther had hung out together for about three weeks. During their first face-to-face date, it had become apparent that she liked to talk. A lot. His limited experience with online dating hadn't flashed the warning lights during their initial messages. He assumed she was an evolved twenty-something woman who liked to talk about, well...herself. None of that was the case. She was just self-involved.

"Oh my god. I ran into someone I used to date as I was coming up the stairs. He was trying to hit on me too. Can you believe that? I was like, sorry guy, you had your chance. Well, I thought that. What I actually did was invite him here. You know me, the more the merrier! I didn't think he would say yes. Oh! There he is." She waved at a guy in a short-sleeve shirt two sizes too small for him. That, or his muscles were two sizes too unnecessary.

Meathead spotted Esther and prowled his way through the crowd. Jace cringed. Mating call received.

"I'll be back." Jace pulled on his beanie and walked out of the apartment before Esther had a chance to respond. He rushed down the three flights of stairs, the air stuffy, and opened the door to a blast of cold that sobered him upon impact.

Jace's earlier whim to invite Esther had seemed less desperate than was actually the case. Having her here only deepened the Jolie-sized hole in his life. And on the heels of yet another unanswered message to Jolie, it had been, quite honestly, a stupid decision to invite Esther.

His phone vibrated—as if it had anticipated his impulse to send Jolie yet another message. He fumbled in his pocket, his breath a plume of white. The urgency to see who it was felt like life or death. Stupid weed.

"Holy shit." His voice bounced off the surrounding buildings while his stomach jumped up into his throat. Grasping his phone, he hit the answer button. "She lives."

Jolie's laugh was a tin-can symphony in the cell phone stratosphere. "And he's relentless."

Not usually, he wanted to rebut. He wasn't one to cause a scene. However, Jolie seemed to possess a natural talent for unearthing his peccadilloes.

"Guilty. But had you responded to my message the first time—"

"Jace. You said boundaries, remember?"

When was the last time he'd heard his name on her vocal cords? "Except you caved."

"A forced hand, or ear, I guess would be the case." The lilt in her tone changed to reserved encouragement. "You have me now."

"I wish I had you," he murmured.

She cleared her throat. "So, is everything okay?"

"Better now." He took a deep breath and forged into the ruins of what had kept him awake at night. "I'm thinking of moving."

She was silent for a beat. "Okay."

The wind picked up and tossed biting ice pellets at his face. "To California." His voice hitched upward as the thought of palm trees entered his mind, stoking a fire in the negative-degree chill. "I was promoted. If you can believe it."

"I can. You work hard."

What he wouldn't give to see her reaction right now.

"That's amazing, Jace. Wow, West Coast living."

"Thanks," he said. He gnawed at his red-tipped fingers. The image of Jolie in his mind had morphed into the pictures he'd tucked away in his closet. He wanted to bring her back into the light. He needed to.

Fuck it. "Where are you right now?"

"Sitting in my car. In my mom's driveway."

"You're visiting your mom on the most bender-forgiving day of the year?" He asked, aware Jolie avoided most major holidays with her mom for this reason.

"Was visiting. I'm leaving now." Her staccato response suggested he should move on to another topic.

"I want to see you," he said in a rush.

"Oh." She elongated the word as if to consider the weight of his own. Which was so unlike Jolie. "But you're moving, or seriously considering it, right? Why invite confusion in the form of...more confusion." She paused. He imagined her readjusting whatever hand-crocheted hat she had on top of her head. "You get what I mean. You could build an entirely new life. *Away.* From all this cold and snow."

"Snow melts, you know."

"Eventually," she said under her breath. "I gotta get on the road though."

He exhaled as his chest deflated. That was it? She had nothing else to say? "Yeah, the roads aren't the best."

"I'm more concerned about the drunk drivers." She went

silent. He was about to end the absence of words when her voice, smaller somehow, sounded out, "But if you still feel the same tomorrow, if you still want to see me, then—I guess we can meet at our usual breakfast spot, around ten o'clock if that sounds good."

"Great. I'll be there." He felt his feet tingle. "See you tomorrow, Jo."

"Tomorrow. Okay. Bye, Jace," she said and hung up.

Every part of his body buzzed. Jace pocketed his phone and then immediately pulled it back out. He would call a cab and go home to sleep. Morning would arrive sooner that way. The double-doors leading into the apartment building swung open. Jace ducked out of view, ninja-style, and watched Esther stumble out with Meathead. They were totally sucking face. Zero jackets. One hundred percent repulsive.

No loss there, he thought as he moved further from the scene.

It didn't take long for his cab to arrive. Jace watched the passing streetlights through the car window while a warmth radiated from the center of his chest. The wait was over. Come tomorrow he was going to see Jolie's real face. And who knew, maybe even kiss it.

The hum of melded voices greeted Jace as he entered the restaurant the next morning, followed quickly by the scent of coffee, pancakes, and fried bacon. He couldn't remember the last time he'd gone out to breakfast. Wait, no he could. With Jolie. At this very place. Not long before they went their separate ways.

"Can I help you?" the hostess asked. Her mouse-like voice matched her baby face. Probably a daughter of one of the owners.

He scanned the visual assault of sun-aged fake plants and rose-colored vinyl booths. Many were empty. Not surprising since it was ten o'clock on New Year's Day. "I'm meeting someone. Although I don't see her."

"Oh, Jolie told me you were coming. She's at the counter in the back."

His jaw almost dropped. Jolie wasn't known to frequent an establishment often enough to be on a first-name basis with the staff. She preferred the comfort of anonymity.

Jace thanked the girl and weaved his way toward the back. He found himself gnawing at the dried skin on his index finger, with zero idea of what to expect. A message or two exchanged with Jolie in the span of twelve months left a lot to be discovered.

He approached the long counter where a line of vintage swivel stools faced the kitchen's rectangular window. The back of an intricately crocheted sweater came into view, and he knew immediately it was her— Jolie always dressed part-hippy, part-trendy.

Jace slipped onto the stool next to Jolie. "Counter-dining. I must be hallucinating." He took her in: glossy brown hair pulled into a ponytail, high angular cheekbones, and translucent skin. Like a come-to-life photograph.

"Can you believe it?" She said.

She swiveled from side to side, her knees grazing the edge of his thigh. He wanted to rotate her into him and soak in the warmth of her smile. "Your girl is now a willing participant in the subculture of weekend brunch. And a paradox to boot!" Jolie tilted her head close to his, her eyes bright.

He blinked a few times, having lost focus after she said *your girl.*

"Way less small talk than I'd assumed. The servers pretty much leave you alone. Get in, eat, get out. We are their least demanding customers." She leaned back. "At least, that's what I've concluded from my limited data collection thus far."

The smile on his face grew in direct correlation to the explanation of her tiny achievement in self-discovery. "Any advice for a novice?" he asked.

She turned toward him so her face filled his view again. He'd missed her slender neck. "Yes. Never put your hand over your coffee mug if you don't want a refill. You'll get burnt. Literally. Just let them pour that coffee."

He was full-on grinning. Her mind worked in the most random way. "Are you speaking from experience?"

"No, thank god."

The server approached, a coffee pot in each hand. "Coffee?"

Jace flipped over a white ceramic mug from the small plate on the counter. "Please."

The brown liquid splashed unceremoniously into his mug while their server rattled off the specials. "I'll give you a few minutes." The server turned to leave.

"Wow, you weren't kidding. What's smaller than microscopic talk?" He watched Jolie blow into her mug.

"I believe it's submicroscopic."

"Well, that's underwhelming in originality."

Jolie's smile was subtle as she sipped her coffee. Her mouth opened and closed a few times, but no words came out.

Finally, she said, "I'm glad we're doing this."

His heart tripped over its own beat. "I always wanted to start the New Year discussing mundane science terminology," he said. "Checking this one off the bucket list. For sure."

"Funny." She bumped his shoulder with hers, and he took the opportunity to pull her in with his arm.

Her lavender smell was the same, but holding her felt very different. The heat from her body retreated much too soon.

"So, how was your New Year's Eve?" he asked.

"Nothing special after I left my mom's house."

"No midnight kiss?"

"Not even close," she said. "I toasted midnight with a cup of chamomile tea. My mom's been in recovery since last February. Well, in and out of recovery. As seems to be the trend with this disease." Her face pointed straight ahead. "So, yeah. No midnight kiss and no real life lived for a good chunk of the year— Well, wait. I moved up the corporate ladder in March instead of quitting. So, there's that. But, I don't know. I've started to wonder if perhaps I'm meant to be doing something else. Like helping others in similar situations to my mom's." She blew out a shaky breath. "Anyway. Yeah. Life. It's been kind of upside down."

A look of sadness rolled over her body like fog. He wanted to reach out and touch her, to comfort the pain seared in her memories.

"A story for another time I think." She looked at him with her chin resting in her hand.

"Anytime, Jolie. I'm always here for you."

"But are you?" Her voice was barely above a whisper as their server reappeared, order-pad raised. Her presence put a stop to further confessions.

"The usual for you, hon?"

A blush crept up from the base of Jolie's neck. "Not today. Yogurt and a fruit bowl instead."

"Whelp, that's a first." The server scribbled on her pad. "And for you?"

"I'm curious. I'll have Jolie's usual." He looked at Jolie as her face fell.

The server whistled and wrote on her pad for longer than he'd anticipated. "He's got your number, this one," she said directly to Jolie before walking off.

Jace hitched his thumb over his shoulder. "You keep strange company these days, Jolie."

"Which explains why you're here." Her fingers worked overtime tearing off bits of white napkin. "I hope you're hungry."

"Sure, hungry enough."

He eyed her pile of napkin confetti. What just happened? She changed the topic before he could dig in further.

"So, tell me about this promotion," she said.

Jace straightened his back and explained what he had practiced in his head the night before. "During my annual review, my boss told me he could reach out to corporate for a promotion, which I'd been all for. I met with a bunch of men last week wearing *literally* the same suit— I swear it was Matrix incorporated, and one of the Smiths mentioned relocation. Not at all what I was expecting. So, I'm supposed to give them an answer, *No later than Monday, J-man.*" He air-quoted and rolled his eyes. "So, I think I might do it. The raise is substantial but mostly to offset the cost of California living. But I swear that dumb nickname is not coming with me."

"Wow, Jace!" Jolie said. "Something good has come from all that overtime. You deserve it." Her coffee mug covered half her face, making it hard to decipher her expression. "A chance at a new start." She shook her head, staring off. "I'd like to get away for a while."

Jace froze. Had she meant to get away with him, or in general? It was hard to tell without seeing her face straight on, or better yet, asking. "I'd take you in a heartbeat."

She abandoned her coffee mug and stared at him openly. "Correct me if I'm wrong, but wasn't it you who called the break? Wasn't it you who wanted to separate?"

He smirked at her rhyme. Where he tended to avoid loaded questions, she made them poetic under pressure.

"Knock it off, I know what I said. I can't help what comes out of my mouth when I'm..." She paused, moving her hands around like a DJ scratching her record. "...free-styling."

He barked a laugh, the familiar spark of their connection present once again. The thought of Jolie moving with him had seemed entirely too antigravity in their world, but maybe they were meant to be together with their feet off the ground, floating around.

"This isn't about me," Jolie said. "Or you *and* me. It sounds like you're not sure. Or processing."

He nodded. "Both."

"So, us getting together after a year apart isn't a random coincidence," she said. Her words were a statement of fact. All he could do was agree. And find a way to tell her what his tongue would surely stumble over. He cracked a knuckle as the words he needed to say came to him.

"I broke the clock on my dresser a few weeks ago. A clock I've had since probably age ten." He paused to make sure he hadn't lost her with the topic change. She remained quiet, his cue to keep talking. "And even though it's gone, I still look for it every morning and night. It doesn't matter how many times I tell myself it's no longer there, I still look for it."

"Why not buy a new one?"

"It's irreplaceable."

"Is it fixable?"

He touched her forearm to encourage a return gaze. "You tell me."

"No. No-no-no." Her hands flew up like a flock of birds taking flight. "Don't do that. You're the one who broke it!"

He saw a few heads turn from the tables nearby. As much as he wanted to remind her of the damage she had caused all those years ago with a single kiss, he also did not want to cause a scene.

"All right." He lowered his voice. "Maybe it just needs the battery replaced."

"Jace." Jolie hung her head. "You compare our relationship to a block of plastic, which may or may not actually be broken or moving to California." She sighed. "Why can't you just be normal?"

"I'd never have a chance with you if I was."

Vibrant green eyes arrested him. "Just give it to me straight, Jace. What is it you want?"

He wanted time to click back in motion, for that proverbial clock to work again, and for the frantic yet snail's pace pursuit to end. He wanted her. Because life was either being with her or missing her.

"I want... food." His eyes landed on the server as she approached. "And apparently lots of it." Three, yes, three plates arrived. The waitress set the plates in front of him, each filled with what looked like the entire front half of the menu. "This is your usual, Jo?"

She was busy pouring granola on top of her yogurt, gaze averted. "I take half home for leftovers." Her hands tried to block the display of red across her cheeks. "You learning of my hearty appetite for brunch food these days does not mean the previous conversation is over."

"Fair enough." He rubbed his hands together. "I feel like I need a map for this meal, or trip destinations. What not to miss, that sort of thing."

Jolie's laugh scattered the previous tension. "You're in for quite the journey."

The fork in his hand hovered over a stack of pancakes while Jolie picked at the granola. A thought, desperate and true and one he wanted to voice, felt so heavy it began to press down on his chest. "Jo, are we making a mistake?"

She turned into him. "I'm not sure I follow."

"I want you to come with me," he said. "I want to start this new chapter with you. I want you to set aside all the pragmatic reasons why you can't or shouldn't and do what you're best at, acting on impulse. I want you. All of you." The feelings he'd kept bottled up were out and in Jolie's possession now.

Don't hurt me, Jo.

Jolie stared at the counter and shook her head. "Oh, Jace. I can't leave my life to enter yours."

He felt short of breath. Or maybe it was the idea of him leaving and her staying, that deprived him of oxygen. "I have no life here unless it's with you."

She didn't even flinch when she looked at him and said, "Then you should go."

The following week he left for California, but Jolie's last words remained.

Twenty

January 2008

"It's time to forget about spacey Jacey!" Carrie's voice rang out so loud that Jolie held the phone an arm's length away from her ear. "Your relationship with him is well past the sell-by date. Move on! He has, quite literally."

"Hello to you too." Jolie pushed open the door to her apartment building and, unable to see anything but white, removed her fogged-up glasses from her face.

"You're coming out tonight, Jolie. End of discussion. You deserve to let loose. Be young, and wild, and free. Besides, what man leaves a clock as a farewell token anyway?" Carrie snorted into the phone—a subtle suggestion she had already nipped at a bottle of wine. "Nothing says 'think of me' like bright-red digital numbers in the middle of the night."

Unless it's a clock from Jace, Jolie thought.

Following her tedious day at work yesterday, where the smell of stale alcohol hovered in the break room, Jolie had trudged up the stairs to her apartment, thankful the second day of the new year had been over with. Exhausted from nursing her day-long heartache, she nearly tripped over the cardboard box resting against the frame of her door.

Jace's long, slanted handwriting looked up at her. She knew before opening the lid that he'd left her a clock.

She placed the box on her kitchen table and had walked away, turned on the kettle, returned to the table, and touched his handwriting. She almost, almost, went for her emergency package of Oreo cookies—nestled high and out-of-reach—but the whistle of boiling water stopped her. She opened the box instead. And sure enough, there it was, tucked inside crumpled newspaper.

It was the same clock as the one Jace broke, except brand new. Jolie wanted to believe it was his way of saying time will work itself out.

But after she said no to his hopeful request to move away with him it was more likely his way of saying, I'm no longer connected to you. Plug yourself in. So, she did. The clock glowed on a table next to her couch.

"Fine. I'll go tonight," Jolie said. "On one condition: no mention of Jace or the clock. Okay?"

Carrie didn't hesitate. "Deal."

Sometime later, Jolie found herself looking at a different clock on her phone. It was past midnight. Late enough for a sober person—her—to witness the overserved crowd up close and personal, but nowhere near closing time. The bar Carrie had dragged her to—through more snow than any sane person should willingly navigate—was loud and stifling. People were everywhere, swaying to the techno music she hated so much.

Jolie craned her neck from her seat at one of the high-top tables. Carrie was somewhere, but not in view. And Jolie wanted to go. She had stayed here against her better judgment long enough.

"There she is." A long shadow from behind covered the table. "Living, breathing, and"—a glass filled with amber liquid appeared in front of Jolie—"in need of one of these."

Wearing a black collared shirt that made him look older than he was, Palmer pulled out a chair and sat down across from Jolie. He pushed his sleeves up and smiled. *Crap*. Jolie had failed to consider the likelihood of running into Palmer tonight. So, of course, her face was heating at the sight of his indented cheeks.

"Hey, I didn't know you were here! But you are, obviously, and buying me a drink 'cause you're nice. I mean you're Palmer. Of course you're nice, and—" She shut her mouth. It was over-talking again.

She hadn't been this close to Palmer since last February when Jolie had hit the stop button on her personal life to take care of her mom. They still worked together, but he was more in the background now, like radio static. An annoyance that might never play music again.

Jolie opened her mouth to finish her sentence. "Thank you." She sat on her hands, forcing a smile on her face.

The corner of Palmer's mouth curved upward. "Anytime. So..." Palmer tapped his fingers on the tabletop. "How've you been?"

Jolie swirled the amber liquid in her glass, stalling. It felt like a disservice to make small talk with a person who took up such a large space in her mind. It hadn't been intentional, keeping Palmer close in her thoughts. Somehow he'd become a fantasy she liked to visit. A harmless break from reality. Except for the guilt that usually followed.

Palmer held up a hand. "Scratch that. You're out. A rare sight since last year. And you look...stunning. You must be doing okay. Are you doing okay?"

A declaration and a compliment, coupled together in what made Palmer so him. Jolie's wits were in serious jeopardy.

"There was hard stuff there for a while, but it'll be alright," she said, looking out the front bay windows of the bar. The sidewalk sparkled against the glow of the streetlight. The snow had stopped. Her eyes returned to his gaze, warm and safe.

"There's light down the line," she continued, "there's so much good stuff in wait."

Palmer's fingers touched the top of her hand. "I love that mindset."

Jolie turned away. Her hand tingled all the way up to her arm from Palmer's touch. She needed it back. Otherwise, her entire body would go numb. She braved direct eye contact again. His hot chocolate eyes looked back at her like she was the marshmallow on top of him.

A blonde head bobbing in and out of the crowd caught Jolie's attention. Carrie rushed up to Palmer's side and pulled him to his feet. "Snow angels," she announced.

Jolie shook her head. Palmer laughed.

Carrie squinted at the space between both of them. "Well, guess what, spoilsports? It's happening! With you..." Carrie closed one eye and pointed at Palmer. "And with you." Her finger swayed and landed on Jolie's shoulder. "And then we all walk home. 'Cause I know you want to go already. Lady-grumps."

Jolie did want to go, but did not want to say goodbye. She pushed her drink aside as a growing impulse coated her inhibitions. "Convince Palmer to walk us home, and I'll make the snow an angel," she said.

Palmer's dimples were back. Carrie turned away, as if she hadn't heard Jolie, and stumbled toward a shout from the bar.

"Snow play and an invitation to walk you home. Who is this?" Palmer said, but his smile suggested he didn't need an answer. He had picked up on all her signals, and who knew—maybe this song was one meant to be played.

She looked up at him and held out her hand. "I'm Jolie. Friend to your cousin, coworker at your company, and soon-to-be angel in the snow."

Palmer grasped her hand. Her stomach danced. "There she is. Living, and breathing, and flirting. With me. How did I get so lucky?"

Jolie tried to push down her growing simper, which was near impossible. Palmer was always the cause of this effect.

Carrie bounded up before Jolie could respond.

"Sorry, had to give that guy my number," Carrie said, staggering to a halt in front of them. "We used to go to high school with him. I think he's older though. Anyway, let's go. Before I change my mind and invite him back with us."

"Is that a normal habit of yours while I'm not around?" Palmer said.

Carrie giggled and shrugged. "Jolie can vouch for me."

Jolie glanced in the direction of the bar, but no one stuck out as familiar. This was a pretty common occurrence, past classmates recognizing Carrie while those same faces couldn't place Jolie.

"I am not getting in the middle of yet another *family* discussion," Jolie said, grabbing her jacket off the back of the stool. Her knees ached. How long had she been sitting down? "I haven't been out in a bar since— Well, you all know how long it's been. So, I have no idea what antics Carrie has been up to."

"Hey! Girl code!" Carrie shouted with an exaggerated laugh.

Jolie watched Carrie point at a man with a fully grown beard and wiggle her fingers. Carrie had gone a bit boy-crazy over the last few months without Jolie, even tip-toeing along the edge of recklessness. Palmer frowned at Carrie then exchanged a glance with Jolie while a silent question passed between them: Was he the older classmate?

Palmer shook his head. "All right. It's time to go."

"She's secured," Palmer whispered while he backed out of Carrie's bedroom.

"Good." Jolie said, averting her gaze from Palmer's fantastic behind and drawing her knees up. She tightened the fleece blanket around her shoulders.

Their walk home had gone from freezing snow angels to snowball fights to Carrie drunk-dialing the first half of her contact list in her phone. Palmer had tried to run interference while Jolie steered a swaying Carrie in the right direction. And while Palmer attended to his cousin, Jolie realized for the hundredth time how easily Palmer lifted her out of her mind.

The couch cushion sank in next to her. "You're warming up, I hope," Palmer said as he placed an arm behind her. She breathed in his pine scent and felt stuck, yet again, in a pattern where Palmer filled the hole Jace continued to leave in her heart. Was that such a bad thing, though, when he fit in there so well?

"And fading," he added. Her body must have grown heavy as her mind settled in. "Don't go yet," he whispered. "It's nice to have you so close. And alone."

He was one of the few people in her life who used words with crystal clear sincerity. Come to think of it, even her own family didn't guarantee what Palmer so willingly provided.

"I know you've gone through things," he said. "You helped repair someone else's life, one that gave you yours. I can't imagine the sacrifices you've made." Palmer's finger grazed under her chin. Her face turned and tilted up, taking him in. "You are quite possibly the strongest, and most beautiful woman, to have graced my life."

Why? Better yet—how? How could he say what so easily burned her from the inside? She risked untying her tongue with his if she didn't speak.

"I'm the opposite of grace under pressure, Palmer." She tried to shake her head, but his hand cupped her cheek instead. On instinct, she leaned into his warm palm. "Or I'm bad at living at maximum capacity. I don't know. You deserve a better...friend, one who doesn't disappear when things get tough."

The pad of his thumb caressed her cheek. "You reached your upper limit," he said. "Most run away at the sight of yet another switchback."

"A mountain of problems," she said, a flutter in her stomach. It felt good, no—it felt deserved, to have someone looking back at her with understanding. Someone who wasn't dependent on her strength, like her mom or even Jace, but marveled in it.

"You know, Jolie, most aren't willing to stand up to one problem in the first place. So, as I said, you're amazing." He released his hold, leaned back, and closed his eyes.

She took the opportunity to study his face, the straightness of the nose she wanted to trace, the shadow of a beard she wanted to feel, and the parted lips she couldn't stop staring at. In the space between her exhale and his inhale, she felt her body move into him, and placed her mouth on his. He groaned, and after a moment of remembrance, she pulled back, her eyes groggy, and said, "Thank you."

Palmer's laugh floated around her. "You're really tired, aren't you?"

The wall of exhaustion was too large for her to step around. She nodded and snuggled further into the fleece blanket. Her head slid down to a throw pillow. Whatever emotions she was meant to feel in this moment would have to wait until morning.

"Sleep," she said, but her mind was already there, drifting around in the blank darkness while Palmer's voice echoed, "I miss you."

Her eyes popped open as if she'd just closed them. She squinted at the brightly lit room. It was daytime. Midmorning, although it was hard to tell with the glare of the sun off the snow. Jolie's body cracked as she uncurled from the position she'd gotten herself into. There, on the armrest of the couch, was a piece of folded notebook paper with her name written in blocky letters. Jolie glanced around. Carrie's bedroom door was closed. Palmer's jacket was gone. Jolie touched the paper, her body buzzing in anticipation. This was better than waking up to the smell of coffee. She unfolded the paper: "I have a mountain of waffles with your name on it."

She didn't stop at her apartment on the way to his to wash off the bar smells, or to remove the impulse that still clung to her from the night before. Jolie walked straight to Palmer's door, her heart in her throat as it opened. Without thought, she rushed into his arms. All she could do, all she wanted to do, was get lost in the rhythm of Palmer's touch and in the release of her own melody. And so, she did.

Twenty-One

March 2008

The flame of a candle, centered on top of the dresser, swayed as Palmer's body cut through the air and approached Jolie in the darkened room. She never replaced the lamp that had broken two years ago. The night Palmer had come to the rescue. A reminder of when her fear had cut right into her, now marked on the edge of her jawline. It'd taken two years for her denial to heal into...this.

She rose onto her tiptoes, reaching for his lips. He kissed her jaw and lifted the oversized sweater above her head. She fumbled with his belt. He kicked off his jeans. Heaviness descended into her pubic bone as he wrapped an arm around her waist and laid her down onto the bed. She ran her fingers through his silky hair.

Earlier that night, Jolie had been sitting alone in her apartment, staring at the clock she couldn't get rid of when her phone pinged. For a moment, she felt a twinge of hope. Had Jace known she was thinking of him as she watched the minutes pass by? Was he thinking of her too? The same answer over the last two months remained. *No.*

Jolie knew who wanted her attention, and he was the reason she stayed in for the night. She'd seen Palmer—naked—almost every day and thought a night off would help settle the developing need for him. Palmer had pried her open and, in the light of the once-dark space, had left a possibility...to fall in love. Maybe. She wasn't sure. So, she watched time pass by. But being with Palmer muted her internal clock, so Jolie responded with a quick '*Come over*,' and unlocked her door.

He peered up at her now, his chin in line with the top of her underwear. "You're holding your breath again," he said. Palmer's touch had become familiar, yet Jolie anticipated his moves as if it was their first time together. He knew how to tease her, where to touch her, and what drove her to the brink of madness. All by pure intuition. Because he was Palmer.

She covered her face with her hands—lying down topless picked at her deepest insecurities—took a deep breath, and brought his face into focus. "Would it be ridiculous to say you take my breath away?" she said.

Palmer dipped his head directly into her most sensitive area and laughed. The heat and vibration from his mouth made her hips twitch upwards. He lifted his head and revealed eyes as dark as an abyss. "Let's take these away instead."

His finger looped underneath the band of her bikini underwear and pulled downward. Cool air hit her inner thighs. She watched the candlelight dance on the ceiling as his tongue circled her navel. The heaviness inside her began to swell and expand. Palmer's mouth was skilled, and he wasn't even talking.

"I've spent a lot of time down here." His lips grazed over her opening, while his fingers explored further. "Do you like me between your legs, Jolie?"

She nodded. Her throat was too dry for words.

"Or do you want me to stop?" His tone teased while his warm breath circled around her breasts now. His mouth made its way up to hers.

"Please, don't stop." She arched her back and captured his mouth then gasped as Palmer pushed inside her, proving once again how capable he was.

Jolie was pouring hot water over her tea bag when Palmer emerged from her bathroom, toothbrush in his mouth, hair damp from the shower. This seemed to be their new weekend routine. He spent the night at her place, showered in the morning—also at her place—and continued to perfect his pour-over coffee in her kitchen. Then they would go find a bagel or donut somewhere.

The ease Jolie felt around Palmer had morphed into domestic comfort. Palmer knew where things went and how she liked her mugs placed upside down in the cabinets. But the short distance to his actual apartment worried her. Was she ready for this level of comfort?

She ignored the pinprick of disagreement she felt somewhere inside.

"Donuts this morning?" she asked.

Palmer held up a finger and mumbled around toothpaste foam before disappearing into her bathroom. She cupped her tea, blowing across the top.

Shit. Palmer had his own toothbrush here, didn't he?

He reappeared with what could only be described as an up-to-no-good, dimple-screaming smile and stared at her. His hands were planted firmly on his hips.

Why did the man have to be so darn attractive? Even in the morning. When most everyone, namely herself, looked like absolute crap. Yet there he stood. Looking too handsome and...still staring. Jolie set her cup down on the counter. "Is it me, or are you acting strange?"

He opened his mouth, and words started flying out as if he'd been talking out loud the entire time. "You're seriously gorgeous, Jolie. I don't know how else to let you know how much I appreciate the view. Other than by staring."

"I, well—okay. Great response." Would she ever get used to Palmer's open appreciation of her?

Palmer stepped into her kitchen and wrapped his arms around her waist.

"Donuts today. But it'll be a little bit of an adventure to get to them if that's all right?"

She looked up and smiled, like a reflex whenever she looked

at him. "I have nowhere to be."

He touched her cheek with the back of his hand. "Sure, you do. Right here. With me." And he kissed away the words her heart had almost convinced her mouth to ask— Was this love?

Or was this simply the next expected step in their relationship? A step she hadn't prepared herself for.

The same two questions ran through her mind forty minutes later. Palmer pulled onto a gravel driveway and pointed to a two-story, white farmhouse in the distance. "Welcome to our Sunday morning donut stop."

Jolie glanced out her window. The ground was muddy, as was typical for late March, a month of thaw and growth. Towering oak trees surrounded the house, their branches long and thick, swaying in the gusty winds.

"It's kind of odd for a donut place to be all the way out here, isn't it?" Jolie squinted at a sign in the ground as it came into view. "Wait a second. That's a for-sale sign." She turned and took in Palmer's flushed complexion. "And you're getting red! Okay. What's going on?"

Palmer slowed to a stop and shifted the gear into park. The wind howled outside, rocking the truck on its tires. She watched him flex his hands on the steering wheel and felt her heart plummet. This could be budding love, but would it be enough for what he was about to say?

"As of this morning, I own this house." His face pointed straight ahead but there was no hiding her dropped jaw. "I know. I didn't say anything. I didn't want to scare you off. And have you overthink. It's equity, first and foremost." He reached his long arm into the back of the cab and returned with a cardboard box. "There's other stuff too, but before that—" Palmer lifted the lid.

Jolie leaned forward and gazed down at a dozen perfectly crafted, glazed, sugared, sprinkled, and *bacon-topped* donuts. Her body tensed. She wouldn't be able to manage a binge-triggering sugar rush in addition to whatever Palmer had planned.

He was a homeowner, and he hadn't told her until *now*—and

he was moving to a town forty minutes away! Her heart galloped as fast as his bouncing knee. And, it looked like he had more to say.

Palmer moved the box in her direction. Jolie plucked the bacon-topped donut from the box, hoping he didn't notice her trembling hands. She inhaled the sweet scent from the sticky, fried dough. This could act as a buffer to whatever Palmer was about to say, right? She shoved half the donut in her mouth and moaned. Salty and sweet—an unparalleled combination and a dangerous plea from a voice buried within.

Palmer laughed. "You're something else, Jolie." He set the box in the middle of the bench seat. Jolie forced a smile—he hadn't the slightest clue of her *something else*—and took another bite.

"So, if all goes as planned, I'll close in two weeks. Move the following week. And ask you to join me...right now."

The dough turned hard in her mouth, yet she managed to swallow it without choking. There was no way he was asking what it sounded like he was asking.

"Join you as in, help you move in?"

He handed her a napkin and motioned for her to set her donut down. She frowned at the half-eaten emotions, placed the donut on her lap, and turned to face him.

Palmer appeared calm but his shoulders had slumped a little, making her all the more nervous. Jolie unzipped the top of her jacket and pulled the turtleneck away from her heated skin. The trees outside bent against another gust of wind and she suddenly longed for the cold.

She heard him suck in a breath. "Imagine a few months from now, everything is green outside, and we're living here, away from the noise of the apartment building and busy cross-streets. Maybe you've even quit your job and have a beautiful and abundant vegetable garden on the property instead." Palmer paused and looked out the windshield.

Jolie didn't follow his gaze because she couldn't move. She was a stray cat caught in the high beams of Palmer's fast-moving future. "I come home to you every night and we have dinner together out on the patio, or in the large, refinished oak kitchen with stainless steel appliances. Or we simply devour each other." He turned to her. "I think you could be happy here, Jolie. You can stay home and run the house, be outside in the fresh air and look after things while I support us and our life. Together."

His eyes darted around her face. Was she still sitting down? Or had she tried to stand up? What was happening?

"I know. It's crazy. But then again, I'm crazy about you. And I think this could be something"—he shrugged and licked his lips—"crazy great."

She opened her mouth, but the look on his face—tentative smile, rounded eyes, raised eyebrows—stopped the flow of words. Had she fallen behind again? This was too fast, right? Or was this the pace set by... Jolie gripped the door handle as the pinprick in her stomach intensified. The thought of becoming Palmer's country *wife* had taken away her ability to breathe, and not in a good way. She had to say something. Anything. Otherwise, she would fling the car door open and run off.

"Thank you," she said.

Palmer leaned back like he'd been punched in the gut. "The two most overused words in the world. Why not give me the one word you know I love?"

This felt more like a surprise attack than *love*.

"I'm flattered and, to be fair, a bit shocked at the moment. I might need a minute to catch up and not feel so overwhelmed. If that's all right."

He crossed his arms. Jolie had never witnessed Palmer pout before.

Because you always give in to what he wants, her mind chirped with unbearable accuracy.

Palmer uncrossed his arms and ran a hand over his chin. The same hand whose fingers had outlined her inner thighs the night before. The same hand attached to an arm that could cuddle her in bed, every night if she wanted, while they discovered each other every day under the same roof.

"Jolie, I'm having a tough time here," Palmer said quietly. "I thought for sure you'd jump into my lap and kiss my face off. I'm offering you a home rent-free with the option to be job-free too. I'm sitting here with all that I have telling you I can provide what you haven't been able to find on your own. Happiness."

Palmer's words stung her in all the places she hadn't allowed him to touch. Jolie shoved the rest of the donut inside her mouth. She didn't want to say anything else. Like how badly she wanted to get out of his truck and hitchhike her way back to the place of her apparent unhappiness. Instead, she swallowed down her needs and said, "I know, Palmer. And I am thankful for your offer."

Palmer glanced at her, the shadow of a dimple forming. Whatever he interpreted in her words was enough for him to think she wasn't totally freaking out on the inside. Nothing about this felt right anymore. "Well, all right, Ms. Polite. Let's get you inside so you can see what you're so thankful for at the moment."

Jolie nodded—careful not to say the one word he'd pressured her for earlier. She pushed open the car door. As she rounded the front of the truck, a gust of wind grabbed her from behind and nearly pushed her to the ground.

"I got you." Palmer secured his arm around her shoulders and walked toward the house. His house. One he wanted to share with her. Palmer released her and ascended the porch steps. At the same moment, her hair whipped in the wind and blinded her enough that she couldn't see the steps she'd have to climb in order to get to where she was meant to be.

Three weeks later, Jolie would find her own way again, as Palmer moved into a house she would never live in.

Twenty-Two

April 2008

"**Y**ou're here! You're here! You're HERE!"

Jolie felt Carrie's hand grip her arm. "You did not prepare me for this," Carrie said, seconds before Alix slammed into Jolie for a hug.

"Hi friend," Alix said. "It's so nice to see you!" She pulled back and looked at Jolie like a grandmother would a long-lost grandchild, then turned. "And Carrie!" She held out her arms. Carrie inched closer to Jolie. "I feel like we've already met and know each other so well."

With expert boundary-crossing authority, Alix forced a hug on Carrie. Jolie couldn't decide whether to laugh at the sight or take a picture with her phone. She watched Carrie pull away from Alix, pat her on the head—yes, the *head*, and attempt to distance herself.

The impromptu girls' weekend had come together shortly after Jolie accepted the receptionist position at a mental health clinic. She hadn't been searching for a new job but stumbled upon the listing while helping her mom find a local Alcoholics Anonymous group. The time away was meant to celebrate her new job, her new apartment, and a long-awaited friend-reunion in the town halfway between her and Alix. Jolie hoped the change of scenery would help clear her overcast mind, too. She needed clarity with all the change upon her.

"Dru is parking the car," Alix said, her eyes darting around. Jolie cocked a brow at Carrie, who shrugged in response. It appeared Dru was joining the weekend festivities.

"A boy is not needed for a girls' weekend," Carrie said in a sing-song, don't-argue-with-logic, tone.

Alix elbowed Jolie in the ribs. "I like her. She's loyal to the cause." She turned to Carrie and said, "I hate highway driving and Dru was coming out this way anyway." Alix paused and shifted her weight from one foot to the other. "To meet up with...someone."

"Right. Noted," Carrie said with a thumbs up.

Jolie looked between Alix and Carrie. "Something's going on. You're both acting super weird. Are Dru and his friend joining us?"

Alix's face deflated like a leaky life preserver while Carrie's head shook once from the corner of Jolie's eye.

What was this?

"Okay. Spill it you two," Jolie demanded.

Alix fumbled with her purse and said, "Dru's meeting up with Jace."

Jolie swung her head in Carrie's direction. A single nod from her supposed best friend confirmed the sordid details.

"I texted Carrie earlier after I found her number in the email about this trip," Alix said as her gaze locked onto something behind Jolie. Alix's smile faltered, but remained in place.

"He's walking up to us right now," Jolie said to no one and everyone. Her hands began to tremble in an infuriating Pavlovian response. She crossed her arms and scolded her body to take a time out.

The distance from Jace, no longer far-stretched, would not cause her to freak out. She'd moved on just like he had, with a new job and new apartment.

And a new rut to perfect.

"Hi, girls!" Dru approached, a megawatt smile fixed across his face. Jace hovered a step behind and waved to the group in general. "We just wanted to say *heeeyyy* before we go do our guy thing."

"Hi, Jo." This came from Jace. Jolie blinked at his wavy hair and tanned skin and cemented her mouth into a smile. A drop of sweat cascaded down her lower back. It was one of those warm April afternoons, where exposed pale shoulders risked getting burnt if left uncovered for too long. Jace's gaze might as well be her sunburn.

"Hey. Wow, this is unexpected." Jolie jerked her arms out of her jacket. "The weather, that is. So warm." Her eyes bounced around the 19th-century brick buildings lining the street in a curve. The town was so immaculate in its preservation that Jolie wished she could transport back to simpler times. A time when Jace was thousands of miles away and not standing right in front of her.

Carrie clapped her hands. "All right. Well, great to meet you, Dru. Jace, hi. We have things to do and wine to drink."

Jolie felt someone grab her arm and move her forward. She caught Jace's eye and saw him mouth the words, *See you later*, right before she turned and walked away.

Jolie peered into yet another window display as her stomach grumbled. They'd walked and stopped and poked around the shop-lined street for what felt like too long. She needed food for her hunger and maybe a glass of wine for temporary memory loss.

Somehow Jace was in the same town as her, and his unvoiced words, cycling in her head, had her trapped. *See you later.* Now that 'later' meant 'sooner', she had no idea how to feel.

Jolie stopped outside what looked to be an expensive shoe and furniture store and declared, "I need answers." She faced her two friends.

"You cannot afford those shoes nor that couch. Let's move on," Carrie said.

Jolie crossed her arms over her chest. Sarcasm would not save her friend from the owed explanation Jolie was about to demand.

"How is it that Jace, of all people, is not only in Illinois, but in the very town of our last-minute girls' trip, and you two were in cahoots about it?" Clearly, the old-timey vibe of the historic town was having an effect on Jolie. She did, however, shout the last part in a very un-ladylike way.

Alix walked Jolie by the shoulders to a brick-lined alley, while mumbling something about chopping Dru's balls off if only she didn't want children in the next five years.

"Are you pregnant too?!" Jolie shrieked.

Alix rubbed her ear. "Ouch, eardrum. No. I mean, we're not trying or anything." Alix blushed. "I was saying he deserves a chopping off because he's the reason Jace is here."

"And the reason why you're kind of freaking out right now," Carrie added.

Jolie spun to face Carrie. "Freaking out! Ha!" She poked her friend in the shoulder. "We just spent three hours in the car talking about why it's so important I'm alone and not in a relationship right now. Were you not in the car with me?!"

Alix raised her hand. "I wasn't, actually."

Jolie caught the smirk on Carrie's face right before it vanished.

"Of course, I was there," Carrie said. "I just thought, maybe if you got all that off your chest, seeing him wouldn't be so intense."

"Oh smart." Alix nodded. "But you *cannot* reverse-psychology Jolie."

Jolie shook her head. "That's not really a good example of reverse psych—"

"Jolie's basically a downed power line post–emotional dump," Alix interrupted. "Like, high voltage, sparks flying every which way, near open water too. That type of danger."

"While I very much enjoy your personality assessments, this one isn't making sense, even to me," Jolie said.

Alix sighed. "The point is, repairs are needed before you, my dear friend, can stand up to another storm."

"So many metaphors." Carrie marched back onto the sidewalk while Alix's legs blurred to keep up. "Let's find shelter already!"

Jolie wondered if waving a white flag would help her friends ease up on their race to fix her.

Carrie stopped in front of an ornate, mahogany door. "How about dinner here?"

The smell of garlic hugged Jolie hello.

"Garlic, bread, and wine. I never say no to that culinary trifecta," Alix said.

"I have no problem with garlic breath all weekend long," Jolie said and reached for the door, not stopping to consider why she mentioned the quality of her breath in the first place.

After menus were opened and drink orders were taken, Jolie looked around. They were seated in the middle of a dimly lit room covered in floor-to-ceiling plank wood. An odd mixture of Americana and Italiana decor filled the walls from floor to ceiling. But the aroma was mouth-watering.

"Do you think this place is haunted?" Jolise said. She'd read earlier, amongst towering musty-smelling bookshelves, that the historic town was haunted in certain areas.

"No ghost would willingly spend time here if unable to eat," Carrie said as she picked at the plastic checkered table with her fingers. "We should totally do one of those night-time ghost tours though. Right?"

"As long as it's not Disney-themed," Alix said. "You know, like a played-out haunted house."

"I hate haunted houses. Although historical hauntings are kind of intriguing," Jolie said, leaning to her right while the server placed wine glasses on the table.

Carrie popped up from her seat. "I'm going to run and grab a brochure. The place is just down the street. I mean, the majority of this town is down the street, but I think they're closing soon." Carrie sprinted out of the dining area.

"Does she have a secret passion for white floating orbs?" Alix said.

"I have no clue. Listen—" Jolie pulled Alix's arm toward her while their server finished pouring wine. "Don't bring up Palmer tonight."

"Speaking of ghosts. Interesting it's Palmer's name you mention and not the ghost that just crossed your path. Whom we call Jace."

"One thing at a time. And this one is time-sensitive," Jolie said, cringing at what she was about to say. "The majority of what's going on there, between me and Palmer, Carrie doesn't know."

"This feels slightly familiar. Like when you didn't tell me about Jace calling you before you came to visit during homecoming."

Jolie drummed her fingers on the table. "I know. But not everything in friendships is meant to be shared. Right? You don't tell me all the gory details of your love life."

"Because I'm basically married and boring," Alix said as her phone lit up on the table.

"Fair." Jolie took a sip while Alix typed.

"This should be interesting," Alix mumbled. "Sorry. I'm back. Go on."

Jolie raised an eyebrow, but Alix's wave suggested she keep talking.

"Okay. Here's the latest." Jolie held up three fingers. "We've slept together. He asked me to move in with him, but I freaked out and said no...eventually—after I found out about my new job. But we continue to spend time together."

Jolie paused, then covered her face with her hand, blocking her view of Alix. "In bed. Naked."

Alix let out a low whistle.

"I know." Jolie groaned. "Not anymore though. He called it off a few days ago." Apparently, her new job in a town stuffed with people and cars posed issues for the man who owned a house on two acres. Never mind the other wants of his, like a wife at home tending to his yet-to-be flock.

It should've been a clean break once their goals had separated their futures. Instead, Jolie had collapsed in the fracture. And there, in all her dusty debris, she plucked out four letters that, when put together, rhymed with *face* and possibly *ache* too. Maybe that was it. She was never meant to fall in love with Palmer, she was meant to crumble in confusion.

"And Carrie knows nothing?" Alix's eyes flickered.

A voice behind Jolie boomed, "I knew it!" The chair next to Jolie scraped back, and a slap radiated from behind her shoulders. "I *knew* you two did the dirty." Carrie's laughter sounded a bit manic. "My god, Palmer is so ruined over you."

Jolie was frozen to her chair but somehow the room was spinning. "You're not super pissed I didn't tell you?"

Carrie took a gulp of wine and shook her head at the same time. She smacked her lips and continued to speak loudly, "You're both adults. Confused, horny, everyone has an itch to scratch down there, adults."

Jolie looked around. "I know this isn't the most ideal location to talk about this stuff, but I'm sitting right next to you. Do you need to shout?"

"I wasn't shouting." Carrie finished off the rest of her wine.

"Just tell her, Carrie," Alix said from across the table. A chill slithered down Jolie's spine as a silent battle took place between her two best friends.

"Fine. Palmer is here. I ran into him outside just now. Apparently, he has a work conference in Dubuque this weekend, but the welcome dinner is here tonight. I had *no* idea."

Jolie slid her arms out in front of her and lowered her forehead on the table. "I'm really tired all of a sudden."

Carrie patted her back. "We'll get you coffee. There's one more thing, which Alix already knows."

Jolie raised her head an inch. "Oh, so that's who messaged you." She glared at Alix. "All right. Just get it over with."

"The dinner is happening in that banquet room. Right over..."

Carrie broke off to point over Jolie's head. "There."

Jolie groaned. "Why is this happening? Someone? Anyone? You there in the back? Why are they both in this town right now? Seriously."

Carrie stepped around Jolie's verbal spill. "And before you suggest anything, he knows we're here and promised us a round of drinks on him."

A memory flashed. Palmer's mouth. Champagne bubbles. A slurp from her navel. Unexpected heat shot straight down her legs. She supposed it *was* her turn to have drinks on him. In public. With his cousin.

Jolie sat up straight, both hands flat on the table. "I bet we'll be long gone before he shows," she said right as a group of twenty entered the dining area. Palmer was in the middle, taller than most and striking in a suit and tie. "Okay. Well, my theory has been put to bed. I mean, to rest. That theory has been put to rest. Because he's here. Standing over—" She swallowed down pine needles. "Over there."

Palmer, dressed in an immaculately cut gray suit, approached their table. Jolie straightened in her seat. Here came another friendly hello with another ex-boyfriend less than twenty-four hours later and she was going to live to tell the tale. Maybe.

"Hi, ladies." Palmer smiled. Jolie's heartbeat threatened the ribs holding it in place.

"You clean up well," Carrie said as she stood to hug Palmer. "You know Jolie." She grinned down at Jolie.

Jolie managed a small wave. Leave it to Carrie to make things even more awkward with an unnecessary reintroduction.

"And this is the remarkable Alix. Don't get any ideas, she's taken." Carrie ribbed Palmer with her elbow.

Palmer laugh-coughed into his fist. "Nice to meet you, Alix." He pinned Jolie with his gaze. "How ya doin' Jolie?"

"Hi," she squeaked. "Good. Hungry."

His eyes lit up. "Me too."

A stout man with a shiny forehead waved, shouting for

Palmer.

"I'll be back, promise." Palmer's wink released all the butter-flies in Jolie's stomach.

Alix rapped her knuckles on the table. "I owe you an apology, Carrie."

Carrie opened and closed her mouth before answering. "Usually, I'm the one who's offending people—"

"Nothing like that." Alix's warm smile mimicked a newly bloomed flower in the sun, which would explain Jolie's sudden chill. Her body's temperature was regulating as poorly as her thoughts were to the situation.

"Your blasé reaction to Jolie's affair totally makes sense now."

"I'd hardly consider it an affair," Jolie said. "Although, I am sorry I kept it from you, Carrie."

"It's okay, Lee," Carrie said softly before turning to Alix. "Pretty obvious, right?"

Alix nodded. "The blind would've seen their chemistry."

"Slightly offensive to those who can't see. But yes," Carrie said.

"Okay, well, you're both not entirely sane." Jolie grabbed the wine bottle and topped off her glass. A bread basket appeared. Jolie reached for a roll, took one sniff of pure garlic, then picked up two more. Anything to keep her mouth from saying more than necessary.

After a series of interruptions—food orders and a wine bottle from *the gentleman in the banquet room*—the spotlight left Jolie and focused on plans for the rest of the weekend. An itinerary for tomorrow started to come together, thanks to Alix's planning and Carrie's adventurous side. Jolie sat back with a smile and watched the exchange between two rapid-fire talkers.

It had been a long time since she'd enjoyed the warmth of a good glass of wine. A hesitancy to drink any form of alcohol had fashioned itself in her conscience. But with friends to laugh with in the midst of insane coincidences, Jolie was relieved to feel an ambivalence toward the drinking, at least for the evening.

Dinner arrived halfway through their second bottle of wine. The noise from the banquet room had increased in volume, carrying with it Palmer's deep laugh. Jolie did her best to focus on her meal, but each bite was a mouthful of anticipation, gamy with a hint of spice.

Hopefully, Carrie would do all the talking once Palmer returned and Jolie could do what she did best: stare at the dessert no longer on her plate.

Except Palmer never showed up and, as the last plate was cleared from their table, Jolie felt disappointment seep into her wine-soaked brain. It was for the best, she reasoned, that he return to the *do not touch* display case in her head instead of her table.

"I'll pop in and try to find Palmer to say goodbye," Carrie said, standing up. "You want to come with, Jolie?"

Jolie's gaze shifted to the back room. It was the adult thing to do, saying goodbye. But she didn't trust her internal filter, it was loosened already. "Can you tell him bye for me?"

Carrie nodded and disappeared into the rowdy banquet room while Jolie followed Alix outside. The little town had fallen into twilight, showcasing the sky's horizon. A cozy haze lined the curved street.

"Off we go!" Carrie announced and looped her arm in Alix's. "You have everything, Lee?"

Jolie patted her bare forearms. "Did I have a jacket? I could have sworn I had a jacket."

Carrie shrugged while Alix looked thoughtful. Both had a slight sway.

"I'd like to take a bubble bath now," Alix slurred.

Jolie smiled. She'd missed Alix's classic go-to excuse to end the night.

"You guys go. No really," Jolie insisted in response to the whining protests. "Two seconds and I'll catch up. Besides, I can see the B & B sign from here." She gently pushed them in the right direction and rushed inside. After a search of the table and a query to the hostess, Jolie was back on the sidewalk empty-handed and cold.

"Here you go."

She turned to see her jacket in the hands of Palmer. "I was about to send you a message when I saw you walk out here."

Jolie peered up. "How'd you find it?"

Palmer motioned for her to turn around and helped her into the jacket.

"I saw it on the floor near your table when I walked to the restrooms. No one else I know owns a green corduroy jacket. Kind of knew it was yours."

"Well, thanks. I would've been sad to have lost it. You know how much I—" She choked on the last words.

"Love it. I know." Palmer smiled. "Where are the other two?"

"Hopefully safe inside where we're staying." Jolie readjusted the cuffs on her jacket. If only she could cover up her overthinking as easily as her body. She opened her mouth to speak. At the same time, Palmer asked her if she would like to meet for coffee on Sunday.

The invitation felt way too satisfying inside her fuzzy head. Palmer might as well be greasy drunk food in human form. She meant to say no—greasy food was only a temporary fix—but her mouth was distracted and a traitor and said yes instead.

"All right, great." He smiled.

"I should make sure Carrie and Alix aren't lost. So, see you Sunday."

"Okay," he said, his thumb pressed against his bottom lip, a glint in his eyes. Jolie felt her mouth crack open, unable to take her eyes away from his lips. "Still my favorite word, by the way," he said, coming closer. The scent of pine mixed with peaty scotch swallowed her senses. "I can't seem to stay away from you, Jolie." He leaned down and brushed his soft lips against her cheek. She was fit to burst into flames. "Can I walk you back?"

She used what tiny bit of brain power she had left and said, "It's right there."

His warmth retreated as he looked to where she pointed. "I could use the exercise. And the peace of mind. Is that okay?"

"Okay," she echoed.

They fell into step. His hand bumped hers but never claimed it. Her mouth remained still but her thoughts kept pace with the fast silence. She left Palmer on the sidewalk, feeling proud to have not kissed an ex-boyfriend after drinking wine. Given the current odds, this was a win. Albeit a burnt dessert to end her night, but even a crème brûlée was torched before being served, right? Little did she know, her night was about to go up in flames.

Twenty-Three

April 2008

J ace watched her freeze the second their eyes locked. He stood up from the sofa in the foyer and swatted away the yellowing lace curtain from his face. The entire room was stuffed with fake flowers and knick-knacks, surrounded by couches with too many flower prints. The sight of it all almost distracted him from the overwhelming smell of mothballs. Taking a full breath wasn't enjoyable, not that he would be able to with Jolie in front of him.

Jolie tracked his movements as he stepped around a flowered ottoman. "Two glasses of wine and I'm seeing things," she said. "Great."

Jace shoved his hands in his pockets and ignored the sinking feeling in his stomach. "I figured Carrie told you what happened."

Jolie moved further into the main room. After several attempts to unzip her purse, she managed to remove her phone. He watched her eyes click along what he assumed was the missed message from Carrie. Who knew the unexpected arrival of Dru and Jace would trigger a tornado of room assignments. It had seemed straightforward enough: Alix with Dru, Jolie with Carrie, and Jace in his own room. But Carrie had refused to move Jolie's suitcase and insisted Jace wait for Jolie to return instead. Which made zero sense. Jace would have proposed a second, equally obvious solution—*move your own shit, Carrie*—but not without back-up. Jace's wingman had retreated upstairs and, from the thumping sounds overhead, had been doing what most people do in a bed and breakfast.

Jolie pocketed her phone and blew out an exaggerated breath.

"Well, that's just silliness, isn't it? Why all the complications, you know? On everyone's part."

"Dru is the epitome of 'good planning'. Remember?" He joked as a longing to hug her came over him. His arms had ached to hold her every night while he was in California. "But it's really nice to see you."

She laughed and shook her head. "I heard you say those words before your voice actually said them." Her back made contact with the wallpaper, also a pastel floral print. Jolie slid down until her butt met the pink carpet. "Or maybe I was hoping you'd say them. I don't know." She looked up at him with tired eyes. "Why aren't you in California?"

"Because I'm here." He sat down next to her, not prepared for the cut-to-the-chase question. She was known for that though, wasn't she? Straight and to the point. When least expected.

It was no different than in January when her sharp words, "*Then you should go*," had cut right through him. He'd signed the receipt for their brunch with a slight hand tremor and said goodbye to her with anger so hot, he was thankful for the falling snow and ice-cold wind.

A week later he arrived in California—sad, but determined. The fine print of his newly-signed contract, which he'd poured over after his brunch with Jolie, had him out of state for only three months. His assignment was to restructure the San Francisco location to something that resembled a profit. For a moment, he thought about calling Jolie to tell her it wasn't a permanent move. Instead, he packed up and left, intent to let it all be. The shadows under his eyes had darkened into the color of bruises during those three months. But he was able to extract enough meaningful data that the location would remain open. He returned last week, elated and edgy. At the insistence of his boss, he took a month's paid vacation. No arguments.

It'd been Dru's idea to come here for the distilleries, an easy sell for Jace. Dru had also said something about spending the time off as a way to realign with what's important in life.

"Like bourbon, right on dude," was Jace's tongue-in-cheek response.

Dru told him they would have to drive separately. Something was off, the quick subject change for one, but also the tone in Dru's voice. Jace figured his lack of sleep was making him paranoid.

But the moment Alix stepped out of the passenger side of Dru's car earlier today, Jace knew, down to his very tired bones, Jolie was close behind. He could have marched back to his car and sped off. The whole situation reeked of drama. Instead, he stayed to see if the girl he couldn't shake might find a way to hold him still.

Jace bumped Jolie's shoulder with his. "You remember that one bed and breakfast with the converted bathroom closet?"

She shuddered. "How does one forget such an inspirational use of space."

"You forgot the best part." He caught the smile on her lips.

"The squeaky bed?"

"Good point." He narrowed his eyes in a playful response. "The second-best part."

She considered him for a beat. "The cat pictures."

He nodded in a single solemn agreement. "The many, *framed* pictures of cats."

She started to laugh. "With every cat dressed in medieval costumes too, right?"

"Yes! And actual photographs. Of real cats."

"Oh my god, I forgot they were real!"

"In hats. With feathers." He placed an imaginary hat delicately on his head.

Her laughter turned wild, giving him no choice but to join in.

She wiped under her eyes. "Wait till you see my room. Think *Secret Garden* in an eighties hyper-colored theme. Actually, let's go up now."

Not missing a beat, he responded, "That's the second-best thing I've heard today."

"Oh yes," she said. "The time-warp *Secret Garden* experience you're about to have is a tale to be told for years to come." Her head tilted. "What's the first best thing you've heard today?"

He grinned. Even tipsy, Jolie's mind was uniquely hers. "When I heard your voice earlier today." He stood and offered his hand to help her up. A distinct chill spread through the middle of his palm as her skin touched his. Once she was on her feet, he added, "Want to do better than best?"

"Does such a thing exist?" Her voice wavered.

He stepped close enough to smell her lavender perfume. "You in that bed with me tonight would make it exist."

"Jace." He imagined his name cradled on her tongue while her tone threatened its eviction.

She shook her head and mouthed no before moving toward the staircase.

"Had to try," he mumbled to her back, but couldn't be sure if she heard.

He awoke with a start, his heart pounding from an unconscious cardio workout. His blurry vision focused on the floral-patterned walls, robin-egg blue curtains, and cotton-candy carpeting. The room was a high-resolution image of an Easter basket and a serious contender with that previous B & B. Except, not really.

Jace hadn't covered Jolie's body in kisses this time. Instead, the night had ended with a half shoulder hug and a closed door. Not a total loss, though. He had told Jolie about his permanent return to the state. The spark in her eyes when she heard the news was all the encouragement he needed to stay the course. He wanted her back in his life. Period.

The clock on his nightstand informed him it was early, but the scent of coffee and maple syrup wafting into his room had him out of bed and into jeans. He was tired, but he knew pants were required.

He walked down the creaky steps and heard Jolie's voice before he saw her. "No, that's fine. Really," she said. Her tone was tentative yet firm. "He can come. I don't know why you think this is up to me, anyway. There are three others here too."

"Four." Jace took a seat next to Jolie in the dining room, his pulse racing at the sight of her two days in a row. He looked across at Alix and Carrie. "Wait, you were right, Jo. I don't see Dru. Three it is." He saw Alix glare while Carrie covered her mouth in what looked like guilt-ridden laughter. Jace continued, "Brushing up on our preschool math this fine morning?"

"Dru went for more waffles. Why don't you help him with that?" Alix asked through clenched teeth.

He agreed, but only out of fear that the petite woman turned coil-spring would release and jab him in the eye. Or the crotch. It seemed Alix had continued her dislike for him, never forgiving Jace for the many party days he had with Dru way back when.

Jace approached Dru, who had what looked to be the entire buffet on his plate.

"Hey J-man, they boot you too, huh?"

"I guess so." Jace grabbed a plate with a floral-etched pattern and went to work covering up the spectacle. "Do you know anything about what's happening over there?"

"They started jabbering about this haunted tour tonight and somehow we got involved. Alix says inviting us"—Dru raised his voice an octave—"falls outside the parameters of the unwritten laws of a girls' weekend. Though I agree with Jo, it all went to shit when we showed up with no place to sleep last night." Dru shoved a slice of bacon in his mouth with a thoughtful expression. "Also, something about Jolie moving out of her apartment and meeting up with Carrie's cousin tomorrow." Dru swallowed. "But I'm not sure."

Jace's head jerked up. "Wait, she's meeting up with him here? In this town?"

Dru shrugged. "Don't know, man. Got distracted when I saw all the bacon."

Jace looked at Jolie from across the room. That long brown braid of hers cascaded over her right shoulder as she chewed and smiled at no one and everyone. He'd never assumed Jolie had sworn celibacy after they broke up—he hadn't. But he'd been sure last night, while his hand hovered over the doorknob, that she had wanted him to stay. He was certain she would have offered her lips to him had he asked. If she was dating this other guy and moving in with him? Then fuck, he and his judgment were seriously sleep-deprived.

Jace walked back over to the table and set his plate down, his appetite gone.

"Can I talk to you for a sec?" He shoved a hand through his hair in an effort to ignore the urge to bite away his thumbnail instead.

Jolie swallowed and placed her fork on the plate. "Sure. What's up?"

He glanced around. It seemed the entire room's activity had paused. "Can we maybe go over there instead?" Jolie nodded and removed the napkin from her lap before standing up. Carrie coughed with an, "*Uh oh.*" Alix sighed and plucked a piece of bacon off Dru's plate.

Jolie looked at Jace like she hadn't heard or seen any of it. "Where to?"

"This way." He led her out of the dining room and toward a back room lined with floor-to-ceiling bookshelves.

He had no idea why the desperate need to have her alone had taken hold. He could barely form a coherent thought—let alone *talk.* He watched her lean against the door as it clicked shut.

A loose strand of hair fell into her eyes, and her fingers grazed along her collar bone.

"What's going on? Everything okay?"

No, he thought. Everything was far from okay. He wanted her. But was the risk worth it? Or would she scare off, again? *Fuck it.*

In two determined steps, her soft face was in his hand. The energy in the room sparked at the contact. Jolie was the electricity to his static. They stood like this for five, ten, maybe one thousand minutes. His breath mixed with hers, a togetherness in their separation.

"I want to kiss you," he said, watching her pupils dilate. The green in her eyes darkened as if clouds had gathered.

"We shouldn't." She leaned into his touch. "You've been gone and now you're not and—" She stopped and shut her eyes tightly, her nose scrunching up in unison, then opened them and licked her lips. "Okay. You can kiss me."

He let out the breath he'd been holding and brought his other hand up to cup the rest of her face. "On the count of three. One."

She sighed, eyes closing.

"Two." He leaned back to take in her flushed cheeks and parted lips, the cadence of her shallow breath. The pulse of anticipation ached inside him, even after all this time.

"Three," he uttered. His mouth grazed hers like a gentle whisper of what had been and a tease of what could be. Jolie's hands slid up his arms and around his neck and confirmed what he had hoped.

Surrounded by her unique scent, everything around him faded into a blur as their kiss deepened. If she were to jump inside his body, he still wouldn't be satisfied. His need to feel her on every part of him took hold. He wrapped his arms around her waist. Her chest heaved against his.

Then, as if lit from the inside, her lips turned to flames and covered him in relentless pursuit until his dried-out heart caught fire. How many times had he tried and failed to contain her wildfire? He matched her heat this time and pressed her up against the door, keeping pace while barely holding on. The fresh burns would be worth it.

"Wait," she placed her hand over his racing heart. "Wait."

He knew what a double *wait* meant and stepped back.

The air was too thin in the space they had just crushed with their bodies. "How are you still able to do that to me?"

"I could say the same about you." She shook her head. "What just happened?"

"I'm not apologizing for that. No way." He'd kissed her like she should be kissed whenever in his stratosphere.

Jolie ran a hand down her now tangled braid. "You said you wanted to talk, not make out with me."

She was right. He'd brought her to this room to talk, to ask for answers she hadn't shared last night. He should have known being alone with her, and after a restless sleep, wishing she'd spent the night in his bed, would sabotage his plan.

"There was no avoiding what just happened there," Jace said. "But I do have questions, and now I have to know. Am I too late? Are you moving in with him?"

A clock ticked in the silence as the seconds passed by.

Tick. Tick. Tick.

And then her voice rang out. "I am moving."

He groaned, but she kept talking. "To a place closer to my new job. A studio, if you're wondering. No roommates. Might get a cat. Or take a course in therapeutic psychology at the college nearby. Or both." She shifted her weight from foot to foot and pulled on her braid again. "I saw him last night, only for a second, totally unplanned, and random, and...weird. And now I don't know what to think because you're back and not leaving." Her eyes seemed to lose focus as she twirled the braid—*And her thoughts*, he mused—around in her hand.

Suddenly the duo of bright-green landed back on him. "But to answer your other question, no, you're not too late. You're usually right on time. I'm the one who's always late."

A knock on the door startled her straight into his chest. She peered up at him, eyes as bright as embers. Swift and with no forethought, he bent down and kissed her again as another knock sounded—this time with a voice.

"That's enough talking, you two," Dru said, followed by the sound of retreating feet.

"Uh-oh. We're in trouble." Jolie giggled against his neck.

He squeezed and inhaled. "So, about this haunted tour..."

"You really want to go, huh?"

"You're going. So, yeah."

Another knock, louder this time.

"He's back," Jolie whispered through another giggle.

"You guys come on, wrap it up already. I've been exiled from the table, and the bacon, until I have you two in tow," Dru whined.

"Just another minute," Jace said over Jolie's head, her body still flush with his. He looked down at her. "I don't want to further complicate things for you."

She laughed and moved away to open the door.

"Okay," she winked, and walked out of the room in a trail of ash, or so he imagined.

Twenty-Four

April 2008

A bell tinkled overhead as Jolie stepped inside the coffee shop the next day. The smell of cinnamon and dark-roasted coffee beans surrounded her like a big, aromatic hug. Jolie suggested this location in response to Palmer's text yesterday. Her pocket had buzzed with his response at the exact time Jace took her hand. He and Dru had joined the girls last night for the haunted tour. A debate that disappeared once Jace's lips touched hers. The voice inside Jolie's head, however, hadn't stopped shouting, *"What are you doing!"* ever since.

Jolie blinked and looked around for a place to sit. Spotting an empty alcove in the back, she walked over and placed her bag on one of two wingback chairs in front of a fireplace. Palmer and his tallness had yet to arrive, so Jolie sat on the edge of the chair and stared at the burning logs.

Her leg bounced as she tried to settle in. Everything that was on her mind would have to find a way down to her tongue, but the task felt impossibly large. Mesmerized by the fire reaching for its invisible life source, Jolie's thoughts floated off as her tired eyes watched the flames.

She had hoped, somewhat naively, that being in a haunted house last night would have distracted her from Jace's hand-holding, and from the thought of seeing Palmer the very next morning. But who was she kidding? Those chills had nothing to do with old dead dudes from the 1800s floating around and everything to do with hovering pheromones. Even the haunted Dowling House, made entirely of stacked limestone and climbing vines, was no match for the ghosts of exes past.

Following the tour, the group walked to another historic establishment stocked with libations from the Prohibition era. Jolie ordered a smoking old-fashioned. The campfire-spiced liquid had gone down quicker than it should have. She found herself snuggling into Jace's side not long after. His hand roamed on her thigh in an act of absent-minded familiarity more than a suggestion. But Jolie was fit to burst, for the second night in a row, and had seriously considered canceling the coffee date with Palmer. For one reason alone: to rest a guilty conscience had she ended up in Jace's bed.

Neither had come to pass. Instead, she overindulged with a large pizza and was left with a throbbing head and tighter pants today. There had to be a way out of the triangle she was trapped inside, but the best exit was not a thick crust of calories and fat. She knew what words would set her free and she planned to release them this morning.

"Hi." Palmer's voice brought Jolie straight to her feet.

"You startled me!" she said, attempting to smooth out her scrunched-up pants while Palmer planted a swift kiss across her cheek.

"How are you?" he asked.

Fumbling for her purse, she wondered if he could sense her rapid heartbeat. "I'm in desperate need of caffeine."

"Please, let me buy your coffee. I'm taking you away from your friends. It's the least I can do," Palmer said.

"All right. Thank you."

"Really? No back and forth today? Oh, I get it. You finally realized I always win that game."

Jolie smirked. "I finally realized spending *your* money is the real win."

"Large coffee, black, coming right up." Palmer winked. She watched his long legs take him over to the counter. How was she ever going to wash off his sticky sweetness from her life?

He returned with two clay mugs and a muffin the size of a child's head. His capable hands managed to set all three down on the table without a drop of liquid lost.

She picked up a mug, inhaled the sweet aroma of clarity, and asked about his work conference. Small talk was like a Band-Aid until the caffeine took hold.

Palmer tilted his head left and right as if to crack his neck, before answering. "Boring. As most furniture store owners are. But necessary. A lot of networking and standard-issued conversation. People really don't listen, have you noticed?"

"Hm? Sorry, what did you say?" She hid a smile behind her cup, both applauding and cursing her wit for flirting with Palmer. Every. Damn. Time.

His eyes shined. "I was saying, every person I had a conversation with this weekend should've been you instead."

Jolie coughed mid-sip, her throat burning while her stomach clenched. "I doubt my conversational skills are that remarkable."

"There you go again, underestimating yourself." He broke off a piece of muffin and offered her some.

She waved her hand. "I'm good, thanks. And what's wrong with holding a realistic view of myself? I'm not deluded enough to pretend I'll reach some super high standard. These arms only stretch so far before muscles begin to tear and...you get the point."

His brows pinched together, either in thought or due to the muffin's taste. "That sunset behind the pool house, remember?"

How could she forget the blaze of a day's end while she ate his grilled corn on the cob, with butter and paprika and...*oh*. What had she said?

"The only thing I underestimate these days is myself."

He had a talent for drawing out her candid side, then and now.

Palmer picked at the muffin and continued. "I couldn't stay away, incapable really. You were shining. And yet, you'd expertly dimmed your light with self-deprecating statements and anxieties. Uncanny, really." He shook his head. "What you fail to realize, even after all this time, is you're already there, sitting on the ledge of remarkable."

His words floated in the emptiness her cynicism had created, like tiny sparkling fairies. "You want my honest opinion?" he said and placed his elbows on his knees. She rubbed her clammy palms together. Her emotions steamed and percolated as she nodded for him to continue. She should have known Palmer would slam her with his own confession first. "You just haven't opened your eyes yet, to take it all in."

"Maybe so." Her voice cracked; she cleared her throat. "Or I'm on the wrong ledge, facing the wrong way, and staring directly at a wall of stone."

The corners of his eyes wrinkled. "Knock it the fuck down, Jolie."

She fisted her suddenly shaking hands. "Metaphorical stone is pretty dense." His back hit the chair while he mumbled to himself before sitting straight again.

"You're stunning, and that's all there is to it. We can talk about something else."

Good god. Jolie needed all the coffee armor to battle this conversation, and with what she planned to say to Palmer, and on the heels of all that he had just said, the thought made her lightheaded. Very lightheaded.

The air around her turned too dense and too thick. She couldn't take in a full breath, while the noise of a coffee shop in motion intensified. She tried to push up the sleeves of her blouse, but she couldn't move. When did it become so hot? Beads of sweat dotted her hairline, and was...the room tilting?

"Hey, whoa." Palmer caught her by the elbow. He kneeled down and centered her into the chair. "What's going on?"

She squeezed her eyes shut from what appeared to be the walls closing in, gripped the arms of her chair, and focused on her breathing.

"Do you need anything?" Palmer asked.

She opened her eyes and blurted, "I need space. I need air.

I need to be alone." She watched Palmer rise slowly from his crouched position. There was no stopping her tongue from taking control now. "You see this strength and courage in me but all I feel is pressure to step into something you claim I already own. And maybe that confidence is there, somewhere, I don't know. But you, you're different. You express yourself in ways both inspiring and daunting. You're not impossible to catch. I'm just not made for your speed. I can never be your country wife or live the life you want to provide. The actual thought makes me want to throw up. No, that's probably from all the food last night." She took a breath, not breaking eye contact. "I made out with Jace last night. And then ate an entire pizza by myself. And I'm pretty sure I'm on the brink of a panic attack. So what I'm saying is, I need to be alone. From everyone. Right now."

Palmer's Adam's apple bobbed as his head tilted to the ceiling, his chest rising and falling. When his eyes met hers again, Jolie fought against a giant shiver. All the warmth had left his face.

"I didn't realize my love for you was so *daunting*, Jolie. And this *need* to be alone—" He laughed sharply. She flinched. "Mark my words, it's not a need, that's a will. You *will* be alone. Because all you do is cause hurt." He swiped his jacket from behind the chair. "You want me to leave?" With a nod of his head, he spat out an 'okay' and walked out the door.

Jolie stared at the picked apart muffin on the table in front of her and swallowed down the bile rising up the back of her throat.

Do not throw up.

Once she was certain she could breathe without releasing her insides, she reached for her purse as Palmer's last words flooded her mind. *All you do is cause hurt.*

Her hands, unstable yet somehow still capable, located her cell phone. She didn't know what she was doing, but she was doing it anyway.

"Hey, you. You disappeared this morning. Last-minute shopping?" Jace's voice shot right through her cracked heart. He sounded so...happy. *All you do is cause hurt.*

"I had coffee with Palmer." Jolie didn't recognize her own voice as it kept talking. "He left. After I told him you and I made out. And now I'm telling you the same thing I said to him."

Jace exhaled. "I know you, Jolie." How quickly his tone went from upbeat to dead tired. "I kind of knew this was coming. But go ahead."

"I need to be alone. From everyone. Right now." She felt robotic and empty having to repeat the harsh truth.

"Christ, Jo..." Jace paused, and she imagined him biting his nails. A habit she hadn't seen in action for a long time. "You and I? We've been away from each other. We've been alone, for the most part, right? I haven't seen you. You haven't seen me. So excuse me if this comes off as crass, but I don't fucking count as everyone. You sure don't in my book. You're...*everything.*"

She slumped under the weight of his words. "I can't be everything to anyone when I'm too overwhelmed with myself, Jace. Don't you get it? This isn't a negotiation of my heart; this is me telling you. I need to be alone. From everyone. Right now. Please."

Her eyes stung. The line on the other end was quiet until it wasn't. And for the second time today, the word she loved the most cut her again.

"Okay." Jace said, and the line went dead.

Twenty-Five

April 2009

"**F**inally!" Carrie's voice tunneled through Jolie's cell phone speaker and bounced off the bathroom walls. Jolie had just returned from a necessary but somewhat cramped run, and was washing the sweat off her face. Over the last year, she had gotten into the habit of running outdoors after sessions of overeating. The clouds formed by her self-generated *yuck* felt less ominous with an endorphin surge. Crisp air and warm sunlight helped too.

"I know you like to disappear," Carrie continued. "But to straight up not answer calls? For like, forty-eight hours? It makes me uncomfortable, and I don't like that. Text next time. Okay?"

Jolie pressed her damp face into the soft fibers of a towel, muffling her response. "You'd know if something bad happened." If only she could feel as comfortable in her own body as the towel did on her face. She patted down her neck. "I'm fine."

Fine, she mused, the one word always said in opposition to its true meaning. She was anything but fine.

What had started as a personal day yesterday had turned upside down and out of control. One year of working at the mental health clinic, and the dizzying pace of coming and going had left her nauseous. An article she'd found on Google profiling the "Bleak Reality of Mental Health Workers" had warned, in big, bold letters, *ninety percent employee turnover.*

But as of late, the empty positions at her clinic were absorbed by the remaining employees, a collection of crumbs advertised as the whole cookie. Jolie had taken on two, sometimes three job titles, which she bounced between for ten to twelve hours daily. She had reached her breaking point. The only title she wanted to fill, at this point, was that of ex-employee. Her perseverance, however, was linked to her independence.

If she left a well-paid job, she would end up back in her mom's basement.

So, instead, she emailed her boss earlier to request—or rather inform him that she wasn't coming in for a second day and had offered no reason why. Once the email was sent, she sat on the couch and ate, and ate...and ate.

Bowls of cereal, rolls of Ritz Crackers smeared in vanilla frosting, bags of tortilla chips, boiled stale pasta with a bag of shredded cheese on top, and spoonfuls of peanut butter straight from the jar. It was a destructive routine of calorie-rich avoidance, as tried and true as silencing incoming calls, while she watched daylight move across her wall.

Once the numbness had been digested, she had forced a bit of mental hygiene and felt slightly more in control of herself post-run. She would do better tomorrow. Because there was always tomorrow, to go into work, to be a responsible adult, to return the calls from her mother, and to buy new pants because hers no longer fit.

Carrie's voice cut in. "The point is, you wouldn't know if something happened to *me*. Now, would you?"

Jolie scooped up her phone. "You're right. I'm sorry. Work has been so demanding. I'm sleeping through my night classes at this point. I just needed to disconnect."

"They still haven't hired Sam's replacement?" Carrie asked.

"My boss said it's no longer in the budget this year." Jolie swallowed down a lump in her throat, the urge to jam a fistful of potato chips into her mouth replacing her earlier calm. "I have to find another job. Or take out a bunch of student loans and go full-time again. I'm too young to hate life."

"You don't hate life. You hate that place because it sucks.

You're a hard worker, and they're taking advantage. I know you'll find something so much better in no time. Or you'll happily go into debt while you become a rock star therapist. You've taken how many classes now? I bet if you transferred to a proper university, your credits would put you halfway through a master's program."

Jolie had already envisioned going after something bigger, better, and...scarier. Fear had stopped her from sharing those plans with her friend.

Carrie coughed slightly then said, "Now, are you going to ask what happened to me?"

Jolie hesitated. When last they spoke, Carrie had been knee-deep with another married man after a month of dating. Correction, separated man. At least this new guy's birth year hovered in the same decade.

"How much could have possibly happened?"

"You know me, the drama I bring in two days could amount to a lifetime for someone else. So yes. There are tales to be told."

"Let me sit down first." Jolie hoped her tone was seasoned with enough humor to cover up her trepidation. Her friend deserved better. "I'm ready."

She heard Carrie's sharp intake of breath. "Lonny moved out of his place. Over the weekend."

Jolie's lips pressed together. She had assumed separated meant separate living too. But what did she know?

Carrie continued, "And now he's kind of, sort of, basically living with me."

"You're living together—"

"Don't with the tone, Lee. It's been amazing."

"It's been less than a week. How can you even gauge a level of anything other than it being different?"

"Well, it's been amazingly different. He's different. I think...like, I might be in love or something."

Jolie stilled in recognition of the monumental confession from her friend. Carrie, notoriously independent, unapologetic in her opinions, and often the pants-wearer in her short-lived relationships, hadn't admitted to any type of romantic feelings since their Christmas cheese expedition years ago, which made it all the more concerning.

"Please don't take this the wrong way..." Jolie knew the buffer was worthless. "But why are you giving one hundred percent of yourself to a man who can only give less than half of himself in return. He's still married!"

"Listen, Jolie." Carrie spat Jolie's name like a fireball from a dragon's mouth. "You've chosen to live alone, after rejecting my cousin repeatedly, and after another offer to move in with him! God, he's so stupidly in love—" Carrie likely tasted blood from biting her tongue. "What I'm trying to say is, you're not allowed to project your unhappiness on me for doing life differently than you."

Ouch.

The line buzzed. What Carrie failed to understand, by Jolie's design, of course, was the well-worn path Jolie had stumbled back onto. She was, yet again, a weary traveler traversing a forest of emotional eating alone over the last year. Jolie wanted to protect Carrie from the pain, not project it onto her.

But she couldn't blame Carrie for taking it that way. It was the result of unspoken boundaries being crossed, a schism in the foundation of their friendship. Carrie was right to be upset. Jolie had rejected her friend's cousin for a second time. An offer she couldn't have seen coming, but perhaps she shouldn't have met up with Palmer last month in the first place.

Palmer had invited her, over text, to meet for after-work drinks as former coworkers. What a hilariously tragic irony, she now thought. When the day arrived, Jolie ignored her nerves and common sense and blotted away the ten-hour grease from her face. She swiped on a second coat of mascara, placed the square, dark-framed glasses back on her face, and showed up five minutes early.

Palmer arrived five minutes late, in a cloud of confidence, and a new, brown leather jacket, which he peeled from his muscled arms in slow motion. Not that she paid close attention. And while he didn't lay it on thick, as they say, it was clear he'd spent time waxing his charm to a gleaming shine.

"Friends flirt," he said with false innocence.

She felt the push-back immediately, that of past lovers trying to be friends. Their attraction had never been their problem—it was an undeniable force. It was their differences that threatened the hold.

They moved on to small talk.

How was her work?

Fine.

How was her mom?

Sober. Recovering. Living.

Did Carrie know they were hanging out?

Yes. She wanted to chaperone.

He smiled and asked, "Why would we need a chaperone?"

If only Palmer had asked what Jolie wanted to flick off the tip of her tongue and into his brain.

How was her life without him?

Dim. Like a lightbulb went out.

Her peach fuzz brain, however, couldn't decipher whose light had burnt out, Palmer's, or Jace's, or...hers.

But Palmer would never ask that type of question. A side effect of engrained Midwestern manners. Instead, he squeezed her down until she was small enough to read between his lines.

The remainder of the evening showcased Palmer's implicit understanding of her while a honey-like substance suffocated her every pore. Sticky and sweet, Palmer flew right in and asked if she would move in with him. Again. She sat unmoving and unable to connect the dots.

She hadn't seen him for any length of time that would elicit the request.

"Well, I had to try, one last time." He shrugged in response to Jolie's stunned silence.

Following the shuffling of goodbyes from the deck of farewell options—*awkward hugs for the win*—she drove home and hadn't spoken to him since. Thank god. The desire to break free from her self-imposed discomfort would only distort her feelings further.

Carrie's voice broke in and said something Jolie had missed.

"Let's touch base tomorrow? Lonny is due back any minute with two carloads."

The tone in Carrie's voice was tight. Jolie felt responsible, *she was responsible*, and knew she had to fix it. "I just want what's best for you, Carrie. That's all. If Lonny makes you happy, then I trust you."

"Thank you, Lee. He really does. You should meet him. You'd like him, I swear. And I want the same for you—to be happy." Carrie's tone brightened. "So, come over and help move boxes, yeah?"

Jolie pinched the bridge of her nose. There was always a catch when it came to Carrie wanting what's best. "Manual labor makes happiness these days?"

"No, but helping your oldest and most treasured friend does. Plus, Lonny has an impressive collection of whiskey. Any bottle. Of our choosing."

Jolie rose from the closed toilet seat she'd been sitting on and looked in the mirror. Her face was puffy. Round. Her hair was unwashed. Dirty. A film of faux wetness. The internal criticism started to boil. Carrie lived close, having moved last year, which removed the drive time as an excuse. Lugging heavy boxes called for grosser-than-usual appearances, right?

Not the best first impression for Carrie's new live-in boyfriend. Oh, hell, what did it matter anyway? Jolie knew she would come out of hiding and into the living world regardless, as was the power of her friendship with Carrie.

So she responded, "See you in a few."

She would stay for an hour. Tops.

Twenty-Six

April 2009

The number of boxes an almost-single man possessed should have been less than half the amount covering the basement floor. Jace was certain of this, being a single man himself. What he wasn't sure about was why he'd agreed to manual labor on a Friday at the end of a long work week.

"An hour, if that," Talon had said following their afternoon staff meeting. The air in the hallway was heavy with sweat and stale fast food. Jace couldn't wait to inhale spring in bloom and sit outside come five o'clock. And maybe flirt with the girl he'd met last week, who said she would be at a happy hour with a group of coworkers. The perfect distraction from the four years spent at a company he was quickly outgrowing. The thought of freelancing had begun to pop up daily. But he would need his Ph.D. first.

"I will literally kill my ex if I spend another weekend in that house with her," Talon continued.

"That bad, huh?" The last time Jace had seen the ex-wife was at a holiday work function in January. She got drunk, admitted to filing for divorce, and slurred a request for him to be her rebound. Jace politely declined while prying her hand off his forearm. That wasn't just shitting where you ate, but shitting on every surface available— *Hard pass.*

"Oh, it is. She found out where I'm moving and didn't take it so well," Talon said as he stopped at Jace's office door and scrunched one eye closed. "She broke all of our wedding china from my parents."

Jace let out a low whistle. "Rough."

"Bad temper, that one. Anyway, we'll need to drive separately to the house. I'll text you the address to my new place."

Why was empathy typically mistaken for agreement? Not that he would've said no.

Which was why he found himself straining to lift yet another box from Talon's basement.

"Hey, you never explained why your ex reenacted a Greek wedding tradition the other night." Jace heard a grunt at the top of the basement steps.

"Not much to explain. I'm moving in with my new girlfriend."

"Yeah, that would do it." Jace puffed up the steps. Those who bounced from one relationship to the next fascinated him. His one-track mind made it impossible for him to flit from heart to bed.

Once outside, Jace surveyed the remaining boxes on the front stoop. "I don't think this is going to fit in one go."

"Huh, you're probably right." Jace heard a tongue click from the rear end of the truck. "Two trips it is then," Talon declared with a clap.

Jace rolled his eyes at Talon's retreat, as his happy-hour plans disappeared through the door.

Thirty minutes and a large coffee later, Jace pulled into the parking lot of an apartment complex he passed daily. He'd considered living here when he returned from California last year, but the noise from a nearby highway had crossed it off the list. His current place was a bit further, but the land backed up against a forest preserve. Much more his speed. Jolie's too. Not that he had chosen it with her in mind.

He was about to get out of his car when he watched, in what could only be described as unmitigated horror, the scene that began to unfold through his foggy windshield. A tall blonde bounded out of the massive apartment building and swung her arms around Talon. Even from a distance, he could make out her wide smile and bright eyes. Jace immediately recognized Carrie's euphoric face.

"What the f—" Jace's mouth snapped closed as a second figure emerged from the building. Even in a baseball cap and baggy jeans, her presence radiated familiarity.

He hadn't asked about Talon's girlfriend. His desire to do his service and get to the face of his latest distraction was more important. Now he saw the error in his lack of curiosity. His stomach blazed with nerves as he opened his door. This big-bad world wasn't microscopic. It was, as Jolie once pointed out to him, *submicroscopic.*

He watched Jolie halt from across a row of parked cars. She spotted him as quickly as he noticed her. The face he would recognize anywhere was cast in shadows. It was as if she had wilted from lack of light.

They'd fallen into a pattern of twelve-month absences, and then, as if the tilt of the earth's axis depended on their reconcil-iation, they were thrown together again. This awareness didn't ease his shock, as gravity seemed to grow heavier with every thrust back into her orbit.

He met her in the middle of the parking lot.

"I have so many questions right now," was her opening line. She looked him up and down. "The first of which is about your current attire."

Jace plucked at the borrowed orange *Salt Life* shirt and readjusted his mesh shorts. Not typical clothing for him, unless running, which happened less often these days.

"We came straight from the office so Talon lent me these. I hadn't planned on moving all his stuff when I got dressed this morning." He left out his original plans, although he was having a hard time remembering what they'd been. To think if he had said no to helping Talon, he would have missed the rare sighting of his runaway heart.

"Oh my god. This all makes sense. Lonny is your coworker.

I've met him. I thought I was losing my mind when Carrie introduced me earlier. He seemed so familiar, but I couldn't place him." Jolie took a step closer. Was she going to hug him? His body hummed at the thought.

She looked down and shuffled backward.

Apparently not.

"New Year's Eve, when you showed up at my mom's house. The swing set. The house. That was Talon's party. Lonny." Relief brightened her eyes while she pulled at her braid.

Jace had avoided women for a good portion of last year, due to limited headspace and a fractured heart. But come January, he'd talked himself into exploring distractions. Those without braids and green eyes.

He nodded. "Right. Yep. Same guy. Carrie calls him Lonny?"

Jolie opened her mouth as Carrie's voice cut in from a distance. "This is so random. Isn't this so random?" Her high-pitched giggles bounced off the parked cars. Jace stared at Talon and Carrie standing together with their arms intertwined, the circumstances that had brought them all together still unreal, then looked at Jolie.

She eyed him before saying, "Your hair is longer. I like it," and walked in the direction of Carrie and Talon with her head down.

The apartment was on the third floor, and lucky for them, the elevator had broken that morning. He refused to count the number of times they'd gone up and down the stairs, but sweat had been involved. Lots of it.

Talon clapped his hands. "That's the last of it. Who needs a drink?"

Jolie sprawled across Carrie's couch, while Jace eased onto one of the kitchen stools and rolled back his stiff shoulders. He had just endured the worst physical and mental workout of his life.

Jolie's legs swung to the floor. "I'm gonna head out actually."

"I promised you whiskey," Carrie whined from inside the galley kitchen.

"I promised you an hour and we're rounding on three," Jolie said, stamping her heel into her shoe and disappearing into the kitchen.

Jace hovered near the kitchen, straining to hear whatever the girls were whispering but it was impossible. He'd barely said two words to Jolie and he wanted her to stay. Jolie emerged, car keys jingling as she waved goodbye.

"Nice meeting you. I'm sure we'll see each other again." Her eyes flicked to Jace. "Sooner rather than later." And then she was gone.

Talon looked between the door and Jace a few more times than necessary, leaving Jace to assume Carrie had filled him in.

"She's not herself today," Carrie said, arms crossed. "Hasn't been for some time. But she wants you to go after her."

Jace frowned. Jolie's hasty retreat had suggested otherwise. Carrie must have sensed his hesitation. "Go, Jace."

Dammit.

He bolted out the door, taking the stairs down two at a time and caught up with Jolie right as she was closing her car door.

"Wait. Jo." He forced the words out between gulps of air, his body exhausted from the exertion. She gave him a full view of bloodshot eyes and puffy ghost-white skin. A tug deep inside had him crouching to her level. "You sure you have to go?"

She blinked at him. "I'm bad company right now, like, the worst."

"Doubt that."

She continued as if he hadn't spoken, "I can't navigate you being here. It's impossible to manage what I'm feeling, like my brain is working overtime, trying to convince me it doesn't mean anything, these random occurrences of ours." She stared out the windshield, knees jiggling. He remained still, not wanting to break the spell. "I just feel stuck in this inability to explain away something that is unexplainable in the first place."

"So don't try."

"You don't think I should try to find the reason why you're still here?" She tapped her chest three times.

He put his hand atop her knee to still the movement. "The explanation isn't important. Us ending the fight with fate is."

Her chest rose and fell. His knees began to ache. Finally, she spoke. "I'll let you know when I end the battle with myself first." She glanced at him, her eyes apologetic, then whispered goodbye.

Twenty-Seven

June 2009

J ace had never considered himself a collector of favorites. Not of colors or books growing up, or even sports teams when sports bars entered his life. Not even his love of music had produced a favorite song; he was an equal opportunity appreciator of all things that piqued his interest. Then, as if right on cue, summer breezed in and released from her grasp the magic of Saturday afternoons. The first weekend in June found Jace falling for that spectacular exception to the rule: his one, true favorite—Jolie.

"I was wondering, if you're not busy, I'm going to a farmer's market this afternoon, and they have a hot sauce stand. And, well, maybe you'd want to meet up, check it out. If you're not busy." Jolie's voice wavered over the phone, pulling at his heart. The location she mentioned was so close to his apartment he felt foolish for not having run into her since April.

He talked himself out of asking her whether the call was a prank and said, "Yes, of course. Tell me when."

They met outside a Starbucks and followed the walking traffic down a line of pop-up tents on the closed-off street. Jolie bought a loaf of cinnamon bread; he bought a bottle of hot sauce. Their pace slowed near the pavilion as an acoustic guitar played in the middle. He followed her lead and exchanged cautious sentiments of work frustrations and of third-wheel dynamics when hanging out with Carrie and Talon.

He joked in response to her apprehension about going out

that night with the couple who defined the acronym PDA. Her shrugged response suggested too much too soon. They approached their original meeting place. Jace was shocked to realize two hours had passed. Jolie offered a loose hug, and they parted ways.

The second invitation came the following Saturday, for the farmer's market again. This time they met in a parking lot. The sun blazed in the rising humidity, Jace's forehead already slick with sweat. Jolie showed up in a thin tank top that stretched across her shoulders when she grabbed a rolled-up blanket from the backseat of her car. Taking the lead, she pointed to a shaded grassy section in the center of all the tents.

He offered to grab iced coffees, and upon his return, saw two bagels on white paper napkins next to a cross-legged Jolie. A dancer dressed in large silk wings drifted into his peripheral vision, but all he could see was Jolie, swaying to the music of a violin, lute, and cittern.

Jolie stretched her legs out on the blanket, leveled him with those green eyes of hers, and started talking of her mom. She told him about the hospital visit that had prompted her mom's recovery two years earlier, and the relapses since. She spoke gently as if the words threatened to break inside her mouth and cut her tongue. He longed to absorb her pain, go back in time, and shield her from it all.

"I could've been there for you, Jo. I would've," he said. He bubbled with emotion, ashamed he felt hurt in the wake of her own suffering.

"I wanted you there so badly. Which was why I stayed away." She offered a sad smile. "But you're here now."

He updated her on his mom and stepdad, still grossly in love, and how his biological father had adopted a baby girl who Jace planned to meet the following month. She listened as her forehead wrinkled in concern. Yes, the absent father during his formative years was planning to raise another, as a single dad. Only Jolie could understand the gritty sting.

He remained quiet on the walk back to the parking lot, reflective, yet not absent of impulses. The bouquet of flowers they'd created at the flower tent squeezed between them as he kissed her cheek goodbye. A moment perfumed with hope and desire.

Then he waited for a third invitation, positive it would show. It felt different this time around. Significant. Number three.

"Three will always be my number. It's lucky for me, I think," Jolie had shared on their third date, way back when. The date of their first kiss. The real beginning.

As if his memory had itched her own, she called him, her tone somewhere between humor and anxiety—humxiety.

"I heard there's a lethal hot sauce with your name on it this weekend. You game?"

Of course he said yes. Inwardly, he wondered if the same magic their past had offered years ago would show up for them again.

He parked in the same lot, Jolie grabbed the same blanket, and as he reached for her hand, she smiled up at him in what looked like relief. *Okay.* The air was heavy, but the sun hiding behind thick, gray clouds muted the mid-June heat.

Jace barely noticed the familiar tents stuffed with local vegetables, fresh farm eggs, homemade candles, and hundreds of stems of flowers in black buckets; all he could see was her. Jolie bought her usual cinnamon bread and a new bottle of hot sauce for him.

"The hottest on the market," proclaimed the bearded man behind the plastic table. They settled on the blanket and listened to the sounds of a banjo and violin playing "Crimson and Clover", a quicker version than the Joan Jett cover. The tin-like quality of the banjo's strings paired with the crispness of the violin created an unexpected harmony.

"So," they said at the same time.

He laughed as a breeze passed over his arms like a page had turned. They were only words away from each other now, or so he hoped.

Jolie took a deep breath. "I can't stop thinking about you. Even in my sleep, you're there, Jace." She pushed back her straight hair. "I'm in a better place, I think. Well, trying to be. And I might be ready to try this again. If you are. I mean, if you want to."

He took in her red cheeks and round eyes. How could his heart not shatter from the weight of the love he'd held for her for so long? The banjoist's cover echoed in his ear.

Over and over. They had loved and lost each other.

"Come here." He motioned with his hand.

She moved between his legs, his heart drumming a lethal beat into her shoulder blade. He dipped his nose into her lavender and cinnamon scent, hovering just below her ear lobe.

"Welcome back," he whispered.

She craned her neck, lips parted, a familiar yearning—one he would never forget. He captured her mouth with his, determined to end their fight with fate for good.

He drove Jolie to the farmer's market the following Saturday. They laughed together, shared food together, kissed together, then adopted two kittens together after visiting the local shelter's pop-up tent for National Pet Adoption Month. And since Jolie's apartment allowed pets and his didn't, they decided to house them with her.

"I can't believe we just did that," Jolie giggled while tucking the adoption paperwork in her purse. "I'm so excited! You're excited too, right? Wow, look at this list. So many things we need to buy!" She waved another sheet of paper in her hand. "We should go to the pet store. Tomorrow. Or maybe like, now."

Jace captured her hand and squeezed it. He hadn't seen Jolie in an anxious burst of excitement for some time. She was as adorable as he remembered. "They won't be at your place until next week. There's plenty of time to get all that stuff. "

"You're right. I'm just so excited. Which I've said already." She blew out a breath. "Oh! We need to name them!"

He raised her hand to kiss the back of it. "I was thinking

Crimson and Clover."

She stopped walking before he realized and pulled him back. He turned, laughing at her frown. "What? You don't like it?"

She wrapped her arms around his waist and raised her face to his. "You're too perfect right now." Her body began to sway from side to side. "And this feels like a dream so...maybe...kiss me?"

"Right here, in the middle of the sidewalk?" He looked around. A man and a woman stood several feet behind them. Up ahead the view was clear. And right in front of him was love. Her beautiful mouth formed the word 'please'.

How could he resist? She wanted him. He brushed his lips against hers and mumbled, "I want you."

Her mouth reached for more. "You have me."

He felt her fingers spread along his lower back, urging him closer. He gripped her waist and, in her moan, deepened their kiss. A low whistle from someone passing by brought him back to reality. They were making out, like horny teenagers, in broad daylight, at a farmer's market, with children running by. Shame on them. Or not. It felt earned, somehow.

Jolie straightened her shirt and pressed her palms against her flushed cheeks.

"So, that happened," she said.

Jace pulled her to his side and kissed her temple. "Long time coming."

A wicked smile took over Jolie's face. "Pun intended?" She blinked once, twice, then a third time.

"What? I mean...no?" He shook his head, mirroring her smile. "Are you suggesting something here?"

She rolled her eyes, grabbed his hand, and marched ahead.

Okay then.

"I think your place is closer," he said from behind.

She threw her head back in laughter. "You bet your ass it is."

Twenty-Eight

July 2009

Two weeks passed and Jolie found herself shaking a bottle of citrus-scented stain remover at a fuzzy devil in disguise.

"Crimson keeps peeing on the rugs," she said as she rose from her knees and stared at the animal conveniently passed out on Jace's lap. She wished Crimson's bladder would grow a pair of wings and fly to the litter box. "And he meows for an hour after you leave. Like, howling meows."

Jolie had been on the phone with her mother the other night, not long after Jace's departure, when the noise had started, like clockwork.

"You're eating enough dear? Getting enough sleep? I worry about you," her mom had said.

Jolie hadn't seen her mom since their weekend lunch in May. It had been a day warm enough to sit outside with lemonades while a lilac scented breeze weaved through the courtyard. Once their salads were eaten, her mom offered gratitude to her only daughter. "Thank you for being there. I would've been lost without you. I'm stronger because of you."

Stunned by the certainty of so few words, Jolie latched on to her mom's determination. It was time to put an end to eating away fear. She would chase it off instead. That night, she applied for a master's program in counseling at Northwestern University. She hadn't touched a single package of Oreos since. Then the following month she called Jace.

But the nature of her mom's disease was a constant test of

Jolie's trust. A burden Jolie hoped would lighten but hadn't yet. Crimson's howls had prompted Jolie to cut the call short and end the conversation with a simple 'I love you, Mom.'

"Look. Is that another stain?" Jolie crossed her arms and tilted her chin forward. Jace reached across Crimson and handed Jolie an off-white throw pillow with cerulean and forest green accents, now damp and stained with urine. She sniffed it and recoiled. Cat pee was the absolute worst.

"You're positive it's Crimson?" Jace asked.

Jolie placed her hands on her hips. In the two weeks since the cats had arrived, Jace had started a creeping takeover of her apartment. First it was his toothbrush situated next to hers. Then, his razor ended up on the soap dish reserved for hair ties. A dresser drawer began to fill with his underwear and socks; even her bedsheets held his lingering scent. But unlike before, she didn't feel debilitated by her own freak-out. There were two kittens to consider, both of which adored him. Still, she spent more time caring for the two little shits than he had.

Clover, their laid-back orange tabby, wove between her legs. "I caught Crimson in the act. So yeah, feeling pretty solid on that accusation."

"I've never seen him do it." Jace rubbed behind Crimson's ears, and Jolie could have sworn the cat sighed. Or farted. Kitten farts were the worst.

"That's because he's fine when you're here," she said. Jolie sat next to Jace and leaned into his warmth—a relief to her constant state of cold, even in the middle of July.

"So, he peed once over the last week?" Jace's chest rumbled into her body. True, Jace had spent six nights in her bed. All of which had ended in a toe-curling finale.

She sighed. "Once is too much. I'm worried it'll get worse, especially if I'm accepted into the master's program. I'll be gone a lot and you won't be able to jump in since you have your night classes."

Jace shifted an inch, careful not to disturb the Prince of

Furriness. "We could try something, if you're open to it."

"I'm open to any and all suggestions."

He stared at her while his thumb tapped a rhythm on her thigh.

Circle. Tap. Circle. Tap.

"I could move in."

Jolie stilled. Of course the thought had crossed her mind. It made sense. She was in love with him. For the third time. Why, then, would the voice inside Jolie's head question her heart's determination?

Now is not the time, the voice whispered.

But saying no to Jace would only cause hurt, she wanted to shout back. The need to eat an Oreo—or five—woke up and yawned.

"I'm here six of the seven days anyway. And Jo," Jace looked her straight in the eyes. "I love you."

She soaked in the face that had captured her heart long before he was aware she existed. A face now framed by slightly longer hair, but with eyes just as bright.

Now is not the time, the voice cut in. Jolie nearly spat out, *But now is all we have!*

"Do you ever think about when we first met?" she said, taking in his expression, certain he would play along and wait out the mystery her mind would reveal.

"Whenever I hear this one Finger Eleven song, I do."

"Really?" She had no idea.

"Yeah. I had it piping through my headphones. Actually, it stopped halfway through, right before you tapped me on the shoulder and scared the crap outta me. Stupid MP3 player, shit for the money back then."

Her memory pulsed like hot coals from fresh oxygen. "That's why you stopped walking out of the lobby."

"Yeah, I had to open the back and roll the damn batteries. Every time."

"Wow." She shook her head, marveling at the tiniest of

threads that had brought them together, at how easily it could have been overlooked.

"Right? iPods revolutionized personalized listening devices."

"No," she laughed. "I mean yes, they did. Obviously. But thank god those didn't exist yet."

"Why not?"

"Because your MP3 player is the reason we met."

Jace looked at her, confused.

She reached down for Clover and placed him on her lap. The kitten began to pad her thighs. "While I waited for you to finish your final, I was so convinced I could do it. Go up to someone I'd never spoken to before but had been so intensely aware of all semester. Once I saw you walk out, with your headphones already on, my nerve went straight out the building."

"Obviously not," Jace said.

"Had you not stopped to fix your MP3 player, I wouldn't have gone up to you. You left me no choice."

The room fell quiet. Jolie stared at him as memories zoomed past her. Their paths had drawn figure-eights for too long. It was time to end the dizzying pace. "Just like now. I'm left with no choice. Because I love you, Jace."

His face lit up. "Then we'll give this a try? This living together thing?"

"Okay," she said.

Jace leaned over and captured her mouth. A promise sealed with a kiss, while Crimson snored underneath.

Twenty-Nine

October 2009

"**Y**ou're next, Lee," Carrie sing-songed from an adjacent salon chair. A hairdresser buzzed around Jolie in a cloud of hairspray and bobby pins.

Jolie coughed away the fruity chemicals. "How am I next? You're the one with the engagement ring." She eyed Carrie's latest accessory, a massive rock as startling as the proposal itself after only six months of living with Talon.

Jolie and Jace had lain in bed last weekend following the engagement party. With covers pulled to their chins and both cats balled at the end of the bed, Jace murmured, "Pretty sure the ink is still wet." He was referencing Talon's divorce papers. "Should we be worried?"

Jolie was relieved to hear a thought she'd tried to push away, voiced by the one person who needed to understand. She turned and tucked her arm underneath the pillow. "I am worried, yes. How long do you think it'll take for her to lose that ring?"

Jace chuckled. "Given its size, hopefully she won't. Are you green-eyed over there?"

"Genetically speaking, yes," Jolie said, glancing at her bare left ring finger. "I don't need an entire constellation sparkling on my finger. Just a little twinkle. At some point. Maybe."

"I can lasso a star for you, Jo."

Jolie flipped onto her back and away from Jace's stare.

"Carrie was glowing," she said.

"I've never seen Talon smile for any length of time. Until tonight," Jace added. And they left it at that.

The hairdresser shoved another bobby pin into Jolie's hair, poking her in the scalp. To Jolie's mention of her ring, the sunbeam that was Carrie responded, "Who knows when I'll walk down the aisle. Lonny wants us to take our time, enjoy our engagement, save for the wedding."

This was news. "Is that what you want?"

"It's fine." Carrie shrugged.

Jolie wasn't convinced Carrie was *fine*, but she also knew now was not the time to keep asking.

"Hey, what about me?" Alix waved her engagement ring like it hadn't been oohed and aahed over for the last nine months. "I'm not married yet. So technically, I'm next in line." An angelic smile took over while the makeup artist painted her face to matrimonial perfection.

Carrie waved her hand. "You're already a victim, Alix. As am I. So, technically, Lee is next."

"A victim of what, exactly?" Jolie said.

Carrie's chair spun to face Jolie, a serendipitous move by the hyperactive hairdresser. "Love, duh. Our dear Alix will be married in less than three hours. At some point, I'll be a bride, too. Which leaves you as the next victim."

Alix laughed while Jolie bit her tongue. She was a victim all right. A victim of perpetual failure. The master's program she'd poured more hope into than she realized had rejected her application. As a result, Jolie restarted the cycle of constant eating during Jace's night classes. She wasn't outright lying, but hiding her secret had bred contempt toward Jace. Living with someone would do that, though, right? Inevitable really. Yet a niggling, deep within the back of her brain, continued to argue with her blame.

It's not him; it's you.

A craving for something deep-fried and salty hit her hard and fast. She pressed a hand against her food-baby bloat, which would soon be on full display in front of hundreds of people in her dropped-waist silk bridesmaid's dress. Thank god for Spanx.

Servicing women who ate their emotions since the year two thousand.

"Well, today has nothing to do with me and everything to do with Alix and Dru," Jolie said.

She reached for the bottle of champagne and topped off her glass, then passed it to Carrie. Maybe the bubbles would distract her from wanting an entire menu of pub food. "To Alix and Dru. May you both continue to be charmed by the disagreements you'll always have."

Carrie's mouth dropped open. "That's bleak, even for you Lee."

Alix sputtered and laughed. "No. It's spot on. We argued from the moment he said hello. Remember, Jo?"

Jolie downed her glass and poured more, nodding in agreement. The passage of time had tampered with her recollections, but she would never forget that day. Her first real conversation with Jace, while Alix and Dru argued in the background. Jolie had felt whole back then as she discovered herself through new love, happy even. Nothing like the scattered pieces she'd become.

Maybe her own happiness had been thrown away with all the other garbage in her life. Or was her chance at happiness hidden under the empty take-out containers and bags of chips in the trash can?

"She's the reason we're together." Alix's doe eyes snared Jolie. "To think, your semester-long crush resulted in my marriage."

"And not mine," Jolie mumbled around the rim of her glass. Neither of her friends heard her sad murmurs over the sounds of their own happiness.

"Hey, come here," Jace said, reaching for the blur passing by. In a maroon, floor-length gown, her slender neck exposed underneath pinned-up hair, Jolie was breathtaking. Earlier, when he'd walked down the aisle with Jolie on his arm, just before the bride, he'd never felt more proud.

Next month, Jace would drive to his hometown and a sit-down with his ninety-year-old grandmother, who had the ring. He planned to return with a band of gold, a humble bit of pressurized rock, and a lifetime of promises for Jolie.

Her body felt rigid as he pulled her into his arms and swayed to the music.

"Have I told you how much I love these lips?" He ran a thumb lightly over her scarlet-colored bottom lip. Jolie almost never wore lipstick, hating the attention it brought. If only she would own her beauty more often.

"I have to get these to Alix." Jolie held up a pair of flip-flops.

He lowered her arm and kissed the back of her hand. "You owe me a dance," Jace mumbled against her soft skin.

Tonight was meant as a break in their grueling reality. The last month had been a series of hellos and goodbyes, with many forgotten I-love-yous in between. Too often, he arrived home well after ten o'clock from his night class, and walked into a dark apartment. Jolie was usually asleep in their bed with the two cats curled up at the bottom of her feet.

He reminded himself while gazing at her peaceful face: six months until his master's degree was complete. Then life would even out. Unless he decided to go all the way. The letters P, H, and D held a certain appeal. The opportunities in career advancement alone, in addition to the salary he could reasonably expect, would be worth the extra grind.

Jolie nodded. "Okay. Soon."

He watched her rush off in a cloud of lavender and anxiety and wondered if her urgency to leave was for more than a bride's sore feet. Or maybe he had put unrealistic expectations on a night notorious for carefree bridesmaids.

A heavy arm fell around his shoulders.

"Who'd've thought," Dru said, his breath soaked in tequila. "Me a married man before the romantic himself."

Jace downed the remains of his lukewarm beer and moved toward the bar with Dru in tow.

Time for a refill.

"I'm happy for you, man," Jace said before he told the bartender his order and turned to his friend. "Where's Alix?"

Dru blew raspberries as the music changed to a pulse-thumping beat, the dance floor substantially less crowded than twenty minutes ago. What time was it anyway?

"I think she's outside with Jolie. There might be a cigarette involved."

Jace sighed. So the night had crossed over into social smoking habits.

"You guys have a room, right?" Dru asked.

Jace gave a thumbs up. He knew the one decision Dru made during the nine-month engagement was the location of the wedding reception. Dru had chosen a historic downtown hotel, complete with renovated vintage touches, but more importantly, footsteps from a room with a bed to safely pass out in.

"Yeah. Although, Jolie hasn't even seen it yet. Hell, I've barely seen Jolie."

Jace inched toward the rear terrace doors. Screw the dance. He wanted Jolie in their hotel room. Dru tried to move his eyebrows. Jace had watched slugs move faster than what he was witnessing on Dru's forehead.

"You're next, bro," Dru said.

Jace took a long drink of whiskey. "If she'll have me."

Dru blew more raspberries. "Shit man, you and Jolie? You're an institution. Just get a plated name already."

For a man drinking his weight in alcohol, the coherence expressed was unexpected. Jace nodded and said, "Soon buddy. Real soon."

Jace pushed open the terrace doors and was greeted by crisp air tinged with a hint of river fish. The noise of rushing water over the dam was loud in an unobtrusive and calming way. Not unlike the river running through his own hometown, or the one meandering through their old college haunts. Jace searched for Jolie while he thought about what Dru said.

An institution.

His smile expanded at the phrase. Jace was a romantic—a previously ignored trait now solidified by each day he spent in Jolie's orbit. Time, he knew, would forever move forward. The past and hidden regrets were the only reasons to wish otherwise.

He found Jolie near the edge of the terrace. The upper half of her body leaned over the wrought-iron fence, her face was lowered toward the river below. Desire swept through him as he stepped forward, took her hand, and turned her into him. He kissed her mouth, slow and deep then walked her to their hotel room. It was well past time for them to be alone.

But shortly after the hotel room door shut, Jolie revealed to Jace what she had sharpened to near perfection all night and stuck it straight into his swelling heart.

"You deserve more and I continue to give less," Jolie said. Two mascara-inked tears raced down her face.

Jace kneeled in front of her. "We've been here before. You know how I feel." His voice cracked as his throat tightened. "I'll never find another you."

A hollow sound escaped her lips. "God, I hope not Jace. I'm no good."

Her hands were ice cold in his. He shook his head. "Where is this coming from, Jo? I thought we had a good night."

Her hands jerked away and began to claw at her hair. "Really, Jace? There's no way tonight was in any way good. Based on the fact that I'm an aimless person who isn't ready for what just happened down there." A shower of bobby pins flew out of her hair and bounced off the floor. Once her hair was released from its hold, she shot up from the bed and grasped for the back of her dress.

"I can help you—" he started.

"No!" she yelled. "I don't want help. I want out." She slumped against an armchair half-naked and slid down until her bare butt hit the carpet. "I need space."

It stung, more than ever before. He would never be enough to eclipse their past. Jolie would rather he disappear than stay by her side. He hated to be facing the one constant of their relationship he hoped had gone away—her ever-changing mind.

"I'll find somewhere else to sleep tonight," Jace said. He would give her time to breathe. It had been an emotional day for everyone. Tomorrow they would talk in a familiar space, with minds clear and fresh, and work through the night's events.

Little did he know how fiercely she would hold on to the words she couldn't take back.

Thirty

January 2010

"When can you come and get him?" Jolie's voice carried a familiar weight.

"I can come by tomorrow," he said. "As long as you're sure, and you think Crimson will be okay." Jace tried to ignore the bloom of optimism. Jolie could still change her mind.

She'd put her foot down in October and insisted Crimson and Clover stay together—which she announced shortly after asking him to move out as soon as possible. Just like that. But now she'd changed her mind. About the cats.

"Either you take him or he goes to a shelter," she said. "It's clear he misses you."

Since his departure, Crimson had peed on the carpet, bedspread, and rugs. Jolie was over it, and understandably so—hence the cat eviction.

"I miss him too," he said. *And you.* "I can come by any time. While you're at work, if that's easier."

The line went silent. He imagined her pushing those over-sized round glasses up the bridge of her nose. "Don't you have work?" she said.

Oh shit. She didn't know. Granted, they hadn't had a proper conversation until now since the logistics of taking Crimson required it. "Nope. They fired my entire department the second day into the new year."

"You're entire...*everyone*?" She sounded as shocked as he had been upon receiving the news last week. Almost. He had added a few choice expletives.

"All thirty of us." He felt his body stiffen. There was more to the story, a plan he decided to set into motion only earlier today.

He weighed whether he should drop the bomb now or later.

No, he would find a way to see her in person and gauge her reaction, rather than pick apart garbled tones over a poor cell phone connection. "Oh, I forgot, I gave you my key to the apartment, so I can't let myself in." That was a lie, he had the key tucked away in his sock drawer. She didn't know any better though and agreed to a handoff after she left work tomorrow.

The next day found Jace belly up at a bar he used to frequent up until his move.

An elegant dive bar, Jolie had declared the first time they'd walked inside back in July. She'd been spot on. About a dozen Tiffany chandeliers hung over high-backed leather booths, casting colorful reflections on the off-white walls.

"Hey man, been a while," said Ryan, a blond and broad-shouldered brute of a dude. Ryan grinned as he placed a coaster in front of Jace.

"It has, yeah. How've you been?" Jace smiled away the tinge of shame trying to free itself from his mouth. A voicemail from Ryan had been sitting in Jace's inbox unheard for over two months.

Ryan had gone to the same college as both Jace and Jolie. Although, the three hadn't met until postgrad, right here at this bar. Ryan was a former rugby player, whereas Jace was a reformed underground music junkie. The two an unlikely mix during their college years.

Jace had been out with Jolie celebrating their moving in together when they stumbled upon this tucked-away treasure, on a night that Ryan was bartending. A quick friendship had formed over their shared alma mater.

At the time, Ryan had a girlfriend too, but broke free from the 'ball and chain'—as Ryan had described it—shortly after their first meeting. The revolving door of doe-eyed girls he brought around turned into a spectator sport for both Jace and Jolie. And further validated in Jace the notion that Jolie was put on this earth for him and he for her.

They had been in love and thriving not too long ago. The thought that he would soon be a stranger to someone who would always feel like his person had him gripping the back of his neck.

"I've been good, man," Ryan said. He poured a glass of whiskey for Jace then leaned his forearms against the mahogany bar. Ryan had twenty pounds on Jace in muscle alone and had zero qualms about throwing his size in drunk people's faces when provoked. "How 'bout you?"

"As well as one would expect, all things considered." Jace heard the tightness in his voice as much as he felt it in his chest. An unavoidable side effect.

Ryan moved his floppy hair away from his eyes and gave Jace a funny look. "Uh oh, trouble in the love nest?"

"Ah, no." Jace fell silent, hoping Ryan would move on to another topic. His open wound could only withstand so much salt.

"But you guys moved, right? That's why you've been MIA?" Ryan continued to look confused.

Jace cleared his throat. "I moved. Jolie didn't."

He grabbed his drink and downed it in one swallow. The burn down his throat danced around the ache in his chest.

"Shit. I'm sorry to hear that." Ryan poured more into Jace's empty glass without asking. "You guys were like an institution."

Jace scrubbed a hand down his face. He'd heard it all before and was over it. "I lost my job last week too."

If all signs weren't pointing to getting the hell out of Dodge before, they sure were now. His bags were packed, well, never really unpacked. All he needed was another drink, his damn cat, and he would be on his way.

"Listen, Bud, you can crash at my place until you're back on your feet. If that helps."

"Thanks. I appreciate it, but I've got it figured out."

Ryan's eyes moved from Jace to a girl gesturing at the other end of the bar. "She's single. I could put in a good word." Ryan swung a towel over his shoulder. His eyes were framed by an expression that could only be described as devious.

Jace waved off Ryan's suggestion. He had no interest in being Ryan's single-dude protégé. His phone vibrated on the bar just as Ryan opened his mouth to say more.

Relieved by the interruption, Jace looked down and saw Jolie's name flash on the screen.

"I gotta take this," he said.

He downed his second glass, sending a silent promise to the bourbon gods above that he would sip and enjoy next time.

"I'll swing by later next week."

"I'll be here," Ryan said. "Come back later tonight and she'll be here too, or some version of her anyway."

Jace shook his head in good humor, swiped to answer the call, and headed out into the cold winter air.

"So I'm home," Jolie said after they both lobbed a stiff hello back and forth. His greeting was a bit more alcohol-soaked than hers. He hoped she didn't notice.

"I was catching up with Ryan. I'll come by now." He started to walk in the direction of their apartment. Her apartment. Just hers.

She sighed and mumbled, "I could go for a drink."

He stopped walking. "It's Friday. Happy hour."

"Not a good idea," she shot back in monotone.

"Why not?"

"I don't know," she said. He recognized the shift in her voice.

"Come on. One last drink together before I—" His voice seized up. If she'd been in one of her more intuitive moods, she would have just caught on to what almost slipped out of his mouth: *move away from you.*

"Okay," she said with another sigh. He heard the sound of

keys. "One drink before you take Crimson. Be there soon." The line went dead. He couldn't decipher what was coursing through his body—*excitement, dread, hope?*—but hated how alive it made him feel.

Thirty-One

January 2010

J olie stepped inside the dimly lit bar and glanced around. The sooner she spotted Jace, the sooner this would be over. It was past five o'clock, which meant a decent amount of bodies occupied the open space already. Jolie's stomach rolled. The air was stale and reeked of old beer and moldy bar mats. She spotted Ryan and his tight graphic-tee standing behind the bar and ducked out of view before he saw her.

With her post-work exhaustion, the thought of engaging in empty conversation sounded torturous. Add in an ex-boyfriend, and a dash of heart-wrenching goodbyes, and you had a Jolie Emotional Mess bottled and ready to hit stores. She would say hi to Ryan later, before she left. *Maybe.* If she survived what was about to happen.

She spotted Jace at a high-top table in the back, his face pointed toward one of the beveled windows, unaware of her arrival. He looked as he always did, and yet, she wished he would blur into nothingness.

She slid onto the metal stool opposite him. "Hey."

He flinched as if startled, which surprised her in return. The need to know what had him so lost in thought felt as if the floor had dropped from underneath her.

"Hey. I didn't see you come in. Here." He pushed forward a glass of what she assumed was her favorite bourbon. A bottle of beer and a glass of water sat in front of him.

"Thanks." She took a sip and felt her shoulders relax.

She would miss this part of their relationship. The knowing without effort. Although the secret she'd kept from Jace had taken all her energy in the end. She cut out the one person in her life who had put up with her and all the baggage she carried. Including the heaviest of locked suitcases.

"So, this isn't weird at all," Jace said. He clicked his bottle to her glass, an upward curve forming on his lips. He was trying to lighten the mood and be the good man he'd always been to her—the man she didn't want to deal with right now. The pit in her stomach moaned. He deserved better than who she had become. It was a realization that had settled into despair in the months following their breakup. All she wanted to do was slip away and find comfort. She would tuck into a box of Oreos once this was over.

"It'd be weird if it wasn't weird, right?"

"Good point." He gazed at her for longer than she could stand.

She crossed her arms over her chest and stared at the table's faded surface. Her glass was too full and all she wanted was for it, and her, to be empty. Releasing her arms, she raised her glass with a slight tremor. *Stupid nerves*. "To Crimson and Clover."

Jace clicked his bottle to her glass again and added, "May they find peace in their new beginnings." He took a long draw from the bottle. The sudden heat of tears from behind her eyes felt as strong as her drink. *Don't freak out.*

His bottle landed on the table with a resounding thud. "Actually, I'm glad you agreed to come out for a drink," Jace said, cracking one knuckle and then another.

Oh, knuckle cracking. Not good. That meant Jace had something to say that had been on his mind for way too long.

"Why? You enjoy the torture of drawn-out goodbyes?" Jolie spoke into her glass.

Jace stopped mid-crack. "I'm going back to grad school full-time." His words fired off like a handgun, one bullet after another.

"Oh!" Jolie's spine straightened. This was happy news, which made the delivery of it a bit odd. "Wow, Jace. That's great. You've always been good at turning a loss into a gain." She'd witnessed him balance school and his full-time job, knowing his heart had craved the study more than the daily grind.

"Wait, you said going back... Back where exactly?"

Crack. Crack.

"I didn't think I'd get in. I applied late and missed fall semester, but it's the best program in the nation and incredibly comprehensive. I'll be there for about four years. And the extra training opens up so many job opportunities. That alone makes the extra time spent studying worth it. I hope so anyway. So I had to try. And it worked. I got in."

Oh no, rambling Jace had just joined their intimate conversation for two. Whatever news was coming next, she knew it was about to rock her world.

"It's in Iowa. I'm going back to Iowa." He peered at her through his long eyelashes and held her gaze. She wanted to move, and run away, and maybe hiss and scream. But she'd gone rigid instead, her breathing shallow. She might as well be a lost cat. Any sudden movements and she would dart off, never to be seen again.

Don't freak out. Don't freak out.

"You're moving. To Iowa," she repeated. It seemed like the safest response. And the only words she felt capable of forming with her suddenly-dry tongue.

Jace nodded. "In about..." He looked to the ceiling, tapping his chin. "Five days." His eyes darted around her face. Her insides felt stone-cold and scorching hot at the same time. She forced a smile while tempering a wave of despair as it swelled into her thoughts.

She had set him free, but her heart was still captive, in a state of constant confusion. It wasn't his fault. She had underestimated how much she still depended on him, on his proximity to her. A move out of state solidified their breakup. Like petrified wood, they would be frozen in terminated decay. For them to cross paths at random would be statistically impossible now.

"Sorry, I'm being weird," she said. "This is huge for you and I'm...just trying to keep up without..." She bit her lip. Tears had become a very real threat.

"Without freaking out," Jace finished. "I know."

Jolie gulped what was left in her glass. She wondered if he felt the sudden suffocation of the public bar as much as she did. They stood up at the same time.

"I'll tell Ryan we had to go, and you said hi," Jace said, as he touched the small of her back and steered her toward the exit. She let out a breath and nodded. One less awkward conversation to endure today.

It was a short and cold walk to her apartment, in the loudest quiet she had ever heard. She fumbled for her keys as they stood at her front door. "I'm going to miss this," she said and stilled, glancing up at him. *Stupid whiskey*. It had dulled the normally airtight filter locked around her thoughts.

Jace didn't budge, and—Was Jace even breathing?

Wrong thing to say. Damage control!

"I'm going to miss this apartment, because I don't plan to stay." She cringed and swung the door open. She couldn't continue to be an ass and confuse Jace into thinking she wanted him back.

She wanted herself back first.

Then him.

She also had no intention to move but now that she said it, maybe it wasn't such a bad idea. Get away from the ghosts in her closets and all that.

A loud meow from further in the apartment provided a well-timed distraction.

"Hey, buddy," Jace said, as he squatted and scratched behind the tabby's ears. Crimson nosed his hand excitedly. Jolie leaned against the wall and smiled. The cats had appreciated Jace's attention more than hers from the very first day. She accepted her inferiority and determined that loyalty was given to the most aggressive scratcher.

Fur was flying. Everywhere.

Jace looked up at her, darkness in his eyes. Yeah, this was hard.

"I have the extra carrier for him," Jolie said and pointed to the plastic rectangle on the floor near the kitchen table. "His favorite mouse toy, cat bed, and some food are in the bag next to it."

Jace was in front of her before she could register his speed, his fingers against her hand, then upon her cheek. He pulled her closer with nothing more than his tender gaze and sandalwood scent. Her lips parted while their faces drew closer together. She wanted to kiss him one last time. The desire was there, as acute as the day they had met. That was never the problem.

She was.

"Bad idea," she whispered, placing her hand on his chest. His heart thumped against her palm. Her forehead touched his as she breathed in his warm breath. She wanted to inhale whatever he was feeling, to somehow absorb the darkness she'd created.

He brushed his lips on hers. Light, and barely there, but stuck nonetheless, like fluffy cottonwood floating on the surface of a lake.

"How will I ever find another you," he muttered against her lips.

His words were barely a whisper. He was so quiet she wondered if he had only meant to think it, not say it aloud.

She wrapped her arms around his neck, pressed her body against his, and gave him a proper kiss—one that would curl her toes for years to come.

He broke off. Thank god. Her self-restraint was apparently non-existent in all matters of...him.

"That can't go any further," Jace said. His voice was rough, like a pack-a-day smoker.

Jolie took a step back. "Agreed." She might as well be cancerous.

"Unless," he paused, Crimson weaving between his legs. "Unless it never stops." The hope in his eyes broke her like a fallen mirror on concrete. "Come with me, Jo. Go back to school in Iowa with me. Get your master's there. We can start again where it all began."

Her vision blurred. How easy it all sounded wrapped in the comfort of Jace's voice. How easily she ruined everything the moment she spoke. "The past is too messy," she said and gently picked up Crimson. With a swift expert shove of Crimson's behind, she handed the carrier to Jace.

"That's just your way of saying there's not enough good between us to outweigh the bad, right?"

She bit her lip, unsure if the urge to argue against the statement was rooted in truth or in codependence. She shook her head and opted to remain silent.

He leaned in, kissed her cheek, looked at her once more, and left.

Clover stared at the closed door longer than necessary. His eyes melancholy. Maybe it was a figment of her imagination. A cat's perceived-sadness had to be impossible, right? The loud hollow meows later that night confirmed she'd been fooling herself, yet again.

What a mess.

Thirty-Two

March 2012
Two Years Later

"We set a date!" Carrie barreled through the front door without so much as a knock. Jolie stood up from the couch, her stomach angry about the movement, and watched Carrie set a bottle of cheap champagne on the kitchen counter. The sound of glass to granite rang out like a well-timed sound effect to mark the day. Carrie was inching closer to holy matrimony.

"You guys finally agreed on a date? I don't believe it!" Jolie moved into the kitchen. Carrie grinned and nodded while unwrapping gold foil from the top of the bottle. When the new year had dawned and progressed, Carrie's complaints had increased in direct opposition to the speed of Talon's dragging feet. The slower he moved, the quicker she was to bitch about it. With good reason, it had been three years since the proposal.

"I needed good news today. What changed his mind?" Jolie squeezed her friend's shoulder. Carrie's noticeable relief warmed Jolie's hand while the smell of jasmine perfume made Jolie feel dizzy all of a sudden.

"I told him to shit or get off the pot." Carrie studied the bottle of champagne and asked, "Do you think ice cubes would ruin the bubbles?"

Jolie reached high in her cabinet for two plastic champagne flutes. Her stomach emitted a loud gurgle upon her arm's descent; its annoyance with movement persisted. She ignored the pain radiating from her midsection and tapped the side of one

flute. "Ice cubes won't ruin the bubbles any more than these."
Decidedly thick with notes of dust.

"Yet another reason to get married, Lee. New champagne glasses." Carrie winked before her head disappeared into the freezer. "Whoa girl, you have enough ice cream and frozen pizza to feed twenty pimpled teenage boys." Carrie reappeared with an ice cube tray. "Have you been hosting Boy Scouts on the weekends without telling me?"

Jolie pretended to focus on washing the dirt off the flutes. "No. I'm the opposite of a do-good Samaritan. You know that." The food was for her, and she would consume all of it over the next few days. Carrie probably wouldn't think twice about it once the freezer was closed, but Jolie offered a stretched truth anyway. "There was a crazy sale at the store, so I stocked up."

"It seems a bit over the top, but all right. Too bad that sale didn't include champagne, right?" Carrie worked the cork out of the bottle with a towel. After a muted pop, she removed the towel with an exaggerated flourish, grabbed the bottle's neck, and poured. Champagne fizz threatened to spill over the flute's rim as Jolie plopped the ice cubes in.

Jolie raised her glass and gave her best friend the best smile she could muster. She was happy for Carrie, of course, but she was also disgustingly full. Of food. "Cheers to your future wedding."

Carrie clinked her glass against Jolie's. "July third!"

Jolie coughed into her glass. Fruity liquid burned up her nose and dripped down her fingers. "As in four months from now? You can't be serious—"

"Calm down." Carrie shook her head and downed her drink in one gulp. "Next year."

Jolie wiped her sticky fingers on her sweatpants—at some point, she would wash the dirty laundry—and cocked her head, unsure if she'd heard her friend correctly. "Did you say—"

"In one year." Carrie shrugged. "Long engagement, remember?

Jolie had assumed long meant two years, max, which had already been met and surpassed at this point. Then again, she wasn't one to judge. How many times had someone, mainly extended family members, asked when she would marry Jace?

"Well, okay then. That's plenty of time to lose some of the graduate school weight." Jolie took her drink over to the couch.

Her new apartment was small, but she loved the main airy room and its slice of a vaulted ceiling, the L-shaped kitchen right off the entrance, the chestnut door to her bedroom, and the barely-there balcony. The neighbors were in abundance and loud, but it had a roof, didn't break the bank, and was close to her school. By the time Carrie married Talon, Jolie would officially be done with her coursework and starting her required supervised hours to become a clinical psychologist. Remarkable really, considering she was as broken as they come at the moment.

"And maybe find a plus-one for your wedding," Jolie added, testing the words on for size. *Nope, too tight.*

Carrie walked into the main room. "As long as they're not related to me. Only one Jolie heartbreak allowed within the realm of my blood relatives, got it?" Carrie smiled over the rim of her glass.

Jolie ignored the sudden sting in her eyes. Carrie hadn't meant anything by it, but *ouch*. Jolie felt exhausted and sat down. Hiding her sour stomach, and the reason behind it, was enough pain to manage for the day.

"So, July third…fireworks and all that hoopla?" Jolie said.

Carrie sipped with a nod. "Lonny's idea. He thinks we can cut deals with the venue and vendors, being Fourth of July weekend and all. There's one other thing." She shifted her weight from one foot to the other. "Since this is Lonny's second wedding, we've decided to forego some of the usual traditions."

"Okay." Jolie drew out the syllable, desperately hoping that one word conveyed, *But it's your first wedding, Carrie!* The look on Carrie's face suggested Jolie's message had been received and translated. "Like what? No garter toss. Always hated those."

"No bridesmaids or groomsmen." The words were barely out of Carrie's mouth before she rapidly continued, "But you'll have special mention in the program and can wear a super fancy dress if you want, and you'll get to wear a corsage of flowers, or a crown or whatever, something with flowers. You're still my maid of honor. You just don't have to sweat up there with us while we say our vows. And kiss."

Jolie stood up as another round of loud gurgling emitted from her stomach. With an eyebrow raise from Carrie, Jolie pulled her into a loose hug. "It sounds perfect. Unlike my body right now." Jolie's attempted laugh sounded strangled. She cleared her throat. "Anyway. I'm better behind the scenes."

Carrie released a long breath and squeezed Jolie tight before letting go. Jolie moved away, her heart beating heavier than moments before.

"There's something else." Carrie twisted her hands. Jolie tensed. Was Carrie going to pry and ask why Jolie's face looked so puffy? Or why her clothes looked too tight on her? Was today the day her secret life ended?

"I saw Palmer the other day. He asked about you." Carrie took a seat at the kitchen table placed inches from the couch. "Right after he told me about this girl he started dating again."

"Oh, okay." Jolie hadn't seen Palmer since Carrie's engagement party, but he'd called her late one night, maybe six months after Jace had moved away, much to Jolie's surprise. Jolie had answered on the sixth ring, after debating with herself if she should pick up at all.

He immediately asked why it sounded like was crying—*because she had been*. He wanted to know if she was okay—*no she was not*. Did she need someone to come over? *Absolutely not*. Jolie could barely breathe through the thick, undeserved love, and asked him to stop calling her.

"Go find someone who has their shit together, Palmer." And

he did, just like that. Both men had listened to her, respected her wishes, and left. She'd released them from the mind games she never meant to play but had put them through regardless. Not because she was better off alone, but because they were far better off without her.

"Remember that tall blonde from my engagement party?" Carrie asked.

Jolie nodded while the scent of day-old garbage from underneath the kitchen sink wafted toward her like a wave of poor life decisions.

"They reconnected after you gave him final notice to move on. Anyway, I told him you're beautiful and thriving and determinedly single."

Jolie lowered onto the couch again. "Two lies to one truth. You're too kind." Jolie tried to be light-hearted, but the words sounded empty.

She chewed on her lower lip. The couch cushion sank as Carrie sat next to her. "You okay, Lee? It can't be Jace, right? You haven't mentioned his name in forever. Is it your mom? Is she having issues again?"

"No, she's great, actually. She just got her two-year token and completed her steps. Now it's maintenance. Which is great. Everything should be great, right? Nothing is wrong. All is...as it should be." Jolie fiddled with the stem of her glass. Her mom's recovery had simultaneously been a relief from what once was, and a magnifying glass over Jolie's own unresolved issues. She was trapped in her toxic thoughts and in clothes that no longer fit.

"But this pressure to find stability in the unstable has been impossible. I keep failing."

Her stomach flipped and gurgled. She leaned forward to set her glass down, the waistband of her pants straining. She felt like shit, constantly, and was tired of it. She'd carried the weight of her long-held secret on her own for too many years. She had to stop lying to herself and her friend. Which meant she would have to step into the truth she'd kept from everyone, even herself.

Jolie folded her legs underneath her and sat up straight. She could do this, even if she felt physically ill. "The thing is Carrie, I'm the one with the problem." She saw Carrie's eyes flick to the glass on the table. "No, not with drinking." Jolie raised an unsteady finger. "With that." She pointed to her freezer and watched Carrie's expression turn to one of confusion.

Jolie moved her trembling hand into her lap. Carrie remained quiet. No one knew. Not a single person. So instead of opening her cabinets to expose the awful truth, Jolie did the harder thing. She opened her mouth and began to talk. "I eat my feelings. All the time. And I hate myself for it," she whispered in shaky tones. "But I can't seem to stop. It's literally ruined everything and I still can't stop."

"Oh, Lee." Carrie reached out. Jolie leaned away, her body wringing with tension.

"It all makes sense now," Carrie said. "Why you never go out. Why you cancel plans. Why you're so...isolated."

Jolie nodded in confirmation as a single tear rolled down to her chin. Carrie wiped the tear away, and whispered back, "Thank you for telling me."

"I want to stop. I want to change," Jolie said, her tongue articulating each word with a confidence her mind had yet to achieve. "Starting today."

"In all my years, I've never seen such determination," said Jace's professor and mentor, Steve.

Jace forced a smile through a sip of whiskey, a necessary distraction from the unexpected praise. The taste of cinnamon and aged oak coated the inside of his mouth.

Hold the first sip in your mouth and let your tongue explore—a tasting trick Jolie had taught him while they'd lived together.

He swallowed down the image of Jolie's fading smile and focused on the man sitting across the table.

"You're ahead in all your classes, caught up on your teacher assistant duties and clocking the longest hours in the research lab." Steve tipped an imaginary hat in his direction.

Jace swirled the liquid around in his glass, unsure of how to respond. Earlier, Steve had caught Jace off guard when he requested they go out for drinks. Jace's steadfast work ethic was no reason for celebration and had nothing to do with determination.

It'd been almost two years since Jace's return to Iowa, and the town still reeked of rotted memories, like living in a broken refrigerator, surrounded by spoiled food. Reminders of Jolie seeped into every pore of this place. How could it be any different?

They had met in the lecture hall he was currently a teacher's assistant in and had kissed underneath the big oak tree in the middle of the quad that he walked by every day.

He couldn't bleach his memories clean of her, that much was clear, but he could bury them with distractions. Even if, at first, it felt suffocating. He'd assimilated to the lower oxygen levels over time.

"Thanks, Steve. It means a lot. But I'm just doing what I'm supposed to." Jace tapped his foot to whatever song was piping through the crappy sound system overhead. All he could hear and feel—aside from the continued discomfort of Steve's prolonged praise—was the thumping bass of an unknown song.

Steve plucked a popcorn kernel from the bowl in the middle of the table and popped it in his mouth before signaling to the waitress. Jace mentally crossed his fingers that Steve would ask for the check. He was queasy from the pungent popcorn smell and had Crimson to feed at home.

"Care for another?"

Damn.

"Sure."

"As I was saying." Steve picked up where he left off—a talent Jace would never master. He preferred to listen rather than lecture. Which meant he had zero intention of using his pending PhD to be a professor. "If you continue at this pace, I have no doubt you'll have a job lined up before your dissertation is completed."

"Music to my ears." Jace smiled as the pretty waitress handed him another glass. "The sooner I'm out of here, the better."

Steve frowned before his usual lopsided grin returned. "I can help you put together the committee for your defense. And you'll need someone to analyze your data after it's all collected, too. All names I can provide if you want."

Jace nodded. "Thank you. I'll make sure your time isn't wasted."

"You're a man of efficiency, Jace. If anything, you've proven how wasteful others are of my time." Steve slapped a twenty-dollar bill on the table, downed his drink, and stood. "That waitress wants to go home with you. I'll leave you to it."

Jace choked as Steve exited the front doors. As if summoned, the waitress reappeared.

"Can I get you anything else?"

"Just the check, thanks." Jace handed the waitress his debit card. She was short and curvy, not his usual type, but pretty, with big, brown eyes. Jace had been so laser-focused on getting his degree that he hadn't considered dating. But maybe it wouldn't be so bad to scratch a casual itch during the home stretch.

The waitress returned within minutes, her face flushed as she placed the black leather check folder onto the table.

"See you soon, I hope." Her eyes darted to the receipts, then she scampered away. There, on his copy of the receipt, was a smiley face, the name *Emma*, and her phone number.

It would take him roughly three days to call Emma, and four

more for them to sleep together. She was an unexpected layer of distraction he could cover himself with. One much more enjoyable than burying himself in work. He finally felt hopeful, like he could well and truly move on from Jolie.

He continued to think this for two years, until Jolie showed up on the morning of his dissertation defense and it all blew up in his face.

Thirty-Three

May 2014
Two Years Later

"I'm late." Jace's voice hit her straight in the chest. A force so powerful the hem of her dress dropped from her fist.

"I'll wait." She barely heard her voice over the thumping of her heart. He may have nodded, she couldn't really tell, and then he ascended the steps into the lecture hall, two at a time.

Don't freak out.

She could hardly breathe, let alone gauge a distanced reaction through her lens of adrenaline. Had Jace recognized her? What if he had and just rushed off to never return? What was she even doing here?

Jolie pushed her toes into the spikey grass, her mind whirling. It had taken some truth-stretching in order for her to be here. No one knew she was here—not her mom, or Alix, or even her boss. Her cat, however, had gazed at her in judgment as she made her way out the door. The side-eye stare from Clover made her sure of the feline's inner dialogue— *Human, you are crazy.*

Her mother, on the other hand, was under the impression Jolie was visiting a friend in Iowa. *Not entirely true.* Her mother hadn't pried—she rarely did anymore—and told Jolie to have fun with Alix. *The innocent power of assumptions*, Jolie had thought.

Jolie's boss had also received a stretched truth, that Jolie was out studying for her state licensing exam. *Not entirely true.* Jolie had taken the exam a week ago and would find out if she passed on Monday.

Her master's in clinical psychology had landed her a solid job in a treatment facility for young women with eating disorders. But following her own healing journey, her career goals morphed into a preference for one-on-one cognitive behavioral therapy. She felt certain this was her purpose, to help others manage the struggles she knew all too well. Which meant a private practice. Which required licensing, and money, and focus. And out of the three, the last one was what she needed to tackle first.

So, she had driven four hours west to crash Jace's dissertation. Well, she'd shown up uninvited with no plan, so maybe the word crash was aggressive. Or maybe not. No matter, she refused to think of herself as the other c-word, *crazy*. She left that to her cat. Crazy felt too simple a term to describe her inner thoughts over the past few months. Unsettled was more accurate. Jace was in her head and refused to exit quietly.

She slipped her sandals on and gazed at the building Jace had just walked into. It was the same building where they'd met ten years ago.

How's that for irony?

She thought back to when she last saw Jace. How her eyes had locked with his as sweat trickled down her temples, while Carrie and Talon said *I do* under last year's hot July sun.

Jolie had gone with Alix and Dru to the wedding instead of bringing the man she was dating. He hadn't known about Jace and she liked it that way. It seemed more logical to go alone. After countless tears, and just as many journal pages, Jolie felt determined to be who she'd transformed into. Someone that no longer numbed herself with food in an effort to ignore the parts of her heart that hurt. It would carry on beating. And it had.

What she severely underestimated were the emotions Jace would dredge up, and how quickly they would seep into her new resolve and her new relationship.

Jace approached her table after the first dance, and her breath caught. There he stood, his hair curled around his earlobes, the sleeves of his teal linen shirt rolled up to his elbows. His exposed forearms were slim and tanned. Her heart pounded against her chest, begging to be reunited with the parts that had gone missing. It was impossible to stay away from him that night. He was a part of her. There was nowhere else to be but by his side.

They spent most of the reception outside the front doors, away from the noise, away from the pressure of dancing, away from the stares of long-time friends. Instead, they sipped on whiskey in dewy glasses, and talked, and laughed, and flirted. Oh, the delicious flirting. She had zero immunity to their chemistry and was infected by him all over again.

They ended the night with a gentle pull of her into his arms and a hug so brief, she blinked and it was over. The familiarity of his smell had left her disoriented. That was all that had happened, and yet, so much had happened.

As for her new relationship and those fabricated high hopes with a man who reminded her way too much of Palmer—hindsight ex-boyfriend vision—well, those collapsed into a pile around her feet. She sat in the mess for a while, digging through the remains of what was left, and found something new and unexpected: a loving commitment to herself. Astounded, Jolie got on her feet, laced up her proverbial boots, and blazed a trail through yet another failed relationship—familiar terrain at this point.

The surprising part was where the path had led her to. Here. In the middle of a grassy knoll, in the middle of the day, in the middle of the week, and in the middle of too many what-ifs. What if she was too late? What if, instead of Jace disappearing, he had erased her from his life instead?

She rolled back her shoulders and moved toward the crosswalk. She was meant to be here, regardless of what would result from the sharing of her deepest vulnerabilities. Jace had earned the right to know, by simply being part—and thus a consequence—of her past. It was her fear telling her otherwise.

She'd worked hard to ignore the doubts her head had tried to drown her in—*don't go back, the past is too messy*—to find herself sitting on a bench just outside the front doors of the lecture hall. This was her heart in longing, her head in confusion, and her decision to act.

"It *was* you."

Jolie popped to her feet at the sound of his voice and turned straight into Jace's eyes, so clear she could see her reflection staring back at her.

"And you came back. Hi." She smoothed her hands down the front of her sundress. "It was—*is* me. And not some random lady with a few screws loose. Which may not be too far off the mark. Anyway. Are you done? How'd it go? Did you kill it?" She clamped her mouth shut against the hostile takeover of nerves.

"The committee is deliberating." He rubbed at the dark stains under his eyes, as if to remove the pigmented color.

"I'll go back in a few minutes, and if all goes well, I will unofficially-officially have my doctorate."

She smiled, and nodded, and pinched her forearms, tempering the urge to throw her arms around him. *Jace was done! Done!*

She hadn't been there for all of it, of course, but enough in the beginning and now, fittingly, the end.

"And after that?" She moved her trembling hands behind her and clasped them together.

He took in a breath. His gaze fixed on her face. His name was called from the double doors as he spoke. "Everything." He turned and raised his hand in acknowledgment then looked back to her, like he was conflicted about whether to leave her or not.

"Go." She motioned toward the bench. "I'll be here."

He extended his hand to hers and squeezed it. Heat shot straight up her arm as he said, "But for how long?"

She pushed him gently toward the steps. "Go." She watched him look back at her, as if she would disappear, and sighed once the doors closed behind him. She would ask Jace what she had to. Because the only way out of this was through it.

The short walk to Java House consisted of Jace detailing the final moments of his defense, when his advisor had proudly announced him as a doctor of philosophy, and what was left: his graduation ceremony next week.

She had no idea what his plans were now that the long road of higher education had come to an end, but she felt fidgety in the unknown. She wanted to be included in whatever his plans were. However far-reaching that may be. She sat across from him at a table near the back of the coffee shop. Far enough from the noise of the milk steamer and the slam of the poorly-adjusted front door.

The walls were painted the same burgundy color. The room had the same low-lit vibe and the tables and the overstuffed, torn couches were still pressed too closely together.

"Why is it always so cold in here?" Jolie gestured down to her dress. "I'm going to be an ice cube in no time."

His eyes swept over her bare shoulders and descended downward to her exposed upper chest before returning to her face with a distinct twinkle. She'd missed his shimmer, which had been in full force last summer, as had the tingle in her toes and legs. They continued to stare, her trying to control what was sure to be a consuming shiver, him crumpling a napkin.

Eventually he reached into his messenger bag, pushed aside a thick set of clipped pages, and pulled out a black hoodie. "This should take the edge off for you."

She hesitated. Her eyes focused on his bag. "Is that your thesis?"

Handing the hoodie over to her, he pulled out the stack of papers. "Two hundred and ninety pages of my blood and sweat."

"No tears? Impressive." She held out her hand. "Can I see?"

"Yes." He pushed the document back into his bag and closed the zipper as fast as a staccato note. His eyes shifted about the room. "But later. When you well and truly need help falling asleep. Trust me, it's a real snoozer."

Jolie shrugged on the hoodie. His familiar scent stunned her out of her insecurities for a moment. "I understand. No problem."

Jace cupped his mug with both hands like it was a lifeline. A few of his fingers sported torn, angry-looking cuticles. His stress must be sky-high, or his hours of sleep were at an ultimate low. It had been some time since she'd seen his self-inflicted wounds. But the same urge to heal him remained.

"This is going to sound nuts," Jace said, as he peered at her through an errant strand of curly hair. Her fingers tickled to push it away. Instead, she sipped her latte and waited for him to continue. "I thought I was hallucinating this morning. When I thought I saw you in the quad. Like, beyond any reasonable doubt, I knew it was you. Somehow I rationalized intuition though, and went into the building convinced it was only an image of you, conjured by a serious lack of sleep." He shrugged in a sheepish way.

She reached across the table and tapped near one of his torn fingers, the physical evidence of his insomnia. "I figured you hadn't been sleeping well."

He flipped her hand and stroked the inside of her palm, his eyes intense. "It's not the first time that's happened."

"What? Not getting enough sleep?" she asked, trying to keep up while not melting into his touch.

"Yes, but I meant, you know—" His shoulders slumped but the hold on her hand tightened. "It's not the first time I thought it was you when it actually wasn't. After I saw you last summer, and the phone call we had...you've been everywhere again."

Jolie looked at their hands wrapped together, *the perfect fit*. It was a thrill to hear she had staying power in Jace's mind, a feeling she experienced not long after the wedding, when Jace had texted her.

Like a digital star in her dark sky, he'd written to say he

enjoyed seeing her at the wedding. She responded in agreement. Then a few weeks later, and on a complete whim, she called him, and he picked up. Their silent understanding of no contact was replaced by their tentative voices, and those unspoken boundaries fell away like a perfectly coiled apple peel. Endlessly satisfying.

But, all too soon, the silence returned and Jolie was left with the stench of rotted fruit. She had hoped, somewhat naively, that her disappointment would decompose into what it had to be—deep, rich acceptance. Except it hadn't.

Her eyes met his and held his gaze. "I wasn't sure what to expect honestly," she said, "Showing up like this. You went silent again and I tried to...to let you go."

Jace removed his hand from hers and twisted his coffee cup on the table. "I got busy with the dissertation."

Jolie nodded in understanding, but her stomach plummeted. The constant wish to go back and slap sense into her younger self haunted her daily. But everything she wanted to say would come out in the wash eventually, right? If Jace was willing to stick around and sit in the laundromat with her.

A memory of their tangled limbs, surrounded in freshly washed bed sheets, bubbled up inside her, and warmed her face with embarrassment. She should know better than to pour memories onto the present. She was going to tell him. *Now.*

"This isn't going to be easy to say, so if I stutter and get all red in the face, just bear with me." She blew out a breath. "After the call and your returned silence, I thought for sure I'd go back to this place of...deep sadness, I guess."

"Jo..." Jace looked at her with pain in his eyes.

"It's okay. I didn't go there this time. I found something, instead, that had probably been there all along. This beautiful kind of conviction. I wasn't going to let you fade away this time." She laughed and shook her head. "So much has changed. You deserve to see me—us—stripped free of our past. You deserve to see the naked truth..." She paused, unable to say the last part:

that she was no longer running away from their love because she finally, *finally*, loved herself.

Jace looked at her, the shadow of a grin crossing his face. Jace looked at her, the shadow of a grin crossing his face. She felt a pull deep within her stomach as she rubbed her forehead. The corners of his eyes crinkled and the energy between them shifted. He glanced down at her mouth, then up. Yes, she wanted to kiss his lips too. So very much.

The sound of the front door slamming broke their trance. Jace's eyes darted around as he cleared his throat. "Listen, I have to pack up my lab this afternoon, which I'd skip in a heartbeat if I knew the custodian wasn't going to toss what I don't pack today. But, you know, loose ends need tying. And I have a few dangling around. Some are a bit of a roadblock actually." He pushed his hand through those lovely curls. "Not you though. You're an open country road on a sunny day."

"Well, what do you know? Someone speaks metaphor now." Jolie tried to play along but the mood had shifted around them. His detailed explanation of why he had to leave for the afternoon felt out of place, even for cuticle-biting Jace. Forced, almost. She recognized how charged everything was at the moment, but also felt like he was blowing her off.

Jace glanced around again, his knee bouncing in double-time. The main door slammed in sync with what he said next. "I'd like to keep talking over dinner tonight, if that works for you."

Maybe it was her adrenaline wearing off that skewed her senses and Jace's weirdness was all in her head. After a slight hesitation, she agreed but couldn't help asking, "Are you okay? You seem...jumpy."

"Yeah." He motioned to his empty mug. "Too much caffeine, you know, spikes the nerves. And the fact that I'm basically done with this chapter in my life. And you're here, in front of me, actually here, and...and all of this..." He waved a hand between them.

The sound of the main door slamming again filled the space

of their weighted silence. She felt responsible for his stuttering and the sharpness of nerve. More than that, she was sorry for all the crap from their past. The urge to apologize bubbled in the back of her throat.

Jace's eyes landed on something from behind her. The color in his face drained.

"What? What is it, Jace?" Jolie rotated in her seat as a woman with auburn hair bumped into her chair. Hot liquid splashed against her arm—thank god it was covered—and dumped down the side of her stomach where the hoodie was unzipped.

"Oh my god, I am so sorry!" The woman stepped back, horrified.

Jolie jumped up and pulled the wet fabric away from her skin. Jace was up and handing her a fistful of napkins, all the while keeping his head angled downward.

"It's okay," Jolie said. "It wouldn't be a true Java House experience without someone getting spilt on." Jolie blotted away the sticky liquid and focused on the woman who wasn't paying attention to her at all.

"Oh, hey!" the woman said to Jace. "I thought you had your dissertation defense this afternoon." Her eyes flicked to Jolie.

Jace cleared his throat. "Emma, hey." The woman took two steps toward Jace and kissed him. *On the mouth.* Jace may have tried to swerve around her, or so it seemed, and ended up wrapping a single arm around the woman's shoulders after the unmistakable kiss. Jolie stopped moving. The weight of Jace's hoodie squeezed around her body as if to strangle her. This had to be his girlfriend.

He released his hold and looked at Jolie, then said, "The defense happened this morning."

"You're done already? Wow, I could have sworn you told me—"

"Listen," Jace said to Emma. Jolie stared at Jace, barely breathing. He had asked her to *listen* only moments before. A quip he had never used before, Jolie had now heard twice in the span of ten minutes. "I'm wrapping up a few things first before I head to the lab. Can we connect later?"

The woman—Emma—glanced at Jolie. Her thin lips formed into a straight line. "Sure. Of course. I'll see you later."

"Sounds good." Jace maneuvered around Emma and motioned for Jolie to follow him. Jolie focused on his back and tried to ignore how quickly Jace exited that train wreck. She couldn't help feeling a bit bad for Emma, however.

She followed Jace out into the early afternoon sun and took a breath of fresh air. The glare from a nearby windshield blinded her enough to diffuse the awkward run-in, with a woman Jace did not want to introduce her to, and brought her back to reality.

Jace had kissed another woman. In front of her. She'd prepared herself for this but had no right, or claim, to what she had let go of anyway. Was she too late? He'd invited her to dinner. Why? As friends? As closure?

Ugh.

Her dress felt hard and sticky and she wanted to go. "I need to get this dress off."

His eyebrows jumped, a glint in his eyes. Before he had a chance to respond and confuse her even more or, god forbid, confirm her worst fear—*you* are *too late, Jo*—she shot her arms around him in what could only be described as a ninja hug. When she pulled back, he looked startled but pleased.

"If you can't meet for dinner tonight, I totally understand." The words rushed out of her mouth. "Just let me know. Okay! Bye." She tried to walk away but his arm stopped her.

"You drove four hours to be here. Of course we're getting dinner tonight." He stepped forward, but then stopped. "I'll text you the place later on."

"Okay," she said again and waved before turning toward her hotel. Whatever happened tonight she knew nothing would be the same after.

Thirty-Four

May 2014

I t *had* been her this morning, against the backdrop of a dream, and not a walking shadow in the foggy morning. *He knew it.* But had reasoned away the image as one conjured by sleep deprivation. He'd headed into the biggest moment of his life, only to come out an hour later to find her seated on the bench, waiting for him.

He watched her now as she walked away from the coffee shop, her body weaving among a swell of oncoming people, while her caramel highlights bounced in a ponytail. He'd never seen her hair so long, certainly never past her shoulders. Midway through their coffee, Jolie had pulled her hair into a ponytail, the movement stirring a hint of evergreen. It wasn't her typical scent, and it took every ounce of his self-control to act like he wasn't affected.

He was well and truly fucked. The second he saw her face and confirmed her presence outside their lecture hall. Totally fucked. As was always the case when it came to Jolie's impulsive nature. A trait of hers that had started their relationship and effectively ended it too.

Yet she'd reappeared, on a whim it seemed, and there were so many words he could not articulate while his mind shouted, *Landmines up ahead!*

He would worry about that later. Right now, he owed Emma an explanation, and a promise to himself to wrap up what he'd started last weekend. It was hard not to wonder, in the midst of all his shit, if the right time would ever come along for him and Jolie.

He found Emma in the back of Java House. Her petite body was nestled into a chair, headphones covering her ears. He rounded the edge of the chair's armrest and sat down opposite her. Her gaze remained focused on the mug in her hand, and it took her a moment to acknowledge he had sat down.

"You're back." Emma pushed the headphones off her ears.

Jace leaned forward and placed his elbows onto his knees. "We need to talk. Or rather, we need to finish our talk from last week."

Emma's smile was small. "So, that's Jolie."

Jace jerked upright. How did she know?

As if she read his mind, she answered, "I've never seen you look at me like that." She shrugged and sipped from her mug. Even in the dim light, Jace could see her eyes mist over.

In the time him and Emma had been together, Jolie's name had come up twice. Once at the beginning of their relationship, during the obligatory conversation about old heartbreak, and then again last summer after Talon's wedding. The wedding he hadn't invited Emma to. He thought for sure Emma would have broken up with him then, but she remained. And endured. And, at this point, she deserved a man with a whole heart to give.

"That's her," he said. "I had no idea she was in town."

"And she wants you back." Emma's tone was clipped. "Or maybe you want her back." She smoothed a strand of hair from the bun pulled tightly at the nape of her neck. "After everything we've been through."

Jace flexed his hands as a dull throb in his forehead formed. They had been through a lot—a lot of unnecessary drama. Most of Emma's free time was spent at the theatre building as a teacher's assistant, so she had a knack for it. She also had a knack for sleeping in well past noon, and complaining about circumstances well under her control.

He took a deep breath. This would be the last time he would

have to witness Emma's zero-to-sixty reactions to situations that weren't in her favor.

"Emma," he started, but the look of hatred tripped him up. "It's not personal, okay? It's just...it's over, it's been over since— Christ. Since January."

She nodded. "January. Right. Well, you're off to Denver anyway. That's the real reason, right? You've got your big fancy Ph.D., and I'm stuck serving drinks to underaged kids with fake IDs."

He stalled, wondering if confirmation of her assumption would make him even more of an asshole. He thought he'd made himself clear.

They were not on the relationship escalator. But then again, Emma heard what she wanted.

"I can come by and grab whatever I have at your place after I pack up my desk at the lab," Jace said. Logistics seemed safer to navigate than emotions at the moment.

Emma nodded and stared and nodded some more. "Sure. Whatever." She paused, and Jace braced himself for her grand finale. "She's going to break the pieces she already chipped away from your heart, Jace. I hope you're ready for it."

Emma stood up. The warning was not lost on him. It was one he'd already considered—how exquisitely painful it could be if he allowed Jolie close enough to touch him like that again.

"Good luck with everything, Emma. You don't need to worry about me. No one does." Or so he kept telling himself.

Jace gripped the arm of his seat as Jolie approached. A cascade of curls he'd never seen before draped over her bare shoulders, and her mascara highlighted one of his favorite features, her eyes. He almost didn't notice those high-waisted shorts, which made her already long legs appear endless.

A sense of longing descended into the pit of his stomach. She was familiar and yet so different. It was the same sensation he experienced briefly last summer when they had spent the evening outside while a roaring celebration echoed from within. A night which demanded poor dance moves and warranted even worse decisions. Neither had occurred. She had been in a relationship at the time. Just like him—something she didn't know, then or now, or maybe never would. The less he revealed of himself, the more protected he remained.

"I like this." She shifted in her seat and looked around the restaurant's courtyard. It was dusk, only a few days from the first of June. A canopy of Edison lights blanketed the space in a soft glow while the Iowa river rolled beyond in all her brown, panoramic, temperamental glory. The air felt sticky and held a distinct damp, earthy smell. A flash of purple lightning in the distance suggested a storm was approaching.

They ordered drinks as well as an appetizer of something with bread. She kept shifting in her seat. A Jolie-ism he still recalled during their time apart.

"I'm trying not to freak out," she said. Her lips shaped her words more so than her voice.

Jace captured her hand on instinct and moved his chair closer to hers. "I noticed," he said, moving his thumb over the pulse on her wrist.

Thump, thump, thump.

She blew out a strangled laugh. "I'll get it together. Once you distract me— How does it feel to be done?"

It took him a moment to realize she was asking about his academic career and not Emma. "I'm not sure," he said. "The same, I would say. I imagine once my new job starts it'll feel different." He stopped himself. She didn't know about Denver. How could she? He would've been the one to tell her and he hadn't.

"That's great! I didn't realize you had a job lined up already. Tell me about it." She squeezed his hand. Her eyes were bright as she watched him.

Jace rubbed his free hand against the rough cuticle of his thumb. He didn't want to see Jolie's reaction to what he was about to say. "It's a lead analyst position at a research company in Denver. I'm moving in three weeks."

Her eyes clouded over as she released her hand from his. "Denver. Wow. And research too. Amazing, Jace. That's seriously just, so great. Congrats."

He nodded but remained quiet. Her tone had been sincere, but her eyes had given away her disappointment. He felt it too, the quick turn to unfavorable conditions because of timing, yet again. But he also felt a slight spark in his gut at the realization that it mattered to her. That he still mattered to her.

She mattered to him, too. Of course, she did. There was no protecting himself from the pieces of his heart that lived right there, across from him.

The wind picked up and laced its muggy air through the courtyard. Jolie shoved a piece of hair away from her eyes. "And the loose ends that you had to tie up this afternoon, was that related to your upcoming move?"

He stared at the river as another wave of dread came over him. After he left Java House, he'd walked straight to his research lab, dumped the contents of his desk into an empty box once used for copy paper, abandoned four years' worth of his life on his front porch, and biked to Emma's apartment across the river. She was waiting at the door—he the idiot for assuming she would make this easier by avoiding him—with a box of his stuff, as well as swollen eyes, and a look he was still trying to shake. Jace would have to tell Jolie what happened. There was no other option.

Their drinks arrived. Jace peered at Jolie over the edge of the glass before taking a generous gulp. She took a sip, then placed the glass down and twisted it on the cocktail napkin. He watched her watch him. He had yet to answer her seemingly innocent question about loose ends. Why did the explanation have to be so complicated?

"I guess you could say it was related to the move. Yeah." He cleared his throat and looked at his drink. He was stalling, yet again.

"Okay, Dr. Vague."

He shook his head and felt a small smile tug on his lips. It was time to rip the Band-Aid off. Arm hair and all. "I'm having a hard time, uh, finding the words, or a good way to tell you that...someone used to be in the picture."

She stilled. "I think you just did. Right there." She played with the corner of her cocktail napkin. "The woman from earlier. Emma. Right?"

"Yes. But she isn't anymore," he rushed on, "and before you jump to conclusions, it would have happened today whether you had shown up or not." He left out a realization he could no longer deny—seeing her last summer had pulled a thread loose and unraveled a once-solid belief that she would never return.

He exhaled and waited. She pulled her lip between her teeth a few times while tapping her index finger on the rim of the glass.

This was a new side of Jolie he had never before experienced: tempered contemplation. Rarely did she weigh her words, but rather threw them around like punches in a sparring match. He'd learned to duck and weave, but certain hits had been unavoidable.

"I'm glad you told me, but you don't owe me an explanation," she said softly, almost like an apology.

"Well, that's incredibly undeserved," he said.

Was she pulling away? Unwilling to get invested? Sure, he was in a moment of instability, but she could certainly be a part of the transition.

Her eyebrows pulled together. "That probably wasn't an easy conversation with...her, after everything else today."

"No, not really. But it was the nail in the coffin, as they say."

He hadn't delivered many rejections in his life but it had sucked as much as receiving one. "I'm guessing since you're here, you also experienced something similar?"

He remembered the brief mention of her new relationship last summer and still bristled at the thought. Jolie had shared herself with a stranger in the same way she had with him. He had wished, and still did, that his heartache would absorb his memories instead of his happiness.

"Oh, yeah. Not recently, but yes. One coffin. One nail." She took a sip. "But when you break it down, it wasn't a good fit. It felt off, even from the beginning. Like the skin I chose to wear around him, the adaptation of myself, wasn't sustainable."

The server appeared with their appetizer and placed it between them. The smell of roasted tomato, garlic, and freshly shaved Parmesan triggered a rumble in his stomach. He'd rushed out of his apartment this morning with a granola bar that was probably still at the bottom of his bag. One of those days.

He popped the bruschetta in his mouth and savored the flavors, as well as the view. A strong wind ripped through the courtyard and lifted Jolie's hair away from her neck. Her squeal of shock faded into the rising chatter of the diners next to them. Yes, it was going to rain, and yes, she was stunning.

"So, tell me," he said after he swallowed. "How do you feel in the skin you're wearing right now?"

"At the moment, I'm pretty darn naked." She choked on the last word, her cheeks flaming a beautiful shade of red. "I mean, obviously not *naked*-naked." She busied her mouth with her drink.

"You know I've seen you—" He was cut off with a wave of her hand.

"Right I know *that*," she said, "but you get my point. It's just me in my own skin, in front of you." Her eyes captured his. "And to be fair, we're in our thirties now, so even if you've *seen* me, as you say, you might not recognize *this* me."

He leaned forward. "I see you, Jolie, and you're more beautiful than ever." And it was true.

Her face glowed, her arms were willowy yet defined, and her long legs shot down from the best ass this side of the Mississippi.

"Jace." A desperate tone painted her voice, one that had him reaching for her bare leg underneath the table. Her skin prickled in his palm.

"Before I lose my nerve—" Her voice broke slightly. "I want to talk about why I'm here. Get it out of the way."

"Okay, right." He leaned back and shoved a hand through his hair as missiles of negative thoughts dropped, one after another. She wanted nothing to do with him. He'd disappeared on her one too many times. He hadn't been worth the drive out here. She regretted her impulse. Denver was a deal breaker. There was no love left between them.

Dammit. Without fail, he could always doom and gloom at the drop of a hat when it came to Jolie.

She caught his arm. "Come back."

She guided his hand back onto her leg. The feel of her smooth skin evaporated all the doubts in his head. He lightly squeezed her thigh to acknowledge the significance of her defenselessness.

"I have so much to say. So much to share with you. But I don't want to ruin this moment," she said. Her gaze drifted down to his mouth. "And I really, *really* like the feel of your hands on me again." She whispered the last part while he fought the urge to kiss her.

He saw she was struggling too.

It had taken four years of countless reminders and a slew of expletives to really hit the point home, that Jolie wasn't coming back. He enjoyed being wrong as much as the next man—which was not at all—but he could admit that in this case, he was pretty fucking ecstatic to have been so very wrong. Doom and gloom be damned.

She was in front of him, in the here and now. Whatever the moment had planned for them, he was ready for it. He refocused on Jolie, on her green eyes, clear from the earlier clouds, and felt a sense of calm in the uncertainty of what sat in front of him.

He squeezed her leg once more before leaning back with folded hands. "Let's get it out of the way then."

Their second first kiss could wait.

Thirty-Five

May 2014

Jace was going to be the end of her, a slow sweet death of gentle touches, heart-shattering words, and arresting gazes. She could barely touch her food; hunger for anything other than him seemed impossible. Food, however, meant delaying what she had come here to say, and fewer alcohol-soaked thoughts, so she popped a piece of toast in her mouth.

She'd taken extra care getting ready at the hotel, as a distraction from what had seemed like a never-ending space of time before she could see him again. When in reality it had taken four hours to prepare herself for one massive, sinking confirmation: Jace was in a relationship. And she had no right to any emotion other than acceptance. Yet, somehow, her worst fears and highest hopes had been confirmed at the same time. He wasn't in a relationship, and he was moving to a state that required a plane ticket.

Jolie looked at him from across the table now, with all his cards laid out, and felt like she was in a freefall. She had no idea what to think, but she felt determined to continue on the path she'd set forth on this morning. It was her turn.

"I guess you could say I have a confession," she started, but paused. She hadn't rehearsed what she planned to share, and now that he was in front of her, she regretted not reciting a few key words to her reflection.

She'd messed up epically four years ago when she kicked Jace out of her life. Then, in the height of her desperation two years later, and on the heels of exposing herself to Carrie, she experienced a moment of crystal-clear consciousness. One that allowed the truth to reveal itself, her life was surrounded by steel bars. Confined. Claustrophobic.

She found herself screaming at the top of her lungs, *I want the fuck out of here.* It was time for her to free the person she'd been so fearful to let go of and come to terms with whomever came out squinting in the daylight.

After admitting to her problems, the path to a meaningful life revealed itself. She was meant to be a therapist to those with similar issues, but she knew her own healing had to come first. With the help of various groups, individual therapy, and meditation of all things, she was able to release her old self. And now, on the other side of the lowest lows, mishaps, soul-searching, and eventual progress to lasting change, she owed Jace an explanation.

He deserved to hear it from the person she was now. Someone he should have known the first time around and not the person who'd been caught in a web of numbing instead.

The weight of humidity attached to every pore on her body as thunder rumbled overhead. She considered suggesting to move inside to save them from the risk of bad weather, or to delay the exposure of vulnerability.

She rubbed her hand against the tightness in her chest, knowing that to remove the layers covering her truth she would have to talk, so she started. "You probably remember all my ups and downs while we were together. That whiplash of happiness to sadness. I mean, obviously. Anyone close to me walked on eggshells most of the time." She watched his eyebrows go up, but he remained quiet. "I blamed my mood swings on anything and anyone. You witnessed the worst of it though. I can't tell you how sorry..." She took a steadying breath in the space of his steady patience. "I'm getting ahead of myself."

Jace shifted in his seat, his face drawn. "Jo, you're not sick, are you?"

She shook her head. "No. I mean, not anymore. But nothing terminal or life-threatening. Sorry. I should have led with that."

His shoulders relaxed. She needed him to hear her backstory, so her apology would mean something other than hollow words.

"Not long after we met, I started hiding my emotional eating. Or, I guess technically, my binge eating." She still had a hard time saying those words out loud, but there they hung, like black exhaust from old lies. Her mouth paused as her mind fought off the word 'pollution'.

Jace leaned into the table. "Wait, so you overate like we all do from time to time, is that what you mean?" To his credit, he looked genuinely concerned.

"At first that's what I thought too. An overindulgent day here and there, or stress eating during finals week, no big deal, right? But my overeating turned into constant to always. The amount of food I would eat in a day... Let's just say it was a lot." She mirrored his stance and placed her elbows on the table. "I blamed everything and everyone else too. My bitchiness wasn't because of my job. And our relationship—all the ups and downs—was not the reason for my unhappiness." She met his gaze as lightning flashed in the distance. "It was all misdirected disgust. With myself. A loop of projection and blame that turned into a never-ending cycle of avoidance."

Jace stared openly. "How did I not know this?"

"I hid it well."

Jace ran a hand through his curls, more pronounced in the moist air. "We never had that much food in our apartment. At least, not in the kitchen." Jolie's foot jiggled as she watched realization come over Jace's face. "You hid food."

Jolie uncrossed her legs and nodded. The unease working up her spine oozed out from the middle of her body, hot and necessary. Only a few others knew all her gritty details, mainly those with similar experiences. But sharing this now, with someone who lived under the same roof at the time and with someone who deserved to hear the truth, was a new, more terrifying level of exposure.

"You know the closet in the hallway? The one where we kept old college shirts, and textbooks, and things we probably should have donated, like that George Foreman grill?"

Jace shook his head. "We barely had a hallway. You're telling me there was a closet somehow too?"

Jolie felt her mouth twitch. He was a brilliant man and yet so comically clueless. "Yeah. We did. I made sure you turned a blind eye to it, though. Obviously. Because that's where I hid the food. Oreos. Mainly. And other stuff too." She eyed Jace. He sat frozen. Stoic. She willed herself to keep talking. "Within minutes of you leaving for your night classes, the first half of an Oreo package would disappear without me even tasting it. And then the rest of the package would disappear because I couldn't stop. I ate for comfort or out of boredom. But mostly to avoid feeling. And I continued to eat, and eat, and eat. And I gained weight. Sometimes I'd go for a run and I'd feel better but mostly I felt gross."

The vibration of her voice in her chest was evidence she was the one speaking, but her ears were convinced otherwise—a stranger had taken over her body. "My cravings for junk food only increased the more I isolated myself in order to feed my addiction to food." She shuddered, thinking back to the sugar withdrawal she had gone through.

"Fucking hell, Jolie. I can't believe what I'm hearing." He scrubbed a hand down his face.

She looked up at the clouds covering the darkened courtyard, then to Jace. The biggest lesson she'd learned, and the most difficult to fully understand, had been the relationship between success and failure. That one change meant success, *just one*.

No one, not herself, not even failure, could take away the step she had already climbed, even if she ended up tripping on the next one. "I was at my worst when I did what I did. When I ended our relationship. But that, in no way, excuses my behavior or how I treated you. I want you to know that." She needed him to know that.

"I can't believe I never knew. We lived together for fuck's sake." Jace brought a finger up to his mouth and began to nibble.

"It's designed that way." She had absorbed enough of other people's hurt and confusion at this point, to know how to respond to Jace's now. "I call it solitary overeating confinement." Jolie reached up and gently moved his hand away from his mouth.

He caught her hand with his and laced their fingers together. "I forgot you did that," he said.

"Sorry. Not my place." It had felt second nature to stop him.

"It will always be your place." He squeezed her hand. "How long has it been since you stopped?"

"Two years." She looked at him and thought of an old photo of them together—his face, with its healthy glow, next to her empty smile and dead eyes. "There are days that beg for the numbness of eating. But I'll never be that person again."

"I wish I would have known, Jo. I could've helped."

"I wouldn't have allowed it. You know that." She placed her hand on his forearm, the coarse hair tickling her palm, the heat of his skin reassuring her. "I would erase our past if it meant we could meet for the first time today, as who I am now."

The look he gave startled her. "You don't mean that." Each word was punctuated with a fierceness she had never heard from him.

His lips twisted as if the words refused to launch. "Don't forget Jolie," he ground out, "I fell in love with the person you're so willing to leave behind."

"Oh." She exhaled as all of the oxygen in her lungs drifted up into the ominous clouds. She looked up, breathless. Within seconds, the sky answered back in an impressive sheet of blinding white rain. For the briefest of moments, she couldn't take her eyes off Jace through the downpour.

She felt him pull her closer, his eyes wild like the wind. She barely felt the rain; all she wanted, in the middle of a raging storm, was his mouth on hers. He touched her cheek with his fingers then ran his thumb over her bottom lip. She lifted her chin, willing him to kiss her, silently pleading for him to show her she was forgiven.

A crack of thunder so loud and so very close shot her straight out of her seat. She rushed with the crowd toward the restaurant's back door, Jace right on her heels. They bounded into the air-conditioned interior in a fit of sputtering laughs. Jace looked at her with bright eyes, his hair dripping from the rain.

She stared at Jace drenched to the bone and wondered if all the dirt and grime from her mistakes and regrets had washed away in the downpour. And maybe, just maybe, she could ask the one question that had brought her here in the first place.

Has our time run out?

Thirty-Six

May 2014

J ace peered out the front window of the restaurant, the buildings across the way a blur in the rain, then turned to Jolie. The room was too large for the number of tables in it and was barely lit by the spattering of wall sconces. "Well, it's definitely not the right time to risk a mad dash through all the rain, that's for sure. So, maybe we should wait it out."

He watched her jaw tremble. The circulated air in the restaurant had chilled his wet clothes, which meant Jolie was probably frigid by now.

She glanced around. "Let me just visit the hand dryer, see if that helps."

"I'll get us something hot, like coffee maybe?"

Her eyes lit up. "Hot chocolate?"

Smiling, he agreed. "Anything for you."

"Well, in that case..." She inched closer and grazed her fingers against his forehead. He held his breath as she moved his wet hair to the side. Bold. Unexpected. Who was this person? "Marshmallows too."

He swallowed down the urge to grasp her wrist and close what little space was left between them. To end his misery of memory and feel those beautiful lips on his once again.

"I'll just be over there," his voice cracked as he pointed to the bar. Her hand lowered from his face.

She shook her head as if to break the spell.

"I won't be long," she said.

She moved in the opposite direction but glanced over her shoulder as if to make sure he wouldn't disappear the second he left her sight. Didn't she know by now?

For her to come all this way with a secret she'd harbored and planned to share with him... To find her way to the other end and seek him out. To apologize. It was unimaginable. If he wasn't careful, he risked blurring dormant love with this new version of old love and—ah, fuck it. She'd possessed his heart the entire time.

Lucky for her and him, the restaurant's dessert menu offered S'mores Hot Chocolate. Whatever the hell that was. He ordered two at the bar and had just set the ridiculously large mugs—with marshmallows the size of his fist—on the table, when Jolie returned.

"How'd it go?" He pushed a mug her way and watched in delight as her eyes grew round.

"I'm still damp but no longer shivering. Whoa. This is impressive." Her fingers cupped the mug and raised it. "To our last firsts."

Jace held her words in his heart and her gaze in his eyes. "Cheers." The drink was warm, deeply rich, and sticky.

She licked her top lip. "Is that Baileys too?"

He wiggled his eyebrows. "We're adults. We drink adult beverages."

She laughed. "With crazy huge fluff cubes on top."

"I always wondered what the technical term was for those things."

"Now you know." She grinned and set her mug down. "Tell me, honestly." Her face grew serious. "How are you feeling about...everything?"

"Well..." He stopped to consider her question, even though the full intention of it was clear. He would rather humor the truth into existence. "I'm a bit concerned about flooding. We've already had a lot of rain this week."

She groaned through a half grin and tapped him on his forearm. "Stop it."

He scooted his stool close enough so their knees touched, then took her hand in his.

"You want to know how I feel?"

She nodded, lips parting.

Focus man.

"I'm a bit shocked you're sitting here in front of me, in a place we went to all the time, over ten or however many years ago."

She pointed a finger at the table. "This used to be Lamont's place?"

"One and not the same." He motioned with his free hand to a wall lined with low-backed booths. "That area was once the dance floor. I believe you dropped it right...there like it was hot."

"Oh my god, you did not just say that!" She laughed, shaking her head.

He tilted his head to the alcove leading into the bathrooms. "And over there is where I pressed you up against the wall and, well..."

Her face changed to the color he would never tire of.

"So, it's a bit of an out-of-body experience, honestly," he said. He reached up with her hand still connected to his and dragged his thumb along her lips. "Except you're real, and incredible, and I need to taste these again." In a single movement, he joined his breath with hers and claimed their last first kiss.

A crack of thunder broke through the ambient noise inside the restaurant and all went dark, as if their touch had shot straight to the heavens and released a celestial sigh strong enough to blow out all the lights around them.

Jolie jolted away from Jace, disoriented. Jace wrapped his

arm around her shoulder. The one person she'd spent countless sleepless nights trying to let go of was now her only grounding.

"This evening is turning a bit dramatic," she said. Her voice was an octave higher than normal. "Did you know Rhode Island has the lowest number of reported tornadoes out of all the states in the U.S.?" she rambled. "I'm not sure about Denver, though. Something for you to look into maybe. Probably less than here, I would think."

"Denver has tornadoes," Jace said, as another crack of thunder tore through the room.

Jolie focused on her chest rising and falling with each conscious breath. "Right. Of course."

He must have sensed her discomfort or remembered how much she hated unpredictable storms. He pulled her in closer.

"Do you remember that one storm we had?" he whispered in her ear. "The tornado sirens were blaring, and the wind, Christ, I was legitimately concerned the roof was going to fly off."

"We took the cats into the bathtub," she said, remembering that night, the rarity of a scare that had reached 'get into the windowless room' status. "Like that would have done any good, had said roof flown the coop."

"We made it out alive."

She huffed. "With my second gray hair, mind you."

Even in the low light, seeing Jace's smile warmed her insides and eased the immediate concern of their meteorological predicament.

"The storm outside is apropos for this time of year," he said. "You know that."

Her head tilted to the left. "Since when do you say words like apropos?"

Jace straightened his shoulders. "Since becoming a doctor, thank-you-very-much. I'm now going to drink my hot chocolate with marshmallow foam. Excuse me." Jace craned his neck and turned his body toward the rain-soaked windows.

Jolie laughed and reached for him. "Don't go."

He turned with a smile and kissed the back of her hand. "I'm not going anywhere. But I was thinking...want to make a run for it?"

She met his eyes, as ruinous in view as his mouth promised to be in taking. Heat radiated from her belly button all the way down to her toes. She wanted him. But he was moving to a new life in three weeks' time. Which colored this weekend with temporary hues of romance. Or could this be something more permanent?

Her chest tightened. They were finally together, talking, touching, and kissing. Yes, she was going to take advantage of it.

"My hotel is two blocks away."

Jace grinned. "Race you there—" And before she could suggest they hold off for a few more minutes, because she would have—it was torrential out there—Jace sprinted out the door and straight into the downpour.

She raced after him but stopped at the front windows, and watched him attempt to moonwalk on the flooded sidewalk. He pointed at her, then waved to join him. She mouthed 'no' as her emotions surged in rhythm with the rain.

Don't freak out.

She had missed him so much. His presence now was a sucker punch right in the gut that stole what little breath she had left at the sight of him. Her person. Someone who was willing to run through the rain and into a future—however short or long—with her.

In a spike of adrenaline, whether from the sky's relentless release or in anticipation of what was to come, she pushed the doors open.

"This way!" she shouted and ran ahead, knowing full well he probably knew where to go. She just wanted the terror of being out in a storm to end as soon as possible.

It was a mad dash, with belly-aching laughter, into the brightly lit hotel lobby; a generator hard at work, no doubt. Jace's feet squeaked to a halt next to her as he let out a low whistle.

"This is way too fancy for a college town."

"Bougie, I believe, is the word," she said. "Oddly enough, the room is the complete opposite."

Jace nudged her shoulder with his. "Since when do you use words like *bougie*?"

Jolie caught his smirk, and his intent, and nudged him back. "Well, that question is apropos, isn't it?"

She smiled at him as the sound of their wet footsteps on the black marble floor echoed off the walls. There wasn't a soul to be found other than the one next to her. They stepped inside the elevator and lifted higher into the stormy clouds. The only noise around them was the beep of each passing floor. She felt tiny drops of wetness fall from her eyelashes and fingertips, as the expectations of tomorrow, or the next day, or the next month, dripped onto the floor below.

They entered the hotel room, a generic floorplan with one hallway, one bathroom, four walls, and one big bed. Jace pointed in the direction of the king bed, which made up the majority of the space, and mouthed 'Wow' while toeing his shoes off. She watched him move around the room, certain her joy would spill out any minute at simply witnessing the act of him being himself.

"This is *niiice*." He pushed aside thick navy curtains to reveal a backdrop of gray clouds. It looked like the rain might have eased up, although it was hard to tell from her angle. Jace's tall frame and broad shoulders took up most of her view.

"I'm going to be honest with you, Jo." He turned and heaved a playful sigh. "These wet clothes need to go."

"You're absolutely right." She approached him as a glow from inside her stomach stretched to the ends of her fingertips. Her hands ran up his arms and began to peel away the wet cotton stuck to his warm skin. She wanted him. No matter their future.

His shirt went first and in record time. He met her urgency, his rough fingertips digging into her thighs, and clawed at her wet jean-shorts. A flip-flopping, fish-out-of-water move occurred before she ceremoniously threw them across the room.

Jace's warm hands circled around her and squeezed her backside, causing her to gasp.

"I've missed the way you feel," he said and walked her backward. His eyes brimmed with lust before they disappeared into the nape of her neck. His teeth nipped a trail up to her earlobe while her need to let go and get lost in his touch became overwhelming.

She gasped again. "Jace."

He captured her mouth as if to absorb the sound of his name. His tongue opened her up, ruthless and reckless, in an intimate and familiar touch.

"May I?" He tugged at the bottom of her shirt—tentative yet firm. She took a step away to lift the damp shirt over her head and, tempering the ingrained habit to cover herself, reached behind to release the clasp of her bra. Cool air hit her chest as Jace's eyes left a trail of wildfire on her skin.

His mouth returned to hers, strong and untamed. The back of her knees hit the down comforter and she fell back, completely bare except for a wisp of cotton between her legs.

"You're here," he breathed from above. "And you're..." He trailed off as his eyes roamed over her body from head to toe. His gaze was a purposeful, slow burn. She hooked her fingers underneath her thong and slid it down her thighs. He deserved to see all of her, completely. He had earned it, after all, having seen her in every other way, but never quite like this.

His Adam's apple bobbed. "And you're different."

She fought against another wave of self-consciousness and breathed into the tension pooled in her raised shoulders.

He must have noticed the shift. "Please don't," he whispered, eyes pleading.

"I'm trying not to." She squeezed her eyes shut and focused on the fuzzy white blurs floating underneath her eyelids. She could do this. She wanted to do this. Let go. "This isn't easy. Blending familiar with anomalous."

He braced his weight with his arms and looked down at her, his hands depressing the soft mattress surrounding her head.

"You're stunning, Jo, and unlike anyone I have known in this lifetime."

His head bent and began a line of kisses, starting from her mouth, down her neck, leaving his sandalwood scent everywhere. He stopped just above her breast and murmured against her skin, "You're an old love with new layers. I'm beyond fascinated, like waking up from a dream, only to realize reality is so much better."

"You're different too, you know."

His voice was rough. "Tell me."

She licked her lips, nervous to say what was on the tip of her tongue. "You undressed your heart the same way I undressed my body. You saw trust through discomfort, just like I had."

His eyes flared and, unable to contain her need any longer, she pulled him down onto her. His bare chest was heavy and satisfying against hers. The stubble of his chin scratched against her collar bone with each taste and lick he gave her.

"And this is so very real, Jace," she said, barely able to catch a full breath. The graze of his lips singed her skin, igniting all the parts he purposefully feathered along the way.

He fixed her with an intense stare before wrapping her tightly into his arms and flipping her so she straddled his waist. It was her turn to kiss and lick and explore. To ignite in him what he had done so well in her. She tucked her nose into the crook of his neck, indulging in his scent, then tasted the salt of his skin on her descent to the sound of his beating heart.

"Jo, please, I'm not sure how much more I can take," he gasped, gripping her shoulders. "Before I lose my mind."

"Okay."

She dragged her body slowly up his torso, leaving a path of wet kisses along the way, until their lips finally met. He kissed her hard, pressing his thumbs into the crevices of her hips, securing her enough to roll her onto her back again. Her hands dug into the muscles in his back, knotted and grounded. The pulsating heat between her legs was unbearable; the stiffness pressed against her promised the necessary relief. She groaned into his mouth and opened wider. He broke away from her, panting.

"Do you...?" she whispered.

He reached toward his discarded pants on the floor. Somewhere in the distance, she heard the pattering of rain against glass, the roll of thunder, the muffled noise of a television, and the tear of a wrapper. Muted but near. His face came back into focus and floated over hers.

He blinked. "You're so beautiful." The tips of his hair touched the edges of his long eyelashes as he leaned down and captured her nipple into his mouth. Hot sparks shot straight up her breast, a kind of white-gold light that reached into the back of her eyes and blinded her with pleasure. She arched into him, her body a floating cloud heavy with rain, and gasped as he entered her. She held his gaze, intense and saturated, while he inched in and out at a deliciously torturous pace.

She propped herself up onto her elbows to absorb his pushes, to endure the building warmth, and to find his mouth.

"Now I'm the one losing my mind," she mumbled against his lips.

"Not lost," he said, increasing his speed. "But found."

Her hands crumpled the sheets as the luscious pulse inside her began to strengthen. His hand touched her sensitive area while the ache inside her surged. The pads of his fingers circled and rubbed in rhythm with his in-and-out motion. Her release was close—insanely and remarkably close.

His chest pressed into hers, slick and damp, and she fell back onto the soft bedding. "Jolie, goddamn, you feel amazing," he muttered into her hair. "Let go. I've got you."

And that's all it took. Her body shook and quivered as she gave in to him in a crushing release. He cupped the back of her neck, not far behind. She held on tightly as his pace quickened.

The sound of her name was a plea for connection and a demand to unleash. She felt herself building again like a breeze on glowing embers. His touch was the lick of a flame.

For the briefest of moments, she floated out of her body and marveled at the sight below, at their ability to meet here, like this, so fully intertwined, after years of disentanglement. They still fit together as if made for the other. She cried out as he filled her deeply with his final push then collapsed by her side. Her chest rose and fell. Everything buzzed and tingled.

"Wow."

Jace groaned and snickered at the same time.

"Yeah."

She rolled onto her side and took in his straight nose and well-defined lips. She wanted him. Right now. All over again. "Will you stay? Make the night ours?"

Jace turned and tucked his arm under his head. "Don't you mean the entire weekend?"

Of course, she'd hoped for this suggestion, to extend their time together, but wondered if too much time had passed? Were there too many changes in front of them? Was it just sex between them now?

"If you'll have me, yes."

She heard him mutter under his breath before he spoke.

"You've been with me since the day we met, Jo. There hasn't been a moment you haven't been a part of me, in some way, either in life or in thought." He kissed her softly. "Jo, I'm sold," he continued to peck her lips between each utterance. Each kiss was a tax for words she'd heard before, once upon a time, when their love had been solid, instead of imploded. "You're the girl I want to marry."

Marry. A word she had never heard him say before. But not just any old word, the most significant word, and powered by Jace's voice, there was only one way for her to react.

Thirty-Seven

May 2014

Her body shot up straight and by sheer force pushed Jace to the edge of the bed. He teetered and almost fell, which would have been a welcome comedic break, but he stabilized himself with the side of the headboard.

Jolie's feet hit the soft carpet, but she remained hunched over. She rummaged for her shirt, or bra, or a blanket. Anything with which to cover herself.

She threw her hands up in exasperation and stared Jace down. "You just delivered a pseudo marriage proposal." She narrowed her eyes. "After thirty-six hours of being in the same town together and countless hours away from each other, and on the heels of remarkable sex. I mean, my goodness, that was amazing." She flexed her toes into the carpet and shivered. "But that's not the point. You're moving to Denver and I"— Her mouth tightened—"am buck ass naked."

To his credit, Jace remained still, as if in a freeze response. The exact opposite of her reaction. She was spooked and confused and ready to attack. Once she found her shorts.

She watched him step into his boxers, then turn back to the bed and lift the comforter. He leaned his head toward the opening. "Get in."

Her arms crossed over her chest as she continued to squint at him. "Why?"

"You're shivering. You need to be covered up. That's all this is. I swear," he said.

"Look, you stay warm here, I'll go over to the chair, and we can talk this out."

She climbed under the covers, while he walked to the armchair next to the bed. She stretched her legs in the lukewarm sheets and released a long breath. Jace sat shirtless, his expression as naked as his chest—which was awfully distracting—and ushered in all sorts of regret.

"What are we doing, Jace?" His eyes descended while his shoulders shrugged. Her stomach dropped. She'd said too much. "I ruined it, didn't I?"

Jace bit around the nail bed of this thumb.

Crap. It was too late to retract the loaded question. Jace sat still but full of motion, gnawing it over.

"Here's the thing," Jace said after he had successfully reddened the skin around his thumb to a color she had coined 'cuticle-apple-red'. "We will always have the ruins of our past relationship, built by us, weathered down by us, but not completely demolished, right?"

Jolie nodded.

"But there's a unique beauty in ruins," he said. "Like Machu Picchu, or I guess the Colosseum."

"Always wanted to go to both," she said with a sigh.

He dipped his head. "I remember," he said, then glanced at her. "There's beauty in ours too, although less Roman and bloody." He paused as he looked down at his torn-up fingers. "My point is, the evidence of a fallen past still standing in the present day is a sight to behold. A display of strength, of tenacity, of a history that refuses to be forgotten, no matter the years of suffering. So, if we're ruined, I say, fuck yeah."

Her own thoughts muted in recognition of his stunning words. "You think we're beautifully ruined?" she asked.

"More than you realize."

She flexed her toes underneath the fabric and watched the material tent as she stalled for however long it would take to slow her heart, to cool her cheeks, and to calm her ravenous lips. But how could she absorb what he said and not sparkle like a brilliant, shooting star?

"So, let me get this straight," she said, wrapping her arms around her naked waist in a half-hearted attempt at decorum. "I make you sit on that seriously uncomfortable-looking chair. In just your boxers. And that's your response?" She shook her head as a lightness bloomed somewhere from inside. "Who is this person in front of me, and where is your shirt?"

He shrugged and rested his elbows on his bare knees, both hands clasped between his legs. "Where's yours?" he smirked, peering at her through his dark lashes.

"No," she wagged a finger at him. "This smoldering look you have going on can wait. I'm trying to apologize for being an ass who's incapable of taking anything you say lightly."

Another shrug. "I feel like an ass for getting caught up in the moment," he said. "That's what makes you-you, and me-me."

She froze. Oh. So, he hadn't meant what he'd said earlier, he'd been caught up in a web of pheromones just like her. Why was she shivering at this realization rather than warming in relief?

"Wasn't that our problem before? Me being me. You being you."

His head jerked up. "This isn't before. This is now. And based on what you told me earlier tonight, you've changed enough to have found love in yourself."

Jolie laughed incongruously, uncomfortable with where the *love yourself* conversation was headed—straight into the hub of pop psychology, something she typically avoided.

He kept on pace. "You hadn't figured it all out yet, before, right? And like I said earlier, you're different. You radiate confidence, which comes through in your presence. This sort of glow... in your appearance, and I can now also attest to your reactions too."

Her jaw went slack. Damn, he'd quickly recovered from the near causality of trendy topics and was now showing off his newly-obtained degree, doctoring his expertise in philosophy.

He had a point though; her outward reaction had been calm. Sure, he had almost hit the ground when she pushed him from the bed, but it hadn't been her words that knocked him to his knees—like so many times before.

The inner strength she'd used to tame that raging sea had taken it out of her, however, and a new wave of exhaustion hit her. Hard. She wanted to ask him if he meant it. That one word. Marriage. But the weight of emotions had piled directly over her eyelids.

"Can I come in?" he asked while a monstrous yawn took over her body. "I'd like to lay with you while you fall asleep."

She nodded and shimmied further under the covers.

"You're not upset?" she asked between yawns.

He motioned for her to lean back and tucked her into him from behind.

The smell of sandalwood circled her as he spoke. "Of course not. You need sleep. I need you right here."

"Okay," she mumbled. Jace's rhythmic breathing tunneled and turned soft as she drifted off.

The following morning was just as Jace had hoped—sleepy at first with a slow start, followed by the same desire they had shared the night prior. They blanketed each other's naked bodies in a silent understanding; breathed in the serenity of their reunion; and avoided any mention of the pseudo marriage proposal, or his impending move, until further notice.

After an indulgent shower together, they got dressed—stiff day-old clothes for him, a flowing sundress for her—and walked east fifteen minutes to his apartment. The white nineteenth-century home came into view. A two-story Tudor-style house with 'character', but really, just an old home conversion sectioned off into multiple, drafty apartments. His section of the house had most likely been a dining room at some point.

He pushed open the heavy wooden door and watched her walk inside. She slipped her sandals away from her feet and tilted her head up. An unexpected breeze spilled through the crack inside his heart and left him shivering as he watched her slowly utter the word "Wow."

The unique use of a very small space had captured him too. The U-shaped loft, which held his queen bed and partially covered the main area below, was accessible only by a ladder leading up to the catwalk. His leather couch, flat-screen television, and a half-kitchen right off the front door made up the main level.

The vaulted ceiling gave the room air, the floor-to-ceiling oak gave it warmth, and Jolie standing in the middle of it all gave it indescribable magic.

"So, this is your place." She eyed him before walking over to the framed artwork that had hung in their bedroom all those years ago—something he'd hidden away to one day be forgotten, until the night before Talon's wedding.

Jace had torn away the bubble wrap from the colorful oil painting, feeling closer to Jolie than he'd thought possible, and hammered a nail into the wall. He hung the painting above his record player, in the spot he knew it would always go, a piece of his heart and hers, listening to music together.

"Hello, you," he heard Jolie say. She turned to him, her smile tight, eyes red-rimmed.

He stepped closer. "You okay?"

Her body moved in tandem with his as if they were magnets. Unaware. Reflexive. And not repelling, like so many times before. "Sure. Yeah."

The last word hung in the air and left him unsure if he should call her out on the falsified response.

"It's just..." She paused. Her eyes were trained on the painting.

"I forgot how much I loved that painting. Yet, when I had the chance to appreciate it every day, even if my days were less than perfect, or downright miserable, I didn't. I ignored it, forgot about it, took it for granted."

She looked at him once again. Her eyes were a pool of unshed tears. His chest burned with an understanding his voice could not give justice to.

"Here." He walked over and took it off the wall. "You can have it." He held it out.

A soft laugh escaped her lips. "Only you can pull off deliberate obtuseness like a comedy sketch."

He placed the frame back on the wall. He would give her anything she wanted. Even if it had always fallen short in the past. Maybe what he had to offer this time around would be enough. "I'm not being funny. And all I want to pull off right now are these crusty clothes."

"Go on." Her smile reappeared, sincere. "I'll wait."

But for how long? he wanted to ask, but stopped himself when Crimson jumped onto the counter and whined.

Jolie raised an eyebrow. "I see his appetite hasn't changed."

"It's gotten worse. I also think he's bored. There was a time I considered getting another cat. But it didn't feel right." Jace reached into his open-face pantry—three rows of two-by-four boards nailed into the wall—and handed a bag of cat food to Jolie.

She nodded but kept quiet. "Anyway. I'll be right back," he said and climbed up the ladder into the loft.

"Well, hello to you too, handsome man," Jolie cooed below.

The tingle of dry food rang out as it hit Crimson's porcelain dish.

Jace found a pair of shorts and a short-sleeved t-shirt and changed. He glanced in the mirror and caught himself sporting a wide smile. Jolie had that effect on him. She left him smiling without even realizing it. He ran a hand through his wavy hair and climbed down the wooden ladder. Crimson was snaked between Jolie's legs, his food untouched.

"I forgot how much his eyes look like Clover's." Her voice was quiet as she looked down at Crimson. "I think he remembers me."

Jace soaked her up from head to toe. "You're unforgettable."

She leaned into him. Her evergreen and lavender scent engulfed him as she whispered, "You're a walking romantic."

"It's all for you." He closed the gap and wrapped himself around her. "It's beyond reason really, how you're standing here and not far away like my mind has trained itself to remember daily. And yet the lack of logic is the only thing that makes sense right now."

Jolie's face returned to the hue he was used to seeing. "If I'm to be the most logical one in this room right now then we're in trouble," she said. Heat sparked in her eyes. "Just kiss me already."

And so he did. A deep kiss, followed by more kissing, and touching, and ass-grabbing. He pulled away. At this rate, they would never leave his place.

"We have plans," he said.

"These mysterious plans, yes." She bit her lip and pressed herself into him. "I hope it involves more of this." Her mouth found his lips and kissed him at a pace absent of patience. Just when he thought she had taken all of his oxygen, she broke free and trailed a line of kisses from his jaw to the nape of his neck, while her hands found the skin underneath his shirt. His entire body came alive and danced in her flames. She backed him up against the ladder to the loft. This was yet another side of Jolie he had never seen before—uncontrollable passion.

It wasn't the first nor the last time he would marvel at his eclipsing love for her. He cupped her face and stared into her hooded eyes. It was impossible to keep his hands off her. So what choice did he have, but to surrender?

Thirty-Eight

May 2014

J ace accelerated onto the expressway, windows open, heart soaring, Jolie's hair wild around her face. She turned the volume up on a song that had always reminded him of her. Their destination was twenty minutes north, off an exit close to the expressway and in the middle of endless cornfields.

"Where are we going?" she shouted above the wind and music.

He mimed zipping his lips and placed his hand on her exposed knee, thanks to the short dress she wouldn't have worn before. She leaned across the console and kissed his cheek. "I'd say you have something up your sleeve but they're far too short for such shenanigans." She turned the volume down. "Although, come to think of it, you casually said you wanted to marry me last night, while shirtless, so I may need to reevaluate your skills in the antics department."

He reached for her hand as heat flared across his chest. She'd opened the door, on the breeze of a joke no less, and had walked right through it. "Would you believe me if I said it would've been impossible to keep those words from coming out of my mouth last night?"

She rubbed her thumb on the inside of his palm. "It's so unlike you though, to speak before you think. I mean, you're moving to Denver. That alone should've stopped you, right? Should I be concerned?" She leaned closer like she was inspecting him. "You didn't have a stroke last night, did you?"

Jace choked on his unexpected laugh. "I think a heart attack would have been more likely after round two this morning." He peeked over to see her grinning. "I'm of sound mind, as far as I can tell. I'm just thinking about a possible future with you. And I know, Jo, you're thinking about it too."

She placed a soft kiss between his knuckles. Her lips hovered for a moment before she placed his hand on her lap. "I have. More than I should, probably. But the logistics of it all..." She gazed out the passenger window. "It's like I'm cut off at the knees right as I take off running with the idea. And yet even though I feel completely lost in you, I still find my way back to you."

"Jo." He squeezed her hand before placing his own back on the steering wheel. It took all his focus to keep the car on the road, to keep from pulling her into his lap, to keep the lump in his throat from turning into something else.

She leaned her head back and turned to look at him. "Anyway. As long as you don't pinch me today, I think we'll do just fine," she said.

He choked on yet another laugh. This was what she meant at dinner last night—her being so purely and consistently *herself* in the wake of all her change. He felt flooded with disbelief to be in her presence. "When have I ever pinched you?"

"Jace." She sputtered out a single 'ha' in the wake of his name. "Your hands. My butt. No pinches today, please."

"That's a tall ask. But I can try if you tell me what you're getting at."

She shifted in her seat. "I want to reduce the likelihood of waking up from this amazing dream. So, tell me. Where are we going?"

Jace turned on his blinker and merged into the exit lane. He understood what she meant; to be with her again was a feeling even his most vivid of dreams had never been able to emulate. The real Jolie, next to the real him, was the dream come true, and a forever-reality worth pursuing—and there it was again. The primal urge to declare his love in the most final of ways. To this time ask her on bended knee.

But it wasn't clear what she was after. Did she only want the breath of the moment or something more? The messages seemed mixed. Or maybe it was his head that was spinning.

His move to Denver could turn out to be a repeat of all those years ago. When they had stared down into the vibrant turquoise water of the quarry, and she'd asked him not to tip the odds in their favor when it came to life decisions. This time, the position he was about to start was far from Jolie's home. But she had also claimed, just last night, to have changed in ways she wanted him to be aware of. So, which Jolie was coming out right now? Old or new?

"We're almost there," he said. "You'll know our destination soon enough."

A few minutes later he rounded the corner and the red barn came into view, a sore thumb atop a hill out of place among the otherwise flat terrain. Jolie popped her head out the open window and shouted into the wind, "What is this place?"

Jace turned onto the winding gravel path. "It's a winery. They also distill their own gin, vodka, and eventually whiskey." The sound of crunching rocks spilled through the open windows as they ascended the hill in a trail of dust.

"Wine made in Iowa." She scrunched her nose and, once he had parked, stepped out of the car. "Is it good?"

"Honestly, it's not bad." He took her hand and moved toward the entrance of the modernized barn. A façade of windows with a distressed wooden door came into view. The hum of crickets serenaded them in the distance while the faint smell of burning wood drifted through the light breeze.

"I've heard good things, as far as young wineries go and all."

He held the door open and followed her straight into the scent of sweet, fermenting fruit. The wide-open room show-cased the steeply pitched ceiling of the converted barn and amplified the many voices from the bodies in it. He moved her in the direction of the steel bar, her back straight, her shoulders noticeably tense. The place was packed.

"It's a soft opening." He rubbed the small of her back. "I know someone though. He'll get us seated away from the crowd." He led her over to the bar and introduced her to Matt, who situated them at a standing cocktail table.

"Jace, my man. I was this close to giving the table to another group." Matt placed enough wine glasses on the table to fill the top rack of a dishwasher. Matt's eyes flicked to Jolie and winked when he caught her looking. He was doing what he did best—giving Jace a hard time and flirting with women. "I figured things must've come up."

Jace coughed at the blatant eyebrow raise and focused on the dark liquid splashing into his glass.

"Thanks for holding the table. We'll let you know when we want to try another bottle."

"You bet." Matt winked—this time at Jace—and left.

"He's charming." Jolie lifted one of the wine glasses with a laugh. "And has a heavy hand. This is more than a taste."

"I have friends in all the right places." Jace swirled the liquid in his glass like he knew what he was doing. "Doesn't taste like grape juice."

"That should go on their label." Jolie took a sip. "He said we're late. Did I mess up your plans again?"

Whatever disruptions came from having Jolie close enough to touch paled in comparison to the disorder he had experienced without her.

"No, not at all." He wanted to ease her mind and to offer assurance that the mess she saw as hers was pure oxygen for his suffocated life. "Wait here a sec."

Jace walked off in search of Matt. It was time to put into motion what he had brought Jolie here for.

Jolie spotted Jace's tall frame moving toward her, a head of loose curls easily found in any crowd. His smile was wide as he approached, her disbelief just as pronounced.

She was here. With him. Close enough now that his breath

warmed the side of her neck as he spoke.

"Let's go explore outside before the sun goes down. Matt will save the table. We can take our wine." Jace took her free hand and weaved a path to the brick courtyard. They padded through lush, green grass, past rows of grapevines, and turned onto a descending path parallel to rows of knee-high corn.

"You seem to know where you're going," she said, intrigued as to where they were headed. At this point, she would follow him anywhere, maybe even to Denver.

"Let's just say I was here for the super-soft opening last weekend." He looked down at her, his eyes illuminated by a sun approaching its set. "It's funny, or maybe sad. I don't know," he went on. "I wanted you here last weekend, for many reasons, some of which I may have drowned in gin or vodka, possibly both. But to hear your reaction to what we're about to see, that's all I wanted." He squeezed her hand. "I never would have thought I would have that wish granted."

The glass in her hand slipped an inch as her foot navigated over a section of exposed rock.

If she wasn't careful, she would end up with spilled emotions and broken glass.

"A delayed wish, anyway," she said, losing her footing again. She was suddenly nervous her reaction wouldn't live up to his expectations.

He tucked her under his arm and moved toward a lone oak tree so tall it appeared to touch the darkening, blue sky.

"Is it even possible for wishes to be delayed?" he asked as he expertly navigated a divot in the ground. "It seems if you make one, it'll show up if and when it's ready." Jace drew her closer and murmured into her hair, "I'm so glad you're here."

Her breathing slowed. The uneven terrain was no longer her main concern now; her weakened knees were, as well as her weekend with Jace coming to an end. Once underneath the shadow of the tree, the sound of rushing water surrounded her.

"We'll leave these here," he said and steadied their glasses in a patch of long grass next to the tree trunk. She watched his shirt stretch over his back and tempered her desire to trace the indents and memorize the feel of him even more. They moved into a thick patch of brush, ducking around sharp branches and waxy, green leaves while his confident stride led the way. She was following him blindly even though she knew her eyes would open to the harsh view of their reality eventually.

Jace's voice rose over the rush and roar of water. "Go on!" His face was childlike as he waved for her to walk on.

She stepped ahead—the air cooling with each foot forward, her skin dampening through the mist of curiosity—and then gasped. There, on the shore's edge of a rushing stream, was a wide berth of white-capped water, tumbling over an edge into a natural pool twenty feet below. The waterfall was loud in timbre and impressive in scope.

"How is this possible, Jace?" She peered over her shoulder. "This is some kind of twilight zone." Her eyes returned to the roaring waterfall at her feet in the middle of a cornfield. The awe she felt from the simple act of nature being itself rooted deep into her belly.

What a rush it would be to fall like this water.

She turned and pointed at his lopsided smile. "You thought the same thing, didn't you? Of time and earth bending."

Jace hooked his arm around her waist, his eyes searching her face. The need to feel his body against hers came over her quickly. He must have felt it too. His warm hands were suddenly on her face, the pad of his thumb stroking her cheek. She craned her neck, urging him to remove the air on her lips. His mouth curved upward then fell onto hers, soft yet commanding, and opened her wide in a dance that sped up and slowed down all at once. Jolie wrapped her arms around his shoulders and dug her fingertips into his back, holding on while she let go.

He pulled back but kept her pressed into him as if she would fall without his support. His voice vibrated into her. "This entire weekend together has been like this waterfall, a remarkable twilight zone in this infinite cornfield of...of life." He shook his head as if he hadn't meant to say his thoughts out loud. "I wish we could spend the rest of our days here, suspended in the deep blue of the water." His arms loosened around her.

The way he had just spoken, with such truth and beauty, was a treasure she hadn't realized she'd been searching for and directly contradicted the downward turn of his mouth. Yet, she found something there, stuck in the spaces between his words: herself, in a sad kind of reverence. Why did it feel like her hope was a shelter for his despair?

He looked down at her and sighed again. "Time hasn't been on our side, has it, Jo? How long have we been separated? How long till we're separated again?"

She flinched as if he had dumped a cup of ice down her back. Had he not felt it as she had so strongly the night before, or this morning, or even right now? A realization she'd thought impossible had shown up right there in front of them, alive and ticking and finally on their side. Her hands squeezed the sides of his shoulders. "We've been pulled apart again and again," she said. "But our connection has never been broken."

Jace nodded but his eyes glazed over. "I just hope after this weekend I will get to see you again, despite our lives taking different directions."

She pulled back abruptly, as the cold she had felt moments before turned scorching hot. The ambient noise of water faded into almost nothing. A low ticking started a rhythmic beat inside her head, one only she could hear.

Tick.

She wanted more than just hope.

Tick.

She wanted more than a future of doubt.

Tick.

She wanted all of her fears to disappear.

Tick.

She wanted all of him. Every day.

All of the hope and doubt and fear could no longer remain contained.

She was overflowing.

She loved him.

Tock.

The alarm bells from within were loud and deafening, the force of her realization overwhelming.

Her stance wavered, while the edges of Jace's body blurred. Pressure warmed her lower back, Jace's arm was supporting her, while a wild type of freedom rushed over the edge of uncertainty and into a glistening pool of absolute clarity.

She drew a deep breath and focused on his face, the deepened lines around his eyes, the gold around his pupils.

"Jace, I need you to know, you never left me. You've been here this entire time." She placed a hand over her chest and felt it expand as she breathed in.

The time apart from Jace was not unlike the movement of her chest. The feeling of him had been kept alive through her deep, nourishing inhales. He was a necessary oxygen that had fed her memories but had hidden her heart in the process. She no longer wanted to hide. She wanted to exhale. Her throat tightened as a burn began to rise.

Don't freak out.

Jace released her and walked toward the water's edge.

Shit.

She had said too much. Again. He might not feel the same this time around. They'd been through so much. Maybe too much. She stood trance-like, her heart beating at a sprinter's pace.

Go tell him, it would say, if hearts had mouths. *Go tell him all the words you've hidden for so long.* No more hiding. No more breathing his memory. No more second-guessing.

Go tell him.

Go!

She finally knew exactly what she wanted, what she needed, what she deserved.

Emotion took over reason, and Jolie launched herself forward. It was only a few steps, but she was out of breath. His back was to her. She felt dizzy and slow, yet acutely aware, as if she'd been here before, had risked it all before, for him. Her hand trembled as she touched his shoulder, the worn gray cotton of his shirt soft underneath her palm. He turned and looked at her with the same sage-colored eyes she had first encountered all those years ago. His expression was unreadable.

"Hi." Her voice shook.

"Hi..." His eyebrows rose slightly.

Tell him, now!

"I love you," she blurted out. "I hid it while you were away, but it's always been there. It has never stopped breathing. It probably never will. I don't want it to. I want it to come out. I want it to feel alive. I want to love you. I want to—" She captured her bottom lip with her teeth, the words right there.

Tell him!

"I want to marry you." She stopped talking and for a moment, stopped breathing too.

He was silent. His eyes were trained on hers. His mouth opened and closed. Twice. His hand reached up and smoothed the hair at his temple.

Goddammit.

She had given her entire heart away without asking if he wanted it in the first place. She watched his head tilt up toward the cloudless sky. Her ears buzzed. What had she been thinking?

"Jace—" His name rolled off her tongue, but before she could continue, his hands reached for her, his mouth claiming hers.

All the oxygen she had held for him during their time apart transferred directly into his living body. She felt weightless. She exhaled.

He continued to peck her lips but remained silent. Her heart raced up her throat nearly to the tip of her tongue as he released her and returned to the water's edge. He stood there for a moment, then his voice rose above the sound as he finally spoke.

"This is time-bending, Jo. You're right." He turned in her direction and smiled. "Somehow the universe has allowed us to go back into the past to arrive in the future that could only be our present." He shook his head. "I'm not making sense."

She couldn't help the smile on her own face or the flutter of eternal butterflies in her stomach. She loved it all, and all of him.

"But you are, to me."

"What I'm trying to say is—" He took her hand and dropped onto one knee. "Time for once," he whispered up at her, "is exactly as it should be." He pulled her onto his lap and circled his arms around her shaking body.

She gazed down into the face she would always love. All they had been through, all the wasted time that had passed them by, this moment marked their true beginning, the official start of their time together. Her vision blurred from the tears she hadn't realized had begun to fall.

"Let's do this, Jace. Let's finally do life together."

His mouth hovered over her lips. His breath intertwined with hers, and just as she couldn't bear the silence any longer, he inhaled her exhale and said, "Okay."

Epilogue

He raced up the steps at a speed too fast, even for him, but he had waited long enough and couldn't wait any longer. Rushing down the dimly lit hallway, he stopped in front of a white door, the gold number three fastened above the peephole staring down at him. She was in there waiting for him; waiting in a space he would enter for the first time, only to leave with her. Finally. He straightened his shoulders and rapped his knuckles against the smooth wood.

She pressed her body against the cool door and peered through the fisheye hole. There he stood, tall and familiar, with his wavy hair and summer tan. His nerves were obvious even through the tiny lens —though it could be a projection of herself in his shoes. The door vibrated against the rap of his hand. Her entire body sparked like a live wire waiting to be reunited with its grounding. She pushed away and reached for the doorknob, removing the only thing left separating her from him.

He froze as the door creaked open. There she stood, familiar and glowing, with her exposed neck and bare shoulders. Sunlight from somewhere in the apartment, streamed around her. She was a figure caught in one of his dreams. She shifted ever so slightly, her long skirt giving her the illusion of weightlessness. He reached up and stroked her cheek with the back of his fingertips. Her voice unfolded like a cat would from a satisfying slumber.

"You're here."

She leaned into his touch, his fingers reassuring, the beds of his nails smooth. His eyes were bright as his hand reached around her neck and tilted her head up. She stared into his face as the sight of her reality replaced her overplayed memory. His breath washed over her, mint mingled with the same sandalwood musk, while his voice filled the empty space between them.

"And you're real."

He traced his thumb over her plump bottom lip and felt the warmth of her breath against his skin. Her unique scent of evergreen and flowery lavender, one he'd wished he could have bottled to inhale during their nights apart, wrapped itself around him as she sighed. Her scent was a security blanket for his bubbling nerves. He kissed her, slow and soft, before he released his hold on her and entered the empty apartment.

"We're late, aren't we?"

She glanced around. The sun through a window to her right began its descent in the western sky, while specks of dust danced in and out of the rays. It was as if the room was suspended in the significance of time, ending so it could start anew with him in Denver, where her career as a professional therapist could begin.

"Not at all."

He hadn't paid much attention to clocks since she had reentered his life. Having hated the passage of it for so long, time held a different significance now. He felt nothing but grateful for the endless hours he would soon have with her.

"Let's go chase the sun then."

He took her hand. She laced her fingers with his. They walked down the steps hand-in-hand, at a speed meant just for him and her. His thumb circled the ring on her left finger. Time, for once, was theirs.

Acknowledgements

First, I'd like to thank you for reading my book and taking a chance on my writing. I'd also like to thank the Instagram writing community for all the encouragement and support. Special thanks to the beta readers and ARC team, too!

In 2017 I wrote a bucket list. Number three: *publish a book.* Thanks to Mike for suggesting I start a list, for protecting my creative time, for understanding why I kept you away from the early drafts, and for being patient as I traversed the learning curve of self-publishing.

To Elliott, thank you for the day when you read the title out loud for the first time in your sweet six-year-old voice. You kept me going.

To my family & close friends, thank you for your support and genuine curiosity as I opened up about my writing and the book.

To Nik, thank you for asking to be a part of the project, for pushing me to finally send you pages, and for hanging in there as we conquered all those plot holes. This book would not have been possible without your keen eye and passion.

Thanks to the wanderer who joined me on this journey and for being a compass along the way.

Thank you to my editor for your guidance and for dialing back my accidental poetic side while keeping the integrity of the words intact.

And finally, many thanks to the faces of my formative years that make up the foundation of this story.

Author's Note

In 2015 I took an online fiction writing course through Gotham Writers Workshop. During the six-week course, I critiqued fellow writers, was critiqued on a story I was drafting, and completed several writing assignments. The prologue in *Time for Once* was inspired by one of those assignments. I stumbled upon the forgotten piece of writing in June of 2020 and felt an instinctual pull to develop it. With giddy excitement, I began to wonder: could I transform the 1000-word assignment into *their* story?

Like many first novels, the inspiration behind *Time for Once* comes from my past.

The beginning is a true recollection of a meet-cute. During the fourth revision, however, it morphed into how Jolie met Jace. Jolie's binge eating is a mirror of my own. Her recovery, however, was different from mine. Part of my healing took place as I wrote the book. Jolie's mom's storyline came from life experiences as well and for a moment, I considered omitting it. After a few conversations with my own mom, however, I was reminded of the value in storytelling and the power of knowing you're not alone in your struggles.

You've heard the saying, "write what you know." Once I typed *THE END*, it dawned on me. I wrote into what I didn't know. The characters built their own story on the foundation of my experiences. I sincerely hope you enjoyed the story of Jolie and Jace. Palmer is up next.

About the Author

Jes Smyth is a Chicago-area native with a degree in Psychology from the University of Iowa. From a young age, Jes has been an avid reader, writer, and dreamer. She's also a small artist appreciator, a budding bourbon connoisseur, an accidental poet, and a lover of fuzzy socks.

When she's not wandering the great outdoors, you can find her acting as a somewhat responsible adult, spouse, partner, and mother. She says she writes every day and hopes the stories she creates will resonate with those who find curiosity in the changes life throws our way.

Join My Newsletter!
https://jessmyth.com/newsletter